MINDHUNT

Michael Schirripa

First edition published 2024 by DoctorZed Publishing.
www.doctorzed.com

Books may be ordered through booksellers or online:

ISBN: 978-0-9756145-0-1 (sc)
ISBN: 978-0-9756145-1-8 (ebk)

Cataloguing-in-Publication entry can be found at the National Library of Australia.

Cover design © DoctorZed Publishing Pty Ltd

rev. date: 26/06/2024

MINDHUNT

Michael Schirripa

DoctorZed
Publishing
www.doctorzed.com

For Lauren, always...

ACKNOWLEDGEMENTS

Even though only my name appears on the front cover of *Mindhunt*, this book could not have come to life without the support, guidance, love and help of so many others.

Sending all my love and immense gratitude back to all of you:

Fiona Murray at Open Door Marketing for that amazing, superb website design and Steve Williss at WriteMind for your fabulous copy. AQ for those cool photos (you even made me look professional!) Tom Moularadellis at Stop 42 for your awesome social media work. Erin Carey and Ellee Lines at ROAM Generation for your brilliant PR, event management and marketing. The best team ever.

To Hari Teah for your incredible editing work that has the manuscript so clean and polished.

Lynette Lodge and Michelle Campbell for being my incredible manuscript alpha readers. Loved your feedback and thank you, sisters, for all of your support.

Sarah and Sam Wellington for allowing me to character name-bomb!

Dr Scott Zarcinas at DoctorZed Publishing. You believed in me and the book when no one in the publishing world would, and I will never forget that. Thank you so much for your advice, encouragement and support with helping me to develop as a podcaster, as a writer, and as a person. Forever grateful, Scott!

Mum and Dad – Joan and Roy Schirripa – thank you for a *lifetime* of love, encouragement and support and allowing me to read all those Stephen King novels as a boy!

Audrey and Edith for your cool video skills, editing and support!

William, Olivia and Tilly for your love, support, encouragement and all your fabulous plot ideas!

My wife, my best friend, my partner in *ALL* things, Lauren. Your belief in me and your encouragement of me is just magical. You always told me to never give up and so I haven't. This book could simply not have happened without you and your support is embedded within every page. I love you with all my heart and mind. Here I run out of words.

_____ **!** _____

PROLOGUE

Case File # CBA-7489-X

'JUST STAY RIGHT where you are, Christina! Don't move! Don't move a muscle and everything will be okay. I promise someone will be right there to...'

She threw the phone as far as possible off the Millennium Bridge.

'...get you!' were the last words she heard as the iPhone disappeared into the Thames.

And then she ran.

Christina Beauchamp-Alard knew all about hallucinations. She knew all about paranoia. She certainly knew all about delusional fears. But she also knew that *this* time what she was running from was real.

Very real.

The twenty-four-year-old daughter of Swiss banking billionaire, Henri Beauchamp-Alard, was on the run—and for once she was not running from the voices or shadows that accompanied the devastating psychotic illness that had ravaged her mind for the better part of a decade.

Right now, her mind had never been clearer.

She was frightened.

Terrified.

But she was *well*.

Or was she.

She just didn't know anymore.

But she knew that she would never, ever be going back.

Once she had made it across the bridge, she allowed herself to stop momentarily and look behind her. She could see a heavy-set man dressed in black making his way through the sea of pedestrians filing over the bridge. He pushed past them, then stopped briefly, making eye contact with Christina. She shuddered with icy fear, then turned and fled in the direction of St Paul's Cathedral.

An image appeared in her mind.

A painting.

Canaletto.

1754.

The image slid from view as she turned left, then left again, then right. Nausea began to set in, but still she ran.

Another left turn. She glanced behind her. The cars, buses, cabs and people had become indistinguishable blurs of colour and movement, reduced to nothing more than shifting reds, blues, yellows and blacks. *Black.* She looked hard for the man dressed in black but there seemed to be thousands of them. Everywhere.

And so she ran again. It seemed as though she was doomed to keep endlessly running through a timeless world—a world that was no longer neatly and accurately measured by the diamond-encrusted Cartier wristwatch her father had presented to her on her last birthday, a gift she had hastily hocked for a measly fraction of its value just a hour ago. Or maybe it was two hours ago. Or three. There was no longer any way of knowing how much time had passed, and the minutes and seconds of her life had lost all meaning, anyway. The only thing giving her life meaning now was the rhythm of her breathing and the pounding of her feet on the hard London pavements.

Now that the watch has been sold, there was one piece of jewellery left on her body—the stylish platinum bracelet on her right wrist. As she ran, she glanced at the small, red light that was flashing on the bracelet, and for the hundredth time that day, she tried in vain to pull the shiny circle of metal from her wrist—but with no success. Every time she grabbed at it, it only seemed to tighten more painfully.

She looked up and saw London Bridge.

Another image came to mind.

An etching this time.

Claes Visscher.

1616.

Christina made another right turn. The lanes seemed to be getting narrower. Her mouth was dry, her legs were shaking. She stumbled forwards, blindly, before doubling-over in agony. Clutching at her abdomen she vomited violently. Her stomach was virtually empty, but she convulsed and gagged for what felt like several minutes. When she had finished, she stared at the rainbow of half-digested tablets that were splattered around her feet.

She straightened up and tried to steady her breathing.

In, out, hold. In, out, hold. Nice and calm.

A psychologist she had seen some years ago had taught her this helpful breathing exercises to reduce her anxiety.

In.

Out.

Hold.

She would try to get to Mansion House tube station and then reassess her options from…

The thought dissolved, unfinished, as very large hand gripped her shoulder.

Without thinking, she summoned whatever strength she had left and kicked up and back—*hard.*

She was unsure how accurate she had been, but she heard a deep cry of pain and the grip on her shoulder loosened, just slightly.

It was enough.

She ran,

Her arms and legs pumped like pistons, and the sights, sounds and colours of London were gone.

All she was aware of was her breathing.

> *In, out.*

She knew she couldn't go much further. With one last effort, she increased her speed. Tears welled in her eyes as a feeling of futility consumed her.

> *I can't go back. I won't go back. I can't go back.*

Before reality kicked in.

> *The moment you stop running, they will take you back.*

Tears streamed down her cheeks.

She closed her eyes but kept in running.

In the distance, she heard Big Ben strike three times.

Big Ben.

Andre Derain.

1906.

Then everything was blocked out.

Every sight and every sound.

Christina never saw or heard the truck that finally stopped her tears forever.

Part 1

Jack and the Brainstalk

1

PROFESSOR NATHAN MORTIMER, the eminent forensic psychiatrist, stared intensely for several minutes at the crisp, passport-sized photograph in front of him. The man in the photo stared back.

Bright, blue eyes.

Wavy, blonde hair.

A warm, engaging smile.

An immaculately knotted blue and white striped tie.

Professor Mortimer dropped the photo onto his leather-topped desk and glanced at his Rolex. There were still a few minutes remaining before the interview began. He turned his attention back to the papers that were carefully arranged before him, wanting to disbelieve the very first piece of information that they contained. Doctor Jack Giorgio was thirty years old.

Thirty! So young! And yet so accomplished.

Mortimer was yet to reconcile the blonde hair and blue eyes with the distinctly Italian surname, but that was a minor issue. The nationality declared in the paperwork was Australian. All the same, Mortimer did not like unanswered questions, and he filed that one away to be resolved later.

His own, less officially authorised documents, revealed that Giorgio was single. He had never married, and Mortimer had discovered no information about any serious relationships. There were certainly no children. No other details were provided about any other family members.

The list of his interests indicated variation.

Giorgio liked opera, collecting modern first edition books, cooking, and marathon running.

Marathon running.

Mortimer shuddered and then checked himself. Maybe it could be seen in a positive light. It certainly indicated stamina, endurance, and discipline: the ability to set a long-term goal and stick to it. The ability to push through pain. And, perhaps most important of all, impulse control. Mortimer leant back in his chair.

A marathon runner must pace himself. Must control the rhythm. Not go too hard too early.

Clearly, Dr Jack Giorgio had all the qualities he was looking for.

It was highly privileged, confidential and sensitive information, but Mortimer also had received Giorgio's medical examination and psychiatric training records. It would be no exaggeration to say that these records were outstanding.

Truly outstanding.

Giorgio had published his first research paper as a medical student in the prestigious *British Journal of Psychiatry*, no less. It was nice work, in Mortimer's estimation. Not overly sophisticated, but nice, neat research nonetheless. The topic was the use of sedative medication for sleep disorders on a population of patients suffering from schizophrenia. More papers were published when Giorgio graduated and became a psychiatric trainee.

Several more papers.

By the time he had completed his training, Doctor Giorgio had over a dozen papers published in a range of esteemed journals, including *The Lancet*. Given the stigma usually associated with psychiatry, even within general medical circles, it was always of major significance to have any sort of psychiatric research published in such a prestigious journal. And Giorgio had done it as a final year trainee.

'Very impressive,' Mortimer murmured softly to himself.

Much against the grain of the political correctness of modern recruitment processes, Mortimer was an interview panel of one. Such was the esteem that he now enjoyed. He did not need an administrator or an allied health professional or, worse still, a member of the general public to tell him who would become the latest member of his team.

And it was *his* team.

He arose slowly from his chair. It was precisely two o' clock in the afternoon when he buttoned his suit jacket, opened his officer door and sized-up for the very first time, in the flesh at least, Doctor Jack Giorgio.

As the heavy oak door opened, Jack stopped the flow of cascading thoughts and stood up.

Jack knew a great deal about Professor Nathan Mortimer— information he had gleaned from the dozen or so textbooks that Mortimer had written, as well as various articles in the media, and some more personal insights that had been shared by some of his medical colleagues.

British-born, Mortimer had studied medicine at Oxford before training in both London and Boston, as a result of which he was credentialed in both countries, as a forensic psychiatrist *and* neuropsychiatrist. He also advised the UK government and the World Health Organization on their mental health policies and strategies.

Jack knew that Mortimer had completed his doctorate at Harvard, under the supervision of the legendary research neuropsychiatrist Robert Berman, on the subject of the interaction between pharmaco-genetics and chronic psychosis. After a brief post-doctoral fellowship in Berlin, Mortimer had returned to the UK, where he worked as a consultant forensic psychiatrist in the National Health Service.

During this period, he also founded his own biogenetics company, *KaryoPsych*, which did ground-breaking work on the genes involved in a range of mental illnesses. Jack knew that he had eventually sold the company to a private equity firm for seventy-five million British pounds—if *The New York Times* was to be believed. That was back in 2012.

After that, he had withdrawn a little from the public eye, holding a variety of academic posts in both the US and the UK. In spite of his attempts to fly under the radar, he was always talked about as a possible Nobel laureate for his work on the genetics of schizophrenia, and *The Guardian* had recently reported that Mortimer was going to be awarded a knighthood for his services to forensic mental health.

Put simply, in Jack's eyes, they did not come any greater than Nathan Mortimer. Working with the professor was the primary reason why he had applied for the position he was about to be interviewed for. It was the once-in-a-lifetime career break that he was desperately looking for.

And then the oak door opened.

Jack was initially struck by Mortimer's height: he stood well over six-foot-five, and his intimidating, powerful posture allowed him to use every inch of his frame to his advantage. He was also much slimmer than the photos Jack had seen, the most recent of which was, admittedly, several years old. He had a slightly receding hairline and his neat, grey hair blended seamlessly into a full beard. His distinctive, powerful face remined Jack of that tall, distinguished, American actor who had been in so many feature films over the past five decades.

The two shook hands firmly, and Jack was ushered into Mortimer's vast office. No refreshments were offered, not even a glass of water, but Jack didn't mind. The last thing he felt like doing was eating or drinking. He looked around the room quickly, expecting others to be there, but found no one.

'Yes, I know,' said Mortimer, picking up on Jack's curiosity. 'It will just be you and me today.' Jack wasn't sure whether this should raise his confidence levels. Or perhaps lower them.

'That's fine,' he said, rather awkwardly. 'I am grateful for the interview'.

Mortimer got straight to the point.

'So why do you want to come and work here, Doctor Giorgio?'

'Well, it's simple really. This is without a shadow of a doubt the most well-resourced inpatient forensic mental health facility in the world. I know it also has a strong research focus, and this is something I am very motivated to pursue.' He stopped himself. He did not want to overplay his academic ambitions. He knew that Mortimer immensely valued clinical work, so he decided to emphasise this.

'I know the facility also gives great opportunities for providing really important treatments and therapies for a severely unwell population. New frontiers for medication are crucial, but, in fact, I have also developed a keen interest in forensic psychotherapy. The forensic mental health population have traditionally been ignored when it comes to the talking therapies, but the growing research provides overwhelming evidence for this type of treatment. I am thinking of the recent review by Howell and Masters on this'.

The professor nodded slowly and deliberately, impressed by the reference Jack had made to the recent academic literature.

'And,' Jack continued, 'if I may say, it would also be an *incredible* learning experience to be able to work with you, Professor'.

Mortimer smiled, as though in agreement.

'Now let me get this right, Jack: you were born in Australia, completed high school there and then went to college and medical school in the States?'

'Yes, that's correct.'

'You studied languages and linguistics as well as pre-med at Stanford. So you can probably read Freud in the original German, then!' He laughed. 'And then...' the professor stopped and looked at Jack. 'Why Stanford?'

'I was awarded an athletic scholarship. Middle and long-distance running. I ran on their track team for four years. My legs, not my brain, paid my way.'

'Yes, yes, but why not just stay at home?'

'Opportunities. Australia, for all its beauty, its wonder, and its charm, is really not a world player in this area. It just seemed as though I could go further, quicker, if I went to swim in a bigger pond. Or run on a bigger track, as it were. I mean let's face it … the economy of California is larger than that of Australia.'

He smiled.

Mortimer looked convinced. He highly valued that sort of drive and ambition.

Going further. Going quicker.

'And then on to medical school?'

'That's correct, Professor. I won a full scholarship, academic this time, to Columbia. I could never have afforded it otherwise.'

Mortimer stared into space.

'New… York… City,' he said slowly to himself. And then casually to Jack, 'How was that?'

'Ahh… great. Wonderful. Extremely stimulating. I found it to be quite a vibrant, dynamic medical school.'

'How so?'

'A lot of cutting-edge work was going on there. Across all fields. The research, the clinical applications, even their teaching methods were extremely bold and revolutionary. Really pushing the envelope.'

Pushing the envelope. Mortimer liked what he heard. He wanted to know more.

'Well Jack, we are all about pushing boundaries here, too. How did you end up in forensic psychiatry? I mean, let's face it, the disturbed, criminal mind is not for everyone, and it seems to me from your resumé that you could have had your choice of specialties.'

Jack was flattered by the assessment, and hoped it was a sign that the interview was progressing well.

'I see the forensic mental health population as the most disadvantaged in society. Not only do they have severe mental illnesses, but they are *also* criminal offenders. A true double-whammy. I felt I could use my skills with this group. For me it is all about working *with* these people. Not *on* them. They have had enough people in their lives working *on* them, exploiting them and abusing them in all sorts of ways. And, to be honest, the chance to work with an inspiring thinker such as yourself is also a strong lure.'

He stopped himself there. That was *two* compliments. He did not want to come across as a star-struck sycophant. He was sure Mortimer would have endured enough of those already.

'I see you have some fascinating interests, Jack. Opera. Fine dining. Rare books. And apparently you also have an interest in designer clothing.' He eyed Jack's suit pointedly. 'One could conclude that you have acquired a taste for the finer things.'

'Well... the benefits of a well-rounded education, I suppose. And travel. These things have certainly opened my eyes to all that is out there.'

'Indeed. But these are all experiences that do not come cheap. Money, Jack. Do you also have an interest there?' Mortimer's voice carried slightly more intensity with the query. Jack thought it was a somewhat odd question for such an interview, but he felt compelled to answer.

'Professor, I did not come from an affluent family. Far from it. We lived in a working-class area. My parents were not educated people: they didn't even finish high school. But they both worked extremely hard and made huge sacrifices to send me to a good school. When I looked around at that school, I did discover the benefits that money could bring. The *opportunities*, mainly. So, to answer your question, I haven't done all of this study, all of this work, just to earn the minimum wage.'

Mortimer chuckled. 'Well, you won't be earning minimum wage here. And as for opportunities, we'll talk more about that at a later date.'

Jack was greatly heartened by these comments. It seemed that Mortimer was talking about their professional future together.

'Jack, do you remember the night before you started your internship in the hospital, after finishing medical school?'

'Yes.'

Everyone remembers that night.

Mortimer gave a short chuckle. 'How did you feel that night?'

'Umm… scared… terrified, in fact,' he said honestly.

'Yes, yes, but what did you really feel… deep down.' He pointed to Jack's abdomen. 'Right in there.'

Jack hesitated. 'Well, actually, I felt like a fraud. A phony. Like I'd been living a lie in medical school. That somehow, I'd bluffed my way through all those exams and now I would be found out.'

Mortimer nodded, as though satisfied with the honesty of this answer.

'Jack, I just have one last question for you.'

'Sure… fire away, Professor.'

'Is there any history of mental illness in your family?'

Immediately, Mortimer saw a look of—not shock, not even surprise… after decades of closely examining the emotional responses of patients, the professor had developed a keen sense of body language, and he wanted to find just the right word to describe Jack's response.

Uncertainty.

Yes, that was the look. '*You simply do not know how to answer that question,*' was the conclusion that Mortimer drew.

Jack tilted his head slightly. He wanted to shout, 'What the...?' But he didn't.

'A history of mental illness?' he repeated. 'Ah... no... no, nothing that I'm aware of.'

The remainder of the interview was taken up by a more mundane and routine discussion regarding administrative issues around Jack's employment.

After forty minutes, the two men rose, shook hands, and said their goodbyes.

Mortimer had decided.

There was no need to look any further than Doctor Jack Giorgio.

2

THE GRACEFUL, FLOWING lines of the brand-new Nicholas Tindal Centre for Forensic Mental Health were as pleasing to the eye as the name was to the ear. There was no question that the architect had succeeded in her brief to design a soothing, calming exterior that was as far removed from the stark, utilitarian 'hospital for the criminally insane' that had previously occupied the site. The only real indication of the elegant building's purpose was the imposing security fence surrounding the centre.

Jack had worked at his fair share of forensic psychiatric facilities but had never experienced anything that came close to the orientation process that marked his first day at the NTC. It was only after Jack was guided through a detailed explanation of the security procedures and hi-tech alarm system that the congenial head nurse, Paul Patterson, appeared, to guide him through the actual facility.

The design of the building was not only contemporary; it was exceedingly clever. A wide, tightly monitored secure corridor effectively split the building in two, with the wards, patient dining rooms, recreation facilities and clinical areas on one side, and the offices and administration areas on the other. This layout allowed staff easy access to any part of the building if a 'Code Black' emergency was called over the public address system.

The tour began in the psychiatric intensive care ward—home to the most acutely unwell patients—and moved through all four secure wards, before finally ending in the step-down unit for those patients being considered for release into the community. *Control* was the word that came to Jack's mind as he was shown around, and by the end, he wasn't sure if he was more orientated or disorientated. On the plus side, he'd had time to fully realise that the amazing facility was his new place of work, and if Paul was anything to go by, he was going to fit right in.

With over twenty-five years' experience working in secure mental health facilities and 'super-max' prisons and a doctorate in forensic mental health nursing, Paul's professional credentials were as impressive as his physical appearance. Standing at an imposing six-foot-seven, Jack was unsurprised to learn that the head of nursing also played a mean game of basketball.

However carefully the architect had crafted the exterior of the building, once you were inside there was no disguising the fact that this was a maximum-security psychiatric facility. Even so, there was a feeling of light and space. High ceilings and vast windows created an ambience of calm and low stimulation.

The only section of the facility that was omitted from Jack's orientation was the research centre. Patterson explained that this particular area was wholly and solely the domain of Professor Mortimer. In fact, although he was responsible for the day-to-day running of the building, Patterson did not even have access to the rooms that lay beyond the heavy, steel door. All he said was, 'He's even got his own MRI machine in there, but you'll have to ask him to take you through – if you're interested,' before ushering Jack swiftly onwards.

***

Doctor Drew Barnard flicked a speck of white dust off the lapel of his grey Armani suit jacket and straightened his striped Hermes tie before shaking hands with Jack.

He had not been looking forward to this moment as he did not enjoy meeting newcomers, especially those as credentialed and potentially threatening as Doctor Jack Giorgio. But he had finally convinced himself that the new guy was probably not that great and his presence would not really make a huge impact on his own life or work, so he would just go with it.

'Welcome aboard,' he said with a tight smile.

'Cheers, Drew. It's good to be here.'

'Mortimer's been singing your praises from the rooftops. Let's hope you live up to your reputation.'

Jack tensed. It was going to take more than a flick of the fingers to shift the chip on Barnard's shoulder. He quickly sized up the older man. Not that he seemed much older. Early forties, maybe. Jack could imagine him being at home on Wall Street or in the casinos at Monte Carlo. The elegance of Barnard's Italian suit was undeniable, although somewhat diminished by his short, pudgy physique. His attempts to compensate for his slightly doughy appearance had extended from his body to his face, which was given the illusion of definition by a short, well-landscaped goatee and carefully slicked-back black hair. Hermes was clearly a favoured brand, because as well as the tie, a pair of spectacles by the same designer sat snugly across his face.

The look was completed by an impressive Patek Philippe watch, which Barnard consulted with excessive performance. Without looking back at Jack, he announced that he was running late and they would therefore need to complete the orientation as quickly as possible. After a whistle-stop tour of the medical staff offices, he ushered Jack through to the research area. Jack's eyebrows raised a little.

'I thought that this was off limits?'

'Yeah, but Mortimer thought you would be interested,' replied Barnard with a dismissive wave of one manicured hand, while the other keyed in the entry code to the private suite.

He led Jack through to a medium-sized room which was dominated by a state-of-the-art General Electric PET scanner.

They both stared at the impressive piece of radiology equipment. It had clearly cost millions and was not the sort of medical imaging device usually found floating around a forensic psychiatric facility.

'Lord knows what he's doing with this!' laughed Barnard.

'You're not part of the research team?' Jack's eyebrows raised a little further.

'*Research?*' Barnard feigned a yawn. 'Who's got time for that? I'm busy enough dealing with all the other crap around here. Most of which comes out of the mouths of the nursing staff.'

He laughed heartily at his own remark and shook his head. Jack decided it was prudent to keep his own research interests to himself. On reflection, it would probably be wise to keep *most* of his opinions to himself when he was around Barnard.

'Anyway,' Barnard continued, as he headed back towards the exit. 'I'm running extremely late now. But with all those impressive credentials I'm sure you can find your own way out of here. Consider the tour complete. Actually, on second thoughts, if you could hold the fort for the rest of the afternoon that would make up for this rather unfortunate distraction that's cut into an extremely busy day. I've been having a little trouble with the Maserati. You know how sensitive they can be? Anyway, the dealer rang earlier to say that they've got her purring like a kitten again and I'm terribly keen to get over there and pick her up before they close.'

Jack opened his mouth to say he'd be happy to help, but Barnard was already halfway down the corridor by the time he'd formed the first syllable.

By the time Jack finished completing the seemingly endless paperwork that he had found neatly piled up on his desk, the day was almost gone. It seemed as though there was a separate form for every single aspect of his job. He was even required to indicate whether he suffered from any food allergies. He dutifully ticked the boxes marked 'macadamias' and 'walnuts'. Stella, the chief receptionist, and a former NHS nurse, laughed when he handed her this final form.

'Fancy that,' she exclaimed. 'A psychiatrist who's allergic to nuts!'

Jack forced a smiled. 'There's no place for those sorts of jokes anymore,' he said brightly.

Welcome to the British health service.

3

JACK HAD ARRANGED to meet with the senior forensic psychiatric training registrar at 4:00pm, to get a run down on some of the patients that would be under his care.

Doctor Sarah Wellington arrived punctually at Jack's office and extended her hand.

'Sarah,' she said with a warm and friendly tone.

After introducing himself, Jack quickly read through her very concisely prepared notes. The case summaries were excellent and contained all the patient histories, offence details, diagnoses, and current management. She had also typed up a separate spreadsheet that summarised their court dates and where exactly in the legal process timeline each patient was currently sitting.

You are going to make life very easy here.

Jack was well-aware that highly organised junior staff were a wonderful asset. He also knew that the reverse was true.

He placed the paperwork down on his desk and stared at her.

'Well, Sarah, it's now seven minutes past four, I think our work here is done,' he said with a smile.

She looked up at him, silently, and then gave a laugh.

'Great. Now that you're here, can I have the rest of the month off?' she said, with a wink.

'Absolutely,' he replied. 'If you can get the rest of the medical staff and trainees here to work as efficiently as you.'

They relaxed and began chatting away about the facility and their lives outside it. Jack could already sense they were going to work very well together. It was clear that she'd more than deserved her place at Cambridge, and he was interested to see how her career progressed once she'd gained her psychiatric qualifications, as well as her sub-speciality certification in forensic psychiatry.

He was aware of her extensive experience in neuropsychiatry and forensic work, and was impressed to discover that she'd even found the time to undertake a twelve-month scholarship, working in Africa with *Médecins San Frontières*.

They spoke for nearly fifteen minutes about her incredible experiences with *MSF*. She explained that she would have loved to extend her time with them, but had returned to the UK when she realised she was pregnant.

'What does your spouse do?' Jack asked, noticing her wedding band.

'Sam? He's a freelance photojournalist,' she said. 'But at the moment he is taking a break and is at home with the twins.'

'Twins!' Jack smiled wryly.

'Oh yes. William and Olivia. Double trouble.'

'I'm in awe!' Jack said emphatically. 'You've slaved through a top medical school, done all your training, worked in Africa, and had twins? That's fantastic. How old are they?'

'Eighteen months.'

'It's great that Sam has time to be at home with them.'

'Oh absolutely. Boys and girls need their dads,' she said, seriously.

   They certainly do.

'We need look no further than a lot of the patients in here for evidence of that,' he said. 'And those among them who did have their dads around probably wouldn't be putting them forward for any awards.'

Sarah nodded in agreement.

'Is it asking too much to see a pic of your kids?' Jack asked, wanting to build rapport, but instantly wondering if it was too soon.

'Oh, for sure,' she replied. With a subtle shake in her hand Sarah rifled through her bag to find her phone.

4

THE FOLLOWING MORNING Jack rose from his chair and surveyed the tall, thin brunette who had been led into the interview room. Dark, wavy hair ran almost the entire length of her back, drawing his attention away from the loose fitting, green, hospital-issued tracksuit.

Curtis, the muscular mental health nurse who brought her in, offered to remain present during the interview, but Jack declined. His instincts told him that one-on-one would be prudent.

Once she was seated, he promptly sat down again. He deliberately left her case notes in the nurses' station as he did not want her to be distracted by them. He knew that psychiatric patients were always very concerned about what was in their notes, and removing them all together from the interview often saved a lot of time and energy. Jack had carefully read them earlier and had a clear sense of her recent background.

'Hi,' he began, as non-threateningly as possible. 'I am Doctor Giorgio, but you can call me Jack if you prefer'.

She said nothing and then looked quickly up to the corner of the ceiling over Jack's left shoulder.

He also looked up to the same spot.

He waited to allow her to speak first. He knew that if he jumped in too soon he would only make her feel more like she was being interrogated and worsen her sense of paranoia. This would no doubt ruin any chance of rapport they might establish, and the interview would be shut down before it even got started. Given what he knew about her he was aware that this was far too important an interview for him to mess up.

She continued to stare upwards.

Her hands were folded neatly in her lap and she sat bolt upright, knees together. Her face was generally expressionless, but he clearly detected fear in her eyes.

He waited.

And waited.

A less experienced or more anxious clinician would have broken the silence. But Jack knew that by waiting, he would save time in the long run.

After almost ten minutes she moved her eyes. They now met his.

She studied his face.

He noticed that her respiratory rate appeared to slightly quicken. Jack interlinked his fingers and placed them on the desk. She did not look down at them.

    Good. So far, so good.

After a further five minutes she spoke.

'Lizzie,' she said, in a bland, monotone voice.

According to the hospital file and police documents, Elizabeth Susan Roberts was twenty-two years old. She lived in Balham, South London, with her parents and her eighteen-year-old sister, Jessica. She was born and bred in London and was a university student in her final year of an economics degree.

She had no criminal record.

Until now.

'Is it okay if I call you Lizzie?'

'Mmmm.' He took that as a yes.

'I would really be interested in talking to you and hearing about what has happened. Is it okay if we talk?'

She stared again, but for a briefer time.

'Yeah… yeah… mmm… I think… so.'

'Do you know where you are, Lizzie?'

Her eyes darted quickly around the room, to every corner, before settling back on Jack.

'Ahhh… no… no…'

And then nothing.

For a further two minutes, nothing.

He decided that she was displaying thought blocking, which was commonly seen in acute psychosis. Her thinking was so disorganised and chaotic that it had almost come to a grinding halt.

Jack cast his mind back to the case notes he had read. Seventy-two hours earlier Lizzie had been arrested by the local police outside of the home of Dr Marc Mollet, a French-born economics lecturer at University College London. Mollet's body was found in the upstairs bedroom. He had been stabbed dozens of times in the chest, back and abdomen, and he was certainly dead by the time the emergency services arrived.

Mollet was a well-respected academic. He was a single, childless man and the house was otherwise unoccupied. The police were alerted by a phone call from Lizzie herself.

She had told them the precise address and that a French terrorist was resident there, but not to worry, as she had executed him and he would no longer cause a threat. She then spoke quickly in a foreign language before hanging up.

When the police arrived, Lizzie was sitting on the front steps of the duplex reading out loud, in German, from an untranslated copy of Karl Marx's *The Civil War in France*. The book's spine and most of the pages were soiled by her bloody fingerprints. A glossy bright red streak also ran from her left ear to her nose.

As the police gathered and stormed into the house, Lizzie sat on the steps and continued reading in a bland voice. She only stopped and raised an objection when her handcuffs were secured, forcing her to drop the book. She did not utter a further word until her interview with Jack.

'Well, you're in a hospital, Lizzie.'

'This... hospital? Why...' Again, her thoughts froze.

'You are here so that we can help you. You are safe here. I really want you to know that. You are *safe*.' He waited for the message to sink in. He was unsure if it really had.

'Why?'

'That's what I really want to understand, Lizzie. I would really like it—and I could help you—if you could talk to me about it. Remember: you are *safe*.'

Again, she stared at him.

He might be okay, he might be, he's okay, okay, okay.

The thought looped in her head, but all she could stammer was, 'Safe...' and then, in a whisper, 'safe...'

'Can you tell me any reason why you might be here? In a hospital?'

'I... don't know.'

Jack thought about the events leading up to her being transferred to the facility. An image came into his mind of her sitting outside the house reading from Marx. His German was reasonable but, unlike his Italian, far from fluent. Despite this he thought it was worth a shot. He decided to ask her if German was what she would prefer:

'Möchten Sie Deutsch sprechen?'

She looked surprised, but then gave a hint of a smile.

'Ja,' she said.

She suddenly seemed slightly more engaged. He felt that their rapport might deepen. The conversation then flowed much better in German.

She told him that she did not know why she was in a hospital because she was not sick.

He complimented her on her German and made self-deprecating comments about his own linguistic skills, which she appeared to warm to.

Slowly, slowly, she began to speak more openly with him and let her paranoid guard down.

Lizzie said that she had learnt the language in high school but then did a twelve-month exchange to a university in Munich which had really improved her fluency. It was there she first discovered Marx, in the original language, and she felt they had a very special connection. It seemed it was during her time there that she first became psychotic.

She denied any illicit drug use, but Jack couldn't help but reserve his judgement about that. He knew, all too well, the extremely close correlation between mental illness, substance abuse and violent crime.

It would also seem that Lizzie had never been treated for a mental illness before. That concerned him greatly, as he calculated she had likely gone over two years in this psychotic state without any medication. He knew that the longer a first episode of psychosis was allowed to continue, the worse the prognosis.

Lizzie suddenly switched into English, much to Jack's relief.

'Sickness … sickness … capitalism is the sickness. Greed is terror and terror is greed.'

'I don't quite follow. Can you explain that to me?'

She ignored the question and looked away.

'Marx was my great grandfather,' she said in a matter-of-fact voice.

'Your great grandfather?'

'Yes. His blood is my blood.' Before he could speak again, she continued, 'Blood... flood... mud... bud...'

Jack instantly recognised this bizarre pattern of speaking as 'clang' associations. He had seen it many times before when patients were extremely psychotic. It was another form of highly disorganised thinking that led to a string of seemingly unrelated rhymes. He felt that the interview was now on the verge of being lost. Lizzie had done well to hang on this long given how unwell she was. In a few minutes he was certain she would completely shut down.

He knew he would have to work fast.

'How do you know he is your great grandfather?'

'He has told me so,' she replied. With wide eyes she looked up to the same corner of the room yet again and smiled.

It then became clear to Jack that Marx was 'speaking' to her right now.

'What is he saying to you, Lizzie?'

There was a further pause before she fixed her gaze back on Jack. Her smile remained, however. She reverted to German.

'He is proud of me. Proud that Mollet is dead.'

'Why *proud?*'

'Because I am doing his work. Eliminating the capitalist threat. The terror.'

'The terror?'

'The greed m...' she stopped abruptly.

Her expression became cold, and a single tear formed in the corner of her left eye. Jack watched the tear as it sat on her skin. Lizzie became frozen like a statue and Jack became gravely concerned that she was heading towards catatonia, a state of severe psychosis that led, essentially, to a psychological and physical paralysis.

It could be life-threatening.

Jack leapt to his feet, opened the door and called Curtis and another nurse standing nearby for assistance. Lizzie continued to sit motionless as the three men gently lifted her to her feet and carried her back to her room.

Jack ordered a stat dose of zuclopenthixol acetate, a highly potent injectable antipsychotic medication that was reserved only for the most severe cases of psychosis. Even though Lizzie was an involuntary patient at the unit Jack still wanted to be thorough and careful with his use of such a powerful drug. He called Paul Patterson and Dr Michelle Campbell to bear witness to his management plan.

'This patient is now catatonic,' Jack announced with confidence. 'My assessment is that I have no choice now but to administer the 'zuclo' injection as a potentially life-saving treatment. Clearly the patient is unable to consent but given that this is a clinical emergency, I believe that I have no choice.'

All other present agreed.

Patterson soon returned with a large syringe filled with clear fluid. After double-checking that he had drawn up the right medication and the right dose he handed it to Jack who proficiently injected it into Lizzie's right thigh.

'She'll be out for a couple of days now,' Jack explained to Angelo, the final year medical student who was staring down at Lizzie with wide eyes.

5

THE DYNAMIC DESIGN of the NTC meant that different patient populations could be catered for simultaneously. Most of the patients were young men, aged between twenty and forty. There were also a number of older men, as well as a handful of women. On very rare occasions, they were required to admit teenagers, the youngest of whom had been just sixteen when he'd arrived at the facility.

The innovative floor plan incorporated heavy, secure dividers that could be repositioned to make 'wards within wards' for these special populations. Three pregnancies and one homicide at the old facility had made this flexible design a necessity.

Lizzie Roberts was being housed in one of these special wards. Not only was she female, but her acutely psychotic mental state made her especially vulnerable. The protection, however, also went the other way. Given what she had been accused of doing, it was essential to keep her isolated from the other patients for *their* protection as well.

Jack took some time discussing her case with the other staff. He wanted everyone to be on the same page. He explained to the captivated audience of nurses, doctors, medical students and social workers that he strongly suspected Elizabeth's 'work' was not done yet. Despite the fact she was heavily sedated, Jack believed her delusions about Marx would remain firmly in place for at least several more weeks.

'She is at extreme risk,' he said.

'In what way?' asked Millie Bowen, a bright and promising second year psychiatric trainee.

'Blood,' Jack replied.

'Huh?'

'She believes that her blood is that of Marx. She killed Mollet by stabbing him—by exposing his blood. It was a purge. In *her* mind, she was literally draining him of his capitalist evil. She wants Marx to be proud of her. The final act will be the spilling of her own blood.'

Jack then pondered over her focus on *blood*. He wondered what else it may signify.

'But why?' asked Curtis, Lizzie's nurse.

'My suspicion is that she will now want to see her blood mixed with Marx's. And I mean that she will literally want to *see* it. With her own eyes. I think the sight of her blood will confirm to her everything that she believes.'

'But why hasn't she done that already?' asked Millie.

'I think there are two reasons. Firstly, she needed to get rid of Mollet. Secondly, she is in hospital now and even though she is floridly psychotic she will be getting the message that people around her do not believe her. So she will need to up the ante, to prove that she is right.'

'So she will cut herself,' concluded Millie soberly.

'Quite possibly,' confirmed Jack. 'When she wakes up in a couple of days, she will have the volition and the energy to go through with it. And I think she will do it at her first opportunity. So we need to be vigilant about anything and I mean *anything* that she might be able to use.'

The discussion continued as Lizzie lay sleeping just a few feet away, a specialised nurse seated in a chair by her bedside, keeping her under constant visual observation until she woke. She breathed deeply and rhythmically.

Jack glanced over at the sleeping figure.

Your brain needs a rest. Then the healing might begin.

6

THE CHAUFFEUR-DRIVEN luxury sedan sped through the empty Munich streets, but Jack's focus was on the back of the driver's head, intrigued by how incredibly still it had stayed throughout the journey.

The road was long and straight, and the car gained speed at an alarming rate. The powerful V8 engine purred away.

Despite the speed Jack felt relaxed. He slumped back in his seat, tilted his head back and closed his eyes. He could have been flying.

His eyes snapped back open as he felt a hand searching around his groin. The muscles around his abdomen reflexively tightened, causing him to recoil. The hand went for his belt and the buttons on his pants.

He pushed it away. But a second hand appeared and took over.

Jack looked to his left, and saw Lizzie Roberts.

She tried to straddle him, barking instructions in German. He could not understand what she was saying, but her actions made her intentions clear.

He pushed her away. She became angry and tried to straddle him again.

She had removed her hospital-issued tracksuit pants.

'Blut! Blut!' she screamed at him.

This was a word he understood.

'Blood! Blood!'

She then leant in close and whispered in his ear, while one hand stroked his face.

'Geblüt. Geblüt.'

Bloodline. Lineage.

'No!' Jack screamed.

'NO!'

'NOOO!'

His own screaming woke him, and he sat bolt upright in his bed. Sweat trickled from his forehead and down his cheeks. He stared at the clock.

3:37 am.

He scribbled down the details of the dream in a notebook he kept on his bedside table for exactly this purpose.

He took a breath and then read back what he had written.

Think, Jack. Think. What is this all about?

Her attempt at seduction.

Blood.

Bloodline.

Lineage.

He grabbed his phone and rang the ward straight away.

'Curtis, it's Jack Giorgio. There is something you must know about Lizzie. And there is something crucial that I want you to do for me.'

7

JACK ARRIVED AT the facility early and headed straight for the acute ward. He'd lain awake following his dream, staring blankly at the clock until 5:30 am when he finally gave up and made his first espresso of the day.

The nurses were performing their early morning handover of patients from the night staff to the day staff.

'Ah, Dr Giorgio,' said Curtis with a smile as he looked up from the case notes he was holding. 'Good morning.' He knew exactly what Jack was after and he clearly perceived the doctor's anxious anticipation.

'Come on, Curtis. Don't keep me hanging.'

'All in good time, doctor, all in good time. We have important nurses' business to get through here and looking down the list there will be… one, two, three more patients until we do the hand over for Lizzie.'

'Now you are just being cruel,' Jack said with a grin as he tried to snatch the notes from Curtis. 'Just tell me the result.'

'It's positive,' Curtis confirmed. 'But I suspect you already knew that.'

He produced the small, elongated plastic device that gave Jack visual confirmation.

Lizzie Roberts was pregnant.

8

'ALWAYS REMEMBER, NO matter how bizarre the delusional idea, there is always a small seed of truth to it. Our job is to dig up that seed and examine it. That is what gives the symptoms meaning to the patient. And if we really want to understand our patients as people, not just as pathology, then we need to understand what gives *them* meaning.'

The medical students and junior doctors were so busy hanging from Jacks' words that they looked noticeably surprised when one of their number broke the spell with a breathless question.

'But how do you do that?'

'Language and listening.' Jack replied, quickly. 'So many of our patients are easily dismissed as crazy – even by our own colleagues. They are never really heard and so it is our duty, our responsibility, to listen. To hear *their* stories. And to hear *their* language. What do *their* words mean to *them*.'

'But won't the antipsychotic medications take care of the delusions and hallucinations?' asked another student.

'Ah, yes, biology! *Medication!* Biology holds all the answers, right? Chemical manipulation will bring about wellness. That's what you guys hear in your lectures from your professors,' Jack said. 'Every year the drugs just get better and better, right?' A few of the students nodded their heads in agreement. 'But that's not even *half* the story. Drugs raise more questions than answers.'

'What do you mean?'

'For instance, why is the response rate so low? Why does one drug seem to work for one person and not for another? Why does the same drug work for a patient one year but not the next? Why is it that side effects can sometimes be worse than the illness?'

'But isn't that due to constitutional differences in people?' asked Millie. 'Their genetic makeup? How they absorb the drug, how their body distributes it, and how much of it ends up getting here?' She pointed to her head as she spoke.

'That's a popular argument, Millie. Where it falls down for me is that it blames the patient for not getting better. *Their* genetic makeup, *their* biology, *their* non-compliance with the pills. But what if the variation in response is explained by factors that the patient cannot control?'

'Like what?' asked a student.

'Like a problem with the treating doctor. Like being given the wrong diagnosis. Like being given the wrong medication. Like not being listened to and understood. Not to mention the more unconscious conflicts that can arise between doctor and patient that can sabotage the treatment.'

'Do you mean transference and countertransference?' asked Millie, with a hint of triumph at having grasped what Jack was talking about.

'*What* and counter-*what*?' Dave scowled, throwing his hands in the air. The small group giggled at his exasperated tone.

Jack liked Dave. He had several admirable traits, including a complete lack of fear about asking questions, even if they seemed stupid. Jack felt that this ability to put his ego aside and admit that he did not know everything would stand Dave in good stead. Jack had seen other, far brighter but far more arrogant students fail badly because they were too afraid to admit their fallibility.

'Good question, Dave,' Jack said with encouragement. 'Transference and countertransference relates to the feelings that doctors and patients can have about each other. A lot of the time these feelings are outside of our awareness, yet they can have a big influence—for better and for worse—on the therapeutic relationship.'

'They can really affect treatment,' Millie chimed in.

'Exactly,' said Jack. 'It is most relevant in psychiatry, but it can be seen in all areas of medicine.' The students still looked a little confused. 'Have you ever been pulled over by the police for a random breathalyser test?'

They all nodded.

'And at that moment, when you see the flashing lights and the officer waving at you to stop, have you ever felt suddenly and inexplicably nervous? Even though you have not been drinking and, in fact, have done nothing illegal at all.'

Again, several more nods.

'That is an example of a transference reaction. You have a feeling of guilt for something, *anything*, that you are not consciously aware of and then, bang, you are suddenly confronted by an authority figure who might punish you. It leads to anxiety.'

He looked around the room. His example appeared to have convinced them.

'Well, exactly the same thing can happen in a doctor-patient relationship. Doctors are perceived as authority figures, and can therefore induce a huge range of emotions. Sometimes positive, sometimes negative.'

'But isn't that just... reality? You feel what you feel?' Dave asked.

Another good question.

'Yes, that's right,' answered Jack. 'Transference feelings *are* real feelings. But the issue is: what are those feelings based on? Where do they come from?'

More confused looks.

'For example, if you suddenly start to feel anxious in the presence of someone you have never met before. Where does that feeling originate from?'

'The past,' Millie responded with confidence.

'Exactly right,' Jack said, inducing a warm smile from the trainee. 'We all build up an emotional memory bank of people, relationships, and past experiences that tell us how to feel in the here and now. That is transference. But those important relationships aren't only formed when we are physically with the other person: they develop in our minds, too. In our heads, often when we are alone, we continue conversations, arguments, and experiences with these other people—even when they are not around. It can even happen after important people in our life have died.'

'So, do you mean like how we got on with our parents when we were growing up? That can affect us now?' Dave asked.

'That is *precisely* what I mean, Dave.'

Moments ago they were laughing at him, but now Dave was enjoying some admiring looks from his classmates.

'Our parents are the very first authority figures we encounter and our relationship with them can often set the tone and build the template for many of the same relationships we have as adults.'

'Is that why I feel nervous around Professor Mortimer?' one of the students asked.

'Yes! And it's also why *I* feel nervous around him!' Jack admitted. The room erupted in laughter.

'I guess the point of what I am saying is that we must make the effort to see all of our patients as *individuals*. Not get sucked in to seeing them as all being the same. Don't clump them together and make a judgment based on what you have seen in the past. Every patient has their own unique story to tell with their own language. To understand the patient, we need to understand *their* words, *their* language. The real question is: are we prepared to listen?'

9

DR THEO STEIN leaned his head against the window frame of his small, elegantly-furnished Upper East Side apartment and gazed out across Central Park. August was his favourite time of year in New York. He closed his eyes momentarily, enjoying the sensation of the late summer heat on his face, before opening them again to delight in the shimmering greens of the trees that graced the large space below him.

The warmth of the sun and the beauty of the foliage were always a pleasure, but what he loved most about summer was the human activity—the elderly strollers, the young lovers, the exuberant children, the energised joggers and the boisterous teenagers. Each of the ninety-one bitter East Coast winters he had endured brought a greater degree of resentment, along with an increase in pain as his arthritis steadily worsened. He wondered how many more winters he could take. But the summers still seemed to make it worthwhile. They could still be relied on.

He ran his bent and swollen fingers through his thick, grey hair and stared down onto Fifth Avenue. A family of five were walking along the edge of Central Park, all busy with their smart phones, ignoring the gorgeous day, the stunning park and, most worryingly, each other.

It reminded Theo that the one thing he hated more than winter was technology. He believed that over ninety percent of it was superfluous to human need and thus its popularity—and profitability—was simply clever marketing.

It was not that he mistrusted technology, as was the case with many of his contemporaries, it was simply that he felt it was of no use to him. It was much like his decision to not own or drive a car. Who really needed such an item in New York City? He had no problem being driven in a cab or even a limo, but to own a car? It was just not necessary.

So it was that he had no computer, no cell phone, no pager and no television. His landline was an adequate means for people to contact him, and adequate was good enough.

He still typed up his own invoices for his patients on the last day of each month, using the grand old Remington typewriter that had been given to him by his supervising psychoanalyst to mark the achievement of his protégé becoming qualified, and it had been a treasured possession ever since. He had maintained it beautifully, with the occasional assistance of the only remaining typewriter repair shop in Manhattan. As such, it still worked as if it were brand new.

All manner of people had urged him over the years to join the twenty-first century: his colleagues, family, accountant, students, bandmates, and even some of his patients. But Theo had always resisted. He was yet to be convinced that these devices could make his life any easier, even if they might make life easier for some of those around him.

What he cherished was still in abundant supply, anyway.

Books, books and more books.

The walls of his apartment were lined with beautifully crafted mahogany bookshelves, which were full to overflowing with thousands of volumes covering a vast array of topics.

Theo also loved hand-written letters and notes. He had an enormous collection of several thousand letters, all carefully catalogued and filed, according to sender. As a treat, he would sometimes head down to Sotheby's whenever an auction contained a collection of old letters or documents that had some significance or interest for him. He loved to pour over the text… the sentences… the words. The *words*. It was all about language and the meanings made in people's lives.

Over the years he had also received numerous letters. In particular, from a young man whom he remembered with great fondness: Dr Jack Giorgio.

He had supervised Jack when he was a medical student and then a resident at Columbia, and found him to be a most intelligent and insightful young man. He had an outstanding intellect, but he had also developed a real understanding of his own unconscious drives and conflicts as well.

Even though Jack never underwent any formal psychoanalysis with Theo, they still often managed to delve quite deeply into Jack's past. Through this process, Theo was able to demonstrate to Jack just how important his formative years had been for him: both personally and professionally.

To Theo, Jack Giorgio stood out in an age when psychoanalysis was on the decline, as 'the talking cure' was gradually replaced by purely 'biological' treatments. But Theo knew that they would not find all the answers in genes or molecules or chemistry. And certainly not in little plastic bottles containing antidepressants.

Theo had been shunned by the psychiatric community for his views, which were dismissed as archaic or old-fashioned. He was written off as a 'dinosaur'—simply too old to keep up with the latest research. But what his colleagues failed to appreciate was his enduring love of reading. He could easily get through four books a week, as well as several journal articles and daily newspapers.

When Theo thought of Jack he thought of dreams, and the young man's fascination with their unconscious meanings. Theo believed that one of Freud's most significant and lasting contributions to understanding the human psyche was the work he did on the interpretation of dreams.

Together, he and Jack had spent many hours in deep, stimulating discussion about dreams and their significance. Jack believed, as did Theo, that dreams were one of the only true measures of what was really going on in people's minds. They were uncensored movie's that portrayed fears, passions, desires and wishes.

As such, Theo and Jack had immeasurable faith in the meaning of dreams *and* the power of language.

> *Always remember, Jack,* Theo would say, *the unconscious and your dreams are structured like a language. The meaning is in the words. Words are unique codes that people use to tell you something special. Listen. Listen. Find the hidden meaning in those words.*

When Jack first came to see Theo, he already had an exceptional understanding of dreams, and this was reinforced by Theo's numerous clinical anecdotes about how the dreams reported to him by patients unlocked the codes to the patient's inner world. This then led to stunning breakthroughs in their therapy.

To this end, he encouraged Jack to keep a written journal of his dreams and to always, always document his dreams—even if he could only recall the briefest fragment upon waking.

'Document your dreams and you will understand yourself and your patients infinitely more deeply,' Theo told him.

Theo was a man of routine. He equated routine with stability and control, and recognised his patients' need for these elements in their lives. Theo always wore the same outfit to sessions with patients, not matter the season or the weather: navy blue corduroy pants, brown leather brogues, a white button-down dress shirt and a brown houndstooth sports jacket. He was this as his 'uniform' and it gave the patients a strong sense of stability, reliability and sameness. When explaining this to others, Theo would often use McDonald's as an example. Why are they such a success? Because you always knew what you would get whenever you walked in there. The burgers, the buns, the uniforms. Always the same. You could be in New York or Berlin: it was always the same.

He was always on time. His fifty-minute sessions with patients lasted fifty minutes. Not forty-six and not fifty-five. Needless, to say, he also practiced with the strictest of discretion and confidentiality.

Theo had no receptionist. He made his own appointments and

did his own billing. He even had a separate door placed in his consulting room so that patients could enter through one door and exit via another. In this way, two patients would never meet. He believed that adherence to such strict standards allowed his patients to have trust in him, and therefore allow them to relax so that they could be completely honest and candid about whatever was on their minds. The proof was in the pudding, and Theo had achieved some amazing results over the years.

He'd accumulated letters from a number of celebrities he had treated over the decades. Actors, musicians, directors, writers, politicians, and even a president—albeit some years before he had taken office.

Theo had loved working as a psychoanalyst. He viewed being given access to the intimate inner worlds of his patients as a true privilege, and one that he never took for granted. He could easily trace his psychoanalytic lineage—the 'family tree' of who had analysed whom during their training, all the way back to Freud. This was important to Theo—and to the New York analytic community at large. At least, it had been. He had to admit that it carried much less weight these days.

Theo sighed and stepped away from the window. It was time to take the short walk down Fifth Avenue to East 73rd Street, where a tiny bakery was located. The same bakery where he'd had his breakfast, every morning, without fail, for more years than he cared to remember.

While he ate, he opened the letter that had arrived with the morning mail, bearing a London postmark. It was with some sadness that he and Jack had said their goodbyes before Jack headed across the pond. He greatly admired Jack's desire to help the mentally ill who had ended up in the criminal justice system. He also found Jack's ideas of applying psychoanalytic theories and practices to such a population as both inspiring and ingenious.

Theo had no doubts that Jack would help a great many under-privileged and unwell people.

10

'I HEAR YOU did some nice clinical work with our new admission,' Mortimer smiled kindly. 'You made quite an impression: even the nurses talked about you in glowing terms. You even managed to make Barnard mumble a few words of praise!' he added with a chuckle. 'They said you're the only one she will talk to.'

Indeed, Lizzie Roberts would only speak to Jack. He knew, however, that due to her psychosis their rapport remained tenuous.

It was late in the afternoon and the two psychiatrists were sitting in Mortimer's plush office— the only one in the building with a balcony. He had just come back inside after smoking an expensive Cohiba Behike. The pungent cigar smell trailed behind him.

Jack felt grateful and relieved by the compliments, in particular what Mortimer had said about the nurses. If there was one lesson Jack had learnt all too well throughout his medical career, it was that no matter where you worked or how senior you were, getting the nurses on side was the single biggest predictor of success.

'Lizzie is a real challenge. She's extremely ill. Almost catatonic.' Jack paused. 'You know what she did to that poor French guy.'

'Mmmm,' said Mortimer, shaking his head. 'Just terrible. The tabloids are having a field day with the headlines.' He opened his desk drawer and pulled out the sensationalised front page.

*LE MERDE-R!*the headline screamed.

And underneath: *French academic slain by crazed student!*

The remainder of the article was filled with half-truths and stigmatising language.

'Christ, those bloody papers set the cause back by about fifty years,' Mortimer sighed.

Jack knew that Mortimer had always been a very strong advocate for the media using non-stigmatising language about mental illness.

'Of course, I wanted to rule out any physical cause for her psychosis before jumping in with the meds. It had never been properly investigated before. But her bloods, urine, MRI and EEG didn't reveal any evidence of physical pathology. No tumours, no seizures, no metabolic disturbances. There were no illicit drugs on board, either.'

'Good work, Jack. I'm a big fan of thoroughness.'

'But the tests did reveal that she's pregnant.'

Mortimer rubbed his palm on his forehead.

'Well that adds a layer of complexity,' he said in a bland tone.

Jack shook his head. These types of clinical dilemmas raised dozens of questions and very few clear-cut answers. But for Jack, at the heart of the matter always stood one simple conundrum:

What is the right thing to do?

After much discussion on the ward it was decided that Lizzie was so desperately ill that her welfare should be put ahead of the embryo. Jack had seen psychotic women in this position before and had often witnessed how the sheer stress of the illness led to a miscarriage.

There were no winners.

Treatment was almost always a judgment call.

A young woman, psychotic, charged with murder, pregnant.

There was no guidebook to turn to that would magically reveal the answers.

'Given that she is pregnant, I've chosen the lesser of all the evils and got her straight on to high-dose intramuscular olanzapine to start getting on top of the psychosis. We've cut back the dosage of lorazepam, but her brain still needs to rest, and this will certainly help. She seems to be starting to respond.'

Jack looked at Mortimer, who suddenly seemed quite disinterested by it all. After a minute he finally replied. 'What we need, Jack, is … *cure!* Don't we? We need a long term … *solution.*'

A long silence.

'Anyway, Jack, keep it up, doctor, keep it up, and you will have a very prosperous career.'

Jack tossed that word around in his mind for several minutes: *prosperous.*

Prosperous.

A slightly odd choice he felt, from a man who used his words precisely and deliberately. He would have expected, or at least hoped for, a word like 'distinguished' or even 'fulfilling', but 'prosperous'?

Either way, it seemed that Mortimer was keen to put Lizzie and her dilemma out of his mind.

'Tell you what, Jack. I'm having a little dinner party at my place this Saturday night with some friends, why don't you come along. I'm sure you'll find the company quite stimulating.'

Jack was flattered.

> *Dinner?*
>
> *With Professor Nathan Mortimer?*
>
> *At his house?*

He almost couldn't believe it. To him, it was the equivalent of the devoted, teenage groupie being invited backstage by the hottest rock band in the world.

'Nell will give you the address. Shall we say eight o'clock?'

'S-s-sure!'

'Do you have a partner you would like to bring?'

'No,' Jack said, with a hint of regret.

11

ASIDE FROM INTERVIEWING the patients, Jack found the weekly ward rounds the most stimulating aspect of his work at the facility. Unlike the rounds made by surgical staff in general hospitals, where the teams moved from bedside to bedside to discuss the patients, psychiatric ward rounds were held without the patients present. This allowed for far more robust discussions of the cases.

Naturally, the rounds were chaired by Professor Mortimer. The rest of the team comprised of forensic psychiatrists, senior psychiatric trainees, residents, medical students, plus the senior nurses and social workers who were directly involved with the patients.

Jack believed these discussions provided a great opportunity to bring together patient histories, clinical skills, and the latest in research to devise highly individualised treatment plans for the inpatients on the wards. He also enjoyed hearing the different perspectives people had on their patients.

It soon became clear to Jack that Drew Barnard was only there to kill time and was happy to delegate as much work as he could to the more junior staff, shielding himself with the defence that 'they have to learn'. He spent most of his time fiddling around with his iPhone while the discussions about the patients took place. Or distracted himself with the coffee and pastries that were provided at the commencement of each ward round, and for which he was invariably first in the queue.

While Jack agreed that the junior staff did need to learn, he still believed that the buck ultimately stopped with the senior consultants, and they should be making the final call on treatment.

Barnard clearly did not share this view, and seemed to actively take pleasure in watching the junior staff and students squirm when he directed them to present the patients. Jack observed that Barnard would unashamedly target any young males who might be a threat to his position. This was a bullying practice that Jack himself had endured at Columbia, and he'd quickly grown to despise it. An environment of fear and anxiety was not, he well knew, conducive to learning.

Wherever possible, Jack would step in and support the floundering junior staff, but Barnard was quite relentless in his quest to avoid doing the work himself.

The only exception to this was when the designer-clad doctor tried to turn on the charm with one of the junior females he'd taken a liking to. They *never* got the tough questions it seemed and were never put on the spot. In addition, Barnard would take the time, *after* the ward round had concluded, to pull them aside and give them a personalised tutorial on the topic of the day.

In contrast to Barnard, Mortimer spoke with a brilliant blend of authority and respect to all in the room. He had an amazing understanding of every single patient in the unit and recalled details of patients' lives and histories that initially seemed trivial, but which would prove to be pivotal in understanding their psychology as the discussion unfolded.

Mortimer also had the rare ability of being able to not only summarise and explain the most recent research in a particular area of psychiatry, but to apply it to the individual cases being presented.

The clinical team had saved the newest and most mysterious patient until last. Sarah, as senior registrar, would usually present these complex patients, but a phone call to say one of her twins was unwell meant she needed to leave early.

Barnard made a strangely snide remark to her as she left.

'Take the rest of the day off, Mummy Wellington. After all, who am I to stand between you and your children's wellbeing?' She threw him a look and stormed out. Jack glared in Barnard's direction.

As such, it was left to a more junior member of the medical staff to describe the case. Jack thought they did a tremendous job of it.

The patient in question was simply known as 'Patient X', as no one knew his identity. Patient X was an Asian male, likely to be Vietnamese, and probably aged in his late teens or twenties, although it was hard to tell. He had been on the ward for over seventy-two hours and still had no formal diagnosis.

He had been arrested by the police down in the Southwest, after he had severely physically assaulted two young women who were returning home from a nightclub. The police report indicated that all he was interested in was a large bag of crisps that one of the girls was carrying. He fractured her spine to get them.

Since being on the ward he'd spoken little. Professor Mortimer had brought in both a Vietnamese and a Cambodian interpreter, but to no avail.

What was clear, however, was that Patient X was extremely compliant with all ward procedures. He did as he was told and had caused no problems at all since arriving on the ward. He only needed supervision at mealtimes when his appetite appeared voracious and insatiable. Despite this he had gained no weight and appeared extremely slim, almost emaciated.

Naturally, the staff believed he had some type of physical process going on, such as a brain or thyroid tumour that was responsible for his behaviour. But all brain scans, blood tests, urine samples and other investigations were completely normal. They arranged for an urgent neurological consult, but that also proved fruitless.

Due to his lack of responsiveness, all formal cognitive testing to assess his IQ and determine any signs of an early-onset dementia had been as much use as a chocolate teapot.

The hypothesis then shifted to a psychotic illness. He demonstrated an extreme kind of disorganisation in his thinking, but to Sarah and the other staff it had a different 'feel' to other cases of psychosis.

When answering questions, Patient X gave only the most basic of answers, usually a monosyllabic sound that barely seemed to warrant being described as a word, regardless of the language. He did not initiate or make any spontaneous conversation. He appeared to sleep well, could maintain only basic hygiene standards and was not obviously behaviourally disturbed in any way.

There was simply a vacuousness to him that almost defied explanation.

No one came forward to claim him. From the time of his arrest to the present day, no relative or friend had identified him. The police had investigated him as much as they could and came up blank.

'We have kept him on the acute ward because there are still so many unanswered questions,' the registrar explained. 'Even though he is behaviourally settled, we haven't sent him through to Dr Barnard's ward as yet.'

Barnard remained silent and simply rolled his eyes before returning to his smart phone.

'You have heard a lot about the patient, Dr Barnard,' said Jack. 'What is your opinion?'

Barnard glared at Jack with a look that said, *'Don't patronise me'*.

'I think it's pretty straightforward. It's a case of chronic schizophrenia with very prominent negative symptoms.' His eyes returned to his phone.

A few of the medical students looked puzzled.

'Who can tell me what the negative symptoms of schizophrenia are?' Jack asked. 'And, Doctor Barnard, you keep quiet because you clearly know the answer.'

The room erupted into laughter. Barnard shot Jack another nasty look, the meaning of which would have raised a few eyebrows if he'd put it into words.

'Isn't that when people with schizophrenia have no emotions?' one of the students bravely suggested.

'In a way,' Jack confirmed. 'Negative symptoms often develop over some years in the context of chronic psychosis. It is as if their brains gradually degenerate to a point where they lose motivation, lose the ability to think clearly, are unable to act spontaneously and where their emotions become extremely dulled and blunted. This is often what leads to the characteristic bland-looking face in schizophrenia, and the very monotonous sounding voice.'

'It is what the illness effectively *takes away* from the patient, hence the term *negative* symptoms,' Sarah added.

She then looked at Jack. 'I think that is probably what's going on here.'

'Even so', Jack said, 'I am very curious about this guy, and it might help to have a fresh set of eyes look over him.'

12

PATIENT X WAS already seated when Jack entered the small interview room on the acute ward. Instantly, he knew this was going to be a different kind of interview to the one he conducted with Lizzie Roberts. Indeed, the patient had a unique kind of ... *blankness* to him, just as Sarah had described.

The patient said nothing.

Jack introduced himself in an informal manner, then waited for a response. The patient just sat.

And stared.

Occasionally he would blink but again, as Sarah described, he would not make any spontaneous conversation.

> *That's okay, I can wait.*

Almost ten minutes went by and not a sound had passed between the two men. Despite the silence, Jack was still conducting what he could of a mental state examination.

The male patient appeared to be Vietnamese. He was probably in his early twenties, around five and a half feet tall and of a very slim build—although not quite skeletal. Jack concluded that the man had probably always been of this diminutive habitus.

There were no visible signs of agitation or distress. He was sitting quite comfortably and was not fidgety or shuffling around in his chair. He was not sweating, and his respiratory rate was around fourteen per minute. Nice and steady.

He did not appear to be responding to any perceptual disturbances, such as voices or other hallucinations.

Jack bet that if he took his pulse rate it would be regular and well within normal limits.

He waited another five minutes.

'How are you feeling?' Jack asked softly.

Nothing.

> *How do I feel?*

Jack knew that at times like this it was important to search his *own* feelings to try to find any clue as to what may be going on with the patient. As he had told the medical students, it was important to listen for any feelings of countertransference.

Jack relaxed and slowed his breathing.

> *How do you make me feel?*

He cleared his head of everything and anything – except the patient who sat across from him.

He soon entered a dreamlike state as he allowed his own unconscious to take over.

Jack half-closed his eyes as he listened to what his unconscious told him.

> *There is blankness. A kind of nothingness.*
>
> *Yet he does still feel emotion.*
>
> *He does breathe. His heart beats.*
>
> *His body functions.*
>
> *So what then is the nothing?*
>
> *I feel relaxed with you, Patient X.*
>
> *I don't feel scared or anxious with you.*
>
> *You won't respond to me.*
>
> *You can't respond to me.*
>
> *You are breathing. Living.*

But…

That is all.

What are you thinking?

All I can hear is your breathing.

Pretty soon Jack's mind became blank. His thoughts became a soft, white sphere of emptiness. Even a casual observer would have noticed that Jack's breathing depth and rate precisely mimicked the patient's, as did his posture.

He does breathe. His heart beats.

His body functions.

But there is no response.

No response.

When are you alive but with no response?

When are y-

A sudden, loud knock on the interview room door startled Jack back to full consciousness.

It was Mortimer.

13

'APOLOGIES FOR INTERRUPTING back there, but I'm about to head off for a few days and have been meaning to ask how you're settling in.' Mortimer raised his coffee cup and took a grateful sip. It had been a few weeks since Jack had started at the NTC and he was starting to feel comfortable with both the geography of the hospital and, more importantly, with his co-workers. He felt he had slipped into a nice routine.

Generally, the ward ran extremely efficiently. Mortimer had assembled an incredibly experienced team, across all disciplines, and it made Jack's working life a whole lot easier. The medical staff, even the junior trainees, were all first rate.

Except for Barnard.

Jack found that he did not cause any specific problems, but given his laziness and appalling treatment of the junior staff he could not understand why Mortimer bothered to keep him around.

The patients were quite an interesting mix of psychopathology. As was often the case in forensic psychiatric units, several suffered with quite severe psychotic illnesses and had experienced poor standards of treatment prior to committing their criminal offence. Others had received no treatment at all.

In addition, several of the patients had quite dangerous antisocial personality disorders all characterised by a complete lack of empathy and a desire to manipulate others in a quest for power. The rest of the world knew them as 'psychopaths' but Jack was always keen to look beyond the label and into the deeper psychological motivations of such disturbed individuals.

Throw in a volatile mix of substance abuse problems, and you have the makings of a forensic hospital.

And then, seemingly in his own unique diagnostic category, there was Patient X.

'Pretty well, thanks.' Jack didn't want to overstate things or come off sounding complacent or cocky.

'That's what I hear too,' Mortimer said with a smile. 'We should talk, Jack. About … *opportunities.*'

'Opportunities?'

'Yes, career opportunities. Financial opportunities. There's a vast world out there for people like you. For instance, have you ever considered doing some private practice?'

'I thought that was pretty limited in Britain.'

'To a great extent, yes. But as with anything, there is always a private… *market.*'

Having trained in the United States, Jack was all too familiar with the interplay between market forces and healthcare. He had seen this function at its best and, sadly, at its absolute worst. He wanted to see where the professor was headed.

'Sounds intriguing and, as you know, I am not completely averse to earning some extra money. London is an expensive city!'

Mortimer did not laugh but stared coldly at him. 'Oh, but it goes far beyond that, Jack.'

What does that mean?

'Doctor Giorgio, with your exceptional skills you certainly won't need to spend all of your time working here. As you have seen, our excellent junior staff can easily carry most of the load. You will be able to put your talents to more… *rewarding* uses.'

Jack was going to ask for clarification when there was a knock on the office door.

'Yes?' the professor called tersely.

The door opened and Nell, Mortimer's personal secretary, popped her head round. 'Sorry to interrupt but your car has arrived,' she announced, without sounding remotely sorry.

'Thank you, Nell, I won't be a minute.' Mortimer walked to the corner of the room and grabbed a Louis Vuitton carry-on case.

'Heading somewhere nice?' Jack asked.

'Yes, Geneva. Just for three nights. I'll see you back here on Monday. We'll resume our chat then.'

His tone had become curt, and Jack sensed that the professor was

not keen to give him any further details about the trip.

14

CERISE NAVARRO STARED intently into the rear-view mirror, made a slight adjustment to her lipstick, rearranged a strand of hair, and then opened the door of the sleek black BMW 220i convertible. She slid out of the driver's seat and strode towards the tall cyclone fence surrounding the secure hospital building with a confidence that belied the height of her stilettos.

In her left hand she carried a Chanel handbag, and in her right a brightly coloured plastic bag with the word '*Positrex*' written all over it in bright gold letters.

The burly security guard smiled broadly as she approached the reception desk and presented her identification. He took some time to look her up and down—under the guise of being diligent about hospital security.

'I'm here to see Doctor Jack Giorgio,' she said politely but definitely.

'Half his luck. Do you want me to buzz you in?'

'No that's okay, we're heading out, so if you could just have him come down to meet me here that would be great.'

The guard picked up a phone receiver and gestured to her to take a seat in the sparse waiting area.

Within a few minutes she was joined by a tall, athletic man in a charcoal suit. He held the business card she had left for him the week before requesting the meeting, and quickly slipped it into his jacket pocket so that he could offer a gentle handshake as she stood up to greet him.

'Jack Giorgio,' he announced with a smile. For a brief moment she lost herself in his intensely blue eyes.

'Oh... hi,' she began nervously. 'Cerise. Cerise Navarro. From

MTR. It's really nice to meet you. Thanks for seeing me. I thought we might take off for some lunch, if that's okay?' She spoke quickly, with a subtle French accent that suggested she had probably been in the UK for some years.

'That sounds good.' He looked down at the plastic bag.

'Oh … we can sort all that out later. I don't really know why I bothered to bring it in, given the fact we are going out.' She laughed nervously and blushed slightly.

Jack handed his security swipe card to the guard, and then they were out the door.

'Don't rush back, Doctor Jack,' the security guard grinned.

***

Cerise drove quickly and confidently through the busy London streets, manoeuvring the convertible with practiced ease, pinpointing small gaps in the traffic and heading precisely for them. He noticed she had opted for the six-speed manual rather than the automatic, and her delicate hand worked the gears like a pro. A few times he felt himself lower his hands to grip the sides of the seat, but decided not to say anything.

They spoke little in the car, and he stared straight ahead for the duration of the ride. Within ten minutes they had arrived at the restaurant.

Stock was the place to be seen for London's up-and-coming executive crowd. It had only been open for three months but was already enjoying incredible patronage. The chef behind it all, a striking South African woman in her early forties, had been the runaway winner on a popular television cooking contest the year before.

The restaurant had adopted the popular 'no-reservations' policy in favour of a 'first-come-first-served' approach and there was already a queue outside the door, despite the fact that it was not yet midday.

Jack began making his way to the end of the queue, but Cerise strode forward and spoke to the maître d', oblivious to the glares of those waiting in line for a coveted table. She turned to face Jack, gesturing for him to join her as the door was held open by the obliging maître d'.

'What did you say to him?' he asked as they were shown to their table.

'That you were the son of the Swedish prime minister, and the bistro could get very favourable press in Scandinavia if you liked it here.'

He looked horrified and didn't know what to say.

She laughed. 'Your face is priceless! I'm just kidding.' She placed a hand softly on his forearm. 'I'm so sorry! My boss has a family connection here and I called ahead to let them know we were coming.'

He suddenly felt self-conscious and looked sheepishly around the room, but the other diners were too engrossed in their conversations and their lunches to notice the queue-jumpers.

Jack smiled and relaxed.

They sat down and ordered drinks. He quickly perused the menu and made a hasty decision. He knew from experience that these drug company sponsored lunches were usually quick affairs. A few minutes of small talk followed by *several* minutes of information on the latest pharmaceuticals. Then came the inevitable handing over of glossy brochures and company-sponsored studies that, surprise, surprise, supported the wonderful claims made by the drug rep sitting across from him about the efficacy and safety of whatever they were plying. He was generally happy to go along for the ride and familiarise himself with the info that the companies were pushing, but he usually found the reps to be patronising and robotic. The whole affair was usually done and dusted in around thirty minutes.

He had to admit to himself that this restaurant was a step above—

actually *several* steps above—any of the places he'd previously been taken to, and Cerise appeared to be more engaging than the any of the previous reps who'd sat across from him, but in spite of this, he expected the same outcome.

She raised her glass when the drinks came, but then did not seem to know what to say.

'Cheers,' he stepped in, to save any further blushes. 'Thanks, this place looks great.'

'How are you finding it at the NTC?' she asked, taking a sip.

'It's very impressive. Professor Mortimer is inspiring and the staff are really good to work with. For the most part,' he said with a wry smile.

It was the first time Jack had the chance to look closely at his companion. Her shoulder-length brown hair was neatly tied back in a ponytail, and although she wore no earrings she had a tiny, silver stud in her nose. It was so subtle that he hardly noticed it, but occasionally it would catch the light and glisten. He just wasn't keen on too many piercings, and while intrigued by the meaning of tattoos never really found them a turn on, but he found her nose stud somehow... exciting... mesmerising... almost erotic. He looked away, not wanting to get caught out staring. But she had noticed the look.

She *had* noticed.

They placed their orders. Jack was suddenly feeling hungry, and was relieved when he saw that Cerise ordered both a starter and a main.

'MTR?' he asked. 'Are they Swiss?'

'Umm... yeah,' she confirmed.

'So how did you come to work for them?'

'I initially did a degree in medical science and then did honours. It just went from there.'

'Great! What was your thesis on?'

She blushed slightly. 'Oh, it's so boring. You don't want to know.'

'Sure I do. What was it?'

She cut a scallop in half and placed it in her mouth.

'Generally, it was on dopamine receptors.'

'And specifically?'

She looked slightly nervous.

'Oh, you know... just how the genes coding for them can sometimes switch on in random patterns. How about you?'

'Me?'

'Yeah, how did you end up here? Why psychiatry?'

'Well, it was just so fascinating—hearing the intimate human stories. These people, these patients, would allow you right into their most inner selves. The self that goes right past the physical and into their soul. Corny, right?'

'No! Keep going! I like hearing this.' The clink of cutlery and glasses filled the restaurant. She moved her head slightly closer across the table.

'Well, I remember once as a med student, I was on a surgical rotation. But not just any surgical rotation – cardiac surgery, with Professor Sandler – you know, the guy who revolutionised work on artificial heart valves.'

Cerise didn't know the name but still nodded in agreement.

'Sandler would talk endlessly about the importance of cardiac surgery and that it's life and death and therefore the purest of all medical endeavours.

'I spent almost eight hours with him while he did a cardiac transplant. He talked endlessly about the heart and how it pumps life around our bodies. It was tedious! But it gives you a lot of time to think and daydream. About halfway through the procedure, it occurred to me that really the heart exists to serve the brain and the brain serves the mind and it's the mind that is where the real purity lies. The real person. After all, you can't transplant someone's mind.'

She was listening intently.

He continued. 'And also, I much preferred to work *with* people, rather than *on* them. The other thing about surgery, about procedures, is that it really forces you to narrow your focus and field of vision, but psychiatry allows to you expand it, you know?'

Cerise nodded enthusiastically. 'Especially forensic psychiatry,' she added.

'Absolutely. It really is psychiatry outside the square. Although, in forensics, you are often judged for the things that do *not* happen. The violent man with schizophrenia who does *not* kill. Managing the threat so that it is *not* carried out. Hoping for things that do not happen can be a bit unfulfilling at times, but overall, I don't think I could work in any other area.'

Their main courses arrived, and a comfortable silence descended upon them while they ate.

After a few minutes Cerise spoke. 'At MTR we are really looking at new ways of developing drug delivery for patients. Pills and even injections, they just seem so... so...' she looked down at her plate, 'inefficient. I mean, so little of the actual dosage of the drug gets to the patient's brain.'

'Yeah, they have their limitations.'

'And then there's the whole compliance issue. We all know that side effects really put the patients off. The pills are even more useless when they just sit there in the bottle!'

'That's for sure,' he agreed with a smile.

'So, we are looking at more advanced and potentially longer-lasting options that could really boost patient adherence to their medication regimes.'

'What, like extended-duration injections?'

'Like nanotechnology.'

'*Nanotechnology?*' he looked at her with wide eyes.

'Sure. Why not? We have two patents for micro-sized mechanical devices that can actually deliver the medication right to the area of the brain that you want to target.'

'Amazing,' he said slowly.

'You know better than most the benefits that can be brought by long-term symptomatic control.'

'But how would that even work?'

'Well,' she looked around the room and then spoke in a quieter voice, 'I can't really say too much, it's all very hush-hush, but we are looking at highly advanced medication delivery systems that may potentially last up to five years.'

'*Five years!* Gee, I really wonder about the ethics of that.'

'What do you mean?'

'Well, let's say someone is initially on an involuntary treatment order that may last say six or twelve months, after which time they get better. Shouldn't they then have the choice about their treatment?'

'But Jack, just imagine five years of wellness. Five years of being free of the torment of voices and delusions. Five years of getting back to a normal life again.' As she spoke, she seemed to become more impassioned.

'It's hard to argue against that, but in an era of patient-centred medicine which shifts away from the paternalistic methods of the old days, I'm just not sure. Patients are better educated now, better informed and they certainly know their rights.' He felt he was making a strong case, but Cerise ignored this and pushed on.

'In fact, we are close to trials on an implantable device, much like you can get for birth control. We are realistic when we talk about the five-year timeframe.'

He felt like chiming sarcastically, *'Hey, I've got a great idea! Why don't you combine the antipsychotic implant with the birth control implant and solve two of society's problems at once!'* but he decided to hold his tongue. In fact, he was pretty much speechless. He'd not read anything about implantable devices for psychiatric patients and he prided himself on keeping up with the latest research, especially in the area of medications used to treat chronic schizophrenia.

Cerise seemed to sense this.

'We've kept it pretty quiet because we don't want to give our competitors a heads-up. But the results are looking quite stunning.'

As are you.

He looked at her right forearm as she sipped the chilled sauvignon blanc. She had a wonderful olive complexion that seemed so natural. *'No tanning salon here,'* he decided.

'Apologies if I am wrong, but do I detect a French accent?' he asked.

'Well done. Yes.'

'But Navarro... is that Spanish?'

She tilted her wine glass towards him.

'Ka-ching. Well done again. Want to go for double or nothing?' She smiled in a playful way. He weighed up what to ask next. He wanted to know more about her but didn't want to push her away by asking too much. He felt the atmosphere was light, and threw a little caution to the wind.

'I know, I know. Your boyfriend is the next Wimbledon champion and spends half the year training in Madrid and the other half developing his immense pastry skills at the Cordon Bleu?' He waited with bated breath.

'Ha, ha, ha!!' she bellowed.

She put a hand to her mouth as a few of the other diners turned around and looked at her. She blushed deeply.

'But that would leave me stuck here in London all alone.'

'Ah, the heartache of distance.'

She suddenly looked more serious. 'Actually, there is no tennis star, no Michelin-starred chef, not even a fourth division football player with a talent for making cheese on toast.'

She looked down at the stem of her wine glass. He wanted to keep the conversation flowing.

'But it's an interesting mix – the Spanish and the French – how did that come about?' He quickly checked himself. 'If it's not too personal, that is.'

'Oh no, that's fine. My father was actually from the Philippines and my mother is French.'

'*Was* from the Philippines?'

'Yeah, he died when I was eight. He was a regional manager for an oil company, and he was a workaholic. He did no exercise and would spend at least twelve hours a day at work. When I did see him, he was great fun though. He went at a million miles an hour, into everything and anything. They would have diagnosed him with ADHD if he was born a generation later!'

She smiled warmly as she looked away and appeared to see long-ago images of her father in her mind.

'He developed a condition like rapidly progressing multiple sclerosis, and it took him when he was only forty-nine,' she added. She stared at him with a tear welling up.

'Oh, I'm sorry,' he looked right into her eyes.

'Thanks, but it's fine. After that my mother and I moved back to

France and lived there for many years before I eventually moved to London.'

She was worried that she was revealing too much about herself, but at the same time she felt so comfortable talking to him. He didn't jump in every few seconds to finish her sentences or try to dominate the conversation by talking endlessly about himself and his achievements. He made her feel like he was genuinely interested in who she was.

Jack glanced down at his watch and could not believe that it was quarter past two. He felt anxious about getting back to work. Cerise clearly sensed this.

'It's a shame, but I suppose we had better get you back to work,' she gave a sigh.

He frowned. 'Yes. It is a shame. I have really enjoyed this.' After she had paid for lunch they strolled back to the car and then wound their way through the streets to the hospital – this time more sedately.

Cerise popped open the small boot of the BMW and placed her handbag and jacket inside. After looking in she moved a pair of running shoes from one side to the other. Jack couldn't help but notice.

'That's pretty hardcore, Cerise. You must be a serious runner. And a good one! New Balance 1260's are not for the amateur!' She didn't know what she found more impressive – his compliment about her running or his knowledge of her shoes.

'Oh... thanks... I love nothing more than a long run.' Jack reached in and grabbed a sneaker.

'They are so light. And the fluorescent pink and yellow is hot.' He believed he could see her blushing. 'What sort of running are you into?'

'Long distance. I have done a couple of half marathons, but now I am in training for the big one.'

'Great, which one are you aiming for?'

'The London Marathon in April. I figured that a hometown marathon was the best one to start with – no travel hassles, familiar route, all that stuff.'

'Mmmm,' agreed Jack. 'How's the training going?' He looked up to the grey sky and made a quick calculation in his head. 'There's about seven weeks to go, how is your weekly mileage?'

'Uggghhh,' she groaned and playfully slapped his left bicep. The touch felt great to Jack. 'It could always be better.'

Jack smiled warmly at her.

'I'm with you on that! I agree that there's nothing more liberating than a long run, but it can seem like a chore at times. If you would like we could take a run together sometime. It can be more motivating if you have someone to run with, and since moving to London I haven't really met anyone to run with yet. We could chat about technique and pacing and all that stuff. I'm always keen to swap ideas.'

He stopped abruptly, worried that he was sounding like a pushy, know-it-all bore.

'Really? That would be great. I would like that. How about this Sunday morning?'

'Sure,' he said with restrained enthusiasm.

I would go right now if you wanted to.

She gave him her address and as they shook hands she leant forward and kissed him gently on the cheek.

15

JACK TOOK THE District line to Sloane Square and walked the rest of the way to Mortimer's in the rapidly fading evening light. He turned onto the private square and followed the numbers on the impressive doors, until he reached a wedding-cake mansion with a striking midnight-blue Bentley Mulsanne parked out the front. He double checked that he was in the right place, but sure enough, there was the number '77', perfectly painted on one of the large entrance pillars. Before he could take it all in, the glossy front-door opened, framing Mortimer's silhouette in the light from the hallway beyond.

Jack hurried up the wide, white steps and shook the professor's hand, before being ushered inside. He had never been in such an opulent residence before. The foyer was tastefully decorated with a few pieces of original art and a beautiful oak hallstand and mirror. The black and white marble floor led them through to a wide hallway, which was adorned with more art. To the right was an impressive staircase that led up to the first and second floors.

As they walked down the hallway, Jack caught his breath as they passed the open door of an immense library. Floor to ceiling bookshelves housed thousands of volumes. On one wall, nestled between the seemingly endless tomes, stood a grand marble fireplace, in front of which had been positioned two large leather armchairs. Jack could not imagine a more inviting place to read.

Several animated voices could be heard coming from further along the hallway, growing steadily louder as they approached. Mortimer turned the handle and gestured for his guest to enter the opulent dining room. A hush descended as Jack crossed the threshold, and all eyes in the room focused on him. The mutual uneasiness quickly thawed as Mortimer warmly introduced him to the assembled guests.

'I'll leave you for a moment, if I may,' Mortimer spoke reassuringly as he steered Jack across the room, 'in the capable hands of Peter.' He delivered his charge and walked away to attend to his other guests.

Jack was slightly flustered to discover that the Peter in question was none other than Peter Ripley, professor of neurosurgery at Oxford. Jack had heard Ripley speak at a conference in the US on neurosurgical procedures for treatment-resistant obsessive-compulsive disorder, and had been in awe of the professor's knowledge of the condition. Ripley was a fit-looking bald man of around seventy and was quite casually dressed compared to the other guests.

'So, you're Nathan's new protégé?' the neurosurgeon asked. For a moment Jack wondered who he was talking about, until the penny dropped. Professor Nathaniel Mortimer was apparently just 'Nathan' to his friends.

'Oh… yes. I suppose, yes,' he hesitantly replied.

'He already speaks quite highly of you, which is saying something,' Ripley added, sensing Jack's nervousness.

'That's kind of him. It's a thrill to be able to work with him.'

Ripley laughed. To Jack's surprise, the eminent man suddenly put his arm around Jack, pulled him in close and whispered, 'Jack, don't say that, whatever you do! Nathan's ego is big enough for *all* of us. If it gets any bigger, I'll have to suction some of it out!'

Before he could think of how to respond, a young waitress entered the room and handed Jack a glass of champagne.

'Cheers,' gestured Ripley, chinking his own glass against Jack's.

Another man then joined them. He was younger, around forty-five, and wore an expensive beige suit with a brightly patterned shirt underneath. He smiled warmly at Jack.

'Well, hello there,' he addressed Jack in a soft Welsh accent, as he extended his hand.

'Doctor Jack Giorgio this is Marty Price, my partner,' Ripley announced proudly. Jack ran the name and the face over in his mind.

Marty Price. Marty Price.

Then it came to him: *M.E. Price.*

'M.E. Price?' he exclaimed out loud. A few guests looked Jack's way. 'Are you *M.E.* Price?' he said again.

'Guilty,' Marty smiled, raising his hands in surrender.

'I know it is a terrible cliché, but can I say that I am a huge fan of your books. The Inspector Jones series is my favourite collection of crime novels.'

'Those kinds of cliches are most welcome!' Marty laughed.

Jack struggled not to feel out of his depth as he quickly surveyed the room to see who else was there. Other than a prominent criminal barrister there were no other familiar faces, but he felt that he would no doubt recognise some of the names when he was introduced.

Jack was almost relieved when Mortimer suddenly announced that dinner was about to be served. The guests made suitably appreciative noises and made their way to the table.

Jack was seated next to Annabel Irvine, a very engaging geneticist, originally from Los Angeles. Her husband, the CEO of a pharmaceutical company, was at the far end of the table, and began intensely debating something that was clearly very important to him with an amused looking Ripley. Annabel, by contrast, was very easy company, and happily exchanged thoughts with Jack about life and work in England versus life in the States. He found her to be incredibly interesting and personable and they spoke for some time whilst their entrees got cold.

At one point during the evening Jack was consumed by an unfamiliar feeling: *he belonged.*

Even allowing for the several glasses of fine wine he had consumed, he was supremely relaxed, and perceived that people were truly interested in him and what he had to say. There was no need to defend himself and his career choice or to set people straight about their pejorative comments regarding the mentally ill. These individuals were so articulate, so worldly and so educated that it was as if their interactions all began on some higher level.

Even though the person closest in age to Jack was the pretty, young red-haired waitress serving the food and wine, it did not matter.

Mortimer also seemed to be revelling in the company. Jack observed that he was quite the affable host and, perhaps not surprisingly, was noticeably more relaxed than when he was at work. After the cheese course, Jack sat back, utterly sated, while Mortimer stepped outside into the manicured garden to smoke cigars with several of the other guests.

Jack opted instead for an espresso, a nip of Port and a chat with Wesley Wong, a successful merchant banker who had moved to London with his family after Hong Kong was returned to China in 1997. The red-haired waitress delivered the after-dinner drinks, holding her gaze on Jack for just a moment longer than necessary, before returning to the kitchen.

Wong also had a passion for books, and he and Jack spoke at length about various rare first editions that had been auctioned over the past few months.

Then came a sudden, brief pause in the conversation when Wong looked deep into Jack's eyes. Jack sensed a tension but was not sure of its origin. Wong looked around the room before moving slightly closer to Jack.

'Does the name Christina Beauchamp-Alard mean anything to you at all?' he asked in a hushed voice. Jack looked up to the corner of the room while he thought.

'No… no, it doesn't. Who is she?'

Wong looked sad.

'Who *was* she, unfortunately,' he corrected, staring across the room towards a Picasso that took understandable pride of place on the opposite wall.

'She's dead?'

'Yes, yes. Here. In London, I mean, not in this house. She was hit by a truck and killed instantly.'

'An accident? Or suicide?'

'I'm not sure. Maybe suicide. I know her father, Henri. We worked together before I left Hong Kong. We kept in touch over the years but since her death I've heard nothing from him.' Wong looked pensive.

'Was she mentally ill?'

'Oh yes. She had paranoid schizophrenia that first took hold in her teenage years. Terrible condition. Henri and his wife did all they could to help her but sometimes...'

'...the disease wins,' Jack finished the thought.

'Precisely,' Wong agreed. 'She was a beautiful girl. She had a passion for art history. It was the one talent that somehow seemed to be quarantined from her illness. And, like her father, she had a photographic memory. No doubt that helped with her incredible knowledge of art.'

Jack wondered where the conversation was headed.

'I guess the thing that doesn't quite make sense to me,' Wong continued, 'is that Christina was in London when she died and yet I thought Henri *always* had her treated in Zurich. The last contact I had from him was about a week before her death, and he told me that she was getting some new treatment, and she had told him that there was real hope on the horizon. But then she dissap...'

Jack felt a firm hand on his shoulder that made him jump.

'With your mutual love of books I am glad that you two boys have had a chat,' said Mortimer in a loud, friendly voice, 'Now come with me to the library and I will show you some absolute treasures.'

At that point, Wong excused himself from the party, explaining that his wife, an obstetrician who had been on call all evening, had just messaged him to say she was on her way home.

Jack dutifully followed Mortimer to the library.

'*Whoa*,' he gasped as they stepped inside. He didn't know where to look first. His eyes darted from the collection of leather-bound nineteenth century English literature to the array of early twentieth century first editions. A cursory glance revealed a wonderfully fine first edition of Fitzgerald's *The Great Gatsby* as well as a mint condition copy of *Soldier's Pay* by William Faulkner.

In a glass cabinet that was illuminated by a soft, ambient light sat a perfect copy of a very rare 1922 first edition of *Ulysses*.

'Spectacular! *Ulysses!* This is beyond belief.' Jack whispered.

'*The* greatest book ever written,' Mortimer said with authority. 'That copy is signed by Joyce and, quite coincidentally, he inscribed it to someone called Nathan. It's probably my *most* prized possession.'

Mortimer settled into one of the two chairs in front of the fireplace.

'Take a seat, Jack,' the professor smiled. Although it didn't sound as though it was an invitation. More like an instruction.

It was then that Jack realised Mortimer had closed the library door behind him, and he could no longer hear any of the other guests.

As he sat down, Mortimer gestured to the small round table between them. It held a bottle of *Penfold's* great grandfather port, with two glasses already poured.

'A little drop from home for you, Jack.'

'Thank you.' Jack reached for one of the glasses, before leaning back into the soft leather of the chair. 'This is truly a wonderful collection,' he spoke seriously, motioning to the bookshelves.

'Cheers. I thought you'd appreciate it.' He raised his glass. 'Anything catch your eye, other than the Joyce?'

'I confess I have a weakness for futuristic, dystopian works,' said Jack. 'You know, Orwell, Huxley, Wyndham, those guys.'

'Ahhh… so you would be a *1984* tragic then?'

'Absolutely!'

No sooner had Jack spoken than Mortimer produced two perfect first editions copies of Orwell's seminal work – one in the famous green dust jacket, and the other in the red. Jack laughed in delighted disbelief.

'Thanks again for inviting me tonight, Professor Mortimer. I've really enjoyed myself. They are an amazing group of people,' Jack gushed.

'I think you can call me Nathan,' the professor laughed.

They both sipped their port.

'Having friends like this is very stimulating, Jack. It opens your mind and gives you access to worlds that you can only imagine. I also find it very comforting to be around them, and this is quite significant because, as I am sure you would know, psychiatrists aren't always…' he looked solemnly at Jack, 'readily accepted.'

Jack knew exactly what Mortimer was speaking about.

'Mmmm,' he nodded in agreement.

'But sometimes these people can go a bit too far, you know, with their questions. They think that we are some sort of mental magicians,' he chuckled to himself. 'Blessed with some kind of supernatural power to know things can never really be known.' Jack was confused and not really following Mortimer's train of thought. The professor sensed this and got right to the point.

'Take Wesley Wong, for instance. A charming guy. A mathematical genius. Knows financial markets like the back of his hand. But can get carried away worrying over things that really don't concern him.'

Mortimer was now glaring at Jack with greater intensity.

'Like young women dying in the middle of London, just to pick an example. Now there's no need for Wong to be asking you about that, in the middle of an enjoyable evening, bringing down the mood.'

The two men quickly finished their glasses of port and stared at the bookcase.

'Come on,' the professor checked his watch. 'I'll give you a ride home in the Bentley.'

***

Once in the car, Mortimer seemed to relax.

'And don't worry about Barnard,' he said, apropos of nothing. 'He's harmless. But between you and me, he's a little on the lazy side.'

'Oh… right.'

'He doesn't cause any problems, as such. Although the nurses can't stand him,' Mortimer said with a laugh.

'Yes, I got a whiff of that,' Jack agreed.

'He's only ever assigned to the step-down ward. That way he doesn't have to deal with the acutely unwell patients, nor is he responsible for those who are about to be released back into the big, wide world. He basically babysits the patients who are stuck in psychiatric limbo, you might say. His trainees do all his work for him, anyway.'

'He comes across as a little…'

'Arrogant? Conceited?' Mortimer cut in. 'You bet. It's in his DNA. He's from old money. Old school tie. Eton. Et cetera. He's actually the twenty-third Earl of Wexbridge. Landed. Loaded.'

'So why does he bother having a job that he clearly has no interest in doing?'

Mortimer chuckled.

'His lands are held in trust. With conditions. One of which is that he must work until he is at least fifty years of age. I guess he figured that if he *had* to work he might as well make it interesting, so he paid his way into medical school and then did his psych training. Perhaps he thought it would easier than being a 'proper' doctor.'

They both laughed heartily.

'And why forensics?' Jack asked, finding himself fascinated with the story.

'To be honest I think it is nothing more than a way to meet women.' Mortimer laughed again, this time more gregariously.

'How's that?' Jack enquired with bemusement.

'Well, I think he likes to talk it up, you know? About how he treats all these dangerous criminals. He always seems to find an audience of young women who will listen to his sensationalised anecdotes about crazed, serial killer psychopaths.'

Jack was puzzled. 'So why do you keep him around then?'

'It's more of an administrative convenience than anything else. He just migrated over from the old forensic unit when it closed. He's on one of those permanent contracts with the NHS that are almost impossible to break. And I have had no legitimate reason to fire him. Unfortunately, hubris doesn't count!'

Both men laughed loudly as the Bentley turned on to Jack's street.

'But, Jack, to balance out Barnard, I did employ Sarah, so you can at least thank me for that one! She is world class.'

Jack nodded in agreement.

Jack thanked Mortimer for a wonderful evening and complemented him on his choice of car. As they said their goodnights, the professor leaned in close and spoke so softly that he almost whispered.

'And Jack… if you want a good deal on something fun for yourself, a little convertible Mercedes perhaps, just head down to the Mayfair dealership and ask for Ronald Richter. He's the GM. Tell him I sent you.'

Jack smiled in an uncertain manner.

'I'm serious, Jack. It will be well worth your while.'

'Goodnight, Professor.'

'Nathan,' Mortimer laughed. Jack smiled again and stepped onto the pavement, where he stayed, staring back down the street as the Bentley slipped away into the night.

16

CERISE WAS ALREADY limbering up outside her terraced apartment by the time he arrived. From a distance he watched her stretch for a minute before approaching. He was fixated by her legs. So smooth, so toned, yet so strong. She had clearly been putting in a lot of training and he began to wonder, for the first time, if *he* would be able to keep up with *her*.

He waved and smiled. 'Good morning.'

'Hiya,' she called back.

'Great day for it.' He was suddenly nervous and small talk seemed the safest option.

She looked up to the skies. 'Yeah, not bad, nice and cool but no chance of rain.'

He'd changed his running outfit twice before leaving his apartment, surprising himself at how keen he was to impress her.

Right before they took off, she produced an iPod shuffle and placed a pair of ear buds into each ear.

'Habit,' she explained.

He felt an immediate sense of disappointment. Had he got the wrong impression? He hadn't thought so. He believed that this run would allow them to chat and get to know each other and… who knew what else? But it seemed that she was going to take this seriously and it was, indeed, all about the run. He told himself that if the worst that happened was a Sunday jog with a beautiful, intelligent woman, that wasn't so bad.

By the time they reached Hyde Park they'd settled into a nice rate and rhythm. Jack was slightly relieved when he realised that he *could* keep pace with her, as it allowed him to run side-by-side with her without expending too much energy on his own form, so that he could focus on Cerise.

Intermittently, he would gesture to her about a subtle change she could make in her stride or posture. She seemed appreciative of the advice, but he was very careful to not overdo it. After a while, she switched off the iPod and they indulged in some light conversation as they ran.

After around an hour of running, Cerise gestured to Jack that she'd had enough, and the pair slowed to a gentle walk. She dropped in behind him and spontaneously laid her hands on his shoulders. He felt her head against his back.

'Piggy-back?' she asked playfully.

Jack feigned an injury and limped forward before responding with 'For sure, a piggy-back would be great—but I don't know if you could carry me!'

She laughed, and they strolled the rest of the way back to her home.

To Jack, it felt as though a magnet was pulling them closer. Cerise slowly placed her hand in his and gently led him up the three steps to her front door. The sweat did not deter either of them.

She fumbled with the key but eventually managed to find the lock. With a firmer grip she pulled him inside and into the kitchen.

Without speaking, she placed a hand on each of his broad shoulders and sat him down at the table. She went to the fridge and grabbed a pitcher of cold water. She filled two glasses, added a slice of lemon to each, and placed them on the table. He watched her every movement. She turned back to the fridge and squatted down right in front of him to get to the freezer.

She returned with two small ice cubes.

Still, no one spoke.

She stood right in front of him, took a wide stance and moved forward so she could straddle his toned thighs.

She ran one of the ice cubes gently over his forehead. He closed his eyes and sighed deeply. She took the other ice cube and ran it up and down his neck and then into the upper part of his back. He leant forward slightly to allow her hand to slide down his shirt all the way to his lumbar area. He sighed again, this time louder. The ice cube made its way back up and found his cheeks and forehead.

He opened his eyes briefly.

Her singlet was just inches from his face. A few beads of sweat sat teasingly in her cleavage. He swallowed, hard.

His skin was still warm from the run and the ice melted quickly.

Jack slowly raised his arms and placed his hands gently on her hips. It took enormous effort to stop them from shaking but he somehow managed to suppress it. His fingers found their way around to her tight behind. Her lycra running pants felt soft but barely contained the firmness underneath.

The ice had now melted, and he opened his eyes. She found the lower end of her running singlet and pulled it off in one quick motion. Her sports bra, also pink, was wringing wet. She unclipped it, and in a moment it was gone, revealing a pair of perfectly formed, round breasts.

She leant forward slowly and kissed his forehead where the ice had been moments ago.

'Hmmm,' she whispered in his ear. 'The ice is nice, but it just doesn't last long enough, does it?'

He could only agree.

'What we need is more water.'

'So what do you propo…' he began, but when he opened his eyes, she was gone. He looked around the kitchen. Nothing. A moment later he could hear the familiar spraying sound of a shower.

'Aren't you coming?' she yelled out, but Jack was already out of his chair.

17

THE IMPRESSIVE FLEET of Jaguars and Range Rovers pulled up in perfect unison outside the hospital. Mortimer and Patterson were ready and waiting to greet the Secretary of Health as he stepped out of his chauffeur-driven car.

'Minister,' Patterson smiled obsequiously. 'Welcome to the Nicholas Tindal Centre. It's an honour to have you here.'

The minister ignored him and fixed his gaze squarely on Mortimer.

'Hello Roger,' said Mortimer, shaking the minister's hand and slapping him on the back.

'Nathan,' he replied. 'Always good to see you.' He yawned widely and looked up to the sign above front entrance before adding, 'Tindal? I was honestly expecting to be visiting the Nathaniel Mortimer Centre. He must have deep pockets to have swung himself a deal of having *your* centre named after *him*.'

Mortimer laughed. 'Come on, old boy. Tindal's not a donor. You should know your history better than that.'

Despite their long-standing friendship, Roger Maxwell bristled slightly.

The two men walked inside, followed by an entourage of government bureaucrats, media advisors, and security personnel. As they walked, Mortimer explained that Nicholas Tindal had introduced the verdict of 'Not Guilty by reason of insanity' to the British justice system.

'It was a monumental case in the history of forensic psychiatry, as well as being a huge milestone in criminal law. The floridly psychotic Daniel M'Naghten had delusions about Sir Robert Peel— you know who he was of course, Roger,' Mortimer teased.

Maxwell bristled again. 'Of course. I'm not a bloody idiot, Nathan.'

The professor laughed. 'Anyway, I'm sure you'd agree that getting access to the Prime Minister isn't always easy, and M'Naghten couldn't reach Peel, so he did the next best thing and murdered a civil servant.'

'Let that be a warning to you all,' Maxwell loudly proclaimed to his staff, who rewarded the minister with half-hearted laughter.

'Roger, please meet Doctor Jack Giorgio, one of my new consultant psychiatrists. Jack, this is the Secretary of Health, and therefore essentially your boss and mine, Sir Roger Maxwell.'

Jack and Maxwell shook hands.

'Now Jack, I hope this old devil isn't working you too hard?'

'Like a slave, Sir Roger,' Jack replied with a wink.

'Well, if you enjoy that sort of thing you can always come and work in my office,' Maxwell smiled dryly. Without knowing why, Jack was gripped with a sudden dislike for the man.

The conversation was interrupted when Maxwell was handed a mobile phone by one of his people. He walked off to a quiet corner, speaking in a hushed tone.

'The Prime Minister, no doubt. She wears him like a glove,' Mortimer whispered to Jack.

Maxwell quickly re-joined them. 'Right ho!' he said, 'I want to see every part of this monstrosity of a hospital. Let's start with the dungeon, shall we?'. Jack was beginning to understand his earlier feelings.

The group was guided through the facility by Mortimer and Patterson, with Mortimer stopping frequently to wax lyrical about the building's design and the clinical services performed within it.

For the most part, Jack thought that Maxwell looked bored, while several of his advisors displayed a mixture of fascination and terror to be walking through an actual forensic psychiatric hospital.

In the twin shadows of Mortimer and Maxwell, Jack soon drifted to the rear of the group, where a pretty young woman had been jostled by her colleagues, presumably as a result of her low status in the pack of aides. The colourful edge of a tattoo playfully poked out from inside her shirt collar. Jack spent almost ten minutes trying to work out what it depicted. She noticed his attention and starting flirting with him, saying, 'I'm glad I'm being chaperoned by you, doctor, just in case anything *happens* with one of the patients.'

He leant in close to her and whispered, 'but I *am* one of the patients.' She smiled uncomfortably and moved away from him.

In order to enable the minister to view one of the acute wards, the patients had been obligingly locked down in their rooms, to remove even the slightest chance of any trouble. Maxwell showed little interest in the unit. However, several of his staff asked some quite pertinent and well-informed questions.

Mortimer clearly and concisely explained that the facility catered for two groups of mentally ill patients: the 'regular' sentenced prisoners, who were admitted for psychiatric treatment and upon discharge from the hospital would return to jail; and those who had been declared by the courts to have been mentally incompetent at the time of their criminal offence. The second group were still committed to detention, but they were admitted to the NTC for treatment, rather than being sent to prison for punishment.

Eventually, the group made its way to the administration area, where a lavish morning tea was laid out. It was at this point that Jack saw the first spark of interest flash in Maxwell's eyes.

Jack ignored the pastries and headed straight for the coffee, with the pretty young aide trotting at his heels. Apparently, his earlier joke clearly had not completely put her off.

'Milk?' he politely asked.

'Uhh… yes, please. And two sugars.' She looked around. 'Is it scary working here?' He looked closely at her. She must have been nineteen, at the oldest. He wondered what she actually did in the department.

'No. It's actually pretty safe really…'

He was interrupted by Mortimer and Maxwell.

'Ahh, Giorgio,' said Maxwell, oblivious to the pastry crumbs flecking his tie, 'I see you've met Zoe.'

'Yes. She was asking me about what it's like working here.'

'Thinking about jumping ship already, dear?' he guffawed patronisingly. The girl smiled awkwardly.

Maxwell turned his attention back to Jack. 'She's my niece. She's only just started work with me in the past few days.'

'God help you, my dear,' chimed in Mortimer with a smirk. 'Politics! Dirtiest business there is!' =

Zoe just sipped her coffee, eyes wide, and remained silent.

The conversation then turned serious, as Maxwell asked Mortimer about the philosophy that underpinned the whole mental impairment defence.

'*Ah, so you have been paying attention,*' Jack mused.

'This whole insanity defence thing, Nathan. I can understand that psychotic individuals have lost touch with reality,' Maxwell began, 'but, at the end of the day, they *have* committed the crime. They performed the act. They pulled the trigger or thrust the knife. I don't see why they should get away with it! And, let me tell you, Nathan, neither do most of my constituents!'

Mortimer sighed and shook his head. He knew that Maxwell was one of those rare members of parliament who was not a lawyer and therefore did not have the jurisprudence background that may have enlightened him about the interplay between criminal law and the mentally ill.

'But Roger, the *act* is only half the story. The *intent* is the other. These very unwell individuals simply do not know that what they are doing is wrong and, at times, they just can't control it.'

'Most of my voters would see the act as the *whole* story,' Maxwell quickly retorted.

'Sadly, so do the tabloid newspapers,' added Jack, not worried that he may be speaking out of turn.

'You're not a bleeding heart too, Giorgio?'

Jack decided to take his chances. 'No. An educated and understanding heart. And mind.' Mortimer nodded in agreement.

Maxwell rolled his eyes. 'Well, I'm yet to be convinced. What do I say when one of my constituents comes to my office and tells me that their husband has been butchered by some mad bugger, and that the perpetrator—*who was caught holding the bloodied knife*—gets sent to hospital rather than to prison?'

'But that's the whole point,' Mortimer shot back reflexively. 'As you so eloquently put it, Roger, they are *mad*. Psychotic. Irrational. Delusional. Mentally incompetent. Their actions are controlled by their symptoms.'

'Yes, Nathan, *their* actions. Nobody else's.'

'Let me put it you this way: a man is driving down the road and suddenly he has a stroke while he is at the wheel. Due to the stroke, he veers off the road and runs down a pedestrian. His *actions*, Roger, but his *guilt*?'

'Oh come on, that's a little different, isn't it.' Maxwell blustered.

'Is it, Roger?' Mortimer said with a glare. 'Or is that stigma talking? Fundamentally, it is *exactly* the same. It's an illness that is directly responsible for a behavioural outcome.'

'And, like it or not,' Jack bravely added, 'the perpetrators actually do need treatment, not punishment. If they get properly treated, then we are all much safer. Including your voters.'

Mortimer threw Jack a grin and a complimentary nod of the head.

'Even though we have an impressive new facility here, Roger, I can assure you it's no picnic for them. The patient's freedoms are significantly curbed. Would you want to suffer from chronic schizophrenia and be confined to a place like this for years?'

'Schizophrenia? You mean split personality?' Maxwell asked in a tangential manner.

'You've been watching too many bad Hollywood movies, Roger,' said Mortimer. Zoe allowed herself a laugh. Maxwell shrugged his shoulders. 'Schizophrenia is a psychotic illness, usually chronic, that presents itself with delusions—bizarre thoughts and hallucinations—often manifesting as hearing voices or sometimes seeing things that are not there. The so-called 'split personality'—if such a condition truly exists—is in no way related to schizophrenia, and usually comes about as a result of severe and ongoing abuse in childhood, leading to a complete fragmentation of the personality.'

Jack was bemused to see that Mortimer had suddenly become quite worked up.

No, more than that. He was highly irritated.

You're genuinely angry.

He observed the beads of sweat gathering on the professor's forehead. Mortimer was so exasperated he almost seemed short of breath.

Sir Roger waved his hand, as if he was attempting to swat a fly. 'Well, you try and sell that to Mr and Mrs Average in suburbia. Now. I need another pastry and more coffee. I just want to know, Nathan, that whatever you are doing here is keeping me and my voters safe at night.'

'Don't worry, Roger, with stars like Jack on the team you can all sleep peacefully in your cosy little beds, dreaming your bigoted dreams without fear of molestation.'

18

'YOU'RE CLEARLY A fan of minimalism,' Jack said as he surveyed Cerise's lounge room.

Even allowing for the fact that her one-bedroom flat was tiny, the furnishings were still sparse. There was a two-seater couch, a small television, a bookshelf with about a dozen books on it, and a few prints on the walls.

'How long have you been here?'

'Oh about six months or so. But with work, well, you know, the days just slip by!'.

She smiled but Jack sensed she was slightly uneasy.

'It's not a criticism. Believe me, I am a fan of the uncluttered approach. Quality, not quantity, right?'

She moved in and kissed him passionately.

'Oh, absolutely… in *all* things,' she said, looking right into his eyes.

The bedroom, which Jack was now getting to know quite well, was similarly decorated. Cerise had a queen-sized bed, one bedside table, a lamp, and a wardrobe. That was it.

The whole place was as neat as a new pin, with nothing out of place and not a speck of dust. He had decided to cook dinner for her, only to find that she had nothing more that the barest essentials in the kitchen cupboards.

'I have to eat out a lot for work,' she said, somewhat apologetically.

'No problem at all,' he said before running around to the corner shop to grab the ingredients for a fettucine carbonara. He managed to also pick up a delightful pinot grigio that paired beautifully.

'I just feel so … so … *safe* with you, Jack. You are so gentle and I am so at ease being near you. And I just love our chats about books and life … and everything.'

While they ate, Jack realised that their relationship had progressed incredibly quickly. He was not one to stick rigidly to hard and fast rules about dating. He didn't have a kind of decision-making algorithm in his head about how rapidly this should happen or that should happen. Not consciously, at least. He was always willing to go with instinct and let things unfold organically.

And with Cerise they had unfolded at a beautiful pace.

It had only been a few weeks, but they had arrived at a level of comfort with each other that he appreciated some couples never experience. But this degree of comfort was certainly not tantamount to boredom or even complacency.

Quite the contrary.

Jack found that as the hours and days went by, the sense of excitement and anticipation was growing. He realised that there was an exquisite intensity of feeling when he was with Cerise that he had not experienced in a long time. If ever.

Was this love?

He wasn't sure. But the possibilities seemed endless with Cerise. She had an energy about her, a particular radiance that washed over him. He stopped eating for a moment just to look at her.

'I should get you to make all my meals,' Cerise wiped the last remnants of dinner from her chin.

'But I must confess that I totally neglected dessert.'

'Don't worry,' she said with a smile. 'I have something in mind for that.'

A moment later she led him to the bedroom.

19

JAYNE BOND WENT bright red as she fumbled and then dropped the digital dictation device.

'Oh *God*—sorry,' she said as she leant forward and retrieved it.

'No problem whatsoever,' Mortimer said with a warm smile. Today she could have thrown a cup of hot tea in his face, and he would not have cared at all.

'Okay, I'm ready,' Jayne placed the recorder on the desk between them and switched it on. She watched anxiously as the small red light appeared. 'Firstly, I want to say thank you for your time Professor... oh, I should now say *Sir* Nathan Mortimer.'

'It's a pleasure, Ms Bond. I have always enjoyed speaking to *The Times*.'

Sir Nathan. Sir Nathan.

'Firstly, congratulations on your knighthood. It's great that people who work so tirelessly in mental health received this sort of formal recognition.'

'Well, thank you. I think it is a sign of how far society has come. There is a way to go yet, but the stigma of mental illness is slowly disappearing.'

Sir Nathan.

'Mmm, yes. But where do you think this stigma arose from in the first place?'

Mortimer grinned knowingly. 'Jayne, it goes back hundreds, if not thousands, of years.'

'*Thousands* of years? Wow, that's amazing.'

'Yes, the history of mental illness is rather fascinating, if generally quite cruel and founded in ignorance. The Greco-Roman philosophers and medics, like Hippocrates, thought mental illness was due to an imbalance of the four humours—the physical elements they believed we were composed of.'

She nodded enthusiastically.

'Sadly, during the medieval period, when the church had ultimate control, it was believed for many hundreds of years that those who suffered from psychosis – what we would call schizophrenia today – were somehow possessed by evil spirits. What was an illness was interpreted as immoral thoughts or some great offense to the Church and led to sufferers being burnt at the stake. Tragically, there are some pockets of society who still hold this belief.'

Despite the recorder, Jayne made copious notes. She had learnt, through an unfortunate prior experience, that technology could not always be relied upon.

'But in your opinion, Sir Nathan, what can be done to change that?'

I like how that sounds. Sir Nathan. Sir Nathan.

He let the words roll around in his mind for a moment. 'Education, of course. Ignorance is always fear's incubator.'

To Mortimer's delight, Jayne made sure she got that last quote down.

He continued, 'Articulate and intelligent journalists, such as yourself, not sensationalising mental illness but rather reporting the truth. The facts. The media, both print and social, has a massive and important role to play here. For better or worse, it *is* where most people get their education as adults. In fact, I have just read an article in the British Journal of Psychiatry that concluded most people get their information about senile dementia from the cinema or TV.'

'That's fascinating. I think that the public are enthralled with issues around mental illness,' she said.

'I agree, Jayne. And that can be of great benefit in terms of advancing people's understanding—provided the media use their powers for good instead of evil,' he said with a smile.

The photographer who had accompanied Jayne snapped a few spontaneous photos of Mortimer as he spoke. He had already posed outside of the facility before the interview commenced.

'And in light of this honour which has been bestowed upon you, what do you hope your legacy to mental health with be, Sir Nathan?'

'Well that will be for others to decide, Ms Bond.'

Oh, you will soon see for yourself, Jayne.

You will see.

20

LIZZIE ROBERTS AND Jack Giorgio sat silently together in the blandness of the ward interview room. She was trying to process what he had just told her.

He did not have to ask her if she already knew.

Pregnant.

'How many weeks am I?'

'We're not sure yet. I was hoping you might be able to shed some light on that.'

She sighed and looked downwards towards her lap.

Towards her womb.

Her head suddenly jerked upwards, and she looked Jack right in the eye.

Then, with coolness: 'Marc and I only did it the one time. I suppose it was a consequence of that.' Jack's body suddenly tensed.

'Marc? *Mollet?*'

'Yes,' she said blandly.

Stay calm, Giorgio, stay calm. This could be crucial.

Her mental state had improved with regular antipsychotic medication, but she was still fragile, and he had to proceed carefully with the questions.

'Were you in a relationship with Marc, Lizzie?'

'Not really. It was just that one night.' She remained expressionless.

'When was that, Lizzie?'

There was a long silence.

Pregnant pause?

'Time has no relevance to the cause.'

Stay with me, Lizzie, please.

'What do you mean by "cause"?'

'The struggle of my comrades.' She rubbed her lower abdomen. 'And now there will be someone else to carry on the fight.'

He was worried that the interview had suddenly taken a turn for the worse. Her capacity to tolerate an interview had improved, but she was starting to deteriorate again in front of his eyes.

Could Mollet really be the father?

Or was he all part of her delusional world?

'Lizzie, are you able to tell me how you ended up with Mollet?'

'I seduced him,' she replied curtly, with a hint of arrogance.

Jack just nodded slowly.

'I waited for him after a lecture and made up some story about needing help with contemporary fiscal policy. It was easy from there. He really had no choice in the matter.' She glared at Jack. 'Typical, weak capitalist male. Giving in to his urges. Instant gratification.'

It was the most Lizzie had spoken during her entire admission. She clearly was convinced, but Jack still questioned the veracity of her story. Even though it was *possible*, he wondered how *probable* it all was.

Especially given the events that followed.

Unfortunately, there was no way of confirming her story with Mollet.

Jack had been in this situation many times before with psychotic patients. Where was the line between reality and delusion? He knew it was dangerous and foolish to dismiss all that the patient said as being simply madness. If he could tease out other details of their 'relationship' it might add some more clues to the questions around her pregnancy.

'Before you slept with Mollet, before you seduced him, what was your relationship like?' he asked.

'Intense. He had been following me.' She paused and then added, 'Stalking me.'

'Stalking you?'

'Everywhere I went. He was there. Waiting. Watching.' She pointed to her right eye. 'He had a hidden camera. In my shower. He liked to watch me.' She gave the faintest of smiles. 'So I let him.'

'Let him?'

'Watch me. See me. I would put on quite a show for him. In the shower.'

'Why?' Jack asked, as non-judgementally as he could.

She smiled again, this time more obviously.

'Know your enemy. Know your enemy.'

'What do you think the reason was for him to be stalking you?'

'He knew my plans. He knew my thoughts. He was reading them. He knew about my great grandfather.'

'Your plans?'

'To eliminate the capitalist terror. It was written by my great grandfather that the day would come when the workers would rise up and overthrow the oppressive bourgeoisie.'

'And is that why you killed Mollet?' he asked.

To his surprise, Lizzie shook her head. She looked almost horrified at the suggestion.

'I did not kill him,' she said quietly.

'No? Then who did?'

She smiled warmly at Jack. It was the first time that he had seen such emotion from her. Strangely, he could suddenly imagine her seducing the economics professor.

'Marx, of course. He used *my body* but it was *his desire*. He has told me that there will be more, but I have to wait. He will direct me again when the time is right.' Again, she rubbed her slightly distended belly. 'And now my body is being used again. For his work.'

'You mean the pregnancy?'

'Yes. The bloodline will continue. The *work* will continue. I know it will be a boy. But not one of you weak men. Strong.'

'Lizzie, how do you feel about being pregnant?' Jack asked tenderly.

She replied without hesitation, 'I think it's wonderful. It will allow me to finish what my great grandfather started. I know that is my purpose. And the purpose of my child.'

Jack was extremely concerned that Lizzie's unborn baby was being incorporated into her delusional system. He knew that was a very poor prognostic sign and it put her foetus at very high risk of harm. Unless there was a stunning improvement, if she carried the baby to term then I would be highly unlikely that she would be able to care for it.

It was a tragic and very painful situation. Jack believed that mothers and their babies should be together whenever possible, as the importance of attachment and bonding was undeniable. But not at any cost. The welfare of both parties needed to be considered and if there was a significant risk posed to the baby then separation was sometimes the only viable and safe option.

He doubted that Lizzie would ever be able to care for her baby. Given her murder charge, she was likely to be confined to the forensic psychiatric hospital for many years, whereas the baby had the right to a life of freedom outside the walls of such an oppressive environment.

These were the dilemmas he hated.

He looked at his medical colleagues who performed surgery all day or read countless MRI scans, and wondered what kinds of legal and ethical dilemmas that they faced. Surely nothing like this.

'Lizzie, other than Marc Mollet had there been anyone else?' Jack asked.

She looked at him sternly.

'Yes,' she replied.

'Who?'

Lizzie looked up to the corner of the room. It reminded Jack of their first interview together. She giggled to herself.

She appeared to be listening to something.

To some*one*.

'He doesn't want me to tell you,' she said.

'Who doesn't?'

But she was gone again.

She had retreated back into her chaotic world.

Her stamina for these sessions was improving but she was still psychotic, and therefore could tolerate only so much. Especially when it came to highly emotive topics.

The nurse entered the room and escorted Lizzie back to the ward. Her hands cradled her bulging abdomen as she walked out.

Part 2

Fight or Flight

21

JOEL LALIC ONLY saw the young mother pushing her pram onto the crossing at the last second, but thanks to the advanced braking system, his gunmetal grey Porsche pulled up within inches of Tayla Burns and her three-month-old son.

She screamed abuse at him, but he simply put the 911 back in gear and tore off again up Bayswater Road, narrowly missing her once more as he did so.

Put simply, Joel Lalic was on the run.

His life was in danger, and he believed the Porsche was the only defensive weapon he currently had. He pushed the sunroof button until it was around a quarter open. He briefly looked upwards.

Nothing.

He closed the roof again and looked back down at the road ahead. He swerved around a Mini and then a taxi. The car hit sixty miles an hour and sounded glorious. Curious onlookers assumed that the Porsche was stolen, but they were wrong. Even though he was only twenty-seven and unemployed, the car belonged to Joel.

He looked up again.

Still nothing.

He briefly contemplated abandoning the Porsche and getting away on foot, but quickly changed his mind.

He was baking under his heavy black leather jacket, but felt secure in it and refused to take it off. He rubbed a sweaty palm over his freshly shaven head three times, in an attempt to self-soothe. As he did so his sleeve slid down, revealing the Breitling Aerospace Evo watch that sat proudly on his left wrist.

On the right, he wore a solid platinum bracelet with a barcode imprinted on the surface. The bracelet was impossible to remove – Joel had tried several times already without any success.

A sharp, blue light flashed intermittently on one edge of the bracelet.

'Heathrow', he mumbled to himself. 'Heathrow.' Suddenly it was clear. He must get to Heathrow and sort this it out once and for all. No more running. Turn defence into attack. They would not be expecting that.

The voice from the cramped back seat agreed.

'Yes. Heathrow. Get to Heathrow. Get to Heathrow. *NOW!*'

'I will, I will,' Joel replied.

'It's the only way to stop the planes, Joel. It's the only way to stop them from killing you.'

Joel hit eighty miles an hour and headed for the A4.

As Joel got closer to Heathrow his driving became more erratic. Keeping his eyes on the road and on the sky was becoming increasingly difficult. He drifted into neighbouring lanes of traffic, causing other vehicles to swerve.

The voice behind him was a further distraction, but just had to be listened to.

Once he hit the M4 the road widened, and he sped up to over ninety miles an hour, zigzagging from lane to lane, passing the other cars as if they were standing still. He had managed to evade the police so far, but he knew they offered him no protection anyway.

Time is running out.

The angry and frightened looks he received from other motorists only spurred him on to speed up. He now knew that they were all part of it.

They wanted him dead.

His sweaty hand rubbed the back of his neck, his fingers passing over the three small silver studs. The very few people that Joel socialised with all thought this was just some cutting-edge fashion statement.

But Joel knew better.

He knew the *truth*.

Joel knew that his piercings were his most crucial link with the outside world. The small studs allowed for the clear and concise transmission of the most powerful commodity of all: information. The piercings directed a range of important and interesting broadcasts straight into his auditory nerves. Usually, this gave Joel the comforting perception that he knew what other people were thinking, but recently the broadcasts had taken a dangerous new form.

It began with a new sound: a soft low hum, like someone had struck a deep note on a bass guitar. It was intermittent at first but then it became louder and more continuous. When it started interfering with his sleep, Joel tried to adjust and rotate the three studs in his neck, but that did not seem to help.

To his relief, three weeks later, the hum eventually died down— but in its place he began to receive cryptic transmissions from a voice who spoke in an unusual language. It seemed to Joel that the language was English, but the *manner* of speaking was bizarre. The individual words made sentences, but the sentences did not make sense to Joel.

Kilo, Foxtrot, Kilo.

Initially it was just a few times a day, but since Monday it had been relentless, almost non-stop.

Tango. Four-niner, Tango, Bravo.

The male voice was a stranger to him, but he realised the voice emanating from the back seat was the same.

Uniform. Whiskey.

Every now and then a name would be thrown in, but it did not make sense to Joel.

Mike. Charlie. Oscar.

At times his own father would be also mentioned, which really concerned him.

Papa. Papa. Whiskey.

Papa.

Papa?

Was his father really involved?

It was only on the morning he took off in his Porsche that it all became clear to him. He had endured over twenty-four hours straight of this voice being channelled through the studs in his neck.

As he drove, he started frantically plucking the studs out of his skin. He knew that his information would be cut off, but at least they might not be able to track him if the devices were removed. He tore his dermal layers as he yanked the second one out and blood trickled down his back.

When all three had been removed he threw them out of the window.

He then sped past a sign that read, 'Heathrow traffic left lanes'. Obediently, Joel directed the Porsche across three lanes of traffic and into the exit lane.

He did not slow down as he hurtled past a police car. Within seconds he saw lights flashing and heard a siren blaring.

He accelerated further, and easily out-ran the motorway patrol. After a minute or so the flashing lights were just a blur on the horizon behind him.

He did not bother to slow down, even when he reached the driveway outside the terminal.

'Yes, yes,' the voice encouraged him. Joel glanced into the rear vision mirror.

Both back seats were empty.

'You're nearly there! The end is in sight, Joel. You will stop them before they stop you. You will kill them, before they kill you.'

'How? *HOW?*' Joel pleaded. His eyes darted all over the road in front of him.

'Get onto the tarmac. Get yourself in front of the plane, Joel. *GET THERE!*'

Joel looked around for any possible entrance to the tarmac.

A black Mercedes delivery van with heavily tinted windows suddenly pulled out in front of him, forcing Joel to slam on the brakes. The screech of his tyres made an elderly couple jump.

A second, identical van pulled in behind him.

He was trapped.

'Run, Joel, run,' the voice urged.

'Where to?' he asked in desperation.

'The tarmac, Joel. Get in front of that plane! You must stop it from taking off. If you don't, YOU WILL DIE!'

Joel saw planes everywhere.

Taking off and landing.

Virgin. British Airways. Air France. KLM. Etihad.

The incessant roar of the jet engines was hurting his ears.

This is it. This will be the end. They have won. I am over.

'No, Joel. There is still time. But you must move now!'

Joel opened the car door and attempted to step out. The moment he got to his feet he was immediately disabled by two burly men dressed in delivery driver outfits. They had his arms pinned by hooking their own under his armpits. The men then effortlessly lifted him a couple of inches off the ground. A third man swiftly opened a rear door of the first Mercedes van. Within a matter of seconds Joel was safely housed within the van and the door was closed.

A further thirty seconds after that both vans and the Porsche were being sedately driven past the departures terminal and were heading towards the motorway.

Other than the elderly couple, no one noticed a thing.

It was as if the entire incident had never occurred.

22

JACK COULD NOT recall a time when Mortimer had left a ward round early, under any circumstances, but when his mobile phone rang halfway through their weekly meeting, the professor promptly rose from his chair and strode silently out of the room.

Jack could see him standing outside the conference room door, looking concerned. Mortimer rubbed his forehead several times as he listened, before appearing to give some very clear and precise directions to whomever was on the other end of the phone. He then saw Mortimer end the call, dial a number, and speak briefly to someone else.

He couldn't be sure, but Jack thought Mortimer was mouthing several expletives.

A moment later, he re-entered the conference room and looked at Jack.

'Excuse me everyone,' Mortimer said. 'Doctor Giorgio, can I speak with you outside for a minute?' His words surged out with a clear pressure behind them.

Instantly, Jack felt his heart rate quicken.

What have I done wrong?

He recalled what he had recently told the students about transference and authority figures. He felt like he was a naughty school kid being sent to see the headmaster. Barnard grinned as Jack dutifully left the room.

'What is it?' Jack asked as they walked towards Mortimer's office. 'Is there a problem?'

Mortimer initially remained silent as he grabbed his suit jacket and looked for his car keys. He seemed quite distracted.

'It's okay, Jack. I have already cancelled your clinic for today.'

Oh really? *Why?* Are we going somewhere?'

He saw Mortimer open his brief case and retrieve a small plastic device that looked to Jack like a garage door remote.

'Yes, we are. Private practice. Come on, Jack, let's go. I'll explain in the car.'

23

PEOPLE WALKING PAST it would have been forgiven for thinking that the South London building, which resembled a disused warehouse, was abandoned at best and derelict at worst. The miserable looking grey relic sat silently among other run-down buildings in an equally miserable street.

The navy Bentley Mulsanne looked entirely out of place as it turned silently onto the street.

'We don't like to advertise,' the professor said dryly as he looked at the building and guided the car towards a heavy black roller door.

Jack looked tentatively out of his window on to the surrounds.

No one.

There was no one around at all.

Where the hell are we?

Mortimer hit a button on the small remote device he had retrieved earlier in his office, and a garage door effortlessly opened for the two men. When there was barely enough clearance for the Bentley to fit underneath, Mortimer eased it inside the garage and hit the button again.

Once the heavy door had closed behind them, Jack and Mortimer were surrounded by complete darkness. Jack could hear Mortimer's breathing. It sounded slightly laboured. As usual, Jack could also sense the faint but distinctive aroma of cigars.

A moment later a circular beam of light was visible, and Jack could then see a small door a few metres away.

'Come on,' Mortimer urged.

The door opened into an elevator and while they waited Mortimer stared intently at Jack. He spoke in a hushed voice.

'We are here to see a private patient.' He looked at Jack. 'A *very* private patient.'

'Who?'

'A young man by the name of Joel Lalic. He is the son of Ivan Lalic.' He looked for a hint of recognition from Jack, but when he saw none, he continued.

'Ivan Lalic made a fortune – an absolute fortune – during the Yugoslavian War back in the nineties.'

'Who? *War?* Fortune? … How?' was all Jack could manage.

'Arms dealing, mainly. For both sides. That was his trick, you see, to be working for both sides. Two bidders are always better than one, and he had such high-spec weapons to offer that both sides substantially knocked up the prices. As you can imagine, it was incredibly dangerous to be acting as that kind of commercial double agent. But the payoff was massive.'

Jack found himself quite mesmerised by the story. Was it really just over an hour ago he was sitting in a sedate ward round back at the hospital? Mortimer clearly sensed his interest and continued.

'Just before the war ended, Lalic fled his homeland, claimed refugee status, and was taken in by Britain. Let's just say that his enormous funds managed to lubricate the machine that is the immigration department. His wife was killed during the war, but he managed to get out with his young son and daughter. Since then, he has been pretty quiet, kept a low profile. He did well during the war but his real talent, his real *genius* has been money laundering. Over time, he gradually invested all his dirty money into quite legitimate enterprises. Business. Shares. Property. Gold. So by now he is genuinely rich. How rich, I couldn't say, but easily well over the three or four hundred million mark. He is a capitalist through and through, and has clearly embraced the Western lifestyle.'

'Gee,' was all Jack could limply say, still not believing how his day was unfolding.

'Yes. His great loves are his antique pistol collection and his kids. Especially his son, Joel. He would do anything for that boy. *Anything*. He apparently named him after Billy Joel – such is his love of the West.'

'You said we are here to see Joel. Is this where he lives? What's wrong with him?'

Mortimer ignored the first question and went straight to the second.

'Paranoid schizophrenia. He started to develop symptoms maybe eight or so years ago when he was around eighteen. Has a nasty version of the illness. Been hard to get under control at times, especially as Joel tends to act on his hallucinations. He can get into some really dangerous situations but so far we have always been able to intervene and prevent a tragedy.'

'Intervene? How?'

'We can now keep tabs on him, electronically. We can get in before he does any damage and, importantly, before the police.'

Electronically? What the hell does that mean?

Mortimer kept speaking.

'But Ivan also loves his privacy, which is understandable given his history. He wants a very *very* discrete service for Joel. Money is no object. He wants his son protected, at any cost. He wants him at home. Wants him safe. And, above all, he wants *no* publicity. He still has many enemies out there.'

'He wants him home?'

'Of course he does. What would you want? To have your ill son rotting away on the secure ward of some Dickensian hell posing as a mental health facility?' Mortimer made quotation marks in the air with his fingers as he said the last three words.

Jack was both shocked and in agreement at the same time.

'So you run some sort of inpatient private mental health clinic for Ivan Lalic?' Jack asked.

'Technically and legally it is not a 'clinic'. It is private health *care*. Whether we like it or not we work in a service industry, Jack. Ultimately, we are no different to the concierge who sits at the desk for ten hours a day at the Savoy. We take care of people's needs. Sure, the needs may vary, and some needs are more…' he looked around for the word before staring at Jack. '*Intense* than others. But if you can fulfil a need, then you have done your job for someone.'

'Uh-huh' Jack said in a monotone voice, unsure of what else to say. Mortimer continued without missing a beat. 'And then it is just a question of economics really. Supply and demand. Pure and simple. The more intense, the more acute the need and the fewer the people there are to meet it, well, the price goes up. It has to.'

'Weapons and healthcare are no exception', concluded Jack.

'Absolutely. Especially in a nation such as this, where essentially all the healthcare is nationalised and in the hands of the public bureaucrats. And *mental* healthcare… well, that is the great untapped industry of the twenty-first century.'

Mortimer was pleased that Jack seemed to be cottoning on.

Jack was not sure that he felt comfortable having mental health described in such commercial terms. Yet, at the same time, Mortimer was *so* convincing in his argument. He could certainly accept that the demand for high quality and comprehensive mental healthcare was enormous, and was only on the increase.

Mortimer's argument then seemed to switch track.

'Come on, Jack, you know the numbers. Especially the one per cent rule.'

'The one per cent rule?'

'The prevalence rate. Give or take. But it all averages out to around one per cent.'

'Of the prevalence rate of schizophrenia, you mean?' said Jack, finally catching on.

Where are we going with this?

'Sure. Black. White. Male. Female. African. American. It's all the same. And, importantly, rich or poor. It doesn't matter. It is all about one per cent.'

'I'm not sure I'm following you,' admitted Jack.

'I can see that,' Mortimer said in a patronising tone. 'I will try to explain. Look at all the World Health Organization projections. In terms of disabling diseases, depression is second only to heart disease. In fact, four of the top ten are mental illnesses. Give it another ten years, I can tell you, we will occupy the top five spots.' Jack wanted to cringe with Mortimer's use of 'we' but at the time same time found himself unable to disagree.

He had read the WHO reports.

He had read the studies.

Mortimer was right.

'But there are some figures that you won't have read, Jack.'

'What do you mean?'

'Well, you know the old story that does the rounds every few years about great people always being related, *closely* related, to people with serious mental illnesses?'

'Sure, everyone has heard of that. The genius-madness phenomena and that they are only this far apart.' He held out his thumb and forefinger a hair's distance from each other.

'Exactly, but you can look as hard as you like and there is actually no hard proof of it in any of the research.' Jack had never looked that hard, but he imagined that the professor was correct.

Mortimer continued, 'After I sold my company, I rubbed shoulders with some really unique and special people. High achievers. Highflyers. People I never imagined I would associate with, but I soon found myself in their living rooms and dining rooms, answering their questions about brains and genes and mental illness. I wondered why there were so interested. But they *were* interested, Jack. Fascinated, in fact.'

Mortimer emphasised these last few words.

'They were such a diverse group. All had achieved in their chosen careers, most were fabulously wealthy, but they all seemed to come from such a range of unconnected backgrounds. Business. The arts. The military. Politics. Sport. Even science and medicine. But, amazingly, so many of them suddenly wanted to talk to me. *Me!*' Mortimer emphasised the last word.

That attention really meant something to you, Professor.

'But why is that so amazing? Look at all you've done, all you've achieved in your own right,' said Jack.

'I guess I didn't see it that way, I mean, who was I compared to these people? Particularly given that I'm a shrink.'

'What do you mean?'

'Come on Jack, you must have noticed. At parties. Social events. Professional meetings. People take one step back when they hear that you're a psychiatrist. And it's even worse when you're among your own medical colleagues. Surgeons are the worst. They usually just roll their eyes and walk off.'

Of course Jack knew what he meant. He had experienced those social and professional rebuffs many times. And Mortimer was right: it was with his own colleagues that he felt it the most. He remembered one colleague, a neurosurgeon, who he had been good friends with in medical school, once berated Jack in a hospital emergency department for '*wasting his fucking career*' in front of staff and patients.

Mortimer continued. 'But suddenly, these incredible people seemed to really want to know. And it soon occurred to me that it was because they had a personal *need* to know, a personal connection to what we do.'

'Why? Had they been ill at some point themselves?'

'Not quite. You see, Jack, the worldwide incidence for schizophrenia is around one percent, but in the families of these high achievers, the *really* high achievers, it is much, much greater.'

'How high?'

'You might not believe it, but it's twenty per cent.'

'*Twenty* per cent!'

Jack recalled his very first interview with Mortimer.

Any history of severe mental illness in your family?

'Yes. I have done the original work myself. I did the research on my own. Spent hours and hours with these people and their families.'

Jack was amazed. 'But why haven't I read it? Why hasn't *anyone* read it? This is of major significance.'

'I never published. It was a condition of the research that it never be published. It was for their own private use.' Jack was gobsmacked. He wondered how such a significant piece of work could be kept from the scientific community.

'Why agree to that?'

'Jack, you have to understand the mentality of the people involved in this. These are important people. Private people. Discrete people. This sort of information, rightly or wrongly, they just didn't want it out in the public sphere. They didn't want to take the chance of being identified or associated with it.'

'Jeez, that's terrible. So stigmatising. I thought we were working to fight those attitudes and bring these issues out into the light.' Jack argued.

'Don't be so fucking naïve!' Mortimer raised his voice, angered. Jack felt nervous. Mortimer sensed this and calmed down almost immediately.

'These people have real influence Jack. They can affect global financial markets and governments, start wars, end wars, influence the mood of entire nations. One wrong word at a press conference or one misplaced handshake can make worldwide news. They had to be careful and so did I.'

'So, are you telling me that these people didn't want it known that they had relatives with schizophrenia?'

'Exactly.'

'It all seems very archaic, almost nineteenth century to me.' Jack remembered reading that before the era of the large asylums, families would essentially be responsible for their mentally ill relatives and would keep them— usually behind locked doors—trapped at home for decades.

'But Jack, I was able to help them, give their sons, their daughters, their brothers, their sisters, sometimes even their parents, treatment. Look after them properly. Look after them at their homes. And let me tell you, they were grateful. *Very* grateful. But not just for the care and for the treatment. But for the way it was delivered, for the discretion. The confidentiality. For lack of a better word, for the *service*.'

'But what happens when they can't be managed at home, what then?'

'That is very rare. These people can afford private staff, private nurses, private security, everything. But on those very rare occasions where more secure care is needed, we have a… facility.'

'A *facility*? What facility? Where?'

The doors of the lift slowly opened, and the two men stepped out.

'You're standing in it, Jack.'

24

THE TWO PSYCHIATRISTS walked into the small, secure interview room and sat down. It reminded Jack more of a CIA interrogation cell from a Hollywood movie than a mental health consulting room.

Joel Lalic was also seated, slumped forward in a chair. His head was resting on his folded arms.

'Joel... Joel...' Mortimer whispered, with a caring tone in his voice.

Without moving from his position, Joel spoke.

'Preffa Morma, s'at you?' In his heavily-sedated state, his speech was slurred to the point of being almost incomprehensible.

'Yes, Joel, it's me. Everything is going to be all right.'

When Joel leant back in his chair, Jack saw that he was wearing a black t-shirt that read, '*Store in a cool, dry place*'. He wanted to laugh at Joel's humour but held it back.

'You've had quite an adventure today, Joel. Wouldn't you say? All that business at Heathrow,' said Mortimer.

Jack detected an arrogant, almost mocking tone in Mortimer's voice. He did not like it.

'You are very lucky, Joel. *Very* lucky. Just think of what you could have done! Just think of the attention that you could have brought to yourself. To your sister. To your father, for God's sake!'

Jack shook his head at Mortimer's patronising manner. At least Joel was sedated and would be unlikely to remember any of it, he thought.

Mortimer moved closer to Joel and spoke into his ear. 'Just imagine if the police had got to you first!' His tone was now clearly frustrated.

It caused Joel to flinch.

Jack watched Mortimer as he paced around the room in a small circle with his hands on his hips.

Joel tried to speak.

'They neeth me… ta… geth Heaf… rooow.'

> *They needed me to get to Heathrow.*

Mortimer ignored the comment.

'Why?' asked Jack.

'Or… they… wa… gon ki- me.'

> *Or they were going to kill me.*

'Who?'

Joel slowly straightened a finger and pointed up to the ceiling.

'Tha play… nnth'

> *The planes.*

'That is all just in your head. You must try to understand that. You are sick. *Sick*, Joel! It is your illness talking. You are going to be with us for some time, Joel,' said Mortimer. 'We can't have you behaving like this.'

Joel looked down. He seemed, to Jack, to be ashamed and embarrassed thanks to the dressing down he'd received from the professor.

Mortimer then left the room and gestured for Jack to follow him.

'Damn stupid kid,' said the professor as they looked in on Joel via the small window in the door. 'After all I have done for him. The incredible treatment I have given him, and he goes and does this!'

Jack was not entirely sure what *'this'* referred to. Surely Joel was not being blamed for his illness?

'I'm really going to have to ramp up his treatment this time. He needs the works. I'm going to prescribe him combination high-dose depot injections. That will slow him down. I am fed up with these relapses.'

How 'fed up' do you think Joel feels?

He watched as Mortimer started typing furiously on the keyboard of an iMac. Jack assumed that the ward had some sort of hi-tech electronic medical record-keeping system, but as he moved closer to the screen, he saw that Mortimer was actually typing an email to an addressee called 'Lalic, Ivan – Private.'

He was giving him a brief run down on what had occurred with Joel and an item-by-item funding schedule for the likely admission cost. Mortimer sent the email before Jack could read the full details, but he managed to see the final item:

Fees – Consultant psychiatrist ward attendances – £50,000.

Jack wondered how Mortimer could legally keep Joel at the ward and give him treatment involuntarily without any sort of order. He then recalled what the professor had told him in the lift:

'Technically and legally it is not a clinic…'

What is it then? A gentleman's agreement?

25

MORTIMER CLEARLY RECOGNISED Jack's unease at what he had witnessed on the private ward. After their work was done, the professor took Jack out for dinner in Richmond in an attempt to mollify his protégé by expanding on their earlier conversation.

Before they had ordered their food, Jack noticed that Mortimer already had two whiskeys inside him.

'These people live in a different world, Jack. They have their own rules and their own hierarchies. If you can enter that world and become accepted there, it opens up fabulous opportunities.'

'What do you mean?'

'Well, there's the money for starters, but that is fairly superficial. I am talking about…' he paused and stared at Jack '…connections.'

'Connections?'

'Let me give you an example. Say you want funding for a research project. You would normally spend days—sometimes weeks even—applying for grants, after which, presuming you're successful in securing the funding you need, you have to go through the laborious process of finding a facility, finding staff, and getting ethics approval.'

Jack nodded in agreement.

'Well imagine a system where the majority of that…' he searched for the right word '…*bureaucracy* does not exist.'

'Hang on a minute. If you're talking about individuals who are at the top of their fields, they're hardly going to part with all of their precious resources lightly. Without any kind of accountability.' Jack felt confident that he had made a very valid point.

'Yes, you are absolutely right. If we were talking strictly about business. But I am talking about family, Jack. Their own flesh and blood. And I am talking about emotion. Different rules apply.'

Jack was not entirely convinced. It made him wonder about his own family.

'Don't forget Jack, a lot of these high-achieving individuals feel incredibly guilty about their success. That guilt can be unconscious, but it's still there, and it drives a great deal of their philanthropy. Often the most charitable are also the guiltiest. But it's with their own family, especially siblings, where the guilt is most intense.'

'What, you mean like a kind of survivor guilt?' Jack was quite familiar with the phenomenon that occurred when people survived traumatic events in which others died.

'Exactly. For all their hard work, dedication, and discipline these over-achievers know that at the heart of it all lies one simple explanation for their success: *luck*.'

'Luck?'

'Absolutely. Your genetic composition is blind luck. Your biological predispositions are blind luck.'

'But environment can have a huge influence, too,' Jack asserted.

'It doesn't count for as much as people like to imagine. And even when environmental factors do play a role, this generally also comes down to luck.'

Jack was finding the conversation fascinating but was not sure where it was all heading. Mortimer's voice was edged with irritation, as though he was frustrated that Jack did not simply accept everything he was saying without question.

Jack had not seen this side of Mortimer before.

'But what about twins?' Jack asked. 'They have an identical genetic makeup, and yet one can live a brilliant, fulfilling life while the other can be completely disabled by an illness like chronic schizophrenia.'

'It depends on what you mean by identical,' Mortimer said with a smirk. 'Sometimes the differences in genes can be so tiny, so subtle, that they are extremely hard to detect. We might only be talking about one billionth of a difference in someone's genome. But this really makes my entire point. That one billionth of a difference could be all that exists between genius and madness.'

Jack circled back to Mortimer's previous point.

'So you're saying that these high-flyers are trying to compensate for their good fortune?'

'Absolutely. Mmmm—this veal is amazing! Compliments to the chef,' Mortimer called to a waiter who was passing by.

'Yes, Professor,' the man replied in a heavy Middle Eastern accent.

'Take that guy for instance,' Mortimer said, gesturing towards the waiter. 'Clearly Afghani. Probably about your age. Certainly a refugee. But the differences between him and you are less than you would care to imagine, Jack. Even though he is a waiter and you are a forensic psychiatrist, I would say that you have both worked just as hard to get to where you are in life. It has taken you both the same amount of effort.'

'I think you are wrong there, Professor.'

Mortimer's eyebrows raised in unison. 'Really, Jack?'

'Oh yes. I think that given all he has likely endured, he has probably had to work a *lot* harder than I have.'

Mortimer called the waiter over to their table.

'Tell me, where are you from?'

The waiter looked slightly uneasy but answered anyway.

'From small village… near Kabul.'

'How long have you been here?'

He looked suspiciously at Mortimer. 'About two years.'

'Refugee?'

Even Jack started to feel uncomfortable with all the questions. He smiled at the waiter to try to reassure him.

'Yes, sir,' he replied, looking down to clear any empty plates from the table.

'How did you get here?' the professor demanded. Jack looked pleadingly at Mortimer in an attempt to bring the interrogation to an end. The waiter knocked over a water glass and took the opportunity to return to the kitchen with the empty glass.

'Fucking idiot,' Mortimer said under his breath as he furiously dried his sleeve.

It was rare that Jack heard the professor swear. In Jack's opinion, it did not suit him.

26

JACK GIORGIO AND Sarah Wellington sat drinking coffee in the staff tearoom. The file of Patient X, growing thicker by the day, sat on Jack's lap.

'So what did you make of him?' Sarah asked, staring with keen interest.

Jack shook his head and took a sip of his Americano. 'Well, he's certainly an enigma. I reviewed all of his physical investigations but there was nothing I could see that was abnormal in any way. It was great thinking on your part to arrange the continuous EEG to get a better understanding of his brain's electricity, but again, I see there was nothing of significance.'

Sarah nodded. 'Yeah, I know, it's all very strange. I even thought about malingering. He is so consistent, so unchanging, if he was genuinely unwell then he would be more volatile, so malingering is up there.'

'I have to agree with those points. I don't want to foreclose on anything too soon, though, so I will keep looking. And if he is malingering, what would his motivation be?'

She drank her coffee. 'True. He has been charged with attempted murder, and a pretty vicious assault at that, but according to all the statements he was pretty much like he is now before and after the assault took place.'

'But what was it that made him so agitated that night? So angry? It was almost like he was an…'

'An animal?' Sarah jumped in.

'Yes. Exactly.' Jack searched through the file until he found the statements from the night of the assault. 'According to the police reports and witness statements, the two girls were headed home after a big night. Young women. High heels. Short skirts. Slightly intoxicated but nothing too extreme. And they were carrying food.'

'Yes, that's right.'

Jack shook his head, 'And there was no sexual assault.'

'No, not at all. No attempt even. Just the nasty assault. But even that was strange. People don't usually just slowly walk away after beating someone half to death. He didn't seem to be trying to evade the police. He was still only about quarter of a mile from the crime scene by the time they arrived.'

'I guess in the absence of anything else, the most likely diagnosis is some type of chronic psychosis. A version of schizophrenia, perhaps?' He smiled wickedly and dropped his voice to a stage whisper, 'Drew Barnard might be right.'

Sarah rolled her eyes and laughed. 'Well, there's a first time for everything, Doctor Giorgio.'

'What about the professor. What does he think of our Patient X?'

'I don't know,' she replied matter-of-factly. 'He hasn't seen him.'

'*Really?* Why not?'

Sarah rose from her chair, walked to the door, closed it, then returned to where they were sitting. Pulling her chair a little closer, she sat down and looked at Jack with an intensity that he hadn't seen in her before.

'There's something you need to realise about working here,' she said quietly. 'Professor Mortimer is very often absent. And when he is here, he doesn't really bother with the patients.'

'But he seems to know so much about them.' Jack frowned.

'I think he bluffs his way through. He has a quick flick through the case notes and picks up bits and pieces of each of the patients' histories from the staff who are working with them. He has decades of experience, and so he can still sound quite brilliant even when he doesn't really know what he's talking about.'

Sarah was right on the mark. When he thought about it, Jack realised that he almost never saw Mortimer on the wards. He was either in his office, involved in some sort of 'meeting' or away.

At his private ward.

'He's more of a figurehead these days, I suppose,' he said aloud, 'but I guess that's important. Someone's got to secure the funding and advocate for the service.'

'Yeah, I guess so,' Sarah replied, but she did not sound completely convinced.

Jack looked around to make sure that they were still alone.

'Sarah,' he said quietly. 'Has Mortimer ever talked to you about doing any private work—at another facility?'

'Private work? No. Never. Why?' Jack thought she looked genuinely surprised.

'Oh, no reason.'

27

EVEN THOUGH A couple of days had passed, Mortimer could see that Jack was still somewhat shocked by what he had experienced at the warehouse.

Reassurance was required.

'It's cutting-edge now, but believe me, this is the future of healthcare Jack—and not just mental healthcare. The population is growing. And ageing. Have you looked at the projected data for dementia and its costs?'

Jack confessed he had not.

'Well! Let me tell you! It's going to be a nightmare, Jack. *Horrific.* Health department budgets are already overblown year after year. Hospital emergency rooms are full. Wards are full. Hospitals, which are designed and budgeted to run at eighty-five per cent bed occupancy, are running at one hundred to one hundred and two per cent occupancy. Aged care facilities are full and waiting lists are growing. Give it another ten years and people will have forgotten about climate change as the greatest problem facing humankind. They will be too concerned about what they will do with their fucking ageing relatives. Not to mention the rest of the population, who will still need healthcare.'

Jack bristled at the professor's use of the f-word.

Mortimer gave Jack an intense look, as if he was trying to ascertain if the younger man had fully understand what he was saying.

'It will be survival of the richest, Jack. It sounds cruel, I know, but that will be the reality. You will see facilities like this everywhere, built by private money as architecturally stunning hospitals, for all to see.

'Eventually, governments will contribute very little to healthcare. I expect that by 2050 private money will fund over ninety per cent of all healthcare.'

'*Ninety* per cent?' Jack was not convinced by this doomsday scenario.

'At least. And forget private health insurance. They will all fold. They will be paying out claims well beyond the premiums they can raise, because it will get to a point when the premiums are so high that people will pull out in favour of their own funding arrangements.'

'Arrangements like your ward,' Jack muttered quietly.

'Exactly. You've got the makings of a perfect storm: a population that is growing *and* ageing, coupled with the spiralling costs of healthcare. How sustainable will the current system be, Jack?'

Jack found it was hard to argue against what the professor was saying.

'The next phase will be deregulation in the extreme.'

'What do you mean?'

'I mean that over time, governments and policymakers will realise what is happening and will stop meeting with public servants and start meeting with private industry. Initially, it will all happen behind closed doors. People like you and me will meet with people like Sir Roger and spell things out to them.'

Jack cut in. 'But won't their own advisors be telling them all this?'

'Oh yes, but we will be able to offer them a *solution*, Jack. A way for them to solve the problem *and* save political face. Their spin doctors will be able to convince the public that governments should not be funding healthcare.'

'I doubt that, Professor.'

'Do you now? The people will believe whatever they are told.

Governments have been taking advantage of this for years. They are already experts at it.'

'But what will be deregulated?' Jack asked.

He was feeling lost in the professor's dystopian vision and needed something solid to focus on.

'Governments will start by slashing red tape. Regulatory and credentialing authorities will be downsized as the private hospitals take hold. There will be no other choice. If you think the general public influences government, then you are a fool. It is industry, Jack. Those at the very top of private enterprise. They have the money. They have the influence. They have the power. When Joe Nobody goes to his local member of parliament and asks for an extra ten thousand in funding for his wife's cancer treatment, what do you think he's told?'

'Th-' Jack's tongue was wedged between his teeth, the first word of his response reduced to nothing more than a deflated hiss as Mortimer abruptly cut him off.

'They are told, very politely, very diplomatically, and with a great deal of sympathy that their situation is tragic, but the fiscal position of the life-saving medicines budget is exhausted, although it is currently being reviewed by a cross-party parliamentary oversight committee in the hope—the *genuine hope,* Mr Nobody—that within the next two, maybe three, budgetary cycles some extra funding may be... blah, blah, blah.'

Jack felt a sudden urge to punch Mortimer in the face, but he knew that the impulse only reflected his own frustration because, ultimately, Mortimer was right.

The professor continued. 'On the other hand, if the CEO of Big Bucks Pharma wants to find a few hundred million to enter into a public-private partnership deal to build an exciting new research facility that may, in twenty years' time, find that cure for Joe Nobody's wife's cancer, then Sir Roger's signing the cheque with one hand

and speed dialling his media advisor with the other, organising a press conference with the CEO as soon as possible.'

Jack needed a moment to process everything Mortimer had told him.

'Look Jack, you are brilliant. You have amazing talents, and you are headed for greatness. But don't be blinded by idealism. My assessment is cold and blunt, I agree, but you have to admit there is no way to sugar-coat this kind of reality. You need to make a decision: are you going to be part of the problem or part of the solution? Because if you are going to be part of the solution then you will be helping to save thousands and thousands of lives.'

Jack smiled to himself at the thought of that.

28

'I REALLY THINK that Lizzie is improving,' the medical student told Jack at the weekly ward round.

'I like that sort of optimism,' he said with encouragement. 'How did you reach that conclusion?'

'Her self-care is definitely better,' the student announced with confidence. Self-care, or lack thereof, was usually a sensitive indicator of the severity of a psychotic illness.

'In what ways?' Jack asked.

'Well, I looked in her room yesterday and noticed that she had really cleaned it up. She doesn't have much, but the possessions and clothes she does have were very neatly arranged and her entire cell … I mean *room*… was spotless.'

Jack thought about what the student said for a moment.

'Any other explanations for Lizzie's newfound tidiness?' he asked the group of students and junior doctors who had assembled for the morning's ward round. Blank faces stared back at him.

He looked back at the student who had made the original observation. 'It's great that you have noticed the change in Lizzie, as it clearly is a sudden and *definite* change. But always remember to ask yourself not only what the change means to *you*, but also what the change might mean to *Lizzie*? If Lizzie becomes tidier you may initially wonder what it means to *you*. But that is projection. More importantly, you need to understand what it means to *her*.'

He was met with more silence.

'What if I suggested that her pregnancy is representative of her being invaded and that, due to her psychosis, she is frightened of being invaded—of having her personal space violated. By having everything in order, she can then see when something is *out* of order. It helps her to feel in control if she believes she can know when there is an imminent threat.'

'But I thought she said she was happy about being pregnant,' another student said.

'Yes, and on the surface that may be true. But it is our job to look deeper than that and always ask *why*. Are the reasons she says she is happy based in reality? Why does she say she is happy about being pregnant? Because she believes that the baby will be able to help her to carry out the work of Marx. Due to her psychotic state of mind, that is the only purpose and the only benefit of becoming a mother.'

A few of the students looked at Jack with horror as it dawned on them just how unwell Lizzie was.

29

THEO STEIN REREAD the letter that Jack had sent him, in which he had detailed a dream about a young, psychotic, female patient who had killed a man. The dream was all about bloodlines, according to Jack. And it was this dream that made Jack realise that the patient was pregnant. Jack wrote that this had been confirmed by the usual blood tests.

Theo closed his eyes and let the thoughts cascade in.

The language.

The *words*.

But Jack was only half right.

There was more to the story.

There was more to the dream.

As Theo reminded him when he wrote back:

> *Remember Jack, place the dream in the context of* your *life. Remember it is* your *dream and we are* everyone *in our dreams, not just the literal representations of the people in them.*
>
> *What does the dream say about* you?
>
> *Yes, you seem to be right about the young lady, but who else raises a conflict within* you *about bloodlines?*
>
> *Who else may be a threat?*
>
> *Who else has recently come into your life with prominent bloodlines?*

The people in your dream have been distorted by your unconscious. I suspect that means that someone is lying to you. Someone is lying to you about their family background. You can't see it yet, Jack, as it has aroused too great a conflict within you to see clearly and your mind knows you would not tolerate the truth. Not yet. But keep working on it, Jack.

Keep searching.

Face the conflict inside you and your fear.

Words can have different meanings, so seek them out.

Bloodlines.

30

'I HAVE AN announcement to make,' Mortimer proclaimed at the end of the weekly ward round. All eyes turned to him.

'I have decided to organise a formal dinner for the medical staff—to mark the Nicholas Tindal Centre being officially opened and to formally welcome Doctor Jack Giorgio to our ranks.'

Jack looked a little embarrassed.

Sarah smiled and patted her colleague on the back.

Barnard rolled his eyes.

'Don't worry, Doctor Barnard, I will be picking up the bill.'

There was muted laugher from a few of the doctors.

'I expect you all to attend,' Mortimer added. 'I will be sure to choose something expensive and "hip", to appease you young folk.' He coughed violently, and it took him some time for him to compose himself. 'Nell will give you the details. And Jack, I want to take this opportunity to thank you for your hard work and for providing so much to this facility in such a short period of time.'

'Hear, hear,' Sarah added with a smile.

'Ah… thank you, Professor… It's a great team. Everyone puts in the hard work. And everyone has made me feel very welcome. So… thanks… to all of you.'

'You're a tremendous addition to forensic mental health in this country, Jack. I really mean that.' Mortimer looked earnestly at Jack, then walked around the table and placed a hand firmly and affectionately on his shoulder.

A few uncomfortable looks were shared between some of the staff.

Okay, you can stop now.

But he did not stop.

Mortimer caught his breath in the excitement of the moment and continued talking.

'In fact, Jack, I can see so much of myself in you. All the drive. All the ambition. The dedication. You are like a young Nathan Mortimer in so many ways.' His hand tightened on Jack's shoulder.

Jack was now going red. But there was nowhere to hide.

There were more curious looks.

'In many ways, I can see that you are really becoming like a son to me, Jack. The son I never had.' Mortimer started tearing up and hastily left the meeting.

'What the fuck was that?' Barnard said to the room.

31

SINCE ARRIVING IN London from New York, Jack had rented a small, somewhat depressing one-bedroom flat in Balham. He kept meaning to find something more upmarket, preferably north of the river, but time had flown and he'd been exceptionally busy at work. He hadn't even unpacked any of his books yet.

When he was not on call, Jack began scanning the rental websites, and had even gone to one or two viewings. But the desirable properties always seemed to be just out of his financial reach.

In theory, a one-bedroom place was enough for his needs, but he wanted a reasonable sized lounge room, a decent kitchen and a second bedroom that he could use as a study. However, as with New York City, all of that came at a considerable cost.

Jack had left his contact details with a few agents, but he was still surprised when a professional-sounding woman by the name of Alice Winton, from an agency he had never heard of, called him one Saturday morning.

'Doctor Giorgio. Good morning,' she began in a friendly and courteous manner. 'I hope I am not disturbing you on this lovely Saturday, but I think I may have a property you would be very interested in. A delightful, modern apartment.'

'Okay,' Jack said slowly and uncertainly.

'In fact, I don't want to seem pushy, but if you are free later this morning, I could show you around.'

As good luck would have it, Jack was off work for the entire weekend.

'Where is it?' he asked, a little hesitantly.

'By the Thames, at Albert Embankment.'

Jack's eyebrows raised. He had assumed anything decent around there would be well out of his price range. It would probably be a dump, the worst apartment in the best neighbourhood, but he had nothing better to do so he arranged to meet Ms Winton at 11:30.

Jack was philosophically opposed to judging books by their covers, but if the facade of the building he was standing in front of was any indication, then this was going to be one swanky apartment.

And a very expensive one, as well.

A smart Audi S6 sedan pulled up a few yards away, and an equally smart property manager stepped out.

'Doctor Giorgio?' she asked, with a pleasant smile.

'Yes. Please, call me Jack.'

'Alice,' she said as they shook hands.

'Beautiful building,' Jack looked up at the façade.

'Isn't it? Only completed late last year. It's five floors. Only twenty-five apartments in total.'

'I had a quick look online before I left, but I couldn't find it.'

'Oh… it's a private offering,' she explained. 'We offer an exclusive, bespoke service for hand-picked clientele.'

Hand-picked?

Jack was distracted by the magnificent pedestrian track that ran between the building and the river, which would be ideal for long runs after work.

Settle down, Jack, don't get too far ahead of yourself

She ushered him to the foyer, pointing out some of the ground floor features, and headed to the lifts. He expected her to hit the first-floor button, so when her carefully manicured finger went for the sub-penthouse level, Jack thought there must be some mistake.

'You are going to love this,' she said as they rode up.

He decided to remain silent and just smiled.

The lift doors opened onto an elegant foyer.

'There are just three apartments on this floor, and two on the penthouse level above. This apartment,' she explained, 'also comes with two parking spaces in the secure basement.'

Parking? Now I know this will be out of my league.

Ms Winton was not exaggerating when she told Jack that he would love it. He adored it. The modern, clean lines and high ceilings gave a sense of space and calm, and the two bedrooms plus study were beautifully appointed. He was especially taken with the bespoke Danish light fittings that hung in every room.

'And anyone who has the faintest of culinary skills could cook up a veritable storm in here,' she exclaimed as Jack was shown through the kitchen. As he leant on the marble benchtop, he could only agree.

The views from the generous balcony were equally breathtaking. Looking across the Thames to Lambeth, and also taking in the Palace of Westminster and Big Ben.

'Best views in London,' she said as he leant on the balcony rail.

Jack turned and faced her. 'I can't disagree. This place is spectacular. It's so far beyond anything else I have looked at.' They walked back into the lounge room.

'It is perfect, but my only concern is the rent. It must be exorbitant. I'm single and therefore only have my income to rely on. To be honest, I'm not sure I could cover it, Alice.'

At that point Jack noticed a tall, older man had entered the apartment. He was dressed in a three-piece Hugo Boss suit, and carried a small black leather satchel. Alice tensed up and looked surprised.

'At ease, Ms Winton,' the man said with a calm and a pleasant smile.

'Ahh... Mr Nicholas,' she stammered. 'What a lovely surprise. Please meet Doctor Jack Giorgio.'

The two men shook hands.

'Good to meet you, Jack. So, what do you think of this little place?'

'It's stunning,' he said.

Alice intervened, nervously. 'Mr Nicholas is the founder and CEO of the company.'

'Yes, and I just wanted to come down and meet you, Doctor. Nathan Mortimer and I are… chums.'

His words were delivered with another warm smile.

'Ah. Right,' Jack said slowly.

'So, do you want to take it?' Nicholas asked, slapping his hand down on the marble benchtop, seemingly not in the mood for further small talk.

'I would love to… but the rent concerns me.'

Nicholas said nothing but unzipped his satchel. He reached in and handed Jack a piece of paper.

The figure written down shocked him.

'Is that per hour?' he asked tentatively.

Nicholas laughed and slapped Jack on the back.

'Per *month*, Doctor. The only condition is that this figure is for a twelve-month contract.'

'That won't be a problem,' Jack said blankly, still staring at the page in front of him.

'Well, that's all settled then. Congratulations, Doctor. You can move in whenever is suits you. If you need assistance with furnishings, then I am certain that Ms Winton here can point you in the right direction.'

Alice nodded. Nicholas gestured towards her, and she promptly handed Jack a business card for a furniture removal company.

32

JACK SAT PATIENTLY at the bar, sipping Bollinger from a champagne flute. His watch told him that she was around twenty minutes late, but he was not overly concerned.

It was a very last minute and rushed decision to dine out, and Cerise had told him she would need to finish some work before she could get to Hyde Park to join him at the Bar Boulud.

'I promise it will be worth the wait,' she teased, 'and the fewer distractions I have, the better for you.'

The sudden *pop* of a champagne cork startled Jack. It surprised him that, despite the alcohol, he was so on edge. He sat back and examined his feelings.

Why so tense?

Even though he loved the new apartment, an honest appraisal of his feelings confirmed that he did not feel entirely comfortable with the *process*.

This led instantly to thoughts of Mortimer and his clearly considerable influence.

Private wards.

'What is *your* process?' he said softly to himself.

And then, 'What do you *want* from me, Professor Mortimer?'

But then came another voice: *Come on, Jack, you deserve this. You've worked so hard.*

And yet, it just didn't feel *right*.

Jack sipped the champagne and let these questions gently roll around inside his mind. The thought soon came to him that he was now part of something bigger. Something grander. It was Mortimer's style, after all, to aim high. But what was he aiming *for*?

A gentle hand on his left shoulder caused these questions to evaporate. He turned his head and saw Cerise standing behind him, looking resplendent in her favourite duck-egg blue cashmere coat and a timeless little off-white dress. She bent down and kissed him softly on the cheek.

'Hiya handsome.'

'Hello, Ms Navarro.'

Jack gestured to the waiter to pour Cerise her own glass of Bollinger. No sooner had it had been delivered, it was consumed.

'Ahhh, that's better,' she sighed with satisfaction, her eyes closed as if recalling the memory of it.

'Another?' asked Jack.

'You betcha,' she replied loudly, causing a couple of their fellow diners to look her way. She quickly downed the second glass and grabbed a menu out of Jack's hands.

'No prices!' she exclaimed. 'Hmmm… always a worrying sign. Can we afford it, Giorgio?'

Jack was about to answer but Cerise suddenly looked very distracted. Her eyes were darting around the restaurant and she was swivelling from side to side on her chair, as though she was trying to pick someone out of the dining crowd. Jack tried to follow the trajectory of her gaze. No one looked familiar.

'Cerise, is everything okay?'

'Yes. Fine. Why?' she replied curtly.

'I don't know. You seem a little out of sorts. Distracted, maybe.'

'Is that your diagnosis, *Doctor?*'

He felt increasingly worried.

'No, I am fine, Jack. All good,' she said briskly, with a smile that Jack sensed was a little forced.

'Okay. Well, here's to the new apartment! And how was your day? Did you manage to get through your work?'

There was a long silence as Cerise seemed to weigh up his questions. He noticed that she then had a tear in her eye as she looked at him longingly. She squeezed his hands.

'Oh, Jack. It's gonna be *so* great. *So great.*' She nodded as she spoke to add further emphasis.

Jack smiled uncomfortably but didn't break their gaze.

'What's going to be so great, Cerise?' he asked softly.

'Dr Jack Giorgio and Professor Nathan Mortimer, of course. Oh my God! It's the perfect fucking combination! It's a masterstroke. *Genius.* With his experience and connections and your mind and energy. The world won't have seen anything like it!'

The couple at the next table stopped eating and stared their way.

Cerise almost seemed to be enraptured.

She ordered a bottle of wine and waited impatiently for it to arrive. Again, she looked around the restaurant.

'Who are you looking for, Cerise?'

'Nothing… ah, no one… I just feel excited, Jack. Really excited.'

He wondered if she was drunk.

The bottle of shiraz arrived and was poured by the waiter. Cerise clutched her glass with both hands. A few drops of the deep red liquid sloshed over the edge onto the table. As she lifted the glass to her lips Jack reached out and put a hand around the stem.

'It's okay, we have plenty of time. There's absolutely no rush. We can just relax and enjoy this wonderful night.'

She pushed his hand away and took a large gulp. The waiter was still standing nearby and raised an eyebrow.

'You must do it, Jack. You simply *must*. You have worked so hard to get that forensic psychiatrist position at the Tindal Centre *and* to work directly with Nathan Mortimer. To be able to collaborate so closely with the professor. Do not pass up any other opportunities.' She looked right into his cool, blue eyes. 'It is also a real opportunity for us, Jack. For *us*.'

Immediately he thought of Mortimer's private ward.

Could she know about that? Surely not.

Her words had become more forceful now. More driven. Insistent.

She looked up and exhaled deeply. Jack could see her relaxing in front of his eyes.

The alcohol must be really kicking in, he thought. He suddenly felt a strong desire to care for her.

She's vulnerable.

'Ahh sorry, Jack. What was I saying?'

'You were excited about the professor and me working together and… opportunities.'

'Mmm, yes! You could do so much good, Jack. So much. End the suffering of so many. What possibilities. The professor can open so many doors for you, you know? I know that you can also work side-by-side with him through MTR on these next generation of antipsychotic medications. These will be a complete game-changer, especially with you and the professor at the helm. I don't think you realise just how important he is.'

'Important?'

'Oh yes! He is so connected, Jack. It is truly amazing. He has contacts like you wouldn't believe.'

Again, Jack's mind wandered back to Mortimer's converted warehouse in London. Maybe she *did* know.

'What sort of contacts?' he asked.

'Politicians, business leaders, scientists, captains of industry, film producers, rock stars…'

'Rock stars?'

'Oh yeah, I remember once he introduced me to…' she suddenly stopped speaking as her phone beeped with a text message. She read the message and her mood completely changed.

She was clearly angry, cursing under her breath, presumably to the sender of the message. Her fingers pounded away furiously on the screen of her iPhone as she responded.

'Everything okay, Cerise?'

She didn't answer Jack immediately, but waited until she had completed the lengthy text and hit send.

'Oh, it's nothing I can't handle. Just work stuff. Frustrations. God, I work with some real idiots, you know?' She shook her head from side to side and smile to herself. Jack wondered what was going through her mind but decided not to ask, as the waiter arrived with their entrees.

'Wow! This looks wonderful,' Cerise exclaimed, seemingly much brighter again.

Jack agreed but found himself struggling to keep up with her mood changes.

33

NATHAN MORTIMER DROVE slowly through the streets of Chelsea, listening to the BBC's midday news report on the outcome of the trial of Elizabeth Roberts.

> '... Justice Berry ruled that university student Elizabeth Roberts, twenty-two, was not mentally competent in relation to the one charge of murder she faced. Roberts, a former economics student, was accused of murdering senior lecturer Dr Marc Mollet at his London home earlier this year...'

Mortimer nodded to himself.

> '... in summing up the case, Justice Berry said she was most impressed with the clear and concise evidence given by forensic psychiatrist, Dr Jack Giorgio, of the Nicholas Tindal Centre...'

This elicited a further nod and a broad smile from the professor.

> '... Giorgio argued that Roberts was acutely psychotic at the time of the homicide and needed long-term psychiatric treatment. And in further news, a boatload of refugees has sunk in the Mediterranean S-'

Mortimer turned off the radio.

'You are going to work out just fine, Dr Giorgio,' he said to himself.

34

THE CLINICAL STAFF were looking forward to the degustation dinner at *The Butler's Pantry* in Soho. True to his word, the professor had made good on his promise to find a classy yet trendy fine dining establishment to celebrate the opening of the centre and to welcome Jack.

How he managed to get a large party booked into the restaurant's private dining room at such short notice was anyone's guess.

Connections.

As he sipped from a glass of 2002 Krug and chatted away to Sarah and Paul Patterson, Jack realised he was easily getting used to this way of life.

In fact, it was a life he wanted more of. Going back to anything less rewarding was becoming unthinkable.

He watched as Drew Barnard pulled up in the loading zone directly outside the restaurant, fashionably late. He barged his way through his colleagues without a word or a smile and made a beeline for the bar, where he demanded a double Grey Goose vodka on the rocks. With drink in hand, he sought out Sir Nathan and led him to a quiet corner for an intense, private discussion about who knew what.

Jack shrugged off the rude bluster of Drew Barnard and returned to the stimulating conversation he was enjoying with Sarah and Paul.

He would have loved to have brought Cerise to the dinner, but Mortimer had made it crystal clear that the event was for staff only. This probably made it easier for him to claim the dinner as a tax deduction, Jack decided.

She would have adored the restaurant's ambience and food, and it would have given Jack a chance to introduce her to his colleagues in a less formal setting, as none of the medical staff seemed to have met her. He briefly closed his eyes and imagined her there with him, looking absolutely stunning.

Oh well, we will just have to come back here on our own.

'Where have your thoughts gone, Dr Giorgio,' Sarah asked with a knowing smile.

He blushed slightly. 'Ah… well… I am just imagining revisiting this place.'

'Dinner for two?'

'Indeed,' he said.

'I thought so! I could tell there was something up with you! Come on, don't keep us in suspense!'

Even Paul seemed interested in the gossip.

'Actually, you may well have come across her. Cerise Navarro. From MTR? Regional manager. Short dark hair. Extremely pretty.'

'Cerise?' Sarah repeated slowly.

'Yes. Navarro. Have you met her?'

'Navarro? No, I don't think so. But one meets so many pharma staff in this game that it can be hard to keep track.'

Barnard attempted to push back past them, vodka in hand. He stopped.

'Allowed out tonight, Sarah?' he asked with a smirk. 'Hope Sam has the twins well looked after. Hopefully no calls home in the middle of proceedings?' Sarah just looked away.

Several, short sharp *clinks* rang out as the maître d' struck a glass with a spoon and informed the party that dinner was served.

They made their way into the inviting space of the private dining room and took their seats around the huge table.

Jack noted with keen interest the numerous fascinating framed photographs that lined the walls of butlers who had served various

European royal families and other dignitaries over the last hundred or so years. He noticed several famous faces and half expected to see a photo of Mortimer on the wall, being waited on by his own personal staff.

During the amazing kingfish entrée, Jack saw that Barnard still wanted the ear of the professor, but Nathan, growing irritated, was starting to swat him away like an annoying fly.

Between courses three and four, Mortimer rose to his feet.

He welcomed everyone and, much to the delight of all in attendance, said he hoped to turn this dinner into annual event. He was immensely proud of the facility that had been opened and he said he had extended an invitation to Sir Roger Maxwell, given the important role the Health Department played in funding the centre, but the minister had declined due to another engagement.

'Thank God,' someone whispered under their breath to muffled laughter.

'Now, now,' cautioned Mortimer. 'I am quite certain he is learning to value the importance of good mental health.'

More overt laughter rang out this time.

'And finally, to you Doctor Giorgio. Welcome, son. Welcome. We are all so fortunate that you have joined us. I know that all the staff look forward to many years of your incredible clinical insights, teaching, and friendship.'

'And drinks on your new balcony, Giorgio!' someone called out. More laughter.

'Thank you, Sir Nathan, and, again, to all of you. It's a thrill to be here,' Jack enthused.

The professor urged Jack to join him. When he did, Mortimer threw his arms around Jack and held him tight.

'You're fucking amazing,' he wheezed quietly into Jack's ear.

Barnard rolled his eyes and ordered another vodka.

35

'WHAT ARE YOU thinking?' Jack asked. He knew that he would get no reply, and the question was more for himself than for the Asian man sitting opposite.

Silence.

A blank stare.

> *What are you thinking? What is going through that mind of yours?*

Jack was desperate for a way to connect with this man, to find a way in and help him. To bring him back. To communicate and understand what was happening. It was not simply a case of chronic psychosis. He had never seen this before.

Jack looked down at the medication chart on his lap. Patient X had been written up for the usual regime of tranquilisers, sleeping tablets and antipsychotics that were often required to settle very agitated patients on the ward on an 'as needs' basis. Usually, the chart was full of dosages, dates, and times that these medications had been administered.

But this chart was essentially empty.

> *As empty as you are, Patient X.*

Not a single dose had been required since the man had been admitted.

> *Not like Lizzie*

The thought popped into his head from nowhere.

'Not like Lizzie,' he repeated slowly, out loud. 'Not like Lizzie.'

> *Why are you suddenly thinking of Lizzie?*

He followed the stream of conscious to see where it would head.

Not like Lizzie.

He looked Patient X up and down. The man sat passively with his arms down by his sides. Slowly breathing. His diaphragm causing his slender chest and abdomen to rise and fall.

Slender chest.

Slender abdomen.

'It is like you are there and you are *not* there,' he whispered. 'But why?'

Once again, an image of Lizzie came into his head. An image of her heavily pregnant. He closed his eyes and the image of her became grossly distorted. Her belly further swollen. Huge. Like a massive balloon. Ridiculous, really. Not possible.

Enormous.

Pregnant. The bloodline will continue. The work will continue. I know it will be a boy.

He stared at Patient X's flat abdomen.

Pregnant. I think it's wonderful. It will allow me to finish what my great grandfather started. I know that is my purpose... and the purpose of my child.

Jack opened his eyes.

Slender abdomen.

There. But not there.

36

'DOCTOR DANIEL BATES!' Jack announced in a loud, enthusiastic voice. 'How is life at the top?'

The two men embraced warmly. When they separated, they grabbed each other by the shoulders and smiled.

'Maybe we should just leave these two alone,' Daniel's wife Katherine jokingly suggested to Cerise.

The two doctors ignored the comment.

'God, it's so good to see you again, Jack,' Daniel's smile broadened.

'You too, mate.'

'Cerise, please meet my med school roommate, best friend, and plastic surgeon to the stars, Daniel Bates.'

Daniel and Cerise kissed lightly on each cheek.

'Lovely to meet you, Cerise. This is my wife, Katherine.' The two women also exchanged polite kisses.

'Well, you've certainly picked a lovely spot for dinner,' commented Daniel as he surveyed the upmarket West End restaurant. 'Not like those student days at Columbia. Remember those nasty all-you-can-eat downtown diners?' Daniel grimaced.

'Oh yeah… we used to try to eat enough to last us for three days,' Jack said with a laugh.

'But I also seem to remember you would take the most basic of ingredients and turn them into those wonderfully tasty meals,' Katherine added with a smile.

'He still does,' Cerise smiled and gripped Jack's arm. Daniel nodded slowly and winked in Jack's direction.

After they placed their food orders, Daniel ordered a bottle of Laurent Perrier.

'To old *and* new friends,' he toasted, looking towards Cerise.

'So how is life in Beverly Hills?' Jack asked.

'Well it's great, actually. My practice is really taking off and it's genuinely fulfilling work,' said Daniel.

'No, not you, Dr Augmentation, I was asking Katherine,' Jack said with a laugh. Daniel threw him a smirk and shook his head.

'Thank you, Jack, I am certainly enjoying the Californian climate. There are worse places to live,' she said, before turning to Cerise. 'As you would know, Jack was always the considerate one of the Fab Four.'

Cerise put a hand on Jack's. 'Yes, I have some inkling of what you are talking about. But tell me about the Fab Four.'

'Aarggh,' said Katherine, taking a generous swig of her champagne. 'The Fab Four. The naughtiest, most annoyingly brilliant students in our year at Columbia. We are quite lucky Cerise, as fifty percent of them are sitting at our table tonight.'

Cerise quickly stood up and looked around the restaurant. 'Where? Where are these fabulous men?'

Katherine laughed out loud. 'Oh, I *like* you,' she said. 'You name the subject, name the semester, and I kid you not, one of the Fab Four would have topped the class. They all made the Dean's list. Awards. Honours. Blah, blah, blah.'

'Names, names, I want names,' demanded Cerise, as she moved on to her second glass of the delicious Perrier.

'Well, obviously there is Doctor Giorgio here, the wonder from down under, with his utter devotion to the human mind and long-distance running, his knack for picking up languages and his fabulous culinary skills. Secondly, we have the good Dr Bates, who, even in medical school, could suture skin better than most attending surgeons at Columbia. Absent from tonight's party is Stephen Heller, who became an intensive care specialist.'

Daniel intervened. 'I ran into him at a surgical conference a few months ago, Jack. He looked great. He's living in San Francisco now and he's *finally* found love. He was very happy.'

'Really?' Jack said. 'That's great. Thank God he finally found someone.'

'Yes. He's a lovely guy. He was at the conference too. Brad. He's a radiologist at UCSF Medical Centre. They looked good together. Heller even splurged on a new Ferrari!'

'No way!' Jack said. He turned to Cerise. 'Heller was *the* biggest Scrooge in medical school!'

'And so who is number four?' asked Cerise.

'That would be Henry,' Katherine said soberly.

'And what did he end up doing?'

Jack quickly answered in a soft voice. 'He didn't quite make it to graduation, Cerise.'

'He dropped out?'

'That's one way of putting it!' Daniel said, but was swiftly slapped in the chest by Katherine.

Jack threw a stern look Daniel's way before turning back to Cerise, 'he took his own life in the final semester. It was a real shock. Tragic.'

'Oh... I am so sorry guys,' Cerise said.

Katherine smiled. 'Daniel and I weren't really that close to Henry but...'. She looked at Jack.

'I was good friends with him. I never saw it coming. I missed it,' Jack said sombrely. He raised his champagne flute. 'To Henry.'

They clinked glasses.

'So did you and Daniel meet in medical school?' Cerise asked Katherine, trying to lighten the mood.

'Actually, just before,' Daniel replied. 'We were both in the same med school entrance exam prep class. I guess she just couldn't resist me.'

Another slap on the chest.

'And what did you end up doing, Katherine?'

'Part time general practice. I'm just the humble, local family physician. I love it actually. I was totally fed up with the hospital system and the endless bureaucracy. I really wanted to see my patients over the long term in a community setting.'

'That's why you should have done psychiatry,' Jack said cheerfully. 'I could imagine you in some nice private practice in L.A.' Katherine rolled her eyes. This was not the first time Jack had made such an observation.

'How long are you guys in London?' Cerise asked.

'Just for the week,' Daniel said. 'I have a two-day plastic surgery meeting, and then we are at your disposal.

The arrival of an enormous seafood platter brought the conversation to a pause. Daniel ordered a bottle of sauvignon blanc, and once they had eaten their fill he leaned back in his chair and asked Jack about what he knew about the local property investment market. The two men entered into an intense conversation.

'I'm just heading to the bathroom,' Cerise said.

'I think I'll follow you,' Katherine feigned a yawn, signalling her lack of interest in the men's conversation.

When the women had left the table, Jack turned to Daniel and spoke in a demure tone.

'You work in the homeland of free markets, right?'

'Hell yeah,' he said with an enthusiastic nod.

'You have a very wealthy clientele. People with money and influence?'

'It's Los Angeles. So, of course,' he replied with a broad smile. 'Almost all of my work is covered by insurance to one degree or another but the patients have to top up the rest, especially for cosmetic procedures, so their contribution can amount to thousands.'

'No, I mean *really* private work. Like, say, an entire clinic that is… under the radar. Procedures done off the record, without any insurance involved.'

Daniel looked puzzled. 'What, like for cash?'

'Yes, but not just that. I mean clinics that aren't officially there, with no regulations and no real patient records kept. Have you ever heard of anything like that?'

Daniel grabbed his wine glass and shook his head vigorously in a confused way before taking a drink. 'No *records*? No way! That's crazy, especially in L.A. It's lawsuit city! Why are you asking about this?' His look of bewilderment turned to one of concern. 'Jack, is everything okay?'

'Yeah. Fine, mate. Don't worry about it.'

The two men made small talk for a few minutes until Katherine and Cerise returned. Jack thought that he noticed a frown on Cerise's face as she approached the table, but when she sat down he didn't give it another thought. Katherine seemed to be her usual vivacious self and once again the conversation flowed smoothly.

> *All the elements are here. Great friends, amazing food, and Cerise. Does it get any sweeter?*

***

Cerise seemed tense during the ride home.

'Are you okay?' Jack asked.

'Yeah, I'm fine,' she answered, before looking down at her hands. 'Actually... *no*. No. I'm not fine. Katherine gave me a really hard time tonight.'

Jack was taken aback and thought he must have missed something. 'Katherine? Really? What do you mean?'

'She made it clear that because I am just a lowly drug company rep, I didn't belong with the three of you.'

How much have you had to drink tonight?

'Really?' He cast his mind back to the evening's conversation. It was like watching a movie in reverse. He didn't recall any comments made to Cerise that were in any way demeaning or hostile or offensive. Nothing came to mind that could have led her to the conclusion she had drawn.

'Yes. *Really*,' she said sharply.

'What did she say?'

'You didn't hear it. It was when we went to the bathroom together. It wasn't anything that she specifically said, but it was the way she looked at me in there. *Ugghhh.*' She shivered.

The frown. I remember the frown when she came back to the table.

'I picked it up from her patronising tone of voice, too. The Fab Four. *Fab Four*. And it's clear she has a giant crush on you.'

'No way,' Jack said with surprise. 'I'm certain that's not true.'

'A woman can tell these things, Jack,' she stared at him.

'Look, Cerise, in all the years I've known Katherine she's been with Daniel and no one else. They are completely devoted to each other.'

'They may be, but she can still have a crush on you.'

He wanted to laugh but suppressed it. He had a sense that may anger her. She was already clearly feeling sensitive.

It was going to sound defensive and corny, but he couldn't think of how else to defuse things. 'Well, I have a huge crush on *you*.' He squeezed her hand.

She still looked angry.

They drove home in silence.

37

WITHOUT ASKING, MORTIMER ordered them both a glass of Martell cognac and, knowing he would refuse, offered Jack a cigar before lighting one up for himself. A very attentive staff member stoked the fire, to ensure the small, private lounge was at the perfect temperature.

Jack settled back into the soft leather chair and stared at the flames. It was pouring with rain outside, and the exclusive club offered a decadent refuge.

'Thanks for the invitation, Professor,' he said.

'It's my pleasure, Jack. They don't usually allow visitors in here at all, but I spoke to the club's president and explained you would soon make a fine member yourself. Between you and me I think the 'no visitors' rule is a tad archaic for modern times, but what are you going to do? You know Aldous Huxley was a member here for a few years. Before he moved to California, of course.'

Jack had been quite observant when they entered the Mayfair Club earlier in the evening and were ushered up into the room.

'No women?' he asked.

'Oh no, not here. It's one the last bastions, you know. But don't worry, they would be quite open to admitting someone with your surname. It was an Italian chap who founded this place, in the seventeenth century. Some sort of coffee importer and connoisseur. So you would fit right in,' he said with a laugh.

The waiter arrived and set down the crystal balloons of cognac. Jack wondered who else had sat by that fire over the last few hundred years. The combination of the cognac and the warmth of the flames made him feel slightly sedated.

Surprisingly, the feeling was not entirely pleasant.

'Have you thought about our recent conversation?' Mortimer finally asked.

'Yes, of course,' answered Jack. Mortimer looked up at a collection of framed front pages from *The Times* that had capture significant moments in world history. The oldest dated back to 1795, with the headline trumpeting the triumph of the British forces, who had just captured Cape Town from the Dutch.

'We don't like to think so, but life was much easier back then,' Mortimer raised his glass towards the framed newspaper. 'Especially for people in our trade.'

'What do you mean?' asked Jack.

'Well, it was all so much more straightforward. People went mad and they were hidden away, either by their family or in an asylum, and our role was really to keep them out of the way. You might have had only a few shrinks looking after a few thousand patients, but you only really needed to see your patients once or twice a year.' He took a sip of his cognac.

'But we've come so far,' Jack retorted. 'We can do so much more now. To help. And as for "keeping them out of the way", well, I'm glad those days are gone. It was a travesty to have so many people unnecessarily locked up. It was all very stigmatising.'

'You're glad, are you? A travesty? We have come so far? Oh, spare me.' He shook his head. 'We haven't come *that* far. The quality of life of patients in the eighteenth century was not that much worse than it is now. At least the patients of the past were given asylum in the *true* sense of the word. Now they are just cast out and told to sink or swim. Care in the bloody community.'

> *That can't be right. It can't be.*

Mortimer pressed on without waiting for a response. 'Don't be naïve. The days of 'doctor knows best' are over, Jack. This so-called patient-centred approach has been so dominant, but its days are numbered too.'

Jack believed in the patient-centred approach. He strongly disliked the paternalistic, old-school methods that saw the doctor as being holier-than-thou and above reproach. He wanted to arm his patients with information, not just drugs, and be a guide in helping them to make choices; not a domineering authority figure who simply demanded that they blindly follow his orders. Even within the strict confines of forensic psychiatry he had found that a patient-centred approach and working *with* the patient could yield incredible results.

'It will be a self-limiting experiment, you know,' Mortimer asserted.

'Why?'

'Think about it, Jack. The global incidence of schizophrenia is subtly but steadily rising. We have records going back decades, although in reality the statistic probably holds true for hundreds of years, that show the incidence of schizophrenia was consistently around the half a percent mark. Diagnosable in one in every two hundred people. After the mid nineteen eighties, it jumped to point eight of one percent. A few years later it was one-point-one percent, with around one in every hundred people being diagnosed. Now, that figure is around one and a half percent and within the next years modelling suggests it will be around one point seven percent. So, the incidence has doubled in thirty years.'

'But what has that got to do with taking a patient-centred approach?'

'Everything. For example, people with serious mental health conditions are not locked away anymore. They are out there meeting people. Having children. The internet and dating apps have made it easier for isolated people to have relationships. To pass on all their pathology. Patient advocates have intervened and prevented schizophrenics from having sterilisations. Just look at Lizzie Roberts. She's the perfect case in point. She's as mad as they come and, well, it didn't stop *her*, did it?'

'Well no, it didn't, but what…' Jack began but Mortimer abruptly cut him off.

'We can't even rely on medications to do the job for us'.

'What do you mean?' Jack was very concerned about where the conversation was headed.

'The old antipsychotics were well-known for causing major sexual dysfunction. Most of the men on those drugs had severe erectile dysfunction and it destroyed their libidos, especially in their twenties and thirties when they were at their most active. And they caused significant infertility in the women. It was great for …' Mortimer turned and stared at the roaring fire … 'population control.'

'And now?'

Mortimer laughed. 'And now, Jack, the antipsychotics have far fewer side effects. And if there *are* side effects, the patients simply head down to their local doctor, call their psychiatrist or go online, so that they can get some Viagra. Problem solved. And we are told that we must facilitate this behaviour. These lifestyles. That it is *cruel* to let these people suffer such a terrible side effect that interferes with their lives in this way.'

Jack finally felt irritated enough to speak up. 'These people are not defined entirely by their illnesses. They have suffered enough and have a right to do the things that anyone else can do. Sex included. Families included.'

'Oh, *do* they?' Mortimer said with venom, raising his voice. 'They have the right to populate the planet with their delusional ideas, their disturbed behaviours, and their defective DNA?'

'I can't believe you are saying this. After all you have done, after all the patients you've helped, after all you have witnessed.' Jack shook his head in disbelief.

'And it is because I *have* witnessed all of this that I can say what I want!' Mortimer stopped there, realising that he had started to lose control of his anger. He quickly composed himself and spoke in a more affable tone. 'Look, Jack, I remember a time, quite vividly, when I thought just what you thought and said just what you said.'

'So, what's changed?'

'I stopped being blinded by my own idealism and started to see things as they *actually are*. Psychiatry can no longer afford this kind of self-delusion. You can really go places, Jack. I can take you places. So can that girlfriend of yours. She can see where all this headed. If she can keep you happy and motivated... well, you and I will have the answer in no time.'

'The answer to *what*?' Jack decided that he been too passive in this discussion and wanted Mortimer to offer some solutions.

'Mental illness, Jack. The answer to mental illness,' the professor said with a faraway smile.

'Oh yes. And what would that be, then?'

'Simple, Jack. We fucking cure them.'

38

THE PROJECTED, MOVING image was typically grainy and initially quite a mystery to the medical students and junior staff present at the weekly teaching session. Jack dimmed the lights to assist in clarifying the video. The fuzzy yellows and blacks on screen suddenly became sharper.

'Why are we watching an ultrasound?' asked one of the sharper junior registrars.

There. But not there.

'Pseudocyesis,' was the single word that Jack uttered to the group.

'*Psuedo-cy-what-the-frig-?*' exclaimed Dave, eliciting raucous laughter from the rest of the medical students.

'Phantom pregnancy,' translated Sarah with certainty.

There. But not there.

'Correct,' confirmed Jack with a smile. 'From the Greek. Pseudo: false. Cyesis: pregnancy.'

The ultrasound showed Lizzie Roberts' empty uterus.

'But... but...' Dave stammered. 'She *is* pregnant! What about the positive blood tests... and haven't her periods stopped?' He looked bewildered.

'You are right, Dave, but the patient can have all the hallmarks of pregnancy, right down to those positive blood tests and even the abdominal posture and shape that mimics the stages of a developing pregnancy. It really demonstrates the power of a delusion. The power of the human mind.'

Dave nodded slowly.

Sarah added, 'The endocrine system can be heavily influenced by the distressed mind and can lead to a loss menstruation. I am sure at least some of the females in this group have had their periods go haywire leading up to med school exams!' There were knowing nods from a few of the students. 'I have even seen women with this condition secreting breast milk.'

'It is likely that Lizzie has lost someone very close to her,' Jack explained. 'That may well have triggered her recent psychotic episode. She has lost what we would call a "love object", and as part of her delusional system she has introjected, or taken inside herself, a memory or a part of that lost person. Essentially, she is allowing it to grow and flourish inside her. To keep the love object alive and connected to her.'

'Could it be the guy she killed? Marc?' asked Millie, one of the registrars.

'Great question. I'm not convinced. But maybe,' said Jack. 'Because she is so unwell it is hard to know exactly what their relationship was. We need to remember that a phantom pregnancy can also be triggered by a loss of fertility. It may be possible that some prescription or recreational drug she has taken caused her to become infertile. Ironically, and sadly, even old-fashioned antipsychotic medication causes infertility in some women. Paradoxically, that antipsychotic can then trigger a delusion of pregnancy.'

'The treatment is worse than the illness,' said Dave, insightfully.

'Indeed, Dave,' agreed Jack. 'Thankfully, with the more modern antipsychotic medications, we have come some way in improving that particular side effect.'

'This news will need to be handled with extreme care and sensitivity,' continued Jack. 'Never forget that for Lizzie, this pregnancy is very real, and it is uncertain how she may react to discovering the truth. Until then, we must try everything we can to get her well again.'

39

THE SPRING SUN shone brightly on the morning of the London Marathon. It was eerie but refreshing to be in the heart of the city with so few cars around. The crowds gradually converged as the professional runners assumed their positions at the front of the enormous pack.

'Shall we try and stick to the edge?' Jack asked to Cerise. 'You can get crushed in the middle, and it can feel very claustrophobic.'

Jack remembered how he had once got stuck right in the centre of the field at the start of the New York Marathon. He was knocked over within the first minute of the race and had injured his knee, forcing him to abandon the run.

'Okay,' she agreed. She seemed quite tense.

Jack put a comforting arm around her shoulders, and she cuddled in close to him, but he could still feel the stiffness in her body. This was not a good sign right before such a long race. Being relaxed and loose, both physically *and* mentally, was key to getting through the run.

'I was really wound-up last night. I must confess that I had a couple of glasses of wine to settle my nerves. But I couldn't sleep anyway. Great preparation, right?' she smiled awkwardly.

'Is everything all right?' he asked.

'I just feel worried, I suppose.' Her voice sounded like it might crack at any minute. He sat down with her.

'What are you worried about, sweetheart? You've done the training. You are super fit. And we can take it nice and easy today. We're not looking to break any world records. We can just forget everything else and run.' He smiled, but she didn't react.

She gripped his hand. 'I keep thinking about Boston and what happened there. That was so terrible. It's really scared me.'

Jack shook his head. 'You mean the Boston Marathon bombing? Is that what you're worried about?'

She nodded.

'Oh, Cerise, everything will be fine. I'll be with you and there is a lot of security here. I mean, a *lot*. Maybe it's just pre-race nerves that are focusing your thoughts on the worst-case scenario.'

'But I think I saw someone over there,' she said, pointing vaguely into the crowd. 'Two guys who looked just like the ones in Boston. And they had large backpacks, Jack.'

He looked into the crowd.

Nothing.

'But remember, one of those guys is dead and the other is locked up. Thousands of miles away. It will be fine, let's warm up, we can do some stretches. It might help to distract you.'

She reluctantly agreed. Jack suddenly felt concerned about the intensity of her fear. She seemed to be genuinely frightened, but he hoped that once the race had started they could just focus on what was immediately in front of them and all would be well.

He watched her out of the corner of his eye as she stretched. He didn't need to be subtle about it, as she was fixated on something— or some*one*—in the crowd.

After what seemed like an eternity, they were finally called to start the race. Jack made sure they began on the opposite side of the road so that at least her view of the spectators was blocked by a colourful sea of runners.

Cerise jumped when the starter's pistol fired and clung to Jack, who steadied her in case she fell.

'Let's just run,' he gently urged.

She followed him, slowly at first, but as the minutes elapsed, they both settled into a moderate, steady pace. Jack began to relax, the tension he had picked up from Cerise melting away from his body.

After around ten kilometres, just when he thought her anxiety was settling down, Cerise suddenly sped up, almost to a sprint. He was worried she wouldn't be able to maintain such a pace for the rest of the marathon. He accelerated, but she was pulling away from him.

He watched her zigzag in a random pattern among the other competitors. She moved deftly between them, and with real purpose. It seemed that within a matter of seconds she had got to the other side of John Wilson Street. She then ran right along the edge of the road for a minute or so, and just as Jack was about to catch up to her she jumped the barricade and headed off into the crowd.

> *'Cerise!'*

As she headed through the spectators, they parted to avoid colliding with her, but as soon as she had broken through the human gap closed up again, like water filling a riverbed.

Jack had no option but to try to follow her, the race now abandoned. He was worried about where she was headed and that she might end up in real trouble.

He jumped the barricade like he was in a steeplechase, then stopped and tried to catch sight of her. It was almost impossible to see with the crowds but when he jumped straight up into the air, he caught a flash of hot pink from her running outfit.

She seemed to be headed for the Thames.

Alarmed, he pushed past the crow and ran toward her. Finally, the numbers thinned out and he was able to sprint without being inhibited.

> *At last, I am gaining.*

She was headed straight for the water, and he had a sudden fear that she was going to jump in.

'Cerise! *Wait! Please!*'

But she just kept running, through a grassed area towards the dark water.

She was headed straight towards the river and, with one final burst of acceleration, attempted to leap over the barricade.

She screamed as she felt a large hand and strong arm wrap tightly around her waist, pulling her back, away from the river.

The two runners tumbled backwards, Cerise falling onto Jack. They hit the ground and Jack was grateful for the soft lawn underneath.

For a minute or so they lay together as they had fallen, their bodies entangled. He could feel her heart racing. Her entire body was pulsing.

  Or is it mine?

Both of them were breathing hard. He kept his arm around her waist, too afraid to let go. She did not pull him closer, nor did she struggle to push him away.

'Are you okay?' he asked breathlessly.

For a long time she didn't respond, and just lay silently on his chest.

'I can't get up,' she finally said.

'It's okay. Just lie here.'

Then she started crying. Sobbing.

He sat up and held her. 'What's the matter?' he asked. 'What has got you so scared?'

'I don't know. I just had to get out of there. There was something not *right*.'

He worried she had experienced a full-blown panic attack, but it felt like more than that.

'Not right?'

'I was thinking about those other bombers. I just felt like it was going to happen again. To you. To all of us. I thought I saw…' She broke off and held him tightly.

'It's okay', he said. 'You're safe. *We're* safe.'

'Am I? Are we?' she asked.

He turned her around and looked into her eyes. 'Of course we are. Look around. We're fine.'

Her breathing slowed.

'I think I'm just overtired, Jack. All this running and training and then there's work. For the past few weeks I don't think I've been sleeping at all well, either.'

Jack knew all about the effects of sleep deprivation on the human body and mind. He knew that a lack of sleep will kill a person faster than a lack of food. Before getting to that point, however, a person enters into a psychological hell. It can make people irrational and confused at first but if it continues then the lack of sleep leads to a severe, acute psychotic state that is pure torture. This is why sleep deprivation was such a common interrogation method.

'That's probably it,' he said. 'You need to rest. Slow down. Catch your breath. After a few days I'm sure you'll feel much better again.'

'Do you think so?'

'Absolutely.'

She did not seem convinced.

***

They slowly made their way back to Cerise's house. She seemed exhausted and they frequently stopped to sit and rest. At times she was like a dead weight in his arms. In spite of her exhaustion she didn't want to take the tube, preferring to walk. Usually this would be fine with Jack, but he remained concerns about her rationale, especially as she was so fatigued.

However, he didn't push her. He could see that she was clearly too frightened to take the underground, although she could not—or *would* not—explain why.

After almost two hours they arrived back at her place. By now, she was almost asleep. Jack carried her inside, taking her straight to the bedroom. He lay her down gently on the bed and removed her running shoes.

'Are you okay?' he whispered.

'Mmmmm,' she quietly replied.

'I'll just grab you a cold drink. Be right back.'

When he returned a minute later, she was sound asleep. He slipped off his own shoes and lay down next to her. She did not stir. Eventually, he went into the lounge room, grabbed a novel from her bookshelf and returned to the bedroom, where he lay on the bed next to her, reading, but not really taking in the words.

Cerise did not wake until seven the following morning.

40

THE FOLLOWING MORNING, Jack flicked on his TV as he sat and drank his morning espresso. He almost dropped his cup when he recognised the face looking back at him from the screen. The glossy host enthusiastically introduced the next guest, who apparently featured regularly as a guest of the magazine show to discuss 'all things mental health.'

Dr Drew Barnard.

The gushing host described Barnard as a 'renowned forensic psychiatrist' and a 'leader in his field'. The camera panned to the excessively groomed Barnard, who was clearly lapping up the praise.

'Good morning, Stephanie,' he said in an upbeat tone that Jack had never heard before. 'It's great to be back again.'

'Well, it's great to have you back,' the pretty host replied flirtatiously. 'And we must thank the kind people at MTR pharmaceuticals for sponsoring this segment. Now, doctor, it would seem that a possible breakthrough is on the horizon in the treatment of bipolar disorder?' Jack was gobsmacked.

What would Barnard know about that?

'Yes, that's correct Stephanie. It's very exciting. Some researchers in Paris have identified a faulty gene that can influence the way certain psychiatric medications are taken up and used by the brain. In this case they have studied mood stabiliser drugs that are very commonly used in bipolar disorder.'

'Uh-huh,' she said with a vacuous smile.

'Now, just for the viewers at home, Steph, bipolar disorder, or what was previously called "manic depression", is a very serious mood disorder where sufferers can experience extreme lows and sustained sadness, and also extreme highs—what we call "mania". As you can imagine, Steph, this combination of highs and lows means that bipolar disorder can be a very disabling illness.'

'Wow, you really have such a great way of explaining very complex medical issues to the general public,' the host said, nodding her head to emphasise her sense of awe.

'Unfortunately, only some of these individuals will respond to the mood stabilising medications that are used to balance out their emotions. The new research from France has identified why this might be the case. It seems that there is a defect in a gene that controls the effect of these medications in the frontal lobe of the brain, which may be responsible for the lack of efficacy of these mood stabilising drugs.'

It was clear that Stephanie barely understood what he was saying. But she kept nodding enthusiastically.

'Sounds exciting! So what does the future hold, Doctor B?'

Jack was amazed at just how polished and relaxed Barnard was in front of the cameras. He came across as extremely intelligent and sophisticated. He was clearly a born performer, and no doubt his television spot was yet another mechanism by which he could meet women. Jack wondered if Barnard had taken things further with Steph than an on-camera flirtation.

Just as Barnard was about to speculate on a diagnosis that may apply to a Hollywood actress who just had an outburst in an L.A. department store, Jack decided he couldn't take it any longer and switched the television off.

Before he'd had the chance to process what he'd just seen, his iPhone rang and the name 'Nathan Mortimer' appeared on the screen.

'Good morning,' The words were barely out of Jack's mouth when Mortimer butted in.

'We need to do some private work after you're done at the NTC today.'

'At the private ward?' Jack asked.

'Ah no, not there. Think of this as PR work— all part of the special service we're providing.'

'I don't follow.' Jack thought the whole point was to avoid any form of public relations.

'You've already met the patient, Joel Lalic. That was the easy part. Now it's time for you to meet his father.'

41

IVAN LALIC LIVED in an enormous penthouse apartment in the imposing One Hyde Park building. Jack Giorgio and Nathan Mortimer were let in via an underground car park that was heavily camouflaged and deliberately difficult to locate. Mortimer punched an eight-digit code into a keypad and the doors slid open. They entered a small lift with only two location buttons: *G* and *PH*.

They rode up in silence.

A small surveillance camera leered down at them from the corner of the ceiling. Jack stared back into the lens, as though he could see beyond his own distorted reflection.

This was going to be a different kind of house call.

When the lift doors opened again, they stepped out into a cavernous but stark reception room. A further security camera followed their movements across to another door.

Two armed security guards in matching black outfits stood watch behind this second door. They were both well over six-feet tall, with closely cropped hair, huge shoulders, and muscular biceps. Jack initially assumed they were both men, but as he passed the imposing figures he realised that it was a man and a woman.

Instantly, he feared the woman more.

'Nathan!' Lalic bellowed from the other end of the enormous lounge room. He held his arms out and walked quickly towards Mortimer. 'My friend! How are you?'

He was smiling broadly, with perfect white teeth framed by a full, black beard. The loose-fitting Prada shirt could barely contain an abdomen that clearly enjoyed the culinary pleasures of life.

The two men embraced warmly.

Lalic was far more flamboyant and relaxed than Jack had anticipated. He would spontaneously break out into a raucous laugh which, Jack had to admit, was quite infectious. It seemed that anything could trigger this laughter, although it was mostly frequently in response to Lalic's own inane, clichéd jokes about anything and everything, from the poor English weather to the London traffic to the Royal Family.

Jack was starting to relax in Lalic's company when they were interrupted by a diminutive figure dressed in a smart black suit, black silk shirt and black tie. In Jack's mind it conjured up images of a jockey attending a funeral. The jockey wore a hands-free device behind his left ear which intermittently flashed with a blue light. He approached Lalic, spoke rapidly and quietly in their mother tongue, and then handed his boss a cordless phone.

'Excuse me for a moment, gentlemen. I must take this. It is Herman Schwarzer'. He said the name as though it belonged to a mutual friend. Jack looked at Mortimer with puzzlement.

'He's the CEO of Rolls Royce,' he whispered.

Lalic overheard and placed the phone on mute.

'Quite correct, Nathan.' He looked at Jack. 'I have an interest in the Park Lane dealership downstairs, and I am in negotiation with Schwarzer to take a look at the Beverly Hills dealership. In USA they had some big troubles in last few years. Ever since GFC. Poor sales. Beautiful cars. *Beautiful!* And much more reliable than English summer weather!' He laughed out loud to himself before walking off to take the call.

When Lalic returned, he was more serious and got straight to the point.

'So, Nathan, how is my beautiful boy?'

'He is not well, but he is safe.'

'What been happening this time?' asked Lalic, holding out his arms to emphasise the question.

'We picked him up at Heathrow. He was about to cause some major damage. Seems he and his Porsche were headed onto a runway.'

We?

Lalic buried his head in his hands. 'Again with the planes! For so many years. Planes this, planes that. Planes in his head. Planes interfering with his thoughts. Pilots plotting to kill him. Airline security staff following him. The airline advertisements have special message for him. I don't understand all this! I thought you give him this… how did you say? This *treatment revolution*.'

Treatment revolution?

'It is his illness, Ivan. His schizophrenia. His mind gets too overloaded with dopamine and his thoughts go haywire. Then he does… *things*… to himself that set this new treatment back.'

'I know, I know, you explain all this to me, but still I do not understand. I know you tell me about this treatment revolution, but I do not understand. Only that it is new injection. You are doctor. You know best. So. I can visit him?'

'Not quite yet, Ivan. He is starting to improve, and I want to keep the momentum going. Which means no visitors. It might get him too excited.'

'Yes, yes, of course Nathan, I see. Joel can be very excitable boy, you know.' He slapped the left side of his own chest. '*Passion* right here. Just like his old man!'

'Don't worry about Joel. He will get better again. We've got him back on some traditional, heavy medication for the time being. All the good stuff, Ivan.'

'Good, Nathan. Good. As a father I just so glad he's safe.' To Jack, Lalic seemed amazingly reassured by Mortimer.

'I am not going to tell you what to do, Ivan, but you might want to think about that powerful car of Joel's. He could have done some real damage with that thing, either on the motorway or at the airport.'

Lalic's brow furrowed and his expression turned sombre.

'No. I want him to have things I never have when I was young man. He have so many problems I can't fix, but one thing I have is money to make my boy's life easy. Fun. He can have car. He love car. I just want you to make him better, Nathan.' This was certainly a firm command, not just a hope or suggestion.

Mortimer nodded in silence.

Lalic sighed. 'Nathan, you just send me bill. You know I pay. I pay for the best and I get the best. Just get him well again.'

Lalic gestured to one of his guards who swiftly returned with a silver tray carrying a crystal decanter of whiskey and three glasses.

'Time for drink?'

'Sure, why not!' Mortimer said.

The three men chinked glasses and sat down.

'So, Nathan, who is this young man?'

'This is my impressive colleague, Doctor Jack Giorgio.'

'Impressive? Well, this is good! It is good to be impressive, Doctor Jack Giorgio,' exclaimed Lalic with a smile.

'Ahh thanks,' Jack said nervously.

Lalic looked over to his security detail. 'Jack, this is Bruno and this is Misha.' The two bored looking bodyguards subtly nodded their heads.

'Jack's a real star,' added Mortimer. 'I brought him here because he is going to be an important part of the treatment team. You will see more of him.'

'Good, good. Trust. If he is okay with you Nathan, then he is okay with me. Not bad this whiskey.' Lalic stared at his glass.

'Fantastic,' agreed Mortimer.

All Jack could feel was a burning in his throat.

42

A DAY LATER, while Mortimer spoke to the nurse on duty in the private ward, Jack sat on the bed next to Joel. His bedroom was as stark and depressing as the interview room.

Joel was wearing the same t-shirt he'd had on when Jack last saw him in the interview room, with the slogan, '*may contain traces of nuts*' emblazoned across his chest. It seemed somehow less amusing today.

'How are you doing?' Jack asked softly.

'Not bad. A bit better, I think.' Pleasingly, he seemed less sedated now. Jack looked around the room. It was so small and bland. Miserable.

Low stimulation

'Are you getting any sleep?'

'Yes, doctor.'

'It's okay Joel, you can drop the 'doctor' bit. Just call me Jack. Now, is it restful sleep or are you having nightmares?'

'A bit of both.'

'Are you eating? It's important to try and eat and very important to drink. You've got to keep your fluids up. Is your medication causing any side effects?'

'What do you mean?'

'Do you think you're experiencing any problems from your meds.'

'I don't know.'

Jack looked over towards the nurses' station and lowered his voice.

'Has Professor Mortimer ever asked you about that before, Joel?'

Joel looked anxious and uncertain. He looked over Joel's shoulder.

'No. Never.'

'Any nausea or vomiting?'

'A little nausea, I feel like I could throw up.'

'Diarrhoea, stomach upset, loose bowels?'

'No.'

'How about dizziness or light-headedness?'

'Yeah. I do feel like I might faint sometimes. I try not to walk around too much because I'm worried I might fall down.'

'I am glad you could tell me, Joel. There is something I can do to help with that.'

'Thank you, that would be nice.' Joel smiled.

Jack noticed that Joel was sweating and kept rubbing the back of his neck while they spoke.

'Is something irritating your skin back there?'

Joel didn't answer, but persisted in touching the back of his neck. This time Jack noticed a tiny smear of blood on his index finger.

'I really need to take a look at that.'

Joel nodded in agreement. Jack pulled down the hemline of the young man's t-shirt and looked at his neck. The first thing that hit him was the smell. He recognised it instantly. An inspection only confirmed what he suspected.

Jack saw swollen and inflamed skin, complete with oozing pus, across Joel's neck.

'Oh, Joel, you've got a nasty skin infection there. Do you know what happened?'

Joel looked down to the ground and did not answer.

Jack had seen numerous examples of self-mutilation previously, especially in the setting of acute psychosis. He knew that it was usually done to stop the perception that outside forces might enter the body or the mind. Occasionally, sufferers would believe they had some type of device implanted inside their body that they would then attempt to remove, by whatever means necessary. The great irony was that these attempts to avoid harm often caused harm.

'This looks very sore. I want to give you some antibiotics to help treat your wounds, Joel.'

Joel nodded, still looking down.

Jack put a reassuring hand on his shoulder. 'It's okay, I just want to understand how this happened so that I can help you.'

When Joel looked up Jack could see tears in his eyes.

'I just needed to stop them, that's all.'

'Stop who?'

'The airlines. They were ruining my life. They were after me and I know they were going to kill me. Making my life miserable with all their noise and messages. So I ripped it out.'

Jack looked again at the small, pungent hole in Joel's neck. He detected what looked like a small surgical incision.

'What did you have done? Did you have sutures? You have had an incision made in your neck, haven't you? Did you rip out your stitches?'

Joel pressed his lips into a tight, white line and looked away.

Jack thought back to the conversation in Ivan Lalic's apartment about Joel's progress.

Injection.

Treatment revolution.

'Did this injury have something to do with the treatment revolution?' asked Jack.

Once again, Joel did not answer.

Jack went looking for a medication chart but could not seem to find one anywhere. He rifled through the files in the nurses' station but came up empty.

'Where are the medication charts?' he asked curtly.

'We don't have physical charts here,' the nurse replied.

No notes. No drug charts. What sort of ward is this?

'Well, how do I order medication?'

'Don't worry, Doctor Giorgio, just tell me what the patient requires and I will be sure that he receives it.'

Jack found some paper and scribbled an order for oral and topical antibiotics.

'He needs these tablets three times a day and I want you to apply the antibiotic cream to the back of his neck twice a day. But before you do, take a swab and send it off for microbiology analysis. He's got a nasty infection there which I am sure is not doing his mental state any favours.' Jack felt angry that this had not been picked up earlier. 'And do some observations. We don't even know if he's running a fever.'

'Yes doctor,' the nurse said.

Jack looked at her. Early sixties, pleasant enough, but he sensed an edge to her. Very efficient. But no small talk.

'How did you manage to come by this work?' he asked. She looked nervous and was about to answer when Mortimer reappeared.

'As I was telling you,' he then said to the nurse, 'Jack here is a real star. He's going to do great things here.'

'I can see that,' she said, staring at Jack.

43

IT WAS CLOSE to midnight when Jack finally arrived home. He undressed and collapsed straight onto his bed, with thoughts of Mortimer's strange, secretive world swirling around inside his head. As he allowed the thoughts to ebb and flow, a pattern began to emerge.

His conversations with the professor had become increasingly intense, with Mortimer seemingly taking great enjoyment in lecturing Jack on his various philosophies. Even though the foundations of these philosophies were ideas that Jack was instinctively repelled by, Mortimer was so damn convincing.

Could he actually be right?

It was too much to contemplate at this hour of the night. Jack closed his eyes and drifted into sleep.

His sleep was fitful, and he drifted in and out of strange dreams. He found himself in a control tower at Heathrow Airport. Thick, grey clouds surrounded the windows, making it impossible to see further than a few feet. He found some earphones and instinctively put them on, but they sent a piercing scream into his brain so he ripped them off.

I am being clouded.

Control... Out of control. Control taken away from me.

My senses are being distorted.

He knew he had to start landing planes, but he could not see them at all. He was effectively blind and deaf.

The pressure was building.

Pressure. I am under pressure.

Then Mortimer was standing behind him, puffing on a cigar. The smoke filled Jack's nostrils as Mortimer barked instructions. Jack could not understand the meaning of his words.

> *'It's nanotechnology, Jack!'*

> *'Twenty percent, Jack!'*

> *I don't understand, Mortimer!*

The clouds then parted and he saw that Joel Lalic on the tarmac, with pus and blood oozing from his neck. It was pouring out. Gushing. Down the back of his t-shirt, down his jeans, and on to the runway.

Joel was frantic. Planes narrowly missed him.

> *Beware of planes, Jack.*

> *But why?*

Joel was running and screaming.

> *Near misses. Running. Getting away.*

Running and screaming.

A scream woke Jack up.

His own.

He looked over at his alarm clock.

4:57am.

Jack made an espresso and pulled out his notebook. He started writing away furiously.

44

'JACK, I WANT you to take over from me,' Mortimer announced as they drove to the private ward in the Bentley.

'You want me to *what?*'

'I want you to succeed me. And I mean in everything we are doing. The NTC *and* the private ward. You belong here Jack. You can't leave. Look at the life you can have.'

You can't leave.

'Prof... Nathan... I don't know what to say.'

> *That's the truth, not a compliment. I don't know what to say to you anymore, Professor.*

'I wasn't joking when I said you are like a son to me, Jack. I look back at my life and it has all been about achievement, success, breakthroughs. Connections. Work. Fucking work. No time for a wife, certainly no time for children.'

For the first time, Jack sensed a deep sadness in the professor.

'You are clearly right on track for a professorship, probably before you turn forty. The way you teach is incredible. The students and junior staff love you. You can do all the research you want. Write books. Do your doctorate. Just name the university and I will make sure it happens. You'll have the best PhD supervisors. You've got the brains and the drive, and, most importantly, you are just so very comfortable in this world. At my dinner party. At the club. You fit right in. Acceptance. Fitting in. I can see it is very important to you, Jack. *Belonging.* These people accept you, Jack, and that is half the battle. You could so easily be one of them.' He put a hand on Jack's shoulder. 'One of *us.*'

Jack felt something very powerful, deep within his being.

One of us.

Belonging.

His eyes lit up. He could not contain his enthusiasm. 'A doctorate? Really? Well … I would want my own choice of topic.'

'Absolutely. Where would you prefer? Oxford or Cambridge? You can do it from London. Minimal inconvenience,' Mortimer said with a cough.

'Well, I would need to think about…' Mortimer cut him off.

'I can sort it out. You won't have any funding problems. Let's just say the NTC budget can offer special *grants* to cover these fiscal issues. You know, I was reading in the paper this morning that some researchers were launching a public appeal to raise funds for their work on viruses. They were offering some sort of auction, and the winner would receive naming rights to their discovery. Can you believe that bullshit, Jack? Is that how little governments and societies value their researchers?' Mortimer shook his head in disgust.

Jack had always dreamed of doing his PhD at a top tier university. He believed in his research skills and knew that his investigation of the human mind could help thousands, possibly millions, one day.

'Remember what we have talked about, Jack. The perfect storm is building. This is the only future, and you could be a crucial part of it.'

Don't worry. There is no way I will forget this conversation.

45

JACK TORE OPEN the small, brown package that he found sitting on his office desk. Inside, a rectangular item was wrapped in two layers of soft, white tissue paper. When he gently removed the tissue paper he looked, disbelievingly, at the dust jacket. It was perfect. Pristine. He quickly checked the sides and back.

No tears. No stains. No fading. No marks at all.

'Just beautiful,' he whispered to himself, not quite able to believe his eyes. The pages were white, crisp and clean. It almost appeared unread.

He read the title again, just to convince himself it was real.

Brave New World.

Aldous Huxley.

Published by Chatto and Windus.

London.

1932.

The *true* first edition of a masterpiece.

He could easily spend days admiring the stylised black and white dust jacket, with the tiny plane appearing to circumnavigate the sphere of the *New World*.

This book was so very hard to find in *any* condition, let alone in *mint* condition.

It must be worth thousands.

He flicked open the cover, and a small, hand-written note dropped out.

'Jack,

Ivan Lalic wanted me to pass this on to you—it is a small token of appreciation from him. He hopes you will accept it.

It seems that Joel has taken a liking to you.

Here's to our "brave new world".

Warm regards,

Nathan'

Jack shook his head and sighed. During his training, he was always taught that gifts from patients, especially gifts of significant value, were never to be accepted. He was also taught that outright rejection of a gift needed to be carefully considered, as it could instantly ruin an important therapeutic relationship that had been established with a patient. As such, in Jack's mind, it was a judgment call. These rules seemed to be particular to psychiatry.

He remembered a cardiologist friend and colleague who regularly boasted about how well his wine cellar had been stocked by grateful patients who had stents inserted into their coronary arteries. Even Daniel Bates had been lavished with gifts by various celebrities in California who were very satisfied with his plastic surgery skills.

He ran through a series of questions in his mind.

Would accepting the book lead to financial hardship for Lalic?

A clear no.

Would I sell the book for monetary gain?

Absolutely not. Never.

Would returning the gift cause a problem in the delicate professional relationship I have established with the patient?

Quite possibly, yes.

And with the patient's father, certainly.

> *So why shouldn't I accept it? Who would know about it, anyway? Anyone who was interested in such an indiscretion would not likely appreciate the book's value anyway.*

He decided to sleep on it.

But not before he took immense pleasure in reading the first few chapters.

46

'JACK, I'VE SAID it before and will say it again, it must be amazing to work with someone like Professor Mortimer,' Cerise declared. They had just been to see the latest Bond film at the cinema and were now cosied up together in a tiny, late-night café in Kensington.

'Amazing is one word,' Jack paused to sip his coffee before continuing. 'It's always interesting to observe how the reputation matches up with the reality.' He thought about his recent conversation with Sarah.

'That brilliant mind and his ability to think outside the box, all coupled with compassion and his love of humanity.' Cerise seemed as starstruck as Jack had once been.

'He certainly has some remarkable ideas.'

'He has done some incredible, inspiring work at MTR,' she added. 'The schizophrenia workshops that he has run for all the non-clinical staff have been inspiring. He's such a gifted teacher, in addition to everything else.'

Jack's interest was suddenly piqued. He set down his coffee and looked at her.

'Really? I wasn't aware that he had done that sort of work at MTR.'

'Oh yes, for quite some time now. He lectures all over Europe. This was how I came to meet him.' She laughed.

'What is it?' Jack asked.

'Oh, I just remember how I snuck into a lecture at MTR and hung around after everyone else had left. I had him all to myself. We chatted and chatted about dopamine receptors and my own research on the subject. That led to us exchanging ideas about an exciting new direction for treating schizophrenia. He could see my vision and I could totally understand his. I was flattered when he liked my proposal, and he asked if I would like to exclusively work with him, in private, on some really cutting-edge treatments. Top secret. It was this work that gave rise to the the new nanotech drug devices. It really is a treatment revolution'

'Yes, of course,' Jack said in a bland tone that indicated he already knew this.

Private.

Private work.

Private wards.

'Next time he heads to Geneva you should tell him you want to go along. I'm sure I could organise to just happen to be there as well,' she said with a wink and a knowing smile. 'There are some gorgeous boutique hotels by the lake where we could stay.'

Geneva.

Lab work.

Nanotechnology.

'In fact,' Cerise continued excitedly. 'You should really think about formally joining a research program. If you do that PhD you told me about it would dovetail beautifully. I'm sure that the professor would love you to join us, and I could speak to the head of pharmacological research at MTR. You would be wonderful, Jack. With your amazing mind and your desire to do good, you could help so many sufferers.' She kissed him on the cheek and cuddled in closer.

'Yeah. Maybe,' Jack said, without clear enthusiasm.

'Well, I think you would be great.'

47

JACK DID NOT recognise the number that flashed up in the screen of his phone, but a very pleasant female voice was on the other end of the line when he answered.

'Good morning, Dr Giorgio, how are you today?'

'Good thanks. How are you?' he said with hesitation.

'I am terrific, doctor, thank you for asking. It is Penelope Green calling from Mayfair Mercedes Benz. I am the finance manager here. I did not get the chance to meet you when you visited our dealership previously, but I wanted to call you and introduce myself. Do you have a minute?'

Jack felt tense.

My finance has been rejected. How embarrassing!

On a whim, he had been into the dealership a few days earlier after finally deciding to splurge on a new car. He felt he had been working hard lately, and that he did not treat himself enough. He wanted to explore some of the gorgeous English countryside with Cerise when he had time off, and he concluded that something with a little style and luxury was in order. Cerise had whole-heartedly agreed with this assessment and had actively encouraged him to go car shopping. She even came along with him. He had initially decided on a sensible, compact Benz sedan.

'Ahh yes, I do, Penelope. Is there a problem?'

She laughed, a little too enthusiastically.

'Oh no, no, doctor. In fact, quite the opposite.'

'Oh okay.' He felt relieved but still uncertain.

'I've had a chance to review your application and I've spoken with Mr Richter. He told me you also fell in love with that stunning AMG V-8 convertible we have in stock…'

'Ah, hang on a second,' interrupted Jack.

> *I see. She's trying the old bait and switch routine. Getting me to sign up for a much more expensive car after I applied for a cheaper one. Even though I can't afford it.*

Penelope ignored his interruption and continued to speak, 'That little C-class you applied for really isn't in the same league. I know you would much prefer the AMG. It's a striking car. A real head-turner. And that engine note! So… we want to treat our very special clients to exclusive offers and, as such, Mr Richter has decided that we can lease you the AMG convertible for the same monthly figure as the smaller sedan.'

Jack's jaw dropped open. He calculated the saving in his head. Thousands and thousands.

'The *same* price? What's the catch?'

'No catch at all. As I said, we are very committed to looking after our clients, and Professor Mortimer, who referred you, is a *very* special customer.'

He found it difficult to take it all in.

'Wow. I really don't know what to say.'

A compelling image flashed into his mind.

> *Jack. Cerise. The roof down. Humming along through the home counties on a warm summer's day.*
>
> *Bliss.*

'Well, a simple *"yes"* will do,' she laughed again.

'Yes! Thanks! That would be incredible!' He ran through the numbers again in his head. 'But how?'

'Oh, don't you worry about that, Dr Giorgio. We can offer these special deals from time to time. Just between you and me, we can claim something of a handsome write-off for it. Nobody loses. And we gain you as a valued client.'

'Well, thanks again. I am thrilled.'

'Excellent. I'll sort out the paperwork and email it through to you right away. Then, whenever suits, come on in for delivery of your gorgeous new obsidian black convertible. How about tomorrow after work? Unless you would like it delivered to your residence?'

'No, that's fine, I'll come to you.'

Connections.

48

JACK ROLLED OVER and saw Cerise still inhaling the deep, rhythmic breaths of slumber. He inched closer and gently curled his arm around her chest. She sighed with contentment and placed her hand over his forearm, pulling it closer.

He closed his eyes again, fully immersing himself in being so close to her.

The previous night had been warm, and they'd driven the new Mercedes out of the city towards Cambridge, blasting Taylor Swift from the impressive stereo and enjoyed the admiring looks of other motorists. When the sun finally set, they headed into the nearest village and looked for the first bed and breakfast place they could find.

The elderly owner seemed slightly annoyed when the couple showed up in their flashy car after nine o'clock. But when Jack offered to pay her a twenty percent tip, she smiled and politely showed them to their room.

The sex that night was slow and gentle. Afterwards, they had both quickly and easily fallen into a heavenly sleep.

Jack pulled away slightly so that he could admire her beauty.

They had not formally defined their relationship. So far, it had been a serious of spontaneous and passionate meetings. Although in the past month these meetings had been occurring with greater frequency. They were very sexually compatible, and all of their dates so far had concluded in the bedroom. It was dinner in an upmarket restaurant followed by sex. A morning run followed by sex. A night at the opera followed by sex. Drinks after work followed by sex.

Sometimes it was even sex followed by sex.

They had managed to weave around the loaded 'f' word: future.

There was no commitment asked for and none made.

He reached down by the side of the bed and grabbed the notebook and pen from the inside pocket of his jacket, which lay discarded on the floor. He flicked through the journal until he found a clean page and began scribbling down last night's dream before it slipped away.

> *'I am on a beach. Seems like the Mediterranean. It is hot. Midday perhaps. Very blue, calm water. White sand. No one around. Peaceful. I am calm. I'm naked. I don't care. Cerise is there, dressed far too warmly. Thick winter coat.*
>
> *"Why are you wearing that?" I ask.*
>
> *She does not answer. I look down at my body. I'm burning. It stings. I hop from foot to foot. The sand is unbearable. I start screaming.*
>
> *"Please give me your coat to stand on. PLEASE!"*
>
> *But she won't.*

The dream disturbed him. He thought about the messages and meaning.

Despite the many hundreds of popular books that promised to 'explain your dreams' he knew that there was no such thing as a universal, generic truth that lay behind what dreams symbolised. They all had to be interpreted in the context of the dreamer.

What was his unconscious trying to tell him?

He was naked. Vulnerable. Cerise had everything he needed but she was refusing to help him.

> *What could she be withholding from me?*

49

FINALLY, AFTER THE third attempt, he managed to get Cerise on the phone. Following the discovery of contraband, there had been a sudden lockdown at the prison, which meant that his regular clinic was cancelled for the day.

Sarah was on the wards, so he decided to head off early to surprise Cerise with an early drink and possibly even dinner.

'Oh. Hi,' she said tentatively when he arrived at her place.

He explained what had happened at work and suggested a cocktail in the bar of the Langham Hotel.

'That sounds great, but I have to go to Paris tonight for work. We have a meeting first thing in the morning and I probably won't be back until late tomorrow night.'

> *Am I over-reacting or does she not sound particularly disappointed?*

He decided he was being overly sensitive.

For a brief moment he thought about suggesting he accompany her, so that they could spend the night together in Paris.

But he stopped himself.

> *Don't sound desperate. She will be totally absorbed with work, anyway.*

But the truth was he really *wanted* to be with her. He really *wanted* to jump on a plane or a train and head to Paris with her. Thanks to Dr Stein, he had learnt to really listen to those feeling and not deny them.

> *So why can't I tell her what I want?*

He knew the answer to that question was overdetermined. In other words, the end result of any complex behaviour was the result of the coalescing of *numerous* factors, not just one or two.

Ordering off a menu was overdetermined.

Buying a new suit was overdetermined.

Falling in love was overdetermined.

Being emotionally honest with others was overdetermined.

And so it was with his feelings about Cerise.

But he also knew that his strong desire to tell her how he felt was inhibited by an equally strong desire not to.

> *A coin always has two sides. Nothing ever exists in a single dimension. Understanding our unconscious is like understanding physics: every action has an equal and opposite reaction. This creates tension and conflict.*

Jack had always found this concept a challenge to fully accept and appreciate, but that proved the point. He needed to understand what lay on the other side of his resistance to accepting the idea.

He closed his eyes and reflected on his emotional resistance to Cerise. He was loathe to admit it to himself, but it was the first thought that came into his mind.

> *Don't ever censor or negate the first thought, Jack. Never. No matter how embarrassing, how revealing or how painful. That is what your unconscious wants you to know. Don't deny it.*

He had learned to harness those thoughts. It took enormous will, but he had trained himself not to push those images and feelings away. And now, he was able to hang on to them, to read them and to allow them to remain.

He opened his eyes.

There is something not quite right about Cerise. I don't know what it is. I can't name it.

But I can feel it.

'Oh, that's too bad,' he said to her. 'Give me a call when you get back and we'll catch up then.'

'Okay Jack. I'd better get to it or I'll miss the flight.'

'Have a good trip and meeting. Bye.'

'Yep. Bye.'

50

'THIS PRIVATE WARD of yours, are there any others out there that I don't know about?' Jack asked teasingly, but Mortimer was clearly not amused.

'Believe me, Giorgio, this place is one of a kind.' He paused for several seconds. 'Seven families provided the initial funding and resources, including this very building, which was gifted by one of the founding members from his vast property empire. There were eight directors at that time; one representative from each of the families, and myself'.

'You're speaking in the past tense?'

'Yes. That formal structure no longer exists. The families still provided the requisite funding to ensure the ward's work can continue, but we've long since dispensed with the red tape.

'Why the change?' asked Jack.

'The ward was established a few years ago now. Some of the original families only needed to use it once, while others are still actively involved.' His expression became serious. 'And despite our best efforts, there is a particular mortality rate when you are dealing with such severe and devastating illnesses.'

Jack knew this all too well. Tragically, and despite all of the so-called advances in medications, the death rate—usually by suicide—remained at uncomfortably high levels for sufferers of schizophrenia.

'Not to mention all of the associated medical illnesses that can lead to a premature death in someone with chronic psychosis,' Jack added.

He paused and thought of the many patients with schizophrenia that he had treated who had suffered heart attacks or strokes or developed severe diabetes and had died decades before their time. The relationship between such chronic mental illnesses and these physical illnesses was well established. What was less clear was the cause of the link.

'The patients who use this ward get very specialised, personal care. And the results have typically been stunning, especially given how unwell some of them have been. But now… I need help Jack.'

'Help?'

'Yes. You have seen the connections I've made. Word spreads, and demand continues to grow..'

'Twenty per cent,' Jack whispered, as he recalled their earlier conversation.

'Exactly. Twenty per cent'.

51

THEO STEIN WAS an avid, obsessional follower of the share market. His interest was piqued while he was in medical school, when some of his more worldly classmates took him to his very first horse race at Belmont Park.

He lost all his money that day, but struck up a life-changing conversation with one of the bookmakers at the track.

'I'll tell you a little secret, young man,' said the incongruously named bookmaker, Curly Smith, as he stroked his bald head. 'The only guarantees at the track are right here.' He pointed to the black and white odds board beside him.

'But I've lost all my money from looking at that board of yours, Mr Smith.'

The bookie laughed, quite taken by the young student. 'My old man is Mr Smith. Call me Curly. And I meant being on *my* side of the board, boy, not on *yours*. You see?'

Theo thought he understood.

Curly reached down and grabbed a crumpled *Wall Street Journal*. He opened it up to the centre pages.

'You see *these*, boy?'

'What are they?' asked Theo.

'These are the share tables, and this is what it means to be on the *right* side of the racetrack, boy.'

Theo looked down at the columns of funny names. He was intrigued.

'If you can't beat 'em, join 'em. If you don't like the price of gas, well, buy yourself a little piece of the gas company. If you and your buddies don't mind a beer, well, buy a piece of the brewery. You see?'

Theo did see. Very clearly.

'This is just between you and me, so don't tell nobody I told you this, but next time you're thinking of placing a buck on number six in race four down here, stick it into Coca-Cola stock or First Manhattan Bank shares instead.' He winked at Theo.

Owning a part of a company! Theo liked the sound of that. He also loved that he could follow its progress in the newspaper every day.

'And one other thing, boy,' Curly said. 'Buying stocks ain't always easy. They can go up, they can go down. A lot of people gamble, it's called speculatin'. Don't do that. Hang on to what you buy. And do your research, boy. Do your reading. The market is all about *information*. As they say: read about it *twice*, but only buy it *once*.'

As soon as he left the racetrack, Theo went out and bought three items: a pencil, a ledger, and a copy of *Investing in the Stock market: A Beginner's Guide*.

Over the years, Theo had treated many neurotic and narcissistic Wall Street brokers, traders, and CEOs. Not once had he ever used information that was given to him on the couch by any of these patients for his own financial gain. He knew the insider trading laws well, and he was not going to sacrifice all that he had for simple greed.

Many times, grateful patients had offered to give him a tip in exchange for his psychiatric expertise. And some of these tips would have made him a fortune. But he resisted each time.

'Paying your bills for your therapy at the end of each month is payment enough,' Theo would always say. 'Nothing more, nothing less.'

What Theo had learnt, however, was that there was really no such thing as a 'corporation'. Not in a psychological sense, anyway. What lay behind the corporate logos, the fancy titles, the clever slogans, the balance sheets, and the long-term strategies were *people.*

People with their own motivations, their own agendas and, most importantly, their own unconscious conflicts. He knew, for instance, that corporations did not *behave* in any particular way.

But individuals did.

In the business world, he knew that greed was a primary motivator— whether conscious or unconscious.

Over the decades, he had read voraciously about companies, the people who ran them, the employees that worked there, the products they made, and the global context in which they interacted.

He had also learnt so much about the *mind* of a corporation from the people who lay on his couch.

And he had never forgotten Curly's advice: 'read twice, buy once'.

Theo had modified it slightly: 'read a *hundred times*, buy once.'

That strategy had paid handsome dividends. Literally. He had accumulated an absolute fortune in his share portfolio. He was not a user of technology, but, boy, did he hold some long-term valuable shares in Apple, Microsoft, Amazon and Google.

> *If you can't beat 'em, join 'em.*
>
> *If you won't use 'em, buy 'em.*

He took a similar view of pharmaceutical companies. He hadn't written any prescriptions for decades, but he saw how many his colleagues wrote, and so he made the lucrative choice to invest heavily in big pharma.

Naturally, he did relentless, painstaking research into each of the companies before buying their shares. He knew all about big pharma, their executives, their researchers, what they had been up to, and how they generated such enormous profits.

Their profits had now become his profits.

Buy and hold.

Indeed, he still had ownership of the first shares he ever purchased. A tiny, fledgling pharmaceutical company from Switzerland who had just opened offices in New York City.

MTR.

52

FOR THE THIRD consecutive week in a row, Mortimer was absent from the ward round. The professor had been around the NTC less and less over the past couple of months, and Jack strongly suspected that he had been spending more and more time in Geneva.

Due to Mortimer's absence and Barnard's laziness, Jack and Sarah took charge of the ward rounds themselves.

'We need to make a few urgent management decisions about Patient X,' Sarah urged. 'At this rate, he's likely to be here for some months, and I don't think we can justify keeping him on the acute ward for much longer. We have real pressure on these beds. My prison clinic is bursting at the seams, and I already have six on the waiting list. They are all people who desperately need to be admitted here ASAP.'

Jack nodded.

'Given how behaviourally settled he has been,' Sarah continued, 'I think we could trial him in the stepdown ward, with a view to getting him out of here sooner rather than later.'

Jack was surprised, but understood the pressure she was under. 'Getting him out of here? As in, *discharged?*'

'Yes. His mental state has really been completely unchanged for the entire duration of his time here. And he has been quite compliant. We aren't providing him with any active treatment, either.'

Jack thought about her proposal. As usual, Sarah made a valid point, and even though they still had no formal diagnosis, which was usually a criterion to move people through to the next ward or to discharge them completely, Patient X's behaviour *would* warrant a transfer.

Doctor Wellington had such excellent clinical acumen and judgement that Jack had no real reason to say no, even though he was not completely certain.

'How about a trial in the step-down and then we could look at discharging him, if all goes well. Drew, do you have any issues with him being sent through to you?'

'No,' Barnard grunted in reply.

Jack turned to the most senior nurse from the step-down ward. 'Helen, any concerns?'

'None that I can think of. Sounds reasonable to me. I can organise a one-on-one nurse for the first 24 hours, if you like?'

'Yes, that sounds great Helen. Cheers. Okay, then it's agreed. Let's move Patient X through after lunch.'

Within a few hours, Patient X was moved through to the step-down ward. Helen had arranged for a nurse to tail him as he paced the corridor. As per his usual pattern, he did not speak or display any discernible emotion.

He just paced.

Helen reluctantly called Barnard's office to remind him of the mandatory psychiatric review that is required following any patient transfer between wards.

'Yes,' he barked as he picked up the phone.

'Sorry to bother you, Dr Barnard, but I am just letting you know that Patient X has arrived on the ward and seems quite settled'.

'Hmmm.'

'So any time you would like to do your review, we are ready.'

'Yes, yes, I know! I haven't forgotten,' he said with a typical snarl, before slamming down the phone.

Barnard marched on to the ward and snatched the case notes from the hands of the junior nurses. He gave them a cursory read before slapping the file back down on the desk in front of him. He then turned back to the young nurse who was almost cowering.

'Just bring me the patient,' he demanded as he strode off towards the interview room.

'Would you like me to attend with you?' she asked nervously, in accordance with ward protocol.

'No. I. Would. Not,' he snapped back.

***

When Patient X was brought into the interview room, Barnard was staring down at his iPhone. The diminutive Vietnamese man sat silently until the doctor was ready.

The usual quiet and calm of the ward was suddenly shattered by a loud, high-pitched scream. Several of the nurses jumped when they heard the shriek, even though they were some metres away. Immediately, Helen hit the alarm and a loud siren blared throughout the facility.

A voice then announced over the public address system: 'Code black… interview room six… I repeat… Code black… interview room six.' The whooping siren then recommenced.

Within seconds, half a dozen staff members stormed into the interview room.

The usually sedate and blank Patient X was now agitated and tense. He was pacing the room and staring at Barnard, who remained seated in his chair, staring back.

Patient X was screaming.

And screaming.

Two nurses tried to calm the patient but with no success. Given how little they knew about him they were wary when they approached him, and did not want to engage in any sort of physical confrontation.

Patient X paced the room but did not take his eyes off Barnard. He also did not stop screaming. His arms hung limply by his side. Given his posture, his marching, and his shouting, he conjured up images of a soldier performing some sort of squad formation drill.

When Jack and Sarah entered the interview room, Jack quickly sized up the situation and looked into the patient's eyes.

He then looked at Barnard, who seemed to be showing no emotion at all.

'Get him out of here,' Jack coolly commanded.

'But we are being very cautious about touching him, Dr Giorgio,' said Jamie, one of the more senior nurses.

'No... I mean Dr Barnard,' clarified Jack.

'Drew,' said Jack. 'Come on, let's get out of here.'

Jamie moved forward and tapped Barnard on the shoulder, then gently grabbed him by the bicep and helped him out of the chair and into the corridor.

Once outside the room, Barnard shrugged violently.

'Fuck off. Don't touch me.'

He then stormed out of the ward and back to his office.

Once Barnard had left the room Patient X instantly calmed down and returned to his usual bland state. He stopped pacing and just stood in the middle of the room. He was gently encouraged to return to his room, which he did without any hint of resistance or distress.

'Let's send him back to the acute ward,' Jack said to Jamie with a look of resignation.

***

Jack sat facing Barnard in his office.

'Will you put that phone down so we can talk?' Jack insisted with more than a hint of irritation.

Barnard dropped it into his lap and sighed. 'What about?'

'About what happened back there. On the ward.'

Barnard shook his head nonchalantly. 'Nothing really. This is a forensic unit. Sometimes patients go off. It happens.'

'But Drew… *why* did he go off like that? He's been here for ages without any hint of a problem.'

'I don't know why. Maybe it was the change of ward, doctor,' Barnard said with clear sarcasm.

Not for the first time, Jack perceived a very subtle downwards glance from Barnard.

What the hell does he keep looking at?

'Am I keeping you from something important?' asked Jack.

Barnard ignored the question. 'Look, I don't know what's up with the Vietnamese bloke. He came in, sat down, and then… bam! He started going crazy, screaming and pacing.'

Not a very sophisticated description, Dr Barnard.

'Did he say anything at all?'

'No.'

'Did you say anything to him?'

'No. I didn't get a chance.'

'So let me get this right: he came in, nothing was said, and he suddenly became very agitated and distressed. Is that right?'

'Yes, your honour,' Barnard said sardonically. 'Can I be excused from the witness box now?'

53

'HEY GORGEOUS,' JACK said into his phone. 'How are you?'

It was just before seven in the evening, and he was finally done for the day. After sorting out the transfer of Patient X back to the acute ward, he'd gone straight to an exhausting meeting with the distraught parents of an eighteen-year-old man who had been admitted following a charge of grievous bodily harm. Their son had firmly believed that the cashier at the local convenience store was an alien who had to be prevented from infecting the globe with an untreatable, fatal virus.

Jack was aware that an increase in delusions centred around viruses had begun shortly after the Covid-19 pandemic took hold.

'Mmm, I'm tired.' Cerise answered listlessly.

'Busy day?'

'Yeah, flat out. The bosses are really at me to get my budgets done, and my marketing submissions in, and my team evaluations completed, and blah blah blah.' She sounded incredibly flat.

'Hey, are you okay?' he asked tenderly.

'Oh yeah, I'll be fine. Just-' she broke off with a yawn. 'Just so tired. I'm having more trouble sleeping lately. And I tripped over today. *Again.* This time I whacked my knee.'

'Oh, ouch! Can I come around? Do anything for you? Make dinner?'

'Oh... um, maybe not tonight, Jack. I just don't feel like *that* right now. My knee is so sore.'

He hadn't meant sex. He simply felt a desire to be there for her. He decided she probably needed sleep, more than anything.

'Okay. Well, why don't you do rest up and get an early night? Work will still be there in the morning…'

He stopped speaking when he heard another female voice speaking in the background.

Had the voice said, 'Sandrine'?

'Who's that?' Jack asked.

After long, tense pause: 'Sorry? What?'

'I thought I heard someone. A woman. Is someone there?' he tried to ask in the least suspicious tone he could muster.

'It's just the TV. I think you're right, Jack, I need to sleep. I'm sure I'll feel much better tomorrow.'

And then she was gone.

54

DESPITE IT BEING an egregious breech of several modern occupational health and safety laws, as well as a direct violation of his own department's 'Healthy Buildings' policy, Sir Roger Maxwell lit up an obese Cuban cigar at his ministerial desk and drew in a long puff.

He waved a facetious salute to the many framed portraits of the previous Health Secretaries who had served the UK in the decades before him. The smoke soon distorted their smug faces.

The vast office was cluttered up by mountains of bureaucracy. Government cabinet meeting agendas, minutes from the global Health Secretaries forum, requests for his time from various health charities and lobby groups, as well as the usual staffing issues, medication submissions, hospital problems, and research funding proposals. One proposal stood out amongst all others, and sat on top of the pile.

But all that could wait.

He was finally at the top and could stop to smell… the cigars.

He chuckled.

Well, *almost* at the top. Word was that the PM was losing favour, and Maxwell felt he was well-positioned to have a crack at the top spot.

But that could also wait.

He reclined in his chair, put his feet up on the mahogany desk, inhaled deeply, and closed his eyes.

A soft vibration deep within his suit jacket pocket temporarily interfered with his bliss. He straightened up in his chair, pulled the phone out, and stared at the screen through the white smoke.

The Nicholas Tindal Centre.

'*Ugh*… what the fuck do you want? It's six o' clock on a Friday evening,' he said to himself. Despite his annoyance, he answered.

'Yes,' he said loudly.

'Now you really need to listen to me Roger,' the angry voice commanded.

'Oh I am *all* ears.'

'You should be. It is very clear that mental health is not your priority but when are things moving, Roger? *When?*'

'They will move, when they move, old friend. Do not worry. It's in hand. I have a research proposal right here in front of me that I am giving very serious consideration to.'

'Well, it needs to be soon. *Very* soon. Things are less stable around here, right? Things are being noticed, especially by someone with too much curiosity. We don't want unwanted snouts sniffing around. I need some certainty from your end. Time is getting short, Roger.'

Maxwell hung up the phone and puffed on his cigar. The thing had gone out. He put it down and dialled another number. The call was answered immediately, and there was no need for pleasantries.

'We're sending three million,' the cold voice said.

'Three. Confirmed,' replied Maxwell.

'The usual route?'

'Yes. Of course. The same numbers. The same everything. I have decided …the *department* has decided… to back this very interesting and rewarding research project. Here's to good mental health.'

'Done.'

He put his phone back into his jacket pocket and turned to the more serious business of locating his lighter.

55

JACK TRIED, ONCE again, to call Cerise. Now her phone no longer rang, it went straight to her message bank. Jack decided that the battery must have gone flat.

> *Hi, you have called Cerise Navarro, UK regional executive at MTR Pharmaceuticals. Sorry that I cannot take your call at the moment, but if you leave your name, number, and a short message, I will get back to you as soon as possible. Thanks.*

Jack heard the piercing tone and hung up. There was no point in leaving yet another message.

She had no business trips that he was aware of, but he had not heard from her at all for several days now.

He checked his watch. 3:28pm. He grabbed his car keys and headed out the door.

When he arrived at the London office of MTR, it occurred to him that he had never actually been inside the front door before and, indeed, had never met any of the staff, other than Cerise.

He parked the sleek Mercedes and walked quickly to the front door, smiling at the thought of seeing her again.

Jack expected the tinted glass doors to open automatically as he approached, but when they didn't, he stood back and located an intercom button on the side of the wall.

'May I help you?' a distorted voice enquired officiously.

'Ah yes, hello, my name is Doctor Jack Giorgio, and I am here to see Cerise Navarro.'

'Sorry, George, there are no doctors here. We are not a medical clinic and we don't have appointments here. Please send an email via our website with your request. Thank you and have a nice day.'

Determined to be understood, he pushed the button again. 'No, no… I'm here to see Ms Navarro.'

There was silence.

He tried for a third time.

'Hello? *Hello?*'

He was about to give up and walk away when the glass doors magically slid open. He stepped inside and was immediately met by a woman whom he assumed to be the owner of the officious voice.

Her name badge told him she was called Mandy.

Jack relaxed his shoulders and smiled.

'Hi, Mandy… thanks so much for coming to rescue me. I'm Jack Giorgio,' he held out his hand.

She did not take it.

'What can I do for you?'

'I am here to see Cerise.'

'*Cerise?* Sorry… who?'

'Cerise Navarro. She works here. She's the regional manager. I'm Jack.' He blushed a little. 'She may have mentioned me?'

Mandy looked puzzled. She shook her head.

'I'm sorry, but we don't have a Cerise Navarro working here. We have two regional execs, both male. I've done this job for four years and never come across anyone here called… what did you say? *Serena?*'

'Cerise.'

'Are you sure you have the right place?' she asked in a gratingly patronising tone.

'Is there another MTR office in London?'

'No. This is the only one.'

He looked around the reception area where they stood. It was impossible to find any clues. There were no other people around. No staff photos on the walls. No staff names anywhere. No directory. The only other door was an opaque glass one that seemed to lead to another corridor.

'But I've picked her u…' he stopped himself.

> *I've always picked her up from the car park. Always. Never from inside the building.*

> *I've never rung her on a landline here.*

> *Never met her workmates.*

'I apologise, Mandy,' he said as he backed away towards the exit. 'I think you're right. I've made a mistake. So sorry to trouble you.'

56

He drove to Cerise's home with their many conversations cascading through his mind. But it was one discussion in particular that he kept coming back to.

And one specific *part* of that discussion.

The very day that they met. At the restaurant.

They had spoken about their backgrounds.

She'd seemed anxious.

> *I did a degree in medical science and then did honours... It just kind of went from there... Oh, it's so boring... you don't want to know... it was on dopamine receptors... how they can sometimes misfire... tell me about your work, Jack...*

She'd wanted to get off the topic of her research as quickly as possible. Jack had known many people who had higher degrees, and in his experience they were always keen to talk about their work. Especially if anyone showed any sort of interest in it.

But not her.

Unusually, for a drug rep, she had also not given him any real information at all on *Positrex*. No research papers on the medication. No glossy brochure. No sample packs of the medication for patients to 'try before they buy'. In fact, the only time they had ever talked shop was briefly at their first meeting, when she had given him a pretty basic information sheet about the drug.

> *But am I looking for things that are not there?*

He dialled Drew Barnard via the hands-free system in the car.

'Barnard here,' came the curt, customary answer.

'Drew… it's Jack. I won't keep you long, but I need to ask you something important.'

'No, I cannot cover you this weekend, I am go…'

'No, it's nothing like that. You know the woman I've been seeing? Cerise?'

There was a pause.

'I remember you mentioning her.'

'Well, anyway, she's a drug rep for MTR, an area manager, actually.'

'*Is* she, Giorgio? *Really?*'

'Why do you say it like that, Drew?'

'I happen to know quite a few of the MTR guys. I've had more than a few big nights out with them, but I cannot remember *her*. And she has *never* taken me out for a company lunch, that's for sure.' Barnard sounded somewhat offended.

Jack gripped his steering wheel tightly.

'Think hard, Drew. This is important. Have you ever heard her name – Cerise Navarro – or come across her before at all?'

There was another long silence. He at least seemed to be taking Jack's request seriously.

'No. Absolutely not. Now what's going on?'

Jack ended the call. His pulse was racing, and he noticed that he was now speeding.

He tried hard to recall any other details.

All that came into his mind was the dream.

> *I was naked and vulnerable. I was burning.*
>
> *She had everything I needed.*
>
> *But gave me nothing.*

57

BY THE TIME he reached her home, Jack felt calmer. The London traffic had forced him to slow down, shifting his attention and allowing him to focus on the road immediately ahead, rather than the thumping pulse inside his head.

He parked around the corner and walked towards her house, with the memory of their first run together playing in his mind. He could still see her so clearly. She looked so strong and fit. She looked so…

He suddenly stopped.

He made a fist and brought it slowly up to his lips and closed his eyes.

> *The run.*
>
> *So very strong.*
>
> *So amazingly fit.*
>
> *I'm training for a marathon.*
>
> *And the driving.*
>
> *So deft behind the wheel, so confident.*
>
> *In and out of the traffic. Changing gears like a pro.*
>
> *Like a pro.*

As he approached the house, he saw that there were no lights on. He tried looking in through the lower windows but there was no movement, no noise.

It was a long shot, but he tried the front door.

Locked.

He tried all the windows.

Locked.

He did not feel justified in smashing a window and he knew that would only bring unwanted attention to himself. In desperate hope he pulled his phone out again. No missed calls. No messages.

He was worried and he wanted some answers.

He wanted Cerise.

Where are you?

Who *are you?*

The sun was setting. Jack leant against a lamppost to consider his options when a figure appeared at the far end of the street. The person took three or four more strides in his direction before stopping dead.

He focused his vision as best he could in the dim, fading light.

A woman. With short, dark hair and a duck egg blue coat.

Cerise!

But at the moment of recognition she turned and fled.

'Cerise! *Wait!*'

He took off after her.

When he rounded the corner, he caught a glimpse of her in the distance as she turned left. He accelerated to catch her, sprinting across the road, narrowly avoiding the traffic. The streets appeared to be getting tighter and more constricted. It felt like he was in an urban labyrinth.

A car horn blared from somewhere around the next corner.

There was a screech of tyres. A deep thud. A high-pitched shatter. Another screech. A loud bang.

Then silence.

But where?

He spun around, racing from one street to another, disoriented in the growing darkness. Time was slipping away.

He heard sirens.

An ambulance screamed past him. He headed after it. Two police cars quickly followed. He sprinted after the emergency vehicles, but could only just keep sight of them.

The broken figure lay motionless in the middle of the road. An elderly man in a small Peugeot hatchback sat motionless behind the wheel of his damaged car, inches from the body. His bonnet was smashed in. Pieces of amber glass were strewn around the body.

Jack could see blood trickling out of her ear. He tried to break through the crowd of people that had now formed, but the police held him back.

'Sorry, sir, but you cannot go through.'

'But I'm…'

What am I? Partner? Boyfriend? Lover? Stranger?

The police officer was waiting for a coherent response, but all Jack could do was stare at the scene in front of him. The group of onlookers stood silently, some with hands up to their mouths. If he was of one of those detached spectators he would probably walk by and think to himself, 'Well, there is no hope there.'

For several minutes he stood paralysed, until the ambulance slowly drove off. There was no need for sirens or lights.

Jack turned and walked away.

The moment he rounded the corner, the tears started to flow.

Part 3

A Cortex in Rome

58

THE INTERNATIONAL SOCIETY for Forensic Psychiatry was renowned for staging stimulating and entertaining conferences, crammed full of high-quality speakers. So when Jack found out that the upcoming annual meeting was to be held in Rome, he jumped at the chance to attend.

It had been three months since he lost Cerise, and he was no closer to understanding who she was or what had led to her death, other than it being a tragic accident.

He'd ventured back to MTR in London and even rang the headquarters in Switzerland, only to be told that she had never worked there. He questioned all his colleagues in London, but none of them had come across her at all.

Mortimer knew her but was suddenly being very guarded and vague about providing Jack more details.

'I meet so many people, Jack, I can't keep track of them all.'

Sarah had been a terrific support to him and could see the pain he was in. He went through the motions at work, but beyond that he had done little else. He hadn't opened a book in several weeks, which was extremely unusual for him. He'd written a couple of letters to Theo Stein, but at much reduced length. He didn't know what to say.

And so the opportunity to leave London had come at the perfect time. He hoped it might be the circuit breaker that would help to temper his grief.

He was pleasantly surprised at the check-in desk at Heathrow when he was told his ticket had been upgraded to first class. The unfriendly woman at the counter told him that it was simply due to overbooking. Even so, Jack could not help but wonder if, once again, Mortimer had something to do with it. Regardless, he gladly accepted the upgrade with a broad grin and headed for the First-Class lounge before boarding.

Once he was comfortably nestled into his opulent, wide, leather seat, Jack wished that he were flying much further than Rome. A long-haul would have, for once, been far more preferable than the relatively short three hours ahead of him. He decided to try to enjoy the flight as much as he could, and had no hesitation in ordering a glass of Dom Perignon as soon as possible after take-off.

Mid-way through the flight he stared across the aisle. In his mind he transplanted the middle-aged businessman who was occupying the seat with an image of Cerise. He could reach out across the space and gently stroke her hand. They'd drink wine and talk excitedly about their upcoming getaway… Roma… Florence… or maybe the Amalfi Coast.

It was there that he stopped himself and opened his eyes. It served no purpose to go any further with what had now evaporated into a mere fantasy.

When Jack finally and reluctantly alighted from the British Airways jet and made his way through the terminal of Fiumicino Airport, he walked straight past the uniformed chauffeur holding the small white sign reading: 'Dr J Giorgio' and stood outside for several minutes to allow the glorious southern European sun to wash over him. It was a relief to be out of London for a few days. He closed his eyes and began to relax. Unlike many native Europeans, he enjoyed the baking Mediterranean heat of late summer. It reminded him of life back in Australia when he was a child and the long, dry summers that always delivered fun, freedom, and plenty of heat.

He was lost in his own memories for a moment, and so he did not notice the tall, young man who was sweeping the sidewalk nearby.

After several minutes he re-entered the terminal and introduced himself to the driver, who promptly and efficiently took charge of his luggage and gestured towards a gleaming white Maserati sedan that was parked outside.

Jack allowed himself to relax even further, as he slumped back into the sumptuous leather seat and stared out the window as the Italian V8 hurtled down the motorway towards the city. A few vehicles behind them, a small green and yellow garbage truck was being driven by the tall man from outside the airport. The blue light on his small wireless earphone blinked rhythmically. His eyes were firmly fixed on the rear of the Maserati.

An hour later, the muscular sedan slowly turned into the crescent-shaped driveway of the Rome Hilton. When it pulled to a stop, an attentive doorman opened the rear door and Jack stepped out.

'*Ciao, dottore!* And welcome to Roma!' the man said with enthusiasm.

Jack replied in fluent Italian, much to the doorman's delight. They exchanged further pleasantries, and Jack entered the hotel lobby.

The garbage truck pulled up on the street below the Hilton. The driver watched Jack intently as he made his way inside.

'Buongiorno,' said the desk clerk in a friendly voice. 'Welcome to Roma. Are you checking in, sir?' His accented English was very crisp.

'Buongiorno. Si. The name is Giorgio,' Jack replied, in Italian.

'Ah, si, si, signore, scusi, *Dottore* Giorgio, I have it right here. *Giorgio?* You speak Italian very well, but your accent... I can't quite make it out.'

'Si,' answered Jack. 'I have spent significant time in Australia, then the US, and now in Britain. So it may get a little confusing!' He laughed, and realised it was the first he had done so for months.

'Ah yes, I see,' The desk clerk replied with a smile.

'I believe I have a standard single room booked for the conference.'

The clerk looked down at his computer screen, made several deliberate keystrokes and then paused for several seconds.

'Everything okay?' asked Jack, hoping he *had* confirmed the booking reminder that was sent to him.

'Si. Si, Dottore. Although, in fact, I see here that you are to be staying with us in one of our premiere suites.'

Jack was surprised.

'Really?'

The concierge noted Jack's surprise: 'Si, and it has all been taken care of.'

He looked over Jack's shoulder to a waiting bellhop. He said something in Italian to the young man, and Jack's bags were loaded onto a small trolley and taken towards the elevators.

'Taken care of? By *whom?*'

'Ahhh… I do not know, Dottore. It does not tell me this. But your hotel bill for the conference is already paid for. I just need your credit card for any incidentals.'

Jack handed over his American Express card and wondered momentarily who could have paid for his suite, although he realised it was blindingly obvious.

Connections.

'Marcello here will show you up to your suite. Your suite comes with complimentary limousine service to anywhere you wish in Roma, and complimentary drinks are served in our exclusive lounge from 4pm each afternoon. Suite guests also have exclusive access to their own pool and gym. Marcello will orient you to these services. Enjoy your stay with us at Hilton Roma, Dottore Giorgio.'

'Oh, I am sure I will. *Grazie.*'

He was led to a bank of elevators where floor ten, the top floor, was selected by Marcello. A subtle 'ding' was heard as they reached their destination and the doors slid open. He was led to the end of a long, carpeted corridor and shown into his suite.

It took Jack several moments to survey the suite in its entirety. It was vast and very elegantly decorated. The large sitting room featured an enormous flat-screen TV, a stereo, and a range of bespoke Italian furniture. There was also a kitchen, the main bathroom leading off the master bedroom, and a smaller bathroom connected to a second bedroom. Several interesting pieces of art hung on the walls in all the rooms. Finally, Marcello showed Jack out onto the balcony, which had stunning views across the city. Jack tried to calculate the cost of staying in such opulent digs.

Must be thousands per night.

'Do you want me to unpack your case and hang your clothes?' Marcello asked.

'No, no, that will be fine. *Grazie.*'

'Is there anything else I can do for you, Dottore?'

'Ahh no, that's okay, I can take it from here.'

He gave the porter a twenty Euro note, and he watched him leave the suite.

59

After the door closed, Jack grabbed an ice-cold San Pellegrino from the fridge and headed for the balcony. He surveyed the street below.

The vibrant hum of Rome.

Vespa scooters and Fiat 500s buzzed by in the late afternoon scramble to get home. A number of elegantly dressed people were also on foot, making their way home or out to the bars, restaurants, and cafés which punctuated the streetscape, where the patrons sat outside smoking and drinking espressos or glasses of wine. Jack became mesmerised by the colour and noise of the scene and allowed himself to drift away in the simplicity of the everyday minutiae of life.

A complimentary bottle of Veuve Clicquot sat chilled on a small glass table in the centre of the living room. Two champagne glasses were placed beside it. He thought about abandoning the sparkling water and having a drink right away but felt tired and somewhat grimy after a day of travelling, so he decided to freshen up in the massive shower instead.

After making use of the extensive range of luxury products, he lay down on the bed and went through the conference registration pack. After removing his name badge and discarding the numerous glossy flyers from pharmaceutical companies he thumbed through the academic program. He wanted to plan his time and work out which keynote addresses were worth attending.

Stravinski, from Toronto, was giving his usual piece on stalking behaviours. And there was Mueller, from Berlin, speaking about sexual offending and psychosis. She always made such a dark topic palatable and even, on occasion, entertaining. Irvine, the psychopathic personality disorder expert from Harvard, was always worth listening to, although Jack doubted that any new information was likely to be shared during his presentation. He would no doubt describe a series of jaw-dropping case studies related to the depths that humans can sink to, then stare sincerely at the audience and tell them that no treatments work and that ultimately, prison was the only effective 'remedy' for the psychopath.

He did see some interesting-looking pharmacotherapy addresses related to treatment-resistant schizophrenia amongst criminal offenders, as well as some interesting work on new directions for the management of acute mania in bipolar disorder. It made him think of Barnard and that damn TV spot of his.

In addition, there were several shorter, less significant presentations on a wide range of forensic mental health topics. Everything from 'supermarket rage in times of a global pandemic' to the use of art therapy among serial murderers. And he realised that every single keynote address was sponsored by a pharmaceutical company. As such, he was certain that each international speaker was flown out first class to Rome by these massive corporations. He shook his head as he thought once again about his own flight.

He skim-read the bios of some of the speakers that he was less familiar with before placing the program down on the bedside table.

Looking inside the satchel one last time, he saw a petite, white envelope taped to the inside of the bag. When he pulled it out, he saw his own name neatly handwritten on the front in elegant cursive.

Inside the envelope was a small, hand-written note. He read it to himself several times:

> *Dr Giorgio,*
>
> *It is extremely important that we meet.*
>
> *The eastern wing of the Colosseum.*
>
> *Friday 17:00. Come alone.*
>
> *I have important information about Cerise.*

The note was unsigned. His first thought was that it was some kind of cruel joke. A set up.

I have important information about Cerise.

He suddenly felt very tired. And sad. He placed the note back in the envelope and the entire contents of his conference satchel into the safe located in his walk-in robe.

Important information.

Surprisingly, sleep came easily.

Unsurprisingly, he dreamt of Cerise.

60

THE LATE AFTERNOON sun radiated a comforting warmth over the city. While many took refuge in the shade, Jack was very happy to walk in the light. It somehow felt safer there.

The loose-fitting, white linen shirt, navy shorts and dark sunglasses allowed him to blend in as just another tourist as he meandered through the ancient streets. Although it was a long walk from his hotel to the Colosseum, he felt it would do him good. He certainly had no desire to be sardined in amongst the locals, the tourists, and the pickpockets on a Roman bus, and taking a taxi seemed unnecessarily indulgent.

Information about Cerise.

Information.

After a good hour of walking, he finally passed the Forum, which he knew meant the Colosseum was nearby. He made his way into the amphitheatre, and found the eastern wing with ease. It was surprisingly quiet, with only a handful of tourists milling around, soaking up the atmosphere.

Connections.

After a few minutes, a man wandered up and stood silently beside him. He was a few feet away but given the emptiness of the vast structure it felt to Jack as though the stranger was uncomfortably close. The two men stared down at the floor without speaking.

Jack stole a quick sideways glance. The man was much shorted than Jack, but much heavier set. Despite the height difference, Jack felt physically smaller. The man was casually dressed, with a touristy baseball cap emblazoned with the word '*Roma*'. Despite the hat, Jack caught a glimpse of closely cropped blacked hair and a thick neck which was attached to huge shoulders and biceps.

> *Probably hits the weights to compensate for his height. Or lack of.*

He could have been thirty. He could have been fifty. Jack could not be more precise than that. He caught a whiff of the man's cheap aftershave.

After what seemed like an eternity, the man began to speak, still without looking at Jack. His accent had a familiar twang. New York.

'It is not widely known, but the ancient Romans would use the mentally ill in the 'games' they hosted here.'

'Really?'

'Yes. It was seen as providing a 'meaningful' role for the sick, as well as entertainment for the masses. Exploitation. It's always been there, in one form or another, and I can't see it changing any time soon.' There was another long pause before the enigmatic man spoke again.

'Giorgio. I'm Portman,' he finally said, staring into the middle distance. Jack nodded, unsure of how to reply.

After another moment of silence, Portman got down to business. He gestured to Jack to take a seat on the ancient stone steps.

'You're running a dangerous practice, Doctor.'

Jack tensed up.

'Sorry? I'm running a *what?* Who *are* you?'

'Sure, on the surface it all looks great. The money, the kudos, the Mercedes, the connections.' Jack listened intently. 'I am sure that Mortimer gave you the speech about supply and demand, and assured you that you are providing a valuable clinical service.'

Jack swallowed hard.

> *How did he know all this?*

Portman was aware of the anxiety he was inducing.

'Surely you must have asked yourself: why does this special ward exist?'

Of course he had, but he had managed to rationalise it with the very convincing argument Mortimer had put forward.

Portman pulled out a cigarette and lit up. Jack coughed.

'Think of me as a friend, Jack. Someone who can give you timely advice. That's what friends do, right? Now I know that you doctors, with all your degrees and fancy pieces of paper, don't normally like to be given advice by people from outside the industry. But I think you should listen to mine. But to answer your question more specifically, I'm an agent with a division of Interpol. A specialist branch, investigating illegal *medical* activities.' He flashed an official looking ID.

'Illegal medical activities,' Jack repeated in a quiet, monotone voice.

'Yeah. Like the trafficking of human organs, the shipping of black-market medications to the developing world, banned surgical devices, movement of individuals for covert medical experimentation.'

Jack raised a hand and stopped him there. He had heard of the first three, but the last, well, that seemed impossible.

'You mean that people—*living* people—are shipped around so that they can be experimented on?'

'Absolutely. Mainly through Africa and Asia, parts of South America, but it happens Jack. It's highly organised. You better believe it.'

Portman was solemn.

'Organised crime.'

'You mean the mafia?' Jack asked.

'Oh, come on, Giorgio, don't be so old-fashioned. It's the twenty-first century. Other than some pockets of domestic drug operations, the mafia is essentially washed up. At least, the *global* version of it.

Large-scale, international, organised crime is now the domain of the Fortune 500 companies.'

'That's pretty cynical.'

'Cynical? How would you know? I'll ask you a question: do your holier-than-thou drug companies make more from legitimate medication sales in the west or from off-loading the failed and expired drugs in corrupt developing countries, such as Africa?'

Jack did some quick calculations. Surely the huge prices charged in the US and Europe in official markets would be more lucrative?

'The first option.'

'Portman made an irritating buzzer sound, as though Jack was a game show contestant who had picked the wrong answer. 'Incorrect, Doctor Giorgio. You want to go double or nothin'?'

Jack did not appreciate the humour.

'I don't understand how they can do that.'

Even through the sunglasses, Jack could see Portman roll his eyes. The special agent didn't directly answer the question but instead asked, 'Ever heard of a psych drug called zinestrapam?'

Jack searched his mental database of psychotropic medication. After a minute he answered in the negative.

'I'm not surprised. It was developed around twenty years ago. A real heavy sedative. Led to short-term amnesia, amongst other things. It was very potent stuff.' He finally made eye contact, raising his glasses and glaring directly at the bewildered doctor. '*Very.*'

'So what about it?' Jack tried to modulate his tone so that he sounded curious, not rude—and certainly not scared.

'It was such a dangerous drug that it was banned from the get-go in the States, as well as in Western Europe. Most of the world, in fact. It was far too sedating and highly addictive. Some patients died during the trials.'

'Respiratory suppression?'

'Exactly. They just stopped breathing. But the company had already invested so much damn money in this drug that they still wanted to find a market. Somewhere. So they started to push it in some of the less stable, less regulated countries. It can be great for keeping political enemies and dissidents under control, and it soon started flooding down to the masses.'

Jack looked at him in disbelief.

'Come on. The masses? They wouldn't have been able to keep that quiet.'

'Oh really, Giorgio? You're all over what happens in Africa and China, are you? If you want to know more, I suggest you ask your guru.'

'My guru?'

'Yeah. The great Professor Mortimer.'

'*Mortimer?* Why?'

'Who do you think developed the drug?'

Jack closed his eyes. He had a thousand questions, but Portman pushed on without waiting.

'Imagine that you are the corrupt dictator of some third world country. You have billions squirreled away and your own private army. The only way you can go is down. And what, or *who*, will knock you off your perch? The masses that you have been suppressing. The people that you have stolen from. If they get educated and organised, then watch out.'

Jack was starting to feel more convinced by Portman. He spoke with such certainty.

'So what are you saying? You just drug them?'

'Pretty much. Give them a little taste, and then more, and then more.

Remember, as a dictator you control both the police force *and* the health system. It's no great leap to see how you can keep freedom fighters at bay. That's where zinestrapam steps in. The dictators are happy to pay a fortune for it, and big pharma can offload it by the tonne.'

Jack noticed that when Portman spoke there was a palpable irritability to his voice. No. It was more than irritation. It was anger.

Was this personal for him?

He no doubt saw Jack as being part of the whole corrupt global medical network. However, as a forensic psychiatrist, Jack was attuned to the subtleties of anger and its many gradients. He couldn't help but wonder where that anger really came from.

'And you think Mortimer is involved in all this… *experimentation*… on people?' asked Jack.

'That's what we strongly suspect. But we still need the hard evidence, Jack.' It was the first time Portman had called him by his first name.

'Mortimer? I just can't believe it.'

'Oh, really? Let me ask you something, Jack. You ever hear Mortimer express some extreme views? Things that don't sound right to you? Any really 'out there' stuff that made you think twice about the guy?'

> *It's the future of all healthcare, Jack.*
>
> *No more government funding… it will all be private.*
>
> *The perfect storm.*
>
> *Literally the survival of the richest.*

Jack didn't have to answer because Portman seemed to know what was going through his head.

'Every now and then a PCS will pop up in the news and make headlines for a day or two.'

'A PCS?' asked Jack.

'A pharma company slave. It's what we call a person who somehow escapes the net of their human experiment system.'

'It's frightening that you have an acronym for such a person,' said Jack, shaking his head.

Portman shrugged.

'We try to get in to talk to these people, but it's difficult. Remember Modisha?'

Of course he did. Modisha was a teenage girl from Sierra Leone who was found wandering alone, distressed, and in a complete daze through the streets of South London. It had been all over the headlines a few months ago. She didn't know her name, where she was from or how she had ended up there. Jack remembered reports of her having very poor and primitive language skills. There was a big media and local police campaign to identify her, and it took several weeks before they did. Even by then she still had no memory of how she'd ended up in London. After that, the media found the next big story and she was soon forgotten.

Jack looked at Portman. 'PCS?'

'PCS,' he confirmed, solemnly. 'As I was saying, we try to get in to talk to them, to piece together events. Maybe even get some firm evidence. But it's damn hard. They remember so little, if anything, plus they're terrified and reluctant to talk.'

Jack thought of Patient X.

Patient X.

Could it be?

'Hang on a minute, Portman. Hold on. When you asked me earlier *why does this special ward exist*, were you talking about the Nicholas Tindal Centre?'

'Yes. Of course. Where else would I be talking about? The NTC is Mortimer's HQ, right?'

Patient X.

Jack felt irrationally relieved that Portman was not referring to the private ward.

His head started spinning. He didn't know where the conversation was headed.

'What we need,' continued Portman, 'is someone with real credibility. Someone who can get their hands on the evidence. We need to target the key players if we're ever gonna make a dent in this horrible business.'

Jack sighed. 'Let me guess. That someone would be me.'

61

IT SEEMED THAT, like an omen, the sunlight had rapidly faded. Portman began speaking far more rapidly. It was the first time Jack sensed an urgency from him. 'Listen carefully. This is what you will do. Next Tuesday, call in sick at work. At elev…'

Jack interjected: 'Call in sick? With what?'

'You're the doctor. You think of something. At eleven o' clock, you will arrive outside the Two Monkeys play café in Notting Hill.' Jack looked at him quizzically.

'Wha…?'

'It's one of those yummy mummy hangouts—somewhere to dump the kids while they sip lattes and bitch about their husbands.'

Jack wondered if Portman was a miserable divorcee who never saw his own children.

'Don't go in. In fact, you won't be able to go in unless you have a kid with you, which is what makes it perfect for our purposes.'

'So what am I meant to do, then?'

'I was getting to that,' Portman said in annoyed voice. 'At eleven, you will be met by one of our young female agents. Maddie. She will be with a four-year-old girl called Charlotte. Don't worry, Maddie will find *you*. You will embrace, kiss on the cheek, make small talk outside, and then head into the café. Nice and relaxed.' Jack suddenly found it hard to keep up.

How did I ever get into this?

'You'll be safe. Maddie's been visiting there over the past few weeks, getting to know the staff. The joint's clean.'

Safe? Clean?

'Maddie will tell you what we need and what to do next.' Portman sensed Jack's hesitancy. 'You're a very bright man, Jack. We know you're an excellent doctor. You've worked hard and you have a promising career ahead of you. It would be a real shame to throw all of that away, wouldn't it? Especially on a guy like Nathan Mortimer.'

Jack didn't know how to respond to that. All he could do was nod.

'Your note mentioned Cerise,' said Jack, with a pleading tone.

'Ah yes, Cerise Navarro. We knew her as Sandrine Besson.'

Sandrine... Sandrine... the name I heard on the phone.

'She was using you. She was one of them. Certain people wanted her to *influence* you, to keep you on a path to *their* thing. They wanted to seduce you into it with all the glitz and glamour. But her bosses felt she was getting too close to you and they couldn't have that. Too big a risk. They wanted her to take the next step with you, bring you right into the fold, but she seemed reluctant to do that.'

Jack was devastated.

'So it was because of me that she died?' he asked, almost in tears.

Portman shook his head.

'No. You were just the poor sucker at the end of the line. She knew what she'd gotten into with these guys. She knew who she was messing with.'

'You really have a way of endearing yourself,' Jack bristled.

'This is a miserable business, Jack. And it comes with miserable outcomes. It's up to you if you want to add to the misery or help end some of the pain.'

Portman seemed suddenly uncomfortable. Jack followed his gaze and saw a man staring at them from some way off. 'That's enough for today, Jack. You will walk away from here first. I'll make sure you get out okay.'

'But I have more questions about Cerise. I mean Sandrine.'

'Jack. That's enough for today. It's time to leave. And Jack?'

'*What?*' he spat back.

'Enjoy the rest of your conference.'

62

IT WAS AFTER nine by the time Jack returned to his lavish hotel suite. He had fought the urge to look behind him for the entire journey back from the Colosseum.

How can I stay here now? My life suddenly feels so… tainted.

But he couldn't just leave. That would be too suspicious.

If Portman was to be believed.

If.

He needed to relax, so he popped open the champagne and quickly down a glass. He then poured a second and headed out onto the balcony. Everything Portman had told him was swirling around inside his head like a tornado.

Interpol… zinestrapam… Mortimer… PCS… Maddie… death… Cerise… Sandrine… Cerise…

He looked down at the street below. Diners and drinkers were out in force enjoying the balmy Friday evening. He suddenly envied them. They were carefree. They were *free*. He felt trapped and alone. The massive suite felt paradoxically claustrophobic. He had to get out. He felt lightheaded and realised he had not eaten all day. He took a quick shower, dressed, grabbed the conference program, and headed downstairs to the hotel bar.

A three-piece jazz band played in the corner of the bar. They seemed to be performing instrumental renditions of a range of eighties hits. Jack took his Bombay Sapphire and tonic and slumped down in a soft, leather chair past the corner of the bar. He flung the food menu back onto the bar. Nothing appealed.

So far, the alcohol didn't seem to be calming the storm in his head.

Portman... Sandrine... Mortimer... drugs... Africa... Cerise... Patient X... Sandrine... Cerise...

Always ending on Cerise.

He closed his eyes and imagined her.

Imagined *them*.

It had been so brief, yet so exhilarating. It was really the first time in his adult life he had experienced such intense loss.

And it hurt like hell. The questions were coming now. Thick and fast. Questions without any answers.

Why, Cerise? Why?

At least he now had Portman. He knew that Portman had more to tell him and had more answers for him. He could *feel* it.

His thoughts were crowded out by a couple who seated themselves next to him and began arguing loudly.

The man's head was covered in curly thick grey hair. He was a smoking a cigarette. His female companion was a very pretty, slim blonde, elegantly dressed in an expensive looking outfit. She held a champagne flute.

'Why can't you, just for *once*, do what I ask you?' he implored.

'I have done just that, and nothing else, for years. For *years*.'

The accents were American. Californian, he guessed. Despite the tone, he found the temporary distraction from his own thoughts welcome.

'I have never heard any complaints. You seemed happy enough to live the life. The homes, the clothes, the jewellery,' he waved his arms around to emphasise his words, 'the luxury vacations. It hasn't been that tough.'

She mimicked him: 'the homes, the jewellery, the vacations... with all the money you were spending on me, I guess I shouldn't have been surprised that the women you were sleeping around with were so cheap…'

He looked around nervously.

'Will you keep it *down*.'

'Why should I? You certainly weren't keeping it down when I walked into your office yesterday and saw you with that slut on your desk!'

'That's it!' he proclaimed. 'I've had enough of this.'

The man reached forward and grabbed his drink from the table. At that moment the woman looked directly at Jack and stared. She looked him up and down.

Intensely.

She looked at his drink. Then looked at his lap and congress program he was holding.

In a loud and direct voice, she said: 'Forensic psychiatry? That sounds fascinating!'

The grey-haired man turned in his chair. He didn't speak but shot Jack a menacing look, before swallowing the rest of his drink and marching off. Jack estimated he was at least twenty years older than the woman. Once he had left the bar, the woman looked as if she might burst into tears.

Again, she looked at Jack.

'Are you okay?' he asked.

She sniffed. 'Yes. No. I don't know.'

She composed herself quickly and looked around, seemingly making certain that old grey-hair had definitely left the bar.

'Ugggh, he's not worth it,' she concluded.

'Your husband?'

'No. We were never married. We lived together for a while a few years ago, but he could never commit to anything more formal. I just can't believe I wasted so much time on him. I wanted to give it another shot, but I feel like a fool flying over here to surprise him. Well... *one* of us got the surprise, I suppose.'

'Ahhh. Yeah, sorry. I heard what you said to him.' He tried to give her a comforting smile. She appeared to relax and kept talking.

'I should have expected it. He's the CEO of an advertising firm back in the States. When he said he was coming over here to finalise some campaigns for Bulgari I should have realised it was just a ruse. He doesn't lower himself to do that sort of work anymore, he farms it out to his underlings.' She stared into the distance. 'I just *wanted* to believe I guess.'

'And let me take a stab: advertising... fashion... Bulgari... models... too much temptation.'

'Absolutely correct.'

'Well, for what it's worth, I'm sorry,' he said.

'That really does look interesting,' the woman said as she pointed at the conference program. 'So, what is *forensic* psychiatry? Is that like in those crime shows on TV?'

Jack laughed. 'Not really. The patients I see are still alive!'

She laughed along with him.

He continued: 'Forensic psychiatry is where mental illness and the law intersect. Criminal, usually.'

Her eyes lit up and she cooed, 'Oooh, like serial killers?'

He smiled. 'You'd think so, but, no, not really. Not really at all. Usually, I see some very unwell people who get into trouble with the law. And I guess I am there to try to help them.'

'Awww,' she said with the same soft voice. Jack noticed her piercing blue eyes for the first time. 'You must be *very* caring to deal with some of those sick patients. Is it dangerous? For you, I mean.'

'Not really. Even though they are very unwell, by the time I treat them they are in a pretty controlled environment. And usually heavily medicated!'

The waiter passed by and asked if they wanted to order more drinks.

'Sure,' she said, without hesitation. 'Another glass of that French chardonnay for me and for… sorry, I didn't catch your name?'

'Jack.' 'And for Jack… is that gin and tonic?'

'Sure is.'

'And for Jack, another G and T. Just book it up to my room.'

She turned her attention back to Jack.

'I'm Laura, by the way. So you're like a psychologist?'

'Lovely to meet you, Laura. And no, I'm a psychiatrist.'

'I've never understood the difference.'

> *Given the little scene before that seems a little disingenuous. Given your taste in men, I bet you've visited your fair share over the years.*

He politely played along. She really was beautiful, and he noted that most of the men walking into the bar looked her up and down as they strolled past. More than that, though, he found that he was enjoying this chat so much more than his earlier conversation with Portman.

'Well, a psychiatrist is a medically trained doctor, just like a surgeon or an obstetrician. We can prescribe medications and order blood tests and brain scans. It's just that we have done extra speciality training in diagnosing and treating mental illnesses. Psychologists are more interested in human thinking and behaviour, like why someone decides to do something. Motivation, that sort of thing.'

She quickly interjected: 'So, like why does someone stupidly follow two-timing loser to Rome to salvage a doomed relationship?'

He laughed. 'Well yeah, something like that. Some *clinical* psychologists provide talking therapies for some mental illnesses, like depression and anxiety. But they can't give out drugs.'

'So you just dish out the pills?'

'Not at all. I believe in the talking therapies too. Like psychoanalysis. You know, unlocking your unconscious mind so you can understand what makes you tick.' He thought she seemed impressed. Or at least interested.

Her eyes narrowed. 'So can you analyse what I'm thinking right now? Like, read my mind and things like that?'

'I wish!' he said with a laugh. 'If I could do that I'd have retired and gone to live in the Bahamas by now.'

She smiled and looked him up and down again.

'But surely you must have some idea of what's going through my head right now?'

He felt his heart rate quicken. He went to speak just as the waiter appeared with their drinks. He grabbed his quickly and took a long sip. He watched her slowly touch the stem of her wine glass before bringing it to her lips, her gaze never leaving his.

63

HE BARELY HAD the lights on before he felt her body up against his. He dropped the swipe card and put his hand around her waist. She spun around and pushed back against his tight abs. He closed his eyes and sighed.

> *That's good. That's good. To feel human touch again. That's good.*

He could smell the citrus aromas of her shampoo. He inhaled deeply.

> *Keep going, please. I am starting to feel alive. Keep going.*

His fingers found the zip to her dress. She leant forward, just slightly, to allow him to pull it down. The subtle, metal sound was all that could be heard in the room. She wriggled her shoulders and the black Chanel dress effortlessly slid down to the floor revealing a slender, lace G-string. He deftly unclipped her bra and that quickly joined the discarded dress on the marble floor.

She turned back to face him and they kissed. Deeply. Her hand found his belt and loosened it.

He felt a brief urge to pull away.

To pull back.

To say: '*I'm sorry. I can't. I want to, but I can't. I have recently lost someone and it still hurts.*'

But he didn't.

He allowed all of the dormant sensations to awaken and devour him.

64

THE SHARP, MORNING light woke him from a deep sleep. It took a moment for him to find his bearings. He felt he had slept solidly but had not dreamt at all during the night. He was still disoriented when he opened his eyes.

The alarm clock read seven fifty-three. By rapid association it all came tumbling back:

> *Portman... hotel... champagne... shower... clothes... conference program... bar... gin.. Californians... more gin... kissing... sex... Laura... more sex... Laura?*

He quickly rolled over in the bed.

Empty.

There was still a faint impression on the sheet where she had slept. He jumped out of the bed and went to the bathroom.

Empty.

The kitchen.

Empty.

The balcony.

Empty.

In the living room there was no sign of her either. No items of clothing. No note.

Nothing.

He realised that other than her first name he knew precious little. He didn't know her last name, her age, or her room number.

He did know one other thing. The previous night had been

unbelievably good. *Great*, in fact. The sex was vigorous and highly satisfying. He was not surprised that he'd slept so well.

It suddenly felt as though he'd been reckless. But he didn't care.

He wandered back to the kitchen and made an espresso, which he took out to the balcony, so that he could savouring the coffee and the morning light. He wondered if he might catch a glimpse of her downstairs, but no matter how hard he tried he could not see her.

In the bedroom an alarm sounded on his iPhone. For a brief moment, he was irrationally excited and expectant.

He frowned as he read the screen.

'*Conference begins in thirty minutes*'

65

WITH HIS THIRD coffee of the morning in hand, Jack wandered through the conference crowd to register for the day's lecturers.

He slid into a seat for the first keynote address of the day next to a morbidly obese man who sternly introduced himself as 'Ivan from Bulgaria'.

Great. Another Ivan. That's all I need.

Jack was not in the mood for small talk and stared ahead at the giant presentation screen in front of him.

Within a few minutes, Jack was engrossed in the lecture and thoughts of Laura began to fade from his mind. The speaker was running through some impressive work that been done on the neurochemistry of psychopathic personalities. He even theorised about what happens at the molecular level when an individual is completely devoid of empathy for others. He made the point that this may—strongly emphasising the *may*—pave the way for future manipulation of such biochemistry, with the aim of altering such antisocial behaviours.

Manipulation. Psychopaths.

Images of Nathan Mortimer suddenly flew into Jack's mind.

Jack was interested but disheartened to learn at the conclusion of the lecture that there was still no effective treatment, either pharmacological or psychological, for the psychopath. He thought about the conversations he'd had with Mortimer and the professor's view that psychiatry had not really made any significant breakthroughs for decades.

When an audience member asked the speaker how they could reduce the number of psychopathic personalities in the community the lecturer said dryly, 'Contraception. And if that fails, build bigger jails.'

By the lunchtime break Jack was feeling more relaxed and managed to rationalise the previous evening as 'just a fun night… no strings attached… it meant nothing.'

It's fine to move on. Cerise is gone. You can move on, Jack.

Memories of the evening before were also a very welcome distraction from the conversation he'd had with Portman. But still, he couldn't help but think about what he had been told.

That can wait. I can deal with that when I'm back in London.

Jack contemplated returning to the bar at the Hilton that evening, but after the final lecture of the day he ran into a group of his ex-colleagues from New York and changed his mind, deciding he'd rather spend the evening with them.

66

PORTMAN WAS CORRECT about one thing. The Two Monkeys play café was a brilliant choice of meeting place.

It was a chaotic, rainbow blur of screaming children, fluorescent play equipment, and sugar-loaded snacks. Even the background noise was psychedelic. Not only were there the shouts, cries, and squeals of children to contend with, but the café's speakers blared out a never-ending playlist of maddeningly catchy kids' songs at deafening volume. Beyond that, there was the chatter of the adults— mainly the West London yummy mummies with their long, blonde hair and their expense activewear, interspersed with a smattering of dads, nannies, and grandparents.

Minutes earlier, at precisely 11 o' clock, he had been met outside the café by Maddie and Charlotte. Jack had no idea what the relationship between the two of them was, but the little girl seemed incredibly comfortable with Maddie, and even gave Jack a warm, natural embrace.

Maddie was a voluptuous, attractive woman who appeared to be in her late twenties. Her long red hair fell fashionably around her ears and shoulders, and she carried a purple child's backpack over one shoulder. She blended in quite seamlessly with the other parents heading through the front door.

Charlotte, with her hair in pigtails, was dressed in a blue pinafore dress and stripy tights, looking every inch as though she'd just stepped out of the pages of a children's story book.

As they entered, they were met by a range of signs that indicated no adult was allowed into the café unless they were accompanied by a child under the age of twelve.

Very cautious. But also very clever.

They found one of the few remaining tables: a booth in the corner of the café. It gave them a view of most of the other patrons and staff. The moment Jack and Maddie had sat down, Charlotte was off, making a beeline for an enormous indoor slide.

'Now,' began Maddie in a loud voice. 'I thought we should look over the details for Charlotte's birthday party.' As she spoke, she slid a handwritten list across the table.

'Umm... yes... of course,' said Jack.

If my friends from medical school could see me now

He noticed that Maddie had an incredible ability to subtly scan the environment while still maintaining a conversation with him.

'I was having trouble deciding on the cake. She's started taking such an interest in Barbie recently, but she loves the Disney princesses, too.'

'Well... I'm happy for... Charlotte... to decide,' was all Jack could think of.

Maddie checked to see if Charlotte was okay and then stared solemnly at Jack. 'The fact that you are here would indicate that you took what Portman told you in Rome seriously.'

Gone was the relaxed mum. Her voice was now that of the no-bullshit agent.

With all the noise, it was difficult to hear her. But it would also be impossible for anyone to eavesdrop on their conversation.

'Yes. I did.' He still had so many questions, but he suddenly could not articulate a single one.

Under the table, her hand firmly grabbed his knee. It looked, to anyone else, like a sign of affection, but it did not feel like a seductive gesture to Jack.

We've got you, was Jack's interpretation of her move.

'That's good, Doctor Giorgio. You've made the right choice.'

'But what do you want from me?' he pleaded.

'It's not you we're after. We know who you are. We think you're one of the good guys. It's Mortimer. *He's* the one we need to nail.'

Charlotte ran back to the table. She was thirsty. Maddie pulled out a *Dora the Explorer* water bottle and handed it to her.

'No… *noooo*. Milkshake, please. Strawberry, please.' Maddie looked slightly irritated, but she acquiesced.

Never work with animals or children.

Within seconds, Charlotte was gone again, back to the thrills and spills of the indoor playground. Maddie continued as if she hadn't ever been interrupted.

'We strongly suspect that Mortimer is running the whole operation. But we need more evidence. We need to know who else is involved and how it is operating. Portman and I feel he is the way in. There is a warehouse here in London that he visits regularly, but the building is so secure we can't infiltrate it.'

'And that's where I come in?'

'Precisely. Mortimer clearly trusts you. He's taken you into the fold—you've even been to his house for one of his dinner parties.'

How the hell did you know about that?

Then a vivid memory flashed into his mind.

The Chelsea dinner… the pretty waitress with long, red hair… that was Maddie.

'But I don't know anything. I haven't been there all that long. I have no *evidence*. What about Barnard? He's been in the system for years. He can help.'

'Barnard,' she repeated as she rolled her eyes. 'There are only two problems with him: Mortimer doesn't trust him. And we don't trust him. He's completely self-absorbed. Mortimer would see right through him.

'As I said,' Jack replied, 'I don't know anything.' This time his voice was stern.

She reached across the table and held his hand. Her grip was firm. Passers-by just saw an attractive couple, happily in love, enjoying a morning out with their oh-so-cute daughter.

'You're a very clever man, Jack,' she said in a soft voice. Her hand then found his cheek and gently caressed it. 'I am sure you would want to protect yourself. Protect your career. Protect your *life*. And I know that you can use that brain of yours to get us all the information we need. Remember what Portman told you. This is very important work, Jack. Innocent and vulnerable people are suffering.'

Why me?!

'What do you need me to do?'

'We need direct evidence of Mortimer's involvement in illegal drug and psychiatric research trials, human trafficking, and black-market medication sales.'

'Is that all?' Jack asked sarcastically.

She gripped his knee again.

Tightly.

Jack did not appreciate the intimidation and felt a sudden urge to get some of his own back.

'How did someone like you ever get involved in this sort of work? I would say you've probably killed someone before. Is that right? Is it? You know, they say that the most traumatised soldiers who returned from war were the ones who actually did the killing. I wonder, Maddie, what keeps *you* up at night?'

She seemed to hesitate. Her eyes widened.

I'm on the mark.

'Oh, spare me your psycho-babble bull...' she broke off as Charlotte arrived back at the table.'

'Are you almost ready to go, sweetie?' asked Maddie in a butter-wouldn't-melt-in-her-mouth tone. The girl nodded and slurped what was left of her milkshake.

Jack felt Maddie pass a small piece of plastic into his hand under the table. Once he had hold of it, he instantly recognised it as a USB stick.

'Cast those beautiful blue eyes of yours over this. We want your psychiatric opinion of the material. But view this on a computer in a public library or an internet café. It will instruct you what to do from here. Do not, I repeat, do *not*, open it at home or at work. Once you've viewed it, destroy it.'

'Okay.'

She grabbed Charlotte by the hand and stood up.

'Now please be a gentleman and walk us out. And remember, Jack, you have a clear choice. Make the right one.'

67

WITH THE ADVENT of smartphones and cheap data, internet cafés were clearly heading the way of video stores, but after some searching Jack finally found an internet café, which thankfully also served drinkable coffee.

As he'd scoured the streets of West London, he'd had the urge to check that no one was following him. For the most part, he'd resisted the temptation, but he'd been unable to resist a few quick glances behind him.

Don't be paranoid. There's no one there.

But still. Trust your instincts. Listen to your unconscious.

The café was not busy. There were a handful of young backpackers who seemed to have gravitated to the place out of a need for kinship as much as anything. He paid for his espresso and carried it to the terminal at the very back of the room, from where he had a direct line of sight to the door and a clear view of everyone else in the café. For once, he felt he had some kind of insight into the terrifying paranoia that gripped some of his patients. He shuddered.

He slipped the flash drive into the rear of the computer, and within a few seconds, a small icon appeared on the screen. He looked closely at it. It resembled a green and white medicine capsule.

Jack clicked on it with the mouse, and it opened.

Initially, it displayed a range of obscure newspaper and internet articles from around the world. Jack read them with interest and horror. They mainly related to missing people who were found, months or years down the track, permanently changed. They had mainly gone missing from third world or developing nations experiencing internal strife, such as famines or civil wars. The stories indicated that their families were relieved to have found them again but were despairing about the psychological condition of their loved ones.

> '*Not the same person...*' '*My brother's body is here, but his mind is gone...*' '*My daughter is now mute...* '*My husband would be better off dead...*' '*No quality of life...*'

It appeared that the devastatingly mental deterioration was permanent. Dozens of articles over the past decade described very similar stories. Each one a tragedy.

Jack then opened a time-stamped video file that showed an African woman being interviewed by Portman in a stark office. Or, more correctly, he was *attempting* to interview her. She was unable to provide any details about herself. She stared blankly at Portman or the camera with no discernible emotion.

Instantly, Jack thought of Patient X.

Other than being an African female, the woman on the video was a carbon copy of him.

The camera then focused on Portman, who explained that the woman was found in Paris, wandering the streets of the Latin quarter. She'd stepped out into the traffic, seemingly oblivious. She was taken to a local psychiatric hospital, and other than her obviously blank mental state, the doctors could not find anything tangibly wrong with her. Physically, she was fit and healthy. After months of tests, interviews, investigations, and treatment, they gave her a less than satisfying diagnosis of early-onset dementia. Jack knew this was exceedingly rare in such a young woman. She was then discharged into the care of a boarding house where she required 24-hour care. Her family of origin was never located.

A second video showed footage of Mortimer having an intense discussion with a woman, her back to the camera, at a café in a European city.

Geneva?

There was no audio, but they appeared to be arguing. The body language suggested exasperation from Mortimer as he started to gesticulate in an angry fashion. He aggressively pointed right towards her chest, knocking over his glass as he did so. A few of the other patrons looked his way, but the woman didn't even flinch.

He then saw Mortimer straighten high right-hand index finger and point to the back of his neck. With hostility, he then used the same finger to tap several times on the woman's forehead.

Jack looked more closely at the screen. There was something familiar about the way the woman moved.

She suddenly stood up and shook her head violently. Mortimer sat back in his chair, looking far more subdued.

The woman turned and started marching in the direction of the camera. Jack held his breath and froze.

Cerise.

The video footage stopped with Cerise in mid-stride.

He wanted to reach out and embrace her. Walk off with her. No, *run* off with her. Take her far away.

It was impossible.

He jumped as the café attendant cleared away his empty espresso cup, snapping him back to the stark reality he now faced.

He closed the video file of Cerise. One file remained. It was titled: 'Dr JG'. He felt anxious.

Oh God, what will this be? Clandestine footage of me? Hidden cameras in my apartment?

Now he really felt like he understood what it must be like inside the mind of one of his paranoid psychotic patients.

When he opened it, he was washed with relief as it revealed Portman staring seriously at the camera. Portman's mouth moved, but there was no audio. Thankfully, small subtitles appeared in a dialect of Italian that Jack had learnt as a boy from his nonna.

You've really done your homework on me.

He checked to make sure no one else could be reading over his shoulder.

Portman was saying that their IT sources had indicated there were secret files located on one of Mortimer's computers, but they were unsure if the computer was at the Nicholas Tindal Centre or at Mortimer's warehouse. The files were heavily password protected and encrypted. They wanted Jack to get into the computer and download the documents. They believed that these files contained the evidence they needed to link Mortimer to these crimes against humanity.

'All you need to do is find that computer and get into those files, Jack. Game over.'

All I need to do.

68

THE INTERNATIONAL CONFERENCE call began at midday on the dot, GMT. All participants were punctual, and as the grandfather clock in the board room struck twelve, the meeting got underway.

A quick roll call was taken to ensure all members were present.

'Alpha-Seven-Four-Nine-Five-Y' a male voice stated in a clear, privately educated English accent.

'Confirmed,' came the reply from an officious-sounding American man.

'Beta-Seven-Six-Two-Nine-Y,' came from a third voice with a strong German accent.

'Confirmed,' said Alpha.

The American spoke again. 'Gamma-Seven-Eight-Eight-Four-Four-Y.'

'Confirmed,' repeated Alpha.

'Delta-Seven-Nine-Seven-Three-One-X,' this time it was an American woman who spoke.

'Confirmed.'

Finally, it was Epsilon's turn, a curt-sounding French woman whose check in was duly confirmed.

Alpha then took charge of the meeting and began working through the agenda using their long-established code.

'The first item is a review of livestock at the farm,' he began. 'The bull who was returned from the abattoir has required the use of the vet but is likely to improve well soon. It is early days, but the signs look promising.'

'Good,' said Gamma.

'Unfortunately, the vet tells me that the ewe remains very unwell and is going to need further treatment. Extensive treatment, in fact, with some new supplements in the diet.'

'How much?' asked Delta.

'He estimates around a hundred thousand. Maybe slightly more. But he is very confident that with the change of diet the ewe will also improve well. I agree to accept the extra fee. Do we have a second?'

'Seconded,' confirmed Beta.

'Passed. The following item relates to transportation.'

'Ah yes,' chimed in Gamma. 'Are the new cattle trucks ready?'

'Yes,' confirmed Alpha. 'And the new highways are mapped out and deemed safe as well.'

'Excellent,' said Delta.

'In fact, we will be expecting our next delivery of lambs in seven days.'

'How many?'

There was a brief pause. It sounded as though Alpha was making keystrokes on a computer.

'I can confirm seventeen,' he said with a clear smile in his voice.

'Bravo!' said Beta. 'That's the largest number of lambs so far in a single shipment.'

'Well done,' said Epsilon.

'And they are of very high quality,' continued Alpha, 'from the Aphrodite breeder.'

In Berlin, Beta scrolled down his laptop screen until he came to the heading 'Breeders'. He looked down the list which further indicated that the Aphrodite breeder meant Cambodia.

'That's fantastic,' he said.

Alpha continued.

'The next issue at the farm concerns a problem of a fox in the henhouse.'

'Hmmm,' grumbled Beta.

'The fox may be scared off with the right noises. But a steel trap may be the only option.'

'I want to try scaring away the fox first,' Epsilon said firmly.

'I agree,' said Gamma.

'Okay. But remember: a sly fox may be hard to scare. And a fox can do enormous damage to the farm.'

69

As HAD BECOME customary, Jack sat in silence with the diminutive Vietnamese man. He checked his watch again. Thirty-seven minutes had passed, and not a word had been spoken. For the entire time, Patient X just stared at him, with the same rhythmic, hypnotic breathing. Jack had been ruminating over Portman, Maddie, and the files he had been given. His mind kept coming back to Patient X. He had to figure out what was going on with him.

What was *wrong* with him?

Paul, the director of nursing, was also present. Jack had asked Sarah Wellington if she would like to sit in as well, but she said she was unable to as she had a training seminar she needed to attend. She told Jack that she did not think his idea would yield any new answers and she forcefully remined him of the pressure she was under to discharge him so that she could admit more acute patients. Jack pushed on anyway.

The senior nurse shook his head and laughed when Jack approached him the day before and asked him to compile a list of items that he wanted brought into the interview with the enigmatic patient. Paul had read down the list of items more than once to make sure his eyesight did not need testing.

'Let's just call it the 'Giorgio Test', Paul. It's a new cognitive assessment tool designed specifically for this one patient. Maybe we could write a research paper on it together!'

More laughter from the nurse.

'Well,' said Jack. 'If Mohammed won't go the mountain, then we will bring the mountain to him.'

'Ahhh, okay Jack. I'll see what I can do,' Paul said, still wondering if the doctor was joking.

The following day, Paul handed Jack the bag of the items with the words, 'Here's your goodie bag. I had a lot of fun filling out the requisition form for this stuff.'

'Thanks, Paul. You're a godsend, mate.'

As they were getting nowhere with the interview, Jack decided to start showing Patient X the items, one by one.

A Vietnamese flag.

He looked at it. Nothing. No response.

A photograph of Patient X that had been taken upon admission.

A blank stare. He breathed in. He breathed out.

A cigarette lighter. Paul felt nervous as he imagined himself explaining to the Department of Health how a patient like this got hold of such an item.

Well, we gave it to him, Minister.

It was handed over to the patient, Jack had to place it in his hands.

The patient looked confused. But there was no other response. Jack took the lighter back.

A model of a handgun.

Again, it was handed to the patient. Again nothing. He held it by the barrel, not the handle.

A pornographic magazine. The pages spread open.

No response. Jack could have been showing him the share tables from the *Financial Times*.

Women's lingerie.

Nothing.

A dildo.

Jack placed the item in the patient's hands. No response at all.

Paul blushed at the thought of what his colleagues would say if they could see him taking part in this strange experiment.

A can of Coke.

Patient X reached out and took it. Jack and Paul watched him with the focus and intensity of a parent watching their newborn baby sleep.

The patient stared at the ring pull. His free hand moved, just slightly, but he then placed the can down on the table. His eyes then fixed back on Jack.

A chocolate donut.

As soon as it appeared, the patient lunged for it, startling Paul and Jack. He snatched the donut out of Jack's hands and hungrily wolfed it down. Within thirty seconds it had disappeared.

He then sat motionless again. Quietly breathing. In and out.

A banana.

He looked at the piece of fruit for slightly longer than the donut, but then grabbed it from Jack and bit into it. Skin and all.

The bag was now empty.

'Let's take him back to the ward, Paul. I think I know what's going on.'

'Well that makes one of us, then,' the bemused nurse replied.

70

Once the patient had been safely returned to his room, Jack strolled back around to Paul's office. The head nurse had his door open in eager anticipation of hearing Jack's theory.

Surely it can't be. But there can be no other explanation. Can there?

He was about to start delivering his theory to Paul when Mortimer appeared from the office and stopped him from entering.

'I hear you have just engaged in an interesting little experiment, Jack.' He did not look impressed.

'We've just been getting nowhere with this guy and I thought I...'

'Yes, yes, you thought you would play some clever game to impress everyone and potentially put you, Paul, the patient, and this entire ward at risk.' Mortimer's tone was curt.

Jack could hear an almost childlike defensiveness in his voice as he shot back, 'But all the investigations so far have come to nothing. I decided to start from scratch. If I can just explain, hopefully you will see that I have really been thinking about what may be going on and...'

'*Hopefully* I will see? Don't fucking patronise me, boy.' Mortimer's anger was rising. Jack was taken aback. 'My office. Now.'

***

'It was a bit of a mystery to me, but only for a short while.' Mortimer's irritable mood had clearly not abated during the walk back to his office.

'What mystery?' Jack thought the professor was going to pontificate about his own views regarding Patient X.

'Your background. Your lineage.'

Jack threw him a puzzled look.

It's suddenly difficult to keep up with you, Professor.

'My *lineage?*'

'Yes. The blonde hair, the blue eyes, the tall, thin body. The Italian surname. If it was Eriksson or Andersen, it would all make sense. But *Giorgio?* Now that was intriguing.'

'What is your point, Professor?' Jack was growing irritated and wanted to get back to the ward to speak to the staff about Patient X.

'It all makes sense now. You're adopted, aren't you?'

Jack gave a subtle nod in Mortimer's direction, as if to say, *'Bravo'.*

'Yes. So?'

'I am curious about the impact that such an *event* might have had on you, boy. How it must have shaped you as a person. Your psychology. Your relationships.'

'Why do you need to know about all of that?' Jack was truly on the defensive now.

Mortimer chuckled. 'Do you feel you need to over-achieve to compensate, Doctor? Like that little game you played back there with my patient?'

Your *patient? Little game?*

Mortimer smashed through his thoughts. 'Need to prove your worth so many times that no one could ever doubt it, do you? Or so that you could never doubt yourself? It must be a terrible burden to go through life knowing that you were an unwanted error.'

Mortimer looked at him with steel in his eyes. Jack felt the coldness.

Why is he so angry with me? What the hell is going on?

'That may be your interpretation of my existence, but it is not mine.'

Mortimer pushed on. 'Oh, *really?* I can't imagine what it must be like. To know that you were rejected by your *own mother*. It is one of the cruellest and rarest punishments that nature can dish out.'

    Bastard.

'Like I said, you have drawn your own conclusions. I have drawn mine.'

'And what might those be, Dr Giorgio?'

Jack thought about his many sessions with Theo Stein. Theo had been extremely helpful in allowing Jack to work through some of the issues around his adoption. But, still, a hole remained. The well-worn cliché of jigsaws and missing pieces rang truer than anything else.

    Look under the surface, Jack. Look at the drives. The motivations. Why is Mortimer doing this?

'And,' Mortimer continued. 'I imagine you found revenge one way or another, didn't you? You would have been mighty popular as a teenager. Tall, handsome, athletic, and with a brain to match. You could run a four-minute mile and then recite poetry to some breathless, drooling little blonde thing. The girls would have lined up for you, Giorgio. Right from high school, I would say. From the earliest days of puberty. Your male classmates would have simply looked on in admiration. "There goes Jack Giorgio, nice guy, the guy we pick first to play for our team. He can have all the girls he wants as long as he's on our side." You would have been young, wouldn't you? Maybe fifteen? In a dark corner at a high school party, the back row of the cinema, on the living room floor when your parents were out. You would have feigned love and a future to get what you wanted. But it wasn't really the *sex* you wanted, was it? Oh no. It was something more meaningful to you. *Revenge.* Every time you screwed a girl and held her afterwards you lured her into a false sense of you – and then, just when she was at her happiest, bang, you dropped her cold. I would say that most of your relationships never even lasted a year.'

Jack did not answer.

'In fact, I would reckon that most of them lasted, oh, I don't know, let's pick a random number... nine months?'

Jack remained as silent and unmoving as Patient X.

'Every time you fucked a girl, literally and then metaphorically, it gave you just that little bit more payback, didn't it? Well, until Cerise, at any rate. Right, Jack? She was different. She was *special*. You loved her. *Finally.* A woman who would love you, too. But, alas, poor Jack, abandoned and rejected once again. That must really hurt.'

'You don't know what you're talking about, Nathan. You didn't know her. Really *know* her.'

'Oh, and you did, did you, Jack? You really *knew* her?'

Mortimer spoke through gritted teeth.

'I'd say you knew as much about Cerise as you knew about your mother. Precious little.'

'Why do you say that, Nathan?'

'I will never forget that first interview. The look of uncertainty that came across your face when I asked you if there was any history of mental illness in your family. You had no idea. No clue. You know fuck all. Tell me, Jack, why haven't you found out? Too frightened she'll reject you for a second time?'

Jack could feel the anger and sadness rising up.

'I really believed in you, Jack. Truly believed. And how do you repay me? By pulling these ridiculous stunts on my ward? What the fuck is wrong with you? Is it your own grief? What you, me, and Cerise could have done together was going to be a new chapter for humanity! And now... now... she is dead and you are... I don't know. What *are* you, Jack?'

71

NO SOONER HAD Sir Roger sat down to light up a cigar than his PA came rushing in. She handed him a thick, paper file marked *'For the Attention of the Health Secretary. Urgent and Confidential.*

He sighed as he took it from her.

Endless bloody bureaucracy.

He started to flick through the file. National Medical Board correspondence coupled with some sort of old hospital records. Not even British. It meant nothing to him.

Then his phone rang.

'Oh, it's you. Yes, I have it, but tell me, why am I wasting my time looking at this old patient file? I've got a briefing with the PM in fifteen minutes about research budgets.'

The reply was curt: 'well, you *are* the Health Secretary, aren't you, Sir Roger? Patient care should be at the forefront of your mind. Your most important job, really. Looking after the health of your constituents.'

'Just what the *fu-*'

'The media can get hold of things so quickly these days. A mobile phone is all you need to broadcast any sort of scandal. You can set up your own fully functioning news channel on Facebook, it seems.'

'Don't you threaten me,' Maxwell spat.

'Settle down, old boy. No one is threatening you. There's no need for us to do that. After all, isn't it *you* posing for photos outside the Nicholas Tindal Centre? Isn't it *you* shaking hands with the newly knighted Sir Nathan Mortimer? Such wonderful advances for mental health. And you are right there, front and centre, riding the crest of a wave, Sir Roger. But one thing always happens to waves in the end.'

A bead of sweat dripped form Maxwell's forehead onto the paper file in front of him.

'Oh yes. And what would that be?'

'They crash.'

Maxwell opened the file in front of him and read it more closely. He flicked back to the other letters and printed emails that sat on top of it.

What the hell?

'Ahh. I see the problem now.'

'*Potential* problem, Sir Roger. I needn't tell you that the voters love a decisive minister. Someone who can take action. Someone putting the needs of the common man first. Not bowing down to these medical elites in their ivory towers.'

'Understood,' was all he could say.

'Make a decision, Sir Roger. Or the decision will be made for you.'

72

JACK WALKED SLOWLY through the sterile, white halls of the hospital. The smell of antiseptic was nauseating. The corridor seemed to stretch on forever. Over the PA system he could hear doctors being paged to attend various wards.

He walked past a bank of beige telephones attached to the wall of the corridor.

Bakelite. Complete with rotating dials. How old-fashioned.

A new message over the PA system urged Jack to answer a call coming through on Line Three.

Obediently, he picked up the receiver of the third beige telephone, but all he could hear was an engaged signal. He held the hard plastic receiver in his right hand and the long, soft, curly cord in his left. As he hung up the phone, he noticed that his left hand was covered in blood and… was that amniotic fluid from a placenta?

He looked down. The phone cord had become an umbilical cord in his hand.

He looked back up. A man stood by his side. Mortimer. But a much younger Mortimer, with longer, darker hair, sideburns, and moustache. He wore a long, white coat and a paisley tie.

'What are you doing here?' he said angrily. 'You should not be here!'

'But I have to answer this phone call,' Jack explained.

Mortimer grabbed the enormous umbilical cord from Jack's hands and placed it around his neck. He pulled tightly on it.

'You should *not* be here,' he kept repeating.

To Jack's surprise, he just stood there and let Mortimer pull on the cord.

Tighter and tighter.

He heard the phone ring.

He tried to reach out to answer it, but Mortimer pulled tighter on the cord.

The phone continued to ring.

Jack opened his mouth to scream at Mortimer. But when he tried to push the air past the level of his larynx, it stopped. Dead.

Jack woke with one hand on his ringing mobile phone and the other around his throat.

He stared at the screen.

Mortimer.

73

'THIS IS SERIOUS, Jack. *Sit down.*'

Jack obeyed.

'I'll get right to the point. As you well know, there are certain things that doctors just cannot do. And there are certain things that psychiatrists *absolutely* cannot do. Not under *any* circumstances.'

After their prior conversation, Jack wondered where this headed. He swallowed hard.

'Ahh… sorry, what are you talking about?'

Mortimer shook his head. 'Oh, I think you may already know.'

An image of Portman's '*Roma*' baseball cap flashed into Jack's mind.

'I don't. Really, I don't.' He could hear a desperation in his voice.

'I just cannot understand why *you*, of *all* people, would do it. You must have known, Jack?'

'Known *what*? Do *what*?'

Mortimer sighed: 'Screw one of your patients!' The words hit Jack like a punch in the face.

'*WHAT!*' Jack's utter shock was genuine. He hoped Mortimer picked up on that fact.

'You have slept with a patient, Jack. That is the number one cardinal rule that can never, *ever* be broken. *Never!*'

Jack took a moment.

Breathe. Breathe.

In a strange way, he felt relieved that *Portman* had not been mentioned. He knew he was innocent of Mortimer's allegation, but such an accusation must be carefully thought about.

Mortimer was angry, and right now, certainty was called for. Jack closed his eyes and went through a lengthy mental database of patients in his head.

Nothing.

He then went through the memories of women he had slept with. After a moment or so, he was sure.

He was clear. He expressly knew '*the rule,*' and he had never strayed from it.

'That is simply not true, Nathan,' he said in a calm, matter-of-fact voice. 'Why would you believe such a thing?'

'Jack,' the professor said quietly, almost in a whisper. 'Don't try to deny it. I have irrefutable evidence. The woman herself has come forward and made a complaint. Of course, I did not want to believe it, but her story checks out.'

'It is simply *not true,*' Jack repeated, on the verge of tears now. But a determined Mortimer persisted.

'Lying will only make it worse. I understand why you would deny such a terrible violation. Your reputation will be in tatters. You could be deregistered and never work as a doctor again. You could even go to jail. So, although I understand your reluctance to come clean, it would be much more helpful if you would be honest with me, Jack, so that we can work out what we're going to do about it.'

We?

'Just hold on a minute,' Mortimer was clearly taken aback by Jack's aggressive tone, 'Who is this patient? What has she said? I need to hear the details before you start talking about making plans.'

The professor opened his laptop. Jack could not see the screen, but he wondered if this was the computer Portman had spoken about.

'The woman's name is Brenner. She says it happened recently. The sex that is.'

Brenner, Brenner, Brenner.

'I've never heard of her.'

'Hang on, Jack, there's more,' Mortimer said with a stern tone. His eyes never left the screen.

An uneasy feeling crawled over Jack's skin. Mortimer was somehow enjoying this.

'We checked the hospital records. She was right. You *had* treated her.'

'Where? When?'

'New York. Let's see… around four years ago.'

'New York? *Four years* ago?'

'Come on, Jack, you know the rules: once a patient, always a patient. It's pretty black and white. We're all human. I understand that. We've all had our moments of temptation, but we must always resist. The power imbalance is too great. Never means never. It doesn't matter how long ago it was.'

Jack recoiled at Mortimer's condescending tone.

He cast his memory back further.

Brenner… New York… Brenner… four years ago…

Nothing was coming up.

'No. Nothing.'

Mortimer fiddled around with his keyboard and then swivelled in his chair. A laser printer sprung to life and printed off a dozen pages.

'It's pretty fucking obvious that you're only going to own up to this if I show you the proof,' he said.

Jack had noticed that expletives had been creeping into Mortimer's vocabulary with greater and greater frequency.

Under pressure, Professor?

Mortimer slid over to the printer and gathered the documents before handing them to Jack. He sighed deeply and gazed out his window as Jack perused them.

He gasped as he read.

'Brenner,' he said to himself. He stared down at the first name: 'Laura,' he whispered. 'Laura Brenner of Los Angeles, California.'

Laura.

Rome.

He felt nauseous and rubbed his forehead vigorously as he read. The notes confirmed that he had treated a Laura Brenner in the Columbia University Medical Center emergency room when he was working in psychiatry in New York City. The documents told him that he assessed her in the ER and then again once more when she went to the psychiatric ward. She self-discharged from the hospital later that same day.

That appeared to be his only professional interaction with her.

Never means never.

He flicked to the emergency room nursing assessment and Laura's identifying features. She gave a residential address in Bel-Air, Los Angeles. Her age was thirty-three. Relationship status was listed as de facto. Her height was five feet and seven inches. Her weight was one hundred and twenty pounds. Boyd habitus was described as 'slim'.

Hair colour: blonde.

Eye colour: blue.

'Hilton,' he said to himself quietly.

'Pardon?' asked Mortimer.

'Nothing,' Jack replied. He flicked through the rest of the documents. Clinical notes were typed and entered into a computerised, digital system, but there was no doubt it was his name and signature at the end of the admission notes.

There was no doubt he had carried out the assessment.

He noted that Ms Brenner had been brought into the ER by a couple of cops who had picked her up from the lobby of the Waldorf Astoria after a call from hotel security. She was initially reviewed by the mental health nurse, and Jack was subsequently called as it was felt that she would require further specialist assessment and probable admission.

His notes indicated that he began the interview at two forty-five in the morning, and he had taken quite a thorough history from her.

The police report described her as 'yelling and making a scene' at the hotel. She appeared to be intoxicated and she was 'abusive to her partner and to staff' and threatening to 'jump from the balcony' if her complaints were not taken seriously.

He returned to his own assessment, which described her as 'very labile, sobbing, somewhat slurred speech, likely alcohol…'

Jack looked further down his notes. She gave a history of a lengthy but tumultuous relationship with her de facto partner and said that they had argued violently in their hotel room that evening about an affair he was having. She told Jack that she had 'savaged the mini bar' and 'thrown a lamp at the bastard.' Jack had written that 'the relationship is clearly on and off.'

He felt that she was distressed, vulnerable, and at risk of harming herself. He had talked her into staying in for the night so that she could be reassessed the following day when she had sobered up. She had agreed.

The notes did not indicate that Jeffrey had called to check on her welfare.

On the next page, he had documented his Mental State Examination, the psychiatric equivalent of a physical. The initial description was of a thin, well-dressed, attractive woman with shoulder length blonde hair who wore numerous pieces of expensive jewellery.

He shook his head.

Why did I have to describe her as attractive?

He realised, in retrospect, it was not great judgement. He also realised that the woman he described in the case notes fitted the description of the woman from the bar in Rome.

Laura.

Laura Brenner.

His heart rate quickened.

He felt lightheaded.

It seems to be true. I am guilty.

He wondered how he could be so stupid. So reckless. He tried to console himself with numbers: what were the odds of being in Italy, in Rome, in the Hilton, in the bar, on the same day and at the same time as one another. A million to one? A billion? He realised he was trying to rationalise what had happened. He could not deny it. This attempt to blame fate did not provide any relief, nor would it likely provide any leniency.

It had happened, and he would need to face the consequences.

'Okay,' Jack finally said as Mortimer returned to his chair. 'Yes, I did sleep with a blonde American woman called Laura in Rome when I was there for the conference. But I truly had no idea she had ever been a patient of mine. She certainly never mentioned it.'

'Given her intoxication and her distress all those years ago, I doubt that she would have remembered you either.'

'Well, how the hell did this ever come to light?' asked Jack.

He was still hoping that Mortimer would suddenly throw the papers in the bin, start laughing, and slap Jack on the back.

'Jeffrey Lear. The man she was with. It seems that she boasted to him about how good you were in the sack. He was the one who paid the bill when you treated her. Don't ask me why, but he remembered the name of the attending psychiatrist on the account. Dr Jack Giorgio.'

'I don't know what to say, Nathan. I just don't know.' That was the truth. He didn't.

'Well, Lear was pretty mad, and now so is Laura. They have both reported you to the medical board and the Department of Health, and they then contacted me, as I am your direct employer. Even Roger Maxwell called me, as he wants action taken about this, given all the publicity this centre has attracted. You must understand, Jack, that no one wants your name cleared more than I do.'

Jack was not convinced about that.

'Other than seeing a lawyer, what else can I do?'

'I'm sorry, Jack, but the powers that be have got me over a fucking barrel. Sir Roger himself, for God's sake! I can't risk any fallout for this centre or for our other work. After all the 'hashtag me too' crap, things like this just can't be ignored. My hands are tied. I have to act. I'm going to need to play the game and suspend you until this is all sorted out. One way or another.'

The last four words did not fill Jack with confidence.

He shook his head.

'I can't believe it.'

'Neither can I, Jack. The suspension is effective immediately. You'll need to hand in your ID and security card.'

74

AS HE RE-READ his own extensive handwritten notes, Theo Stein realised that he still had seven more days until the next scheduled international conference call.

Just enough time.

His notes demonstrated that his extensive research *and* his ability to draw together numerous pieces of seemingly unrelated information had allowed him to piece it all together.

A huge hand-drawn web of connections stared back at him.

Connections.

It had taken some time, but it was Jack's work in London that had provided him with the final clue.

Theo stared down at the broad list of references he had used to put it together:

The boring and lengthy product disclosure statements of share offerings from big pharma companies.

The figures gleaned from the *Wall Street Journal.*

The Annals of European Neuroscience Research.

The World Health Organization policy 6.23R on refugee health.

The International Guidelines and Protocols for Commercial Shipping in the Atlantic Ocean.

UK immigration and population statistics.

MTR research briefing 232(A).1

No one had connected the dots.

No one had connected the neurons like Theo had.

It's amazing what could be achieved with a ballpoint pen and a landline phone.

>*If you can't beat 'em, join 'em.*

>*If you won't use 'em, buy 'em.*

He had walked around to his local First Manhattan Bank branch and transferred the required deposit into the Swiss account needed to secure a transplant.

Three million US dollars.

The remaining balance was substantially more, but Theo knew he would never need to make that final payment.

Theo took great satisfaction in the game he had played. He'd convinced them that he was just another wealthy old New Yorker who could not cope with his own mortality. He'd given a very plausible story of gradual-onset dementia, telling them he was becoming more forgetful, that his family were complaining more and more about his memory lapses and that he was having trouble finding the right words nowadays. Couldn't do the *Times* crossword anymore. Found his fresh underwear stored neatly away in the refrigerator. He was worried he would need to stop practising soon, unless...

>*Unless.*

Something could be done.

If only there was a definitive treatment out there.

A miracle cure.

A brand-new mind to call his own.

He knew he could not be too choosey when it came to the type of mind he would be receiving. He knew it would be a young male who was free from neurological or genetic disease, and that the tissue typing would be matched to his own sample.

Beyond that, he just needed to be patient.

Wait for the next harvest.

Then, with the help of Jack, he would be able to expose it all. He would have the concrete proof that linked all of the players.

They would all come crashing down.

The share prices of big pharma would tumble, but he had gotten out before the fall.

Buy and hold.

Theo had held a fortune in MTR shares for decades, and in all his years he never once sold a single stock.

Until now.

The best three million I have ever spent.

75

SARAH WELLINGTON WAS quite out of breath by the time she sat down next to Jack in the espresso bar. She'd received his message at short notice and had to run half the way.

'So... sorry... I'm... late,' she stood with her hands on her hips until she'd regulated her breathing.

'That's fine, Sarah. I'm just so grateful you would come,' he replied.

When she'd composed herself, she looked Jack up and down. He was clearly exhausted, with enormous bags under his eyes. He was unshaven and wore an old pair of jeans and a creased t-shirt. He looked like he'd lost weight—which he could ill afford to do, given his naturally thin physique.

'Are you okay? I haven't seen you or heard from you at all since... well since...'

'I was suspended.'

'Yes. I was worried, Jack. Things at the NTC haven't been the same without you. The whole mood is miserable. Even Lizzie Roberts seems to be deteriorating again. She will only speak to you, she says. At least we were finally able to discharge Patient X and get some more of the acutely unwell prisoners admitted. Now, what's going on?' She had so many questions, but had a sense that their meeting would be brief.

The waiter arrived with a strong half latte with one sugar, Sarah's usual, and a double espresso for Jack.

'I took the liberty,' Jack said, gesturing to the coffee.

'Oh thanks! Nothing wrong with your memory!' she said awkwardly, trying to lighten the mood.

He didn't smile, but picked up the espresso and knocked it back in one hit.

'I don't have a lot of time. I need your help.' Jack was incredibly distracted, his eyes darting around the coffee shop.

Careful. She might think you're paranoid.

'Anything, Jack. Just name it. I trust you. As do others. We've seen your fabulous work. You don't deserve... *this*.'

Jack ignored her attempts at solidarity.

'It's not so much your help I need,' he spoke rapidly. 'It's your husband's.'

'*Sam?* What do you want with *him?*' She looked concerned.

'You said he is a photojournalist, right?'

'One of the best.' She thought of his award-winning shots of the devastation and heartache that followed the London terrorist attack from a few years earlier.

Jack was startled as the door to the café swung closed with a bang. 'Is he still off work, at home with the boys?' he asked, hopefully.

'Yes. Why? What's this about Jack? What does Sam have to do with it?'

'I'm sorry, but I can't give you the specifics. I just can't. I want to employ him for a short-term job. I need some photos taken... discretely. I will pay handsomely for his time and his skills. It's incredibly important. I promise he won't be in any danger. I really wouldn't ask unless it was so...'

'Danger? Why would he be in danger?'

Jack was standing already. He slid a small piece of paper into Sarah's palm and kissed her lightly on the cheek. And with that, he was gone.

Sarah finished her coffee. After a few minutes, she unfolded the note. It indicated that Jack wanted to meet Sam at an address in Notting Hill.

She read the final sentence three times to make sure she was not seeing things:

And bring the twins.

76

'IN MY HOMELAND we have saying, Jack: the tongue is enemy of the neck.' As he said this, Lalic smiled and made a slicing gesture with his index finger across his throat. 'People usually make big mistake when they talk. When they not quiet. Quiet people live longest.'

Jack had called Lalic a few hours earlier and suggested they meet. Alone. No Mortimer. No bodyguards. Just a doctor and a father with one common interest: Joel. He agreed instantly.

Bruno, the guard, dressed in his customary black, had met Joel downstairs and accompanied him up to the penthouse. He then promptly disappeared, leaving the two men alone.

'I can't accept this,' he said sternly.

It broke his heart to do so, but Jack threw the rare, first edition copy of *Brave New World* down on to the coffee table that sat between them. He could never take any pleasure in it now, knowing how it had made its way to him.

Lalic grimaced. 'You should be careful with that, Jack. Nathan tell me that is some valuable book.'

'Joel is…' Jack began, but he was cut short by Lalic.

'Jack, Jack, Jack. Don't be in rush. Come. Sit. Have drink. Easier to chat when throat not so… *dry.*' He pulled out a couple of crystal glasses and a rare Remy Martin cognac.

Jack watched Lalic like a hawk as the big man poured the drinks. It seemed safe.

Seemed.

His throat was certainly dry.

'Cheers, Doctor.'

Lalic drank first, then Jack. The warmth of the strong alcohol was a welcome comfort.

'My boy like you. This is important. He tell me you listen to all he says and he feel better.'

'He is an incredible person, Ivan. Courageous. And, yes, I can get him better. He is already sta…' Lalic cut him off again.

'Yes, yes, you will. But what is *better?* What this mean? I tell you what I think it mean. Better mean he not cause *problem*. He just be very quiet. He not talk so much. Not cause problem for him. Not cause problem for me. Not cause problem for *you.*'

'I don't see how…'

It was clear Lalic had his own script to follow.

'Because you already have big problem, yes?' He stared down at Jack's groin, pointed, and laughed. 'This is where you have problem! You like to fuck! Big problem for you. Big problem.' He laughed again, much harder.

> *How did he know? It could only be through Mortimer, surely. But why tell Lalic?*

Lalic pressed on, 'You are good listener, Jack. You hear much. You see much. Maybe too much. In my country, I am problem solver. Problems is good business. I can make problem. I can end problem. In London, I am in same business: make problem, solve problem.'

Jack took another sip of his cognac.

'Joel is love of my life. But he also big problem. So you see, Jack, we can make little business for ourselves. You solve problem for me. Keep Joel quiet. And maybe I solve problem for *you.* Everybody win.'

Lalic finished his drink.

'You want him kept on the ward? Sedated?'

'Bravo! Make problem. Solve problem. Easy.'

77

JACK WATCHED AS the slim, casually dressed man pushed the side-by-side pram along the West London street. He had recognised Sam Wellington immediately, even from a distance. He was the picture of organisation, just like his wife.

As Sam reached the designated meeting place, Jack made the first move, to encourage a sense of familiarity for anyone who may be watching.

Following.

'Sam. It's nice to see you again,' he said brightly, with an outstretched hand. Sam shook it, and, thankfully, returned the enthusiasm.

'Jack,' he replied. 'Great to see you too.'

'And how are Olivia and William?'

'Very well. And thankfully…' he gestured down to the two sleeping toddlers.

They headed inside. The children remained asleep as they made their way to the same corner table where Jack had met Maddie.

'Thanks for coming, Sam. I really appreciate it.' Jack surveyed the room anxiously.

'That's okay. Sarah speaks very highly of you, but this all seems a bit…'

A bit what, Sam? A bit weird that I've been suspended for sleeping with a patient and then I ask to meet up with you out of the blue?

'… a bit… *worrying*. All this cloak and dagger stuff.'

Jack surveyed the room again.

'Yeah, I know. I can't explain right now. Just trust me, Sam. It's something that could help many, many people. The less you know, the better. So I'll be brief. I need some photos. Some covert surveillance. You won't be at risk. I'll cover your expenses, including any babysitting you need for the twins.'

Sam Wellington looked unconvinced and gravely concerned.

'Sam, I really wouldn't be asking if it wasn't critical.'

Jack could see he was considering what had been requested.

'Who is the subject?' he eventually asked. Jack slid a small black and white photo across the table to him.

'This man.'

'Professor Nathan Mortimer! Obviously I know who he is, although I've never met him in person.'

Jack nodded. 'That's good. He seems to spend a lot of time in Switzerland. Geneva. I really need to know why.'

'Geneva? I'm definitely going to need a babysitter, then.'

78

PACING AROUND HIS apartment only seemed to make matters worse. Other than meeting Sarah at the café, he'd had no contact with anyone from work. No one wanted to risk being associated with him.

He had contacted a defence lawyer about his suspension and the complaints made by Lear and Brenner, and was told it would take time to build a case for him. Until then, he was stuck.

Waiting.

He was never any good at just sitting around, even as a kid.

His suspension meant he was unable to get back into the Nicholas Tindal Centre and do any digging for Portman. The timing of his liaison with a former patient, and the subsequent 'discovery' of what had taken place seemed suspiciously coincidental, given what else had happened in Rome. It seemed as though they must have been aware of his meeting with the Interpol agent and taken immediate steps to get him out of the way.

The monotony of the morning was broken by a long run, followed by the arrival of the post. He flicked through half a dozen bills and various scraps of junk mail before discovering a small envelope at the bottom of the pile. His name and address were handwritten in a distinctive style that he instantly recognised.

After reading the short note inside he grabbed his laptop and flipped up the screen. He went straight to the British Airways website and booked himself a seat on the next flight to New York.

79

JACK WAS ALREADY on his third espresso of the morning as he gazed out of the window of the small Manhattan café. He had slept poorly the night before and he needed the caffeine like he needed oxygen. Despite the jetlag, he was restless and agitated. He had arrived early and didn't know what to do with himself.

He checked his watch again. Still three hours until he could see Theo Stein.

He would know what to do.

Jack looked around the café. An assortment of newspapers, magazines and brochures for Broadway shows were stacked up on one end of the counter. He walked over, grabbed several of the brightly coloured pamphlets, and started making his way through them.

Cats. The Producers. Frozen. Hamilton.

At the bottom of the pile there was a black and white newspaper promoting off-Broadway shows in the smaller theatres around the city.

He thumbed through it, barely taking in the titles as he moved from page to page. A dried coffee stain marked page thirty-five. It caught his eye. Ever so briefly. But even that split second was long enough.

Two faces looked back at him from under the coffee stain. One was strangely familiar.

The photograph was part of an advertisement for a production of *Waiting for Godot* which was playing at the small Odeon Star Theatre in Greenwich Village.

'Standout performances... 4 stars!'

'The best Godot in years!'

'Stanton and Bale are unbelievable!'

He looked back at the faces. The older one, the one on the left, he knew that face.

I've seen you before.

But where?

He read the name underneath the picture. *Stephen Bale.* He repeated it silently to himself a dozen times, but continued to draw a blank. He closed his eyes momentarily, and then stared again at the serious face, trying to think what was familiar about it.

Was it the eyes?

The nose?

The mouth?

The chin?

The hair?

The hair!

Yes, that was it. That thick, full head of curly grey hair. That hair. That face.

Jack opened his eyes.

Rome.

Jeffrey Lear.

Laura.

He pulled out his phone and Googled Jeffrey Lear. The photos of him bore no resemblance to the actor in the newspaper in front of him.

Jack was now certain. It was not Jeffrey Lear who was in that bar in Rome. So it stood to reason that his female companion was not

Laura Brenner. She might have been a pretty good facsimile of Laura Brenner. But it was not her.

So, who was she?

An actor as well, no doubt.

He pulled out his phone again and Googled Stephen Bale. The results led Jack to a theatrical agent's website where Bale was listed as a client. There were more photos of Bale which only confirmed Jack's suspicions. The actor's career had been quite varied career. No major roles but several minor parts, including some television work, which appeared to have sustained his career.

No doubt the fee for the 'one night only' performance in Rome would have been irresistible for Bale. Jack looked through all the female actors on the agent's website, but there was no one who resembled 'Laura'.

He went back to the page dedicated to Bale and scrolled through his recent roles, looking for any younger, blonde, female co-stars.

He drew a blank, but right at the bottom of the page there was a link to 'baleactingschool.com'. Jak immediately clicked in the link. He scrolled past Bale's biography, the class programs, the tuition fees, until he finally found the testimonials page, with accompanying headshots of the studio's recent attendees.

And there she was.

Imogen Davis.

A few months prior, she had completed Bale's 8-week course on 'character acting' and gave her teacher a glowing endorsement in her comments.

'Stephen offers the best-value courses in New York. A true professional and a wonderful teacher…'

I hope it was worth every fucking cent.

80

TOWARDS THE END of his regular session with Tilly Wilson, Dr Theo Stein did a very rare thing: he interrupted his patient and stopped her from speaking.

He had no choice. The pain had become unbearable.

His chest was burning.

'I'm sorry…' he stammered. 'I … need… you… to stop.'

The patient dutifully stopped speaking. She knew how unusual his request was. She heard the therapist gasp for breath. Instantly, she sat up on the couch and spun around to look at him.

'Oh, Dr Stein! Are you okay? You don't look well at all.'

His breathing had become laboured, and the colour had drained from his face.

The pain had spread lower, down into his abdomen. Intense nausea engulfed him.

He had read numerous articles over the years on poisonings. His thoughts were interrupted by a sudden need to vomit.

He then lost control of his bowels.

When he regained his composure, he resumed the search in his mind. He listed the symptoms to himself.

He stared at the empty teacup on his desk.

Polonium.

He was done for.

The patient was now on her feet. 'What can I do, Dr Stein? Call an ambulance?'

'Yes. Ambulance… and…'

It was becoming a struggle to speak. He knew that very soon it would also be difficult to think and then…

While Tilly was calling the ambulance, Theo stumbled to his writing bureau. He scrawled a brief note to Jack, placed it inside an envelope, and wrote his friend's address on the front.

'Post this. Vital…'

He handed the envelope to his patient and then collapsed to the floor.

'Post this? Oh, I don't think so, Dr Stein.'

Theo stared up at her helplessly.

'Your three million is not refundable, either.'

Theo was unable to speak.

Tilly had genuinely called the paramedics, although she knew it was pointless. Just a necessary part of the charade. She stared down at the dying man for a moment, then casually walked over to the mirror, where she gazed at her reflection as she worked herself up into a state of 'distress'. Then she walked over to the consulting room door and opened it, in anticipation of the paramedics' arrival.

She jumped when she saw a tall, young man with blonde hair and wide, blue eyes standing in the waiting room.

81

Jack was speechless at the scene that confronted him.

A shaking female patient.

Theo close to death.

His dear friend and mentor.

Dying.

He had travelled to New York to seek counsel with Theo, but reality had now slapped him hard. And in the most painful way. Tilly stuttered that the paramedics were on their way.

She looked stunned.

Jack ran to Theo. The old man looked very pale, the colour had drained from his sunken cheeks.

Jack grabbed his wrist. The pulse was thready and weak.

And very irregular.

'Theo. Theo,' he whispered into his ear as he supported his head.

'*Tihhhhl*'. But his voice faded softly into silence.

Jack asked Tilly what had happened, but she seemed too upset to explain.

He stood up and saw she was holding an envelope from Theo's own personal stationery. With his name on the front.

He grabbed it from her hand.

'I'm Jack Giorgio,' he said.

She was about to speak when the paramedics burst in.

82

EVEN THOUGH THE handwriting was messy and bordering on illegible, Jack instantly recognised it as Dr Stein's. The numerous letters they had exchanged over the years allowed Jack to pick out the distinctive style.

He was not sure what to make of Tilly. She seemed to be genuinely shocked, but there was something that didn't feel quite right. The paramedic crew who declared Theo dead took her to the local ER for an assessment. He'd have to let it go, for now.

When Jack tore open the envelope, a small piece of Stein's personalised writing paper fell onto his lap.

Jack carefully folded out the note and stared down at the scrawled message.

It took him some minutes to decipher it, but he was confident that it read:

Palermo 2000.

He tossed the message around in his mind for several more minutes. The first image that came into his mind was of the city in northern Sicily. But he had never been there and had no connection to the island. He had never discussed the city with Theo, either. And as for 2000, was it referring to the year? Or an event? Or a particular model of some kind of device? Or did it have some cryptic meaning and he was being too literal?

Whatever the meaning of the message, he couldn't decipher it.

Jack's heart rate quickened when he Googled the phrase 'Palermo 2000' and over twenty-two million results appeared in a fraction of a second.

Twenty-two million!

'Talk about needles and haystacks,' he muttered to himself.

He started making his way through the results.

Initially, he found himself looking at images of Palermo and its associated features, such as the city's coat of arms, the geography, the architecture, and the beloved football team. Being a devoutly Catholic region there were also several hits related to the various religious activities that occurred in Palermo in the spiritually significant year 2000.

By the fifth page of results, he was almost ready to give up, when he spotted an obscure-sounding reference to the United Nations and key international legislation. He clicked on the link.

The page he landed on was part of the UN website, and described a conference that took place in Palermo in 2000. As Jack read on, he realised that a convention had been drafted at the conference that dealt with international organised crime.

> *Nice touch. Hosting a convention on organised crime in Palermo, Sicily! I wonder if the mafia were invited along to give a keynote speech.*

More specifically, the convention addressed the devastating issue of human trafficking by organised crime networks, along with other illegal activities such as the manufacture and trade of firearms.

> *Firearms?*

He instantly thought of Lalic.

His eyes widened when he saw the heading of the section that followed.

> *Illegal Organ Trade.*

He thought of Portman.

There were details of tragic case studies describing individuals who had been trafficked from their homeland to other nations in order to give up a kidney or part of their liver. Sometimes they were paid a pittance, and at other times the organs were simply harvested— stolen, essentially—and the donor was then discarded.

Several donors died soon after their surgery.

Jack was intrigued to read the vast legislation that related to human trafficking and illegal organ transplants. There was an enormous amount of detail relating to the criminal offences associated with the trade. Despite that, he wondered how all of this was relevant to him.

> *You clearly wrote this for a very important reason, Theo. What is it?*

He stared at the screen, then closed his eyes, relaxed, and threw the words around inside his mind.

> *Palermo.*

> *Firearms.*

> *Lalic.*

> *Trafficking.*

> *Organs.*

83

SIR ROGER MAXWELL was completely absorbed by the boxing on the big screen TV. The cheers that erupted from the pub's other patrons were irritating, but not as irritating as Chaz King's right hook, which was connecting with his opponent's jaw every time he took a swing. The health minister gripped his pint of bitter and watched on.

Come on you fat fucker. I've got a lot riding on you.

He loathed getting out among the common man, especially in such putrid surrounds. He was appalled that Horatio had picked this place to meet. At least here, among the more stupid of his constituents, no one had recognised him. Or if they did, they didn't bother to acknowledge it.

Suits me fine.

Another blow was landed by King, and the bell mercifully rang to end the second round. Chatter broke out in the busy pub, full of amateur analysis of the fight.

Maxwell turned back to the bar and ordered another pint when a firm hand landed on his shoulder. He jumped.

'Take it easy, old boy, you'll give a chap a heart attack sneaking up like that.'

'I'm quite sure you would be given a priority angiogram,' Horatio laughed at his own quip.

'*Ha ha,*' Maxwell mocked. 'Drink?'

The two men sat at a small corner table. Maxwell looked around nervously, but the fight had started again and the other patrons were wholly distracted.

'So how's the farm?' Maxwell asked quietly.

'The weather conditions are just right, it seems. Harvest is on track.'

Maxwell nodded.

'Any disease among the cattle this season?'

'None that we can detect. The vet has given them a thorough once-over. All healthy. One or two came back with a few issues, so we naturally put them down right away. The cattle truck is fuelled up and ready to go.'

Horatio sipped on his vodka.

> *Only you would order a drink like that in a working man's pub*

'My team and I would be grateful if the proposal for the next phase of our research could be given the go ahead. Viruses are very sexy right now, Minister, as I'm sure you are aware, 'said Horatio.

Maxwell nodded. '*Very* sexy right now. I have looked at your proposal and I'm sure there will be no problem securing the funds from the exchequer. I've already made a strong case to the cabinet. Research into viruses is just what these idiots want to see.' He gestured towards the other drinkers as he spat these last words.

'Excellent,' said Horatio. 'I'd like to give the farm hands a time frame, of course.'

'Seven days.'

Horatio finished his drink.

A raucous cheer went up when Charlie King landed a knockout blow.

Maxwell grimaced.

84

SAM HANDED JACK a brown envelope. Jack had returned to London the day before, and he could not meet Sam fast enough.

'Your man certainly does spend a lot of time in Geneva,' he said.

'MTR?' Jack asked.

'No. Never.'

Jack was shocked. 'So what *does* he do there?'

'He seems to attend some sort of medical clinic. He was in and out of there several times. It's clearly a private clinic. Very discrete. No signage out the front. Darkened windows. No external indication of what the building is used for. It was definitely not the sort of place where you can just walk up to reception and ask what goes on inside.'

'So how do you know it's a medical clinic?' asked Jack.

'It's a glorious old building. I put a couple of cameras around my neck and told the receptionist I was an architecture student and wanted to know something about the building's history. I asked if I could take a few photos.'

Jack nodded.

'She agreed that I could take some pictures of the *outside* of the building.'

'I see,' said Jack.

'As I was snapping away, a waste truck arrived. A medical disposals waste truck with a black and yellow radiation sign on the side. You know the ones?'

Jack did.

'I followed the truck around to a rear entrance, but it quickly disappeared behind a security gate. About thirty minutes later, the gate slid open. I stopped the driver as he was heading out and flashed up my press ID. I said I was doing a story on the new congestion tax introduced for heavy vehicles in Geneva, and asked how this was impacting him. Would he switch to an electric truck. That sort of crap.' Sam could see Jack had suppressed a laugh.

'Talk about thinking on your feet!'

'Yeah, well I managed to hold him up with the gate open for a few minutes and I just caught a glimpse of a few blokes in white coats. I also saw a guy in a hazmat suit. Totally covered.'

'Interesting. And confusing,' Jack said, wide-eyed.

'I asked the driver what sort of waste he was carrying, but he just growled at me and drove off. When I walked around to the front again, I almost bumped into your man, Mortimer. He just snarled at me, *Watch where you're fucking going.* Didn't even look at me.'

'You've done a great job, Sam. I have a hunch about what is going on.'

'Well here are the pictures. As you can see, he stayed at the Woodward Hotel. In a suite overlooking the water. Staying there for one night costs more than I make in a month!'

'Was he up to anything else?'

'Not that I could see. He went from the Woodward to the medical place and back again.'

'Thanks so much, Sam. You've been a huge help.'

85

JACK KNEW ABOUT the multi-million-dollar lawsuits that had been successfully filed against the big drug companies. Many of these actions were successful and uncovered the propensity of big pharma to falsify research and cover up instances of adverse effects, and even deaths, in their own drug trials.

'But what you know about, what you see in the papers, that's just the tip of the iceberg. These companies are doing deals to settle claims every single day. And because these claims are settled out of court, you just don't hear about them. The patients and their families sign water-tight confidentiality agreements, so they get their money on condition that they keep their mouths shut,' said Portman with authority.

He looked at Jack to make sure he was fully engaged, before continuing. 'Complaints are so common that the companies even have special funds set aside to deal with these claims. Hell, they have entire departments just to manage all of the lawsuits.'

Both men sat and stared out into the glorious green expanse of Hyde Park. The blue skies and afternoon sun were a welcome break from the crowded indoor spaces of London.

'But ultimately, the executives of these corporations don't lose much sleep at night. What they pay out is a drop in the ocean compared to their overall incomes and profits. The public may be shocked from time to time when they read about the latest hundred million dollar fine or fifty million dollar compensation payout, but that is pocket change to these guys.'

'I would have thought they would care a great deal about having to hand over that sort of money.'

Portman rolled his eyes.

'Not compared to the tens of billions they pull in each year in revenue. It's all about sales, Jack. And believe me, sales are strong.'

'But surely in this day and age of corporate responsibility and transparency, big businesses buying their way out of problems can't go on forever, Portman?'

'Why not? It's like the great codeine paradox!'

'The great *what?*'

'Think about codeine, Jack. Wonderful stuff, right? Tried and tested for hundreds of years in one form or another. It's brought pain relief to millions and millions of sufferers, of that there can be no doubt. But what they don't tell you about is the hyper-analgesia response that gets people hooked for decades.'

Portman looked away for a moment and sighed deeply.

'It's a codeine-induced pain hypersensitivity syndrome.'

'A what?'

Clearly, this was one area of medicine where Portman held superior knowledge. Jack wondered if part of this knowledge came from personal experience.

'The very drug that you are taking to relieve the pain, the drug that you become addicted to, actually makes the pain worse. So what do you do? You take more… and more… and more.'

Jack nodded.

'Big pharma knows about this, of course. And after centuries of use, why has codeine addiction really only become a widespread problem in the past thirty years?'

Jack was not entirely sure of the answer.

He took an educated guess: 'Because it is cheap and available?'

'No, Jack, no. *Because people are in pain.* And the drug companies will remind you of that if you happen to forget it.'

Portman then switched his tone to mimic that of a smooth and slick advertisement voiceover.

'Aches? Stiffness? Soreness? Pain? You don't have to put up with that! No one has to suffer any longer, including *you*... thanks to... codeine!'

'So it's marketing, then?'

'Yes, Jack, but the primary focus of the marketing isn't the drug itself—it's the *problem*. You sell the problem, the symptoms, the disease, and the illness. Give people a name for their self-perceived misery. Give them a *diagnosis*.'

'And then step in with the solution. The cure.'

'Precisely.'

'But how did they do that with codeine?'

'Jack, we live in a world where every problem is now medicalised and pathologised. Every problem has a medical explanation and therefore a medical treatment. Minor lower back pain, which normally just gets better in about six weeks, is fixed *right now* with codeine. And, of course, when someone takes it when they are in acute pain they feel much better, physically and psychologically, and so they keep taking it... and taking it... and taking it...' his voice trailed off as he looked into the distance.

Jack was familiar with the marketing strategies...

> *'If you're not feeling one hundred per cent all of the time, there's something wrong with you!'*

'But the irony is,' Portman continued, 'that if you take enough codeine for long enough then you end up with two problems: an addiction *and* chronic pain.' He sighed: 'Fucking big pharma.'

A couple walked past, hand in hand. Jack's mind found its way back to Cerise.

He realised he was fed up with being swept along in this mess.

Being used as a pawn by Mortimer and Portman, and God knows who else. Suspended from work. False allegations. Career in tatters. Cast aside. All for what?

No more.

It was time to take some action.

'I can't get Cerise out of my mind,' Jack confessed. The Interpol agent looked down, clearly uncomfortable about the unexpected admission.

'You knew a lot about her, right?'

'Well… yeah.'

'Kept a close eye on her?'

'Yeah,' Portman said slowly, uncertain where Jack was going with this.

'Surveillance, right?'

Portman nodded.

'Including her flat?'

Both men suddenly became very aware of the implications of that question.

'Save your modesty, Portman. I don't care about *that*. But you must have had access to her place, right?'

'Where are you going with this, Giorgio?'

86

JACK SLID THE housekey that Portman had reluctantly given him back into his pocket and looked around. The house was just as he remembered it. Sparsely furnished and neat as a pin. *Minimalist.* The lounge room had a sterile, display-home feel. He walked through to the kitchen. Immaculate. Unused.

After all, no one really *lived* there.

Likewise, the bedroom was untouched. The bed was made and not a single crease mark could be seen on the crisp white quilt cover. The pillows were fluffed. The wardrobes were now empty. He stared longingly down at the bed and the memories flooded back. It was too much. He turned and began to walk out.

He stopped.

Swivelling around, he stared back at the bedroom. He took a short, quick breath as his eyes captured one small yet significant difference.

The single bedside table now sat on the opposite side of the bed. He was sure of it.

He looked inside. Empty.

His fingers slid down the back of it. Nothing.

Why would she have moved it?

Jack gripped both sides and moved it towards him. Nothing but floorboards were revealed.

He stared down at the floor and noticed that the tiny gap between two of the boards appeared slightly wider than the rest. He grabbed a knife from the kitchen and prised up the board closest to the skirting. It came away easily, revealing a cavernous space under the floor.

He flicked the iPhone torch on and gazed down into the vault below.

Laid out in organised piles under the bedroom floor were numerous newspapers, magazines, documents, and books. There were also printouts of pages from various websites.

At first glance, there seemed to be a randomness to the publication dates and contents. The only thing that appeared to link them was that someone, presumably Cerise, had highlighted certain sections with a bright pink fluorescent marker. She had also made notes in various places adjacent to these highlighted areas.

Jack pulled the papers out of their hiding place, so that he could examine the notes more closely. The first item that caught his eye was a newspaper article about polio vaccinations in Africa. She had not highlighted complete sentences but specific words.

> *Virus.*
>
> *Poverty.*
>
> *Charity.*
>
> *MSF.*
>
> *Charity.*

Jack looked up to the ceiling with his eyes closed and allowed the words to run around inside his mind.

He found more words highlighted.

> *Big pharma.*
>
> *Drug companies.*
>
> *MTR.*

These papers were sitting on top of a neatly stacked pile of articles referring to one specific subject: Professor Nathan Mortimer. Newspaper articles, magazine stories, financial information, documents about his previous companies. A complete catalogue of his career and his success. She had annotated some of these.

NM – believer.

Funding.

Implants – Positrex??

He then studied a neat assortment of newspaper clippings and printouts from various news websites. They were all written by the same journalist: African correspondent, Cerise Lyon.

The articles were mainly focused on corruption in certain African nations and the impact this had on the general population. Other stories covered healthcare in Africa, and the pharmaceutical companies—including MTR—that had offered to vaccinate children against a range of infectious illnesses. Some articles even described the race to perfect the world's first HIV/AIDS vaccine and the relief that this would bring to the continent.

The name Cerise was also highlighted in pink. There were several pictures of the journalist that had been cut out and placed among the papers.

The final story was a magazine article, in which Cerise Lyon had interviewed the chief of medical research at MTR about the future of the pharmaceutical industry. On the first page, there was a photo of Lyon with the scientist. Jack stared down at the caption that read: Cerise Lyon interviews Jose Navarro of MTR by Lake Geneva.

Navarro was highlighted.

Jack sat and read through the entire piece. Navarro spoke optimistically about the next ten to twenty years of pharmacological and genetic research and the benefits it could bring to billions of people. Navarro also spoke about the potential for nanotechnology to precisely deliver medications but, in his opinion, this was realistically at least a decade away.

Jack recalled his conversation with Cerise at *Stock*.

Nanotechnology.

'We have two patents for micro-sized mechanical delivery devices,' she had told him.

There is always a seed of truth.

At the article's conclusion, Jack was sad to read that it had been published posthumously, as the journalist, Cerise Lyon, had been killed a week after the interview by Sudanese militants in a bungled extortion attempt.

He rifled through the remaining documents and discovered birth certificates, driver's licences, and passports. Two of everything. The tattered, faded passport of Sandrine Besson sat on top of the newish-looking passport of Cerise Navarro. The photographs were identical. To Jack's eye they both looked absolutely legitimate, although the only explanation was that the more recent documents were black market acquisitions that 'Cerise' had exchanged for cash in some seedy Sudanese backstreet.

He suddenly started to cry.

87

ONCE JACK HAD composed himself, he looked down at the annotations that had been made in the margins of the texts. Most of it was an illegible scrawl. There were various names written that he did not recognise.

In several places, she had simply written *MTR* in various fonts and sizes.

In other areas she had written:

MTR = Money Through Robbery

MTR = Murder Through Research

MTR = My Tomorrows Returned

Buried in amongst another pile of papers he found a car rental receipt for a black BMW convertible. He checked the date. It was the day he first met Cerise. The day they went out for lunch together.

Before replacing the floorboards, he took one last look around with the torch. The beam glinted off something at the bottom of the hole. He reached down, pulled out a small glass container, and held it up to the light. It held a tiny white plastic rectangle. He carefully slipped the container into his jacket pocket.

Jack found himself thinking of a dinner that Cerise had organised around three months after they'd met. She'd sent him a text message with the name of the restaurant and a demand for him to be there.

She had chosen a very expensive French establishment, which was more than fine with Jack, but when he met her out the front she was wearing a very sexy, very short white dress and had really gone to town with her makeup, which was unlike her. It seemed a bit like a role-playing fantasy and, truth be told, although Jack found it very playful and highly arousing, he was not sure the maître d' would be as understanding.

They had been promptly shown to their table in a dimly lit corner of the restaurant. Jack started to relax as they sipped their Dom Perignon.

Cerise had been effervescent that night. Chatty, witty, and seemingly very happy. She had been extremely busy with work, and Jack had found it reassuring to see her so relaxed.

'I want you to order anything you like, baby,' she insisted. 'Tonight is on me.'

'Well in that case, I might go for a bottle of the vintage Bordeaux,' he joked as he read the eye-watering price. Instantly, she moved to hail the waiter, but Jack stopped her. 'Just kidding,' he had laughed.

After they'd ordered, Cerise excused herself and went to the bathroom. Jack, and several other male diners, watched her longingly as she walked away.

Jack quickly swallowed the last of his champagne.

When she returned, Cerise walked right past the chair that was being held out for her by the waiter and kissed Jack on the cheek. She bent down and whispered in his ear.

'I *want* you. Right now.'

He smiled as she sat down.

When the waiter had left he said softly, 'Mmm… I wish.'

'Right now,' she repeated, more forcefully.

He looked nervously around the restaurant, which was starting to fill up. 'Right now?'

She turned and looked in the direction of the bathrooms.

'Oh absolutely.' She found his hand under the table and slid something silky and soft into it.

'I took the liberty of removing these. To make it easier for you.'

Jack found himself blushing. She was serious. He had always considered himself to have a healthy libido, but he'd never been a risk-taker. He was also well aware of the potential implications for his career if he was ever caught in the act in a public place.

Implications for your career.

Retrospectively, the irony didn't escape him.

'Cerise, you look utterly gorgeous and you're really turning me on, but what if we get caught? Let's skip dinner and go back to my place,' he pleaded.

A wicked grin spread across her face. 'Don't worry, I've checked, and there's a large disabled bathroom that no one dining here is going to use.'

Jack was both appalled and aroused.

Cerise slipped out of her shoes and her foot found his shin under the table. Then his knee, then his thigh.

Sweat had formed in the palm of his hand. He could feel it being soaked up by her underwear.

When her foot rose even higher, he grabbed it with his free hand.

'Okay.'

What am I doing?

'Give me a thirty second head start,' she said excitedly before disappearing towards the bathrooms.

When he felt that no one was watching, Jack casually strode towards the door. When he opened it, she was waiting. He made sure the door was locked and quickly slid up her tight dress.

She had waxed.

His mouth went dry. His pulse quickened as he quietly moved toward her.

The classical chamber music that flowed from a speaker in the corner of the bathroom made Jack feel like he was in a cheap porno.

She reached out and undid his belt. They kissed feverishly before Cerise spun around and braced herself against the immaculate porcelain vanity unit. She looked up at her own image in the mirror.

She spread her legs and bent, ever so slightly, at the knees.

'Fuck me, Jack,' she whispered breathlessly.

An image entered his mind of the entrees arriving and the waiter looking around for them.

> *I don't think I can do this.*

She rocked back against him. A hand moved around and attempted to guide him into her. He was sweating profusely.

> *I can't… I just can't.*

His thighs felt weak and fatigued. He turned his head and looked at the door. He was sure someone was right outside. He started to quiver. Cerise misinterpreted this as desire.

'Come on, baby,' she urged. '*Come on!*'

> *It's going cold out there. I've gone cold.*

'Come on, honey. Do me.'

He backed away. 'I'm sorry. I just can't.'

She looked at him blankly before turning around to the mirror and readjusting her dress and hair. She marched out of the bathroom without looking at him. He waited a minute before joining her back at the table.

She was already getting started on her entrée when he sat down.

'I'm sorry,' he said. 'I was just too anxious.'

'That's fine,' she said in a bland tone as she munched away on her mushroom crepes.

He could tell that she was annoyed.

Give me a break, Cerise.

He reached out and grabbed her hand. 'But when we get home, I'm sure it will be a different story.'

'The moment has passed,' she said coldly.

The rest of the meal was eaten quickly, her annoyance remaining palpable. They made superficial small talk right up until the bill was paid. The drive home was just as icy.

As they neared her home, she turned to him and asked, 'Is it me, Jack? Is it that you just don't find me sexy?'

He was stunned. 'That's ridiculous! Of course I find you sexy. I don't understand how you would think otherwise. What happened tonight was my issue.'

That entire evening now took on a whole new significance. The extreme impulsivity, the disinhibition, the sudden anger and paranoia about their relationship. All were hallmarks of her psychotic state of mind. Pressure and stress seemed to exacerbate this inside her ill mind.

He looked back down at the articles, the passports, the scrawled handwriting. *Cerise. Sandrine.* Africa. He then knew that her delusions did not just stop at paranoid thoughts about corporations but had infected and changed her very identity. He had seen this so many times in severe psychosis.

Oh Cerise.

88

JACK WAS SURPRISED to see Portman drinking a pint of lager when he walked into the Clapham pub. Given Portman's line of work, Jack imagined there would be rules about drinking, especially on the job. Portman noticed Jack staring.

'You don't need to worry. It's allowed.'

'Half-full, or half-empty?' Jack asked with a smile, pointing at the glass.

Portman shook his head. 'Very funny. But don't try and analyse me, Doctor Freud.'

'Doctor Freud? I'm flattered! But am I a half-empty or a half-full Dr Freud?'

Jack grabbed a San Pellegrino and the two men settled into a booth. Much like Maddie, Portman had the well-developed skill of being able to keep focused on the conversation while simultaneously scanning the room.

Jack got right to the point. 'You know more about Cerise than you let on, Portman. I want to know everything. I am owed that, at least.'

Portman remained silent.

'Tell me,' Jack demanded.

'There are more pressing matters at hand, Doctor.'

'Not for me. Why won't you tell me?'

'Because it is classified information, Giorgio. That's why.'

> *Time to roll the dice, Jack. Let him think you know more than you do.*

'I know about Africa. I know about the *real* Cerise. Cerise Lyon. The journalist who was murdered...' He was on the edge of revealing more, but stopped himself.

Just hold back, Jack. Don't over-reach.

The play proved to have been well worth it, as he got the desired response. Portman's eyes widened just a touch, but enough to tell Jack he was on the right track.

'How do you know about that?' Portman asked quietly.

'Sorry, that's classified information.'

'Don't be smart with me, Giorgio.' Portman emptied his glass. He placed it carefully back on the table and sighed. 'Okay. But what I'm about to tell you does not leave this room.'

'Of course,' Jack said sincerely.

'Does. Not. Leave. This. Room,' he said slowly and clearly. He signalled to the bartender. He was going to need another pint.

He spoke quietly. 'Sandrine... Cerise... was *not* one of the bad guys.'

Jack was stunned, but also relieved. 'But you had said that...'

'Yeah, I *know* what I said,' interrupted Portman. 'She was with Interpol, a senior agent. She was assigned to Africa four months before Lyon was killed. We were close to a major bust. MTR. It was going to be huge, Jack. *Huge*. We were looking at major indictments. Sandrine had done some amazing work gathering the evidence. She really *did* have the fancy science education. She knew a lot about pharmaceuticals and neurochemistry and all that jazz. Super bright girl. Which was exactly why we approached her. We didn't need to give her the hard sell. She believed her father had been poorly treated by the drug companies before he died, and she wanted to do the right thing. So we recruited her into the Interpol sub-branch that I manage.'

Jack was stunned.

Portman continued. 'She met Lyon in Khartoum a month before her death. Lyon had been based in Africa for some years and had some important contacts. Sandrine tried to persuade her to become an informant, but Lyon resisted.'

Portman stopped talking as the bartender came over with his beer.

'Sandrine found out that Lyon was going to do a feature story on a scientist, a guy called Navarro, from MTR. He was a key target of our investigation. We didn't know it, but a security firm used by MTR was trailing Lyon. They knew she had met with Sandrine, more than once, and so they assumed she was cooperating with our investigation.'

There's always a seed of truth.

'The interview went ahead, but a few days later, well, it seems you know what happened. It was a professional execution. No one was ever arrested in connection with Lyon's murder.'

'And Sandrine? She must have felt immense guilt,' Jack concluded.

Guilt. Pressure. Stress.

Psychosis.

'I assume so. Sandrine disappeared after that, along with all the evidence she had gathered.'

'Disappeared?'

'Without a trace. We put an APB Alert out, as we'd assumed she'd fled Sudan, and that her next move would be to try and get out of Africa altogether. It was only later that we realised she hadn't gone anywhere.'

'She was still in Sudan?' Jack asked.

'Right in Khartoum. Fuckin' unbelievable,' he said, looking up to the ceiling in exasperation. 'Needless to say, the whole operation was compromised. We had to shut it down.'

'Along with Sandrine's career.'

'Our next sighting of her was at an MTR conference.'

Jack cut in. It all made sense.

'I think the guilt and trauma caused her to form a delusional belief that she really *was* part of MTR, and to develop a hybrid identity which fused Cerise Lyon with Jose Navarro.'

'I can see that now. All we know is that a woman matching Sandrine's description walked onto the stage during the CEO's opening speech, grabbed the mic, and started talking about drug company corruption. MTR's security removed her from the stage, threw her out, and we didn't hear anything more about her until she showed up in London.'

'Anyway, it's all academic now, isn't it? Her death means that we'll never know the truth,' Jack said with sadness.

A subtle, indecipherable look flickered over Portman's face.

What did I just say, Portman?

Jack decided to explore what might have provoked that micro-reaction.

'There's got to be a personal cost when you lose a fellow agent. When one of your colleagues dies. You said yourself that the agents looking into medical crimes are a specialist division of Interpol, so I imagine it's a relatively small team.'

Portman just stared.

'So that would mean you'd be working closely with the other members of that team. You'd get to know each other very well, wouldn't you?'

Portman could not hide a look of discomfort.

'Especially one you *personally* recruited. What was it you said about her? Such a bright girl?'

Portman drank his beer and looked away.

'What is it? What are you not telling me?' Jack demanded. For a moment, he thought that Portman might start crying.

Are you that grief-stricken?

Portman took one last sweeping look around the bar.

'Jack, I'm sorry, but...'

'But *what*?'

'Sandrine is still alive.'

89

JACK COULD BARELY contain his rage. He clenched his fists under the table. The vitriolic hatred that he felt for Portman would have completely overwhelmed him if it wasn't for the sense of relief that was washing through him, knowing that she was still alive.

This time it was Jack who ordered a drink.

A double whiskey.

He knocked it back in one.

'You need to understand,' Portman tried to explain. 'She was too unstable. She was undermining our work. And we didn't want her to compromise you.'

'*Compromise me!*' Jack spat angrily. 'What the hell does that mean?'

'You became the best person to help us get the evidence we needed on Mortimer. We knew he had contacts, so we were silently watching him from a distance. He was suddenly back and forth from Geneva. Then Sandrine showed up out of the blue. At first, we had no idea what she was doing. So we just watched and waited. He had such a positive, public profile we couldn't rush in. We needed irrefutable evidence. Sandrine would meet Mortimer and we thought she might have found a connection. We were damn confused.'

Jack ordered another double and thought back to the documents he found in her flat about Mortimer.

Funding. Believer.

'But then you started falling in love with one another. We couldn't risk you having your judgement impaired. By then, *you* were then too important. We had to find a way of getting her out the picture. There were too many lives at risk.'

'Don't fucking patronise me!' Jack shouted. The bartender looked their way.

'Calm down,' Portman said in a quiet, controlled voice.

'We wouldn't want any attention coming your way, would we?' Jack said sarcastically. 'So you staged the accident? Made me believe she was dead. So that there was no risk of my judgement being impaired. Is that right?'

Portman nodded.

'Tell me where she is. I've stuck my neck out for you. The least you can do is tell me where she is.'

'I don't think that's a good idea, Jack.'

'Tell me where she is,' Jack repeatedly forcefully.

90

JACK WALKED INTO the foyer of the austere-looking building. His feet didn't seem to want to carry him any further.

I can do this.

He forced himself to take a few steps forward, and then hesitated again. He turned around and faced the front door.

I must do this.

He spun back around and headed to the reception desk.

'Welcome to St Margaret's Psychiatric Hospital. How may I help you?' asked the friendly young woman.

'Hi. Yes. My name is Jack. I'm here to visit a... a friend. Ceri... sorry... Sandrine Besson.'

The receptionist looked at Jack quizzically and then focused her eyes on the screen that sat just to her left. She scrolled down a list before returning to Jack.

'If you will just fill in this visitor's form, I'll be right back.'

She handed him a sheet of paper attached to a plastic clipboard with a pen that dangled from a thin metal chain.

He completed the paperwork with a nervous, shaking hand. When he was finished he realised that what he had written was barely legible, but when the receptionist returned she didn't even look at the form, and simply handed him a visitor's pass.

Jack had given expert evidence to the supreme court in murder trials, interviewed psychopathic killers in maximum security prisons, and taken specialist medical examinations in front of panels of professors, but as he entered Sandrine's ward, he had never felt so nervous in his life.

91

JACK SAT TENTATIVELY on the edge of an uncomfortable chair in the communal lounge. An old television set reflected a darkened version of the room back at him, and a miserable-looking plant sat drooped in the corner, desperate for sunshine and water.

In front of him was a small wooden coffee table covered with a messy pile of magazines, most of which were several years old. He reached out for a dog-eared copy of *National Geographic* when a petite set of feet came into view.

He didn't need to look up to know who they belonged to.

> *It feels like the very last moment before something changes forever.*

He looked up. Into her face.

Into her eyes.

His first impulse was to gently pull her down onto his lap and hold her tightly. But instead, he stood up.

'Cerise... I...'

She looked blankly at him and did not speak.

'Sorry,' he said. 'I mean Sandrine.'

She blinked slowly.

Without shifting his gaze, he reached out and took her hand in his. Her fingers felt stiff... hard... and they did not close around his own.

'Can we sit? So that we can talk? I'm sorry if this is a shock, but I needed to see you.'

She sat down on the couch next to him. Her hands were folded neatly on her lap. He leant forward with his elbows on his knees, then shifted, so that he was sitting back. He ran his fingers through his hair, and sighed.

He looked at her, longingly. 'It's incredible to see you. How are you? How are you feeling?'

'Not too bad.' It was the first she had spoken. 'Tired. I'm sleeping too much. I seem to stumble a lot.'

Her hair had grown long and a wispy tress fell forward as she spoke, covering one of her eyes. He slowly moved his hand up and brushed it back behind her ear. She didn't flinch.

She didn't respond at all.

She continued to sit there, staring ahead.

'Sleeping too much? Off-balance? Are you on too much med...'

No, Jack, no. Don't be the psychiatrist.

He softly placed his hand in the middle of her back. 'I've thought of you every day and dreamt of you most nights. What we had felt like such a beautiful thing. And then it was gone. I'm sorry. But I just had to see you.'

She looked towards him for the first time since they sat. 'You are a gorgeous man.' She rubbed his cheek with an open palm, slowly. He closed his eyes.

I remember this. Can't we please go back there? Can't you be Cerise again?

When he opened them again, he saw that she was smiling. A moment later she was giggling. He initially found it infectious and joined in with her. He convinced himself that it was some kind of happiness poking through. He reached down and took both of her hands in his.

'What is it?' he asked with a warm smile.

'It's amazing. They told me you would be coming and now you're here!' she said.

His smile quickly dissolved. '*Who* told you?'

'*Sssh!*' she put a finger up to his lips. 'I have to hear this.'

Jack quickly looked around the room. They were completely alone. The television was dark and silent, although he realised she was staring at it intensely. She continued to smile.

'What is it?' he whispered.

She tilted her head towards him but kept her gaze fixed on the TV. She laughed heartily again.

'They think you're gorgeous, too. They want to have you, but I will not let them.' She turned towards him suddenly, her expression had changed. 'But what have you really done with him?' she asked coldly.

It was as though she was surrounded by a glass wall. He could *see* her clearly, but he could no longer *feel* her.

'Sorry, I'm not following you.'

'Where is the *real* Jack?' She pointed an accusatory finger at him. The giggling was long gone.

She was angry.

He had seen this anger before.

'Tell me right now! What have you done with Jack?!'

'It's me. I am Jack!'

He jumped as the door to the lounge swung open..

'So sorry to interrupt you,' the nurse said. 'But it's time for Sandrine's afternoon medications.'

'Oh… sure,' he said.

Sandrine continued to glare at Jack.

The nurse looked at him sympathetically. 'And then she will need to rest.'

'I understand,' he said. 'I'll leave.'

He backed away, slowly, and cautiously waved goodbye.

Sandrine stared straight ahead, blankly, as unmoving as a statue.

92

AFTER HE LEFT Cerise, for she would always be *Cerise* to him, Jack headed home and immediately changed into his running gear. Some people drink. Some people smoke. Some do drugs. In times of crisis, Jack Giorgio would get out and run as hard as he could for as long as he could. Often to the point of vomiting.

He couldn't get out fast enough.

Jack soon found himself running at a rapid pace along the pedestrian track adjacent to Albert Embankment. The Thames, which sat to his left, became a blur. He passed walkers and even other runners as if they were standing still. The cloud cover made the conditions cool, spurring him on. He wondered how long he could keep going at such a speed, but the thought was quickly left behind as he pushed on.

He just ran.

He wanted to be arms, legs, and lungs. Nothing more.

> *Stride, stride, breathe.*

Despite his desire to shut his mind down, he knew that when he ran it was the meaningful conversations and experiences of the past that seemed to cascade through his head. Initially, they appeared random, but Jack knew that if he relaxed and just let them flow they would soon assemble themselves into an orderly pattern that would make sense.

A pattern that could be interpreted.

Within minutes, he was not surprised when he heard Cerise's words enter his mind.

> *Where is the real Jack?*
>
> *Where is my father?*

My father was a workaholic.

He died from multiple sclerosis.

Into anything and everything.

How much have you had to drink tonight?

Katherine really gave me a hard time tonight.

Where is the real Jack?

I stumble a lot.

Off-balance.

I'm worried about what happened in Boston.

I can't get up.

Off-balance.

I tripped over again.

Clumsy.

My father.

Boston marathon. Worried.

And then suddenly:

Keep running, Jack. You are burning fat.

Burning fat.

Fat.

Fat.

He shook his head as he ran. *Fat?* But before he could make sense of it:

Run harder.

Feel the acid in your legs, Jack. Feel the acid burn.

Fat.

Acid.

Burn.

Acid.

Fatty acids. Fatty acids.

Worried. She was hard on me.

He shook his head and quickened his pace.

My father. Workaholic. Multiple sclerosis.

I think they would call it ADD now!

He was forty-nine.

Dead at forty-nine.

I stumble a lot.

Off-balance.

That is young. Even for MS.

I had a few glasses of wine last night.

Great pre-race preparation.

I can't get up.

So scared.

Clumsy.

Fell again.

I couldn't sleep.

I'm tired.

Tired.

Off-balance.

Suddenly he stopped running and stared into the Thames.

93

JACK WAS BREATHING hard by the time he arrived back at the South London psychiatric hospital. He walked around outside for a few minutes in order to compose himself.

He doubted that anyone would listen to a sweaty, agitated, breathless man, no matter how convincing his argument. He went into the bathrooms in the foyer and washed his face. He looked at himself in the mirror and wondered exactly how he had ended up like this.

He was grateful that the first person he encountered when he entered the ward was the same nurse who had been caring for Sandrine earlier that day. She recognised him instantly.

'Visiting hours are over for today,' she informed him. 'And even if they weren't, Sandrine was quite agitated when she saw you earlier. She needs to get some rest. She is not up to seeing anyone at the moment.'

'Yes, I know,' Jack said. 'I'm not actually here to see her. I was wanting to speak with her treating doctor. I have some very important information. It is vital that I speak to the doctor who is looking after her.'

Stay calm, stay calm.

The nurse looked him up and down.

'Is this some sort of personal information?'

'It relates to her illness. My name is Doctor Jack Giorgio. I am a forensic psychiatrist at the Nicholas Tindal Centre. I apologise for my current appearance, but I feel I have something crucial to tell you all about her diagnosis. It could save her life!'

The nurse did not seem convinced. Jack could see she was weighing up whether she should call the doctor or the security guards. He needed to nudge her in the direction of calling the doctor.

'Is there something about Sandrine that you can't quite explain? Some of her balance issues and other symptoms that don't quite fit with a typical psychosis?'

She stared at him, thinking.

'Wait there,' she replied dryly, without any indication of what she was going to do. She disappeared onto the ward. Jack paced around in circles.

Get control of yourself. Pacing is not a good look.

A few minutes later, a tall, lanky man with thinning black hair and spectacles was standing beside him.

'I'm Doctor Stevenson, one of the senior registrars here. Can I help you?' he asked.

'I'm Doctor Jack Giorgio,' he offered a hand and Stevenson reluctantly shook it. 'Can we talk somewhere?'

Stevenson gestured towards a small interview room that sat just off the ward. Once they were seated, Jack wasted no time in getting to the point.

'Even though I have had a personal relationship with Sandrine, I am here in a psychiatric capacity,' began Jack. 'I don't know how much you know about her family history?'

Jack could tell that Stevenson was extremely reluctant to divulge information about Sandrine, which was quite reasonable under the circumstances. It was a situation Jack had found himself in many times. Breaching patient-doctor confidentiality was very serious and only reserved for the most extreme of situations.

'I'm sorry about my appearance,' Jack said, 'but it has just occurred to me, and I thought I should get straight over here.'

'*What* has just occurred to you?' Stevenson asked with concern.

'What may be underlying Sandrine's psychosis. I don't think she has schizophrenia. I am not here to tell anyone how to do their job, and I am sure that all of the usual physical screening checks have been done.'

Stevenson nodded but did not say anything. It became clear that he was not going to tell Jack anything.

Fine, I'll just lay it all out for you.

'Sandrine told me that her father died at forty-nine, from multiple sclerosis.' Stevenson's look did not indicate whether he knew this information or not. 'She has described him to me as someone who would have been diagnosed with ADD if he was a generation younger.'

Stevenson looked blankly at Jack.

'And now Sandrine has this very nasty psychosis which appears to intensify after exercise and with alcohol. Exercise and alcohol! And when you add in the worsening insomnia, the falls, and the balance problems, well it all starts to make more sense.'

Stevenson squinted like he was looking for something on a far-off horizon.

'You've done a CT scan of her brain?'

Stevenson nodded.

'And no anatomical problems or strokes showed up on the CT. No altered brain waves on the EEG either. So, therefore, no signs of seizures or epilepsy. And because they were both normal you didn't bother getting a more sophisticated and detailed MRI scan of her brain, did you? Save the public health system some money by not wasting it on unnecessary investigations?'

Another nod.

'She suffered a major trauma a few years ago in Africa, which I think was the emotional stressor that unleashed the psychosis,' explained

Jack. 'But I also think there is another, more significant underlying *biological* influence here.'

Stevenson nodded his head yet again, and finally spoke.

'Like what, doctor?'

Jack could feel himself growing frustrated.

'I think we are dealing with a neurological illness, not strictly a psychiatric one. I think she has a degenerative condition. A leukodystrophy, like ALD. I think she has an X-linked adrenoleukodystrophy. It is mimicking a psychosis.'

Jack recalled several cases in New York during his training when he was attached to a neurology unit for six months. These patients had been admitted with a perplexing combination of physical *and* psychiatric symptoms. He knew all too well that patients could present with quite florid psychosis that was easily treated when the underlying *physical* illness was addressed. He knew that adrenoleukodystrophy, or ALD, although rare, was such an illness.

Stevenson pulled out a small notepad that Jack had not previously noticed. He started scribbling down notes but kept his gaze on Jack the entire time.

Thank God you are at least listening to me.

'Can you at least tell me that you will look into it? At least do the blood test to measure her long-chain fatty acids. It is still early enough in the course of her disease to consider a stem cell transplant. It could save her life,' he pleaded.

Stevenson looked him right in the eye.

'It's Doctor Jack Giorgio, right?'

'Yes.'

'The forensic psychiatrist?'

'Yes. Yes.'

'Didn't I hear on the grapevine that you have been suspended from practising following a sexual transgression with a patient?'

Jack was speechless.

You bastard.

'Ms Besson. Was *she* the patient?'

'No! No! Of course not! There was a false allegation made. This has nothing to do with…'

'I think we are finished, Doctor Giorgio. I'm sure you can find your way out of here.'

Stevenson stood and towered over Jack.

'Okay,' Jack said with resignation. 'But please think about what I have told you today.'

And with that, he turned around and marched out of the hospital.

Jack did not notice it, but as he walked away from the building, a pretty, female face watched intently him from a gap in the curtains of one of the patient bedrooms.

94

JACK NESTLED INTO the plush leather chair that sat in front of the huge iMac. He turned the computer on and, as expected, was confronted by a screen that required him to enter a password before continuing. Jack had been keeping track of Mortimer's schedule, and if the professor was sticking to his typical cycle, he should currently be in Geneva.

Should.

God, I hope so.

Jack had managed to convince one of the more pleasant security officers at the Nicholas Tindal Centre that he needed to get into the building to quickly retrieve some important personal belongings.

He'd always taken the time to say good morning and goodnight to all the security staff before his suspension, and had often stopped to have a chat at the end of a shift. He was grateful now that he'd invested time in these people—people that so many of his colleagues didn't give a second thought to—as the guard on duty let him in without even a moment's hesitation.

Once inside, Jack made his way up to Mortimer's rooms. It was around seven in the evening and all the admin staff were long gone.

He punched in the five-digit door code he had seen Barnard use when he gave Jack the orientation tour.

That seems so long ago now.

Once he was in Mortimer's office, he'd wasted no time in booting up the iMac. And now, he sat staring at the empty, expectant password box.

What would you use, Mortimer.

He closed his eyes and imagined the professor seated at the desk.

What did Mortimer want?

What was important to him?

Science and biology. He was always emphasising the molecular and genetic causes of mental illness.

Jack began typing: G-e-n-o-t-y-p-e

The password you have entered is incorrect. You have 2 more attempts.

'Damn,' he said out loud.

He closed his eyes again and conjured up the same image of Mortimer. Jack reconsidered. He would not be likely to use a password that was work related. Too obvious. He thought about his own interactions with Mortimer outside of work.

He typed again: B-e-n-t-l-e-y

Another failed attempt.

Despite the rejection, he felt he was on the right track, but he had only one chance left. What was so meaningful and personal to the professor that it encapsulated his sense of greatness? An image of Mortimer's home entered Jack's mind.

Probably my most valued possession, Jack.

He stared down at the keyboard and typed: U-l-y-s-s-e-s

There was a brief pause, and Jack held his breath. The password box was replaced by the words, '*Welcome, Professor Mortimer.*'

Jack exhaled and sat back in the chair.

Start at the start.

He initially began searching through the hard drive for any reference to Christina Beauchamp-Alard.

Nothing.

Mortimer had an extensive range of neatly and precisely catalogued scientific journal articles related to a range of endeavours, including genetics, biochemistry, pharmacology, and neuroimaging. Some of the research was still unpublished and had been sent to Mortimer for his opinion. Jack was sure the articles would make fascinating reading, but right now he was after cases.

He was after patients.

Jack then found an enormous database of papers related to the basics of research design. Placebo versus non-placebo. Active versus controls. Random versus non-random trials. Many of the papers were quite rudimentary, and some of them dated back several decades.

> *Why would you need all of these, given your extensive history in research?*

He put the papers aside when he stumbled across a folder called 'Subjects', buried inside six other folders.

Jack clicked on it.

The folder did not contain any documents but rather a series of video files. All the files appeared to have an unusual labelling system. A curious mixture of letters, numbers, and hyphens.

And there it was.

CBA-7489-X.

He opened up the video and sat back.

The screen revealed a very thin young woman, Jack guessed she was in her early twenties. She had several small holes in her left ear, presumably where earrings had once hung, but none in her right ear.

A voice from off-screen, instantly recognisable as Mortimer's, spoke to her.

'Christina, I was wondering if you could start by telling me a little about yourself?'

She looked hesitant and paused for a few moments, but then decided to comply with the request.

'My name is Christina Elisabeth Beauchamp-Alard. I am twenty-three years old. My father is Henri Beauchamp-Alard and my mother is Colette Beauchamp-Alard. I have no siblings. I was born and raised in Geneva, Switzerland.' Jack noticed that she spoke with a very cultured voice and a subtle French accent. Nonetheless, there was still a forced, robotic quality to her speech.

She stopped, clearly unsure what else she should be saying about herself. She was quickly prompted by Mortimer.

'Perhaps a little about what you do, what your interests are.'

There was a longer pause this time before she said, 'I do not currently work. Most recently, I have been a student in London. I enjoy films, fashion, and reading. I love art and history. I love paintings.'

'And now, Christina, are you able to describe your illness?'

Without hesitation she replied.

'I have been diagnosed with chronic paranoid schizophrenia. I first became unwell when I was fifteen years old. Since then, I have had many years of treatment; both in and out of hospitals.'

Jack had a sense that what she was saying was somehow rehearsed, possibly even scripted. The interview then continued for some time with Christina documenting for the camera her history of symptoms and treatment. She gave a checklist of paranoid delusions, hallucinations, and disturbed, disorganised behaviour that any medical student could easily diagnose as schizophrenia.

She then reeled off a long list of various psychotropic medications that she had received over the years. Jack was astounded by the sheer number of antipsychotics, antidepressants, and tranquiliser drugs that she had been prescribed.

In addition, Christina had also been given two courses of electroconvulsive therapy, or 'shock' therapy, without any success.

She had even been placed on the antipsychotic wonder drug, clozapine, for around eighteen months until she developed life-threatening side effects, at which point the medication was stopped.

'And how are you feeling now?' asked Mortimer, off camera.

Christina gave a broad, warm smile. As far as Jack could tell through the detached vision of a video camera, it appeared genuine.

'Much, much better.'

'In what ways?'

'The first thing I noticed was the voices. They just stopped. Went away. One day I heard them, screaming in my head, and when I woke the following morning they were gone. Completely silent. And they have not been back since.'

'How long ago was that?'

'Around four months now.'

'Excellent, Christina. How else are you better?'

'The fear. The fear that dominated my life just... vanished.' She smiled again and chuckled to herself in a relaxed way. 'My life was dominated by terror. For years I thought... no, I *believed,* with absolute conviction... that my life was in danger. That *they* were after me. Following me. Bugging my phone. Putting cameras in my apartment. In my shower. I was never alone. I knew that they were always watching me.'

'And now?'

'And now I can see that I was unwell. It was the schizophrenia that tricked me into believing all those horrible things.'

Jack was impressed. She was more spontaneous now and was articulately explaining all of the improvements that any psychiatrist would dream of hearing from a patient who had been as unwell as Christina.

To hear and see that she was better.

Cure was a strong, emotionally loaded word that was hardly ever used in cases of schizophrenia. Phrases like 'symptomatic control' and 'illness management' were far more realistic. But listening to Christina made Jack wonder if 'cure' *was* an appropriate word in her case.

Mortimer spoke again. 'And what else?'

She appeared to tear up. 'I just have my life back now. I can think. I can move freely. I can leave the house and do my shopping and not worry that the supermarket scanners are reading my thoughts. I can sit in a café and drink coffee without wondering if it has been poisoned. All of the things that people take for granted, I can now thoroughly enjoy!'

'And why has there been this improvement, Christina?'
'Positrex,' she said, without any hesitation.

'Can you elaborate further?'

'It's been wonderful. Complete relief. I have been given the new Positrex implant.'

Mortimer's voice cut in again. 'Christina has been given the new therapeutic device known as Positrex Scion. Please continue, Christina.'

'Yes, that's right, Professor. Scion. Such a beautiful word. *Scion.* For the first time in nearly ten years, I have received a treatment that actually works. A medication that finally takes away all of my maddening worries and symptoms.'

'And what was it like for you, as a patient, to have Scion administered?'

'Very easy, really. I had a simple procedure and when I woke up the next morning I was better.'

'Was it painful, Christina?'

She smiled. 'Oh no, not at all. A doctor put me to sleep and I did not feel anything.'

Mortimer then spoke and described how she was given a light, brief sedative with midazolam and then a small incision was made in the skin at the back of the neck. The *Positrex* was then implanted allowing the nanotechnology particles to migrate directly from her cervical spine into the brain. The entire procedure took fifteen minutes. He had perfected the technique so that the procedure could be carried out in a matter of minutes, with no need for assistance, in the same way that an injection might be administered.

He then returned to Christina. 'And have you noticed any side effects?'

'No, none at all. Which is both welcome and surprising.' Jack felt that phrase seemed a little contrived.

She continued, 'I think that every other treatment I have ever had gave me some nasty side effects. Sedation, nausea, a foggy head, weight gain, tremors, headaches, my hair even started to fall out at one stage. And then there was the nasty blood problem I developed when I was on clozapine.'

Jack knew that she was referring to a dangerous and sudden drop of her white blood cells which would have made her extremely vulnerable to infection and even put her at risk of death. Although it was uncommon, it was known to happen with clozapine.

Christina turned around and the camera then focused on a tiny scar high up on her neck. It was hardly visible and could easily have been missed unless it was pointed out.

Mortimer's voice then began again. 'As you can see, a small incision is made in the neck and Positrex Scion is inserted under the skin.'

At the end of the video the screen went blank for a few seconds before two dates appeared on the screen.

The first read: *Date of video recording – February 11.*

The second: *Date of death – February 12.*

95

'COME ON, JACK. Be *realistic*. You cannot get any meaningful research done now without the financial backing of the drug companies. You need billions. *Billions,* Jack! Where else would you get that sort of money, if not from Big Pharma? Do you honestly think that governments are going to pay? Even if they could afford it, mental health is not politically sexy enough. Especially forensic psychiatry. Supporting the people who support the criminally insane is simply never going to be a priority for any government.'

It had been several weeks since Jack had seen Mortimer, but the professor seemed to have aged several years.

Jack put the matter of funding to one side for a moment, as it clearly wasn't going to get him anywhere pursuing it, and changed the subject to Laura Brenner, aka Imogen Davis. He hoped that the new information, which clearly demonstrated he had been set up would force Mortimer to lift his suspension. But the professor was solely focused on the difficulties of obtaining funding, and completely ignored everything Jack had said about the allegations that had led to his suspension.

Mortimer coughed violently and continued to pontificate.

'Do you know what it took to get this monstrosity of a hospital built? *Do you have any idea?* If you really want to highlight the difficulties with obtaining government funding, you need look no further than the Covid-19 response. That scared the shit out of the whole planet but was it the UK government, or the mighty US government that produced a vaccine? *Hell no!* It was Pfizer and Astra Zeneca... it was CEOs making thirty million a year, making the big calls and paying their own, private scientists millions a year to get the fucking job done!'

Jack nodded slowly.

Mortimer, encouraged, pushed on, 'And no government agency or regulatory body is ever going to give you the ethics approval either. Not for this sort of research. I am talking about world-changing work here, Jack. Not this 'baby-steps' bullshit that has been happening for the past thirty years in mental health.'

'But how can you experiment on innocent people?'

'You have to sacrifice the few to save the many, Jack. And billions could be saved, my boy. Fucking *billions!*'

> *Sacrifice?*

Mortimer wheezed. 'Think back to the great wars of the twentieth century. They were the moments in history when we saw the largest medical breakthroughs. Global trauma led to global advances. Right across the board—in all areas of medicine and surgery. So yes, boy, the end justifies the means. When the world sees the outcomes, *my* outcomes, the benefits, the fucking cures, they won't care how I got there. *I* will be saving every family, every health service, every government, in every country around the world, hundreds of billions of dollars.' Mortimer's fists were clenched now.

'You're more deluded than your patients.'

Jack had lost all desire to hold his tongue.

Mortimer's laughter quickly descended into a coughing fit. 'No Jack, not mad... *brave*. Mental health—the broken mind—is the new frontier, and I will be seen as a true pioneer.'

96

JACK COULD NOT drive home fast enough. He desperately wanted to leave Nathan Mortimer, Patient X, Portman, Cerise/Sandrine, Laura/Imogen, and the ward behind.

The sun was just starting to set as he headed out along the Embankment for a run, and within minutes he felt better. Calmer.

The events of the day played in his mind as he hit his stride. His mental self-cleansing mechanism was at full tilt as the conversation with Mortimer went around and around in his mind. There was something familiar about what the professor was saying. He'd heard it before. But where?

Mortimer. Mortimer.

Drug companies. Research.

Saving billions.

Monstrosity of a hospital.

No government will pay.

The criminally insane.

Not sexy.

Government.

Sexy.

Crimes.

Ethics approval.

No government.

Sexy.

Government.

97

'I REALLY LIKE speaking to you,' Joel said. 'You are an easy doctor to talk to. You really listen.' The two men were sitting in Joel's small room on the private ward.

Joel wore a t-shirt that read: *Store in a cool, dry place.*

Despite being suspended from his role at the NTC, Jack was still able to access and work on the unregulated private ward, which gave him a chance to keep looking for evidence for Portman. He also wanted to make sure that Joel was being treated appropriately. Jack worried a great deal about him.

'That's good, Joel. It's easy to listen to you, and I guess my job is to listen to my patients.'

Joel looked around anxiously. 'Yeah, well someone should remind Professor Mortimer of that,' he said in a quiet voice.

'You feel that he doesn't listen to you?'

'No, not really. He just wants to tell me off and remind me who my father is. Like I needed any reminding of that!' Joel looked pensive.

Jack nodded. He sensed that Joel had more to say. He sat back to see what might spontaneously come next.

After a minute, Joel tentatively began to speak. 'But at least he's better than that other arsehole.'

'Who are we talking about?' asked Jack.

'The other doctor. Dr Barnard.'

'You know Dr Barnard?'

'Yeah, from a few years ago. It was my very first admission. The one where I was diagnosed with schizophrenia.'

'Was that here, Joel?'

'No. That was in the *real* world,' he said with a sarcastic note. 'It was back in the old hospital, the one they closed down. My father was appalled and horrified that I was locked up there.'

'The old forensic hospital? What had you done to end up there, Joel?'

Joel looked embarrassed. 'Driving offences.'

'That's okay, Joel. You were very unwell. But it was Dr Barnard who looked after you then?'

Joel looked confused. 'Yes... no... *kind of.* He was a nasty prick to me. He hardly ever saw me, and on the rare occasions when he did, he would criticise me and then just walk off. I mainly saw a junior doctor who didn't know what he was doing. And I was given heavy-duty doses of medication. I was a fucking zombie most of the time.'

'I'm sorry you had to suffer through all of that, Joel. Let's hope you can have a better treatment experience from now on.'

'Thanks, doctor... I mean, Jack. One other thing I do remember about Barnard was that he seemed quite interested in my father.'

'Your father?' Jack asked.

'Yes. When Barnard *did* speak to me for longer than a few seconds, it would be to ask me endless questions about my father—most of which I couldn't answer. I think he spent more time talking to my father than he did to me. He was always arranging to meet him.'

'Why do you think that was?'

'I don't know. At first, I thought he might be interested in my background. I was pretty sick at the time, and I wasn't really able to talk much about my past. But I doubt he was truly interested in me.'

'Have you seen Dr Barnard since then?'

'No. Never. Since then, it has only been Professor Mortimer. And now you.'

'Has your father ever talked about Dr Barnard to you?'

'No, not recently. Although I do remember that after my first admission my father said he was very, very impressed with Dr Barnard. He thought Barnard *had great ideas and smart mind.*' Joel mimicked his father's accent as he said these last words.

'Really?'

'Yes, and I remember one other thing: I overheard Barnard talking to my father at length about his private lab, and how many important medical and scientific papers he had published. Of course, my father was impressed. He also explained how my father could get generous tax deductions if he agreed to fund Doctor Barnard's research. Needless to say, my father was *very* excited about the prospect of that.'

Jack thought back to his first meeting with Barnard at the NTC.

Research? Who's got time for that?

Jack strolled back out to the nurses' station. Barry, the congenial septuagenarian night nurse, had just clocked on for his shift. He always carried a stack of crime thrillers with him to read overnight. He nodded in Jack's direction. Jack knew that Barry would soon be distracted enough that he could have a look around.

Walking through the building, he found that there were several unlocked rooms which were completely empty. He assumed that these could accommodate more patients, if required.

There was no sign of a computer anywhere.

One room contained boxes of old patient files, but these appeared to relate to previous patients on the private ward and had nothing to do with trafficking, experiments or drug companies. Jack was shocked to see the high dosages of medications that had been administered to these patients—they were way outside the guidelines. It would seem that the long-suffering family members of the rich and powerful were basically sedated and kept out of the way.

For a whopping fee.

It was scandalous.

The only item seemingly out of place was a large, yellow envelope with the name of a local radiology service printed on the top left corner. The contents revealed what appeared to be a series of MRI scans of the brain. It was extremely hard to make sense of the highly detailed images in the dim light of the ward, and the scans only had a date, which was quite recent, and a patient ID number. There was no name and no date of birth. Something told Jack to take a closer look.

He grabbed the scans and walked back out past the nurses' station. He was sure to keep his arms low, and he had removed his suit jacket so that it was draped over the yellow envelope. As expected, Barry was engrossed in his latest thriller. Joel seemed to be fast asleep.

'Night,' Jack called as he walked to the exit.

'Hmm,' Barry grunted, his eyes not leaving the page.

98

'AHH HELLO… HI … it's Jack, here. Jack Giorgio. Sorry to bother you, but we have met before. Do you remember? The tour… at the Nicholas Tind…'

She quickly cut him off.

'*Jack!* Yes, of course I do! Hi yourself, how are you?' she sounded bright. Her voice carried a smile.

'Oh, I'm good thanks, Zoe.'

He'd been trying to reach Zoe Maxwell at the Health Secretary's office for weeks now, and he was extremely relieved, not only that the call had finally made it through to her, but that she seemed to be happy to hear from him.

'Still keeping us all safe from all those serial killers, Doctor Giorgio?' she said with a giggle.

The ones with knives, or the ones in suits?

Jack grimaced. 'Ha ha! Doing my best.'

Well, I would be if I wasn't bloody suspended.

There was a brief, awkward silence.

'*Soooo…* what can I do for you, Jack? I think you must be the first person to ring this office and ask for me by name.'

He imagined her twirling a strand of her hair with a pencil as she spoke.

'Well I was after a bit of a favour, actually. It's a bit of boring admin, really. But I would be incredibly grateful for your help.'

'Oh sure… just how grateful are we talking?'

He wasn't expecting that.

'Oh. Very. You've already had the tour of serial killer central. So... I don't know... how about I take you out for coffee?'

There was a further pause.

'Make it a drink. A *proper* drink, then.... yes.'

'Deal!'

'Okay then, what do you need?'

Good question, Zoe. Good question. What do I need?

'Well, it relates to a psychiatric colleague of mine. The Professor has asked me to supervise him, write up performance appraisals, that sort of thing.'

'Oh yeah?'

'Yeah. So I just need a bit of background on him. You know, from an employment perspective. Dates of service, medical board registration, education, previous appraisals. Pedestrian stuff, but it would save me so much time.'

He could hear keystrokes. 'No problem. Let me fire up the database here. All the medical staff employed in the NHS. One sec. Ah, there we are. So... name?'

'Last name, Barnard. First name, Drew. Psychiatrist. Sorry, I don't know his date of birth. He would be about forty or so.'

'Okaaaay.' Then after a pause: 'Huh. Hmm.' More hair twirling.

'Everything okay, Zoe?'

'Yeah but... weird. Nothing is coming up.'

'Oh. Sorry, try Andrew. I think it must be *Andrew* Barnard.'

'Ah, yeah, with you now. Annnd... no. Nothing. Well, nothing in psychiatry. We have a Dr Andrew Barnard, pathologist in Manchester. Andrew Barnard, cardiac surgeon in Birmingham and... Andrew

Barnard, radiologist in London. But he is sixty-eight. God, that's old. Older than my uncle! He should be retired.' Another giggle.

'Can you just search by way of last name and specialty?'

'Ahh yes. Good thinking. Hang on.'

A moment felt like an hour.

Zoe returned to the conversation and said, 'Well we have a couple of Barnards in psychiatry. Ian Barnard, who is a child psychiatrist in Bath. He is fifty-seven. David Barnard in Cornwall, who is thirty-six. We have a Stuart Barnard in London who is only twenty-nine. Wow, that's young! He'd be about your age, right?' Jack could sense her winking down the phone line.

'But no one in forensic psychiatry?'

'Ahh… no.'

> *Well that makes no sense.*

'So, Zoe, just to be clear. What you are telling me is that there is *no* psychiatrist employed by the forensic mental health service in the UK by the name of Barnard… Andrew or otherwise?'

'Correct.'

99

His shoes echoed on the marble floor as Jack walked into the Royal Genealogy Library in London and approached the elderly librarian.

'I want to do some research on a family line,' he said.

'Certainly,' she replied in a friendly tone. 'What is the lineage you are interested in?'

'Wexbridge. In particular, the current Earl. I think he is the twenty-third.'

'Follow me.'

She led him through to a smaller, private library that branched off from the main library.

Jack was in awe and thought that this was easily one of the most beautiful places he had ever been. He suddenly wished that Cerise was here with him. The walls of the smaller library were lined with magnificent oak bookshelves, all the way from the floor right up to the lofty, vaulted ceiling. Thousands of leather-bound volumes filled every conceivable nook and cranny. A huge Persian rug sat in the centre of the room on top of immaculately polished wooden floorboards, and several small oak tables and chairs had been placed on top of the rug.

Each wall had a wooden ladder attached, that allowed the librarians to ascend right to the highest shelf. Jack was tempted to ask the librarian if he could climb up.

Just once, please.

The room was not completely devoid of technology. The librarian went to a computer that stood in the corner of the room and typed in the details.

'I tried to Google this information, but there was nothing online,' Jack said with interest.

'Yes, I hear that at lot. We just don't have the funds to digitise it all and, to be honest, some of the aristocracy don't want their family histories on the internet. Now let's see. Ahh, yes, here we are. Wexbridge. That is located at… F… twenty-seven. Oh. Bother.' She looked worried.

'What's the matter? Is there a problem?' Jack asked, concerned.

'Well, the volume *is* here. But it's in the second row from the top. Over there.' She pointed up towards the other end of the library.

'Is that a problem?'

'I'm not much good at climbing the steps these days. It's not really allowed, you know, health and safety nonsense, but could you possibly climb up and fetch it for me?' She smiled sweetly at him.

He returned the smile. 'It would be a pleasure.'

When he descended, volume in hand, she directed him to take a seat at one of the tables.

'So this volume gives a social, familial, and economic history of the Wexbridge region, and has quite an extensive description of the Earls,' she said. 'What is it you would specifically like to know?'

'The current Earl. In particular, who that might be.'

She thumbed through the pages of the book.

'Ah. Well, that's interesting. You learn something new every day. Even at my age!' she said.

'What's that?'

'The lineage ended around forty years ago. See… here.' She showed Jack the entry. 'The last Earl died with no heir.'

'So there is *no* current Earl of Wexbridge?'

'Exactly.'

<u>100</u>

BACK AT HIS apartment, Jack placed one of the MRI scans over a light box that he had picked up in an art shop. He almost took a step back when he saw the image of the brain light up in front of him.

Even though he had seen his fair share of CTs and MRIs, he was no expert on the radiology of the brain, but he was quite confident that even a layperson could look at the image in front of him and determine that things had gone horribly wrong.

Jack looked closely at the frontal lobes, the section of the brain responsible for emotion, impulse control, and high-level decision-making. Then he shuddered.

Three ugly masses—malignant tumours.

He shook his head and sighed. Given that there were three distinct tumours, they were highly likely to be metastases or 'mets' that had spread from another organ, most probably the lung or the breast.

Is this the brain of Patient X? Or Joel?

There was no name on the scans, only a coded number used for cross-referencing. Jack rang the radiology service that had performed the MRI. Thankfully, it was one he was familiar with.

'Hello, it's Dr Jack Giorgio here at the Nicholas Tindal Centre. My registration number is 72748G. I was reviewing an MRI scan and I wanted to be certain the code matched up with the right patient.'

He waited anxiously for a response.

'Yes. The code is 65Y78RX. Thanks.'

The woman on the other end of the line was typing.

When she gave the patient name that corresponded with the MRI, Jack dropped the phone.

101

JACK COULD NOT stop thinking about what Joel had told him, and he was desperate to find out what Barnard's role may be in all of this.

Barnard had clearly been lying.

But who the hell was he?

With Joel's recent disclosure in mind, he went to the PubMed website, which contained all of the medical, neuroscientific, and psychiatric research published in academic journals.

Frustratingly, an author search over the past ten years did not reveal anything by Drew Barnard.

He relentlessly searched again, under psychiatry, neurology, neuropsychiatry, and neuroscience.

Nil.

It would take hours, but he expanded the time parameter to the past fifteen years and broadened the search term to the name '*Barnard*'.

As expected, several hundred papers emerged spanning the entire breadth of medical research: Abdominoplasty through to Zygoma.

Jack brewed a strong espresso and started to sift through them all. After more than three hours he couldn't believe his tired eyes.

At one in the morning, his search finally revealed a series of papers published a few years ago by one Horatio Andrew Barnard, PhD *and* Sarah Kate Wellington, psychiatric registrar.

Fundamental neuroscience work.

He had to reread it several times to make sure his eyes were not deceiving him.

Sarah?

Jack further discovered that Barnard had an impressive bachelor's degree in neuroscience from Oxford, followed by a masters in neurochemistry and then a doctorate from no less than the Massachusetts Institute of Technology in Boston. He had worked with easily the most prestigious neuroscience research team on the plant. His doctoral thesis was on the cholinergic receptor regulation of the cerebral cortex.

Basically, a PhD on the molecular and chemical building blocks of human thought.

'Incredible,' Jack said to himself. 'So, you *are* a doctor, Barnard. Just not a medical one.'

That's why you don't show up on the medical register.

'But how the hell did you end up with the psychiatric job you have?' he whispered. 'And *why?*'

He then read that Barnard and Sarah had co-authored original neuroscience research on not only the genetics of the brain, right down to the molecular level, but also on the receptors in the brain that are responsible for higher-level thinking.

The research of cognitive functioning.

The research of the mind.

The research of what it means to be human.

He was amazed by what they had produced. Truly pioneering work. Paper after paper. Uncovering the basic building blocks of the mind. They appeared to be inching closer to locating the specific molecular receptor sites, the neural 'lock and key' responsible for human thought.

And then it all seemed to stop.

Around two years ago. No further papers were published by either of them. The research trail went cold.

So why did you stop?

He scanned the articles again. He noticed that in the author credits, Sarah Wellington was variously described as working for the East London Mental Health Service, the Oxford University Mental Health Clinic, the Birmingham Psychiatric and Neurology Centre and, of course, for twelve months with MSF. This was fairly typical, he thought, as a training registrar would move posts every six to twelve months.

When he checked Barnard in the author credits at the end of each paper it always read the same: *Delegate, UK Department of Health and Private Research Facility.*

Jack had never read anything quite like that.

> *What did that mean? Who was behind him?*

Jack realised that it was true: Barnard was never officially employed in forensic mental health. Zoe's information confirmed that he was never paid by the Department of Health. A detail that, stunningly, no one seemed to have detected.

He knew of people who had masqueraded as medical practitioners. Some had got away with it for many years. They had devised very convincing forged degrees and complicated networks of fake referees. Eventually, they were found out, but some of them were so skilled that they had risen to the lofty and powerful position of unit directors before they were discovered.

They were usually cunning, intelligent psychopaths. But what of Mortimer's role? Did he even know?

So many layers of bureaucracy, and no one had even noticed.

> *Or had they?*

Someone with authority must have got Barnard into that forensic unit. Someone on the inside.

> *But who? Mortimer?*

Just then, his phone rang.

102

'I KNOW WHAT's been happening to these missing refugees.'

After the intrusion by Mortimer and his suspension, Jack hadn't been given the opportunity to explain his theory regarding Patient X to the clinical staff at the NTC, so the first person he could explain his idea to was Portman.

'We know that already, Jack. The pharma companies are using them as guinea pigs for their own drug research, so that they can develop new medications.' Portman rolled his eyes.

'No. You're wrong.'

'I'm *wrong*?'

'Well… half wrong.'

To Jack's surprise, Portman let out a laugh. 'So am I half wrong… or half *right*, Dr Freud?'

'Very funny. But listen, it's not that. It's not new drugs. Actually, I don't think it involves any of those big pharma companies at all. At least, not *directly*. It's not about new medications. It's the illegal organ trade, Portman.'

Portman raised his eyebrows in surprise. '*Organ* trade? *What the fuck?* There's no evidence of any kind of surgery.'

An image of the blank Patient X came into Jack's mind. 'That's because it's their minds that are being harvested,' he replied with absolute conviction, his eyes fixed on Portman.

'Their *minds!?* Are you *serious*, Giorgio? How is that organ trafficking. How is it even *possible!*' Portman shook his head.

'It *is* trafficking. Think it through. You have *seen* these victims. You have interviewed them. I have tried to assess one of them. Their minds are *gone!* Vanished! The victims are alive, but just existing, with no capacity for higher thought. And under any *modern* definition of an organ, the human mind would certainly qualify.'

'I don't know...'

Jack interrupted. 'They have the perfect premise. These refugees are already presumed missing, dead, drowned. No one is looking for them. No government, no navy, no family members. And with their minds gone, the victims can't speak up or identify the perpetrators.'

'Vanished,' Portman whispered as he watched Jack intently.

'Yes, and given what we understand about the brain and its biochemistry, we can easily argue that the mind is a tangible, identifiable organ. Just like a kidney or a heart.'

'How can you prove that?'

'In several ways. For instance, with functional MRI and PET scans.'

'With what?' Portman shook his head.

'High tech, high-definition scans that light up specific parts of the brain when people are given a certain stimulus. It can detect changes in blood flow in different areas of the brain. You can clearly show when people are afraid, content, craving a drug or horny. You can effectively capture an image of someone's mind. You can prove its physical existence.'

'You might need more, Jack.'

'Okay then, think about this: the pancreas is an organ, and it secretes insulin. The thyroid is an organ, and it secretes hormones too. The mind is an organ, and it secretes thoughts and emotions.'

Portman seemed puzzled and unsure. 'Yeah, but insulin and hormones can be measured. How can you measure a thought?'

'You can measure thoughts and emotions quite easily,' Jack said.

'Really? How?'

'There are dozens of very credible, very reliable psychometric scales and tests that can easily be used to measure products of the mind. They are just as valid as any 'physical' measuring device. Think back to the psych evaluations you did when you joined Interpol.'

Portman nodded and looked off into the distance like he was trying to identify some far away landmark.

'In addition to thoughts and emotions, these people are being robbed of something else,' continued Jack.

'What's that?' asked Portman, with genuine curiosity.

'*Language.*'

'Language?'

'Yes, the ultimate expression of the human mind. And in all of the victims, it is missing.' Jack felt wholly satisfied with the argument he had made.

'Trafficking of human minds,' Portman said to himself, with a further shake of his head. 'Okay, you've convinced me that minds could be considered an organ and therefore, if 'stolen', would be subject to severe international criminal laws. But how the hell would they even be able to steal someone's mind?'

'They have developed a technique, a procedure, that can remove the very essence, the molecular basis, of a human mind,' Jack explained. 'They implant a small device in the base of the neck. My suspicion is that they enter the top of the spinal cord and use the implant to remove all of the neurotransmitters and receptor sites that control executive functioning and our higher mental functions—our more complex thoughts and emotions. The physical structure is left behind, the nerve cells and so on, which is why the MRIs always look normal, and the more primitive, deeper part of the brain is left completely intact. That is why the patients remain alive but seem to exist in a fugue-like state.'

'What the *hell!*' Portman exclaimed.

'I know it sounds unbelievable, but I have *seen* the effects. Tested them out. And so have you. As I told you, we have a patient at the

NTC who has had this done to him. And I have looked closely. There is indeed a tiny scar at the base of his skull. This guy is a zombie. He is a victim of organ harvesting. But they didn't take out anything anatomical, Portman. They took his *mind!*'

'But why would they do this, Jack? What's the point?'

'The *point!?* Come on, Portman. We are talking about the essence of human existence here. To be able to capture it and *use* it. The possibilities are endless. One use may be to test out new psychiatric drugs at such a precise level that success would be almost guaranteed. That is where the drug companies may be involved, as a buyer of the product.' Jack looked soberly at Portman. 'And then there is the illegal transplant market.'

'The *what?!*'

'Transplantation. That's what I believe the *real* purpose is. They are using these stolen minds to transplant into people whose own minds are failing them. For a massive fee, of course. My old mentor, Theo Stein, in New York was onto it. He tried to warn me but they got to him first.' Jack's voice was heavy with sadness.

'I just can't believe it,' Portman paced around in a circle with his hands on his hips. Jack had never seen him like this before. 'But it all makes sense now, Jack. Mind transplants. All those missing people. The ones who turn up without a brain. I guess if you live long enough you get to see everything. But who is behind it? It must be Mortimer!'

'I don't know, Portman. Maybe, but I'm not convinced it *is* him. Stein was close to uncovering the truth, but I don't think he got to the top of the chain before they got to him. It could be Mortimer, but I believe we need to think bigger. Grander.'

'*Bigger?* But he has the resources, the genius, *and* the connections. It *must* be him. Jack. If what you are saying is true then this will be enormous. You must find the evidence that uncovers who is doing this.'

'I think I already have a lead on that, Portman.'

103

WHEN HE CAUGHT a glimpse of Mortimer side-on, it suddenly occurred to Jack that he had lost more weight.

A *lot* more weight.

Mortimer coughed violently into a handkerchief. As he pushed it back into his pocket, Jack noticed small specks of blood on the white fabric.

You are sick. Extremely sick.

Mortimer finally caught his breath and continued.

'My grandfather and my father were screwed by a massive corporation. It killed them. But I knew that to beat them, I had to join them.'

He coughed again. More flecks of blood.

Jack had already put it together before he'd seen the MRI of the professor's brain. The weight loss, the relentless cough, the breathlessness, the blood, there had been enough tell-tale signs even without the scans.

'How long do you have, Mortimer? A month? Three?'

'Long enough,' he replied with a sly smile.

'Where has it spread from? Your lungs?' Jack already knew the answer, but for some reason he wanted to hear Mortimer say it.

The professor did not speak, but with a straightened index finger he simply pointed to the side of his head.

Jack had to admit to himself that his feelings were a complex mixture of sympathy and anger.

'This is my time, Jack. *Mine*. In a week from now, I will be hailed as one of the greatest medical geniuses of the past century. Scion, it will be my idea, my glorious creation, will be the start of a complete change in *all* of medicine, not just psychiatry. With Cerise Navarro gone, it will be all mine and the Nobel Prize that comes with it. With this nanotechnology, *I* will be the one who finally cured schizophrenia and who led the way in treating all serious illnesses. They will all be lining up to shake *my* hand and pat *my* back.'

Jack gazed down at Mortimer's bony, blue hands.

Not likely

'Just like you did with Christina Beauchamp-Alard? Was she one of your little success stories? Will they be slapping you on the back over her?'

'That was an accident, boy. She was well. I had cured her. Scion worked brilliantly for Christina.'

'Then why was she on the run? If she was doing so well, then why was she so terrified?'

Jack looked at Mortimer with wide eyes, waiting for a response.

'I don't know,' he said slowly.

'You don't know? *You don't know!?* How the hell could you not know?'

The words had barely left his lips when the answer struck.

> *Of course. The changes in Mortimer's manner and speech. His use of profanities. The emotionality. His anger. The grandiosity. He couldn't control his feelings anymore because those nasty brain tumours had eaten holes in his frontal lobes.*

'It's true, you really don't know, do you? Oh Nathan, it was all a con. A huge lie. Scion is nothing more than your own grandiose fantasy. There is no nanotechnology that can do what you claim. It doesn't work because it doesn't bloody *exist!*'

Then a realisation smacked Jack in the face.

It was more than a fantasy.

It was a delusion.

The eminent professor had truly gone mad.

'There will be no more trips to Geneva, now, Nathan,' Jack said.

'No,' Mortimer conceded glumly. 'No more trips. There is nothing more that they can do.'

Jack was confused.

'Nothing more they can do?'

Mortimer said nothing, but pulled out a cigar from inside his jacket pocket and lit it up.

You might as well. No point quitting now.

Part 4

Freud by the Sea

104

THEY WALKED SLOWLY and silently through the streets of Southampton under a crescent moon that hung suspended in the cold, clear sky. They only dared move at night. During the day they remained hidden, out of sight. Fear kept them imprisoned in one of the many derelict buildings that were sprinkled throughout the east of the city.

It was difficult to estimate their numbers. Ten? A dozen? More? From a distance, their shuffling gait created the impression that they were elderly. But most were under forty. They moved as a pack, always together. Most were shrouded in worn, grey blankets—not to keep out the cold, but to keep out the world.

They were the walking dead. The media had killed them off months ago, with headlines such as 'Asylum Seekers Drown' and 'More Boats Sink'. They would have chosen death over their current existence.

There was no common language that united them. They were Iraqis, Iranians, Cambodians, Africans, and Vietnamese. Men and women. Old and young.

They came out at night to scavenge for food and any scraps of wood that could be used to keep their fires going.

They were the forgotten people. Dead to their own families and dead to the rest of the world. No one was looking for them now. No one was going to saving them. The police no longer bothered them.

There was one common element that united them. If you were to look closely enough, each of these vacant souls could be observed to have a tiny lump under the skin at the base of their skulls.

A tiny implant.

The few memories that remained were as broken as they were. Simply, there was *before* and there was *after*. Of before, there was virtually nothing left. Recollections were like faded, grainy photographs projected briefly onto the back of the eyes. An image of home, a birthday, a loved one. Then nothing.

Vanished.

What remained only slightly more vividly was the journey. The crowded boats, the wind, the waves, the hunger, the thirst, and the emotions; all of them negative. Fear. Terror. Hopelessness.

But then came the hope. The sun emerging from the darkness. Out of nowhere came the miracle. An enormous cruiser, sleek, black, and shark-like.

It could have been the Mediterranean, between Africa and Italy. It could have been the Indian Ocean, between Indonesia and Australia. It did not matter.

The *black shark* would somehow be there.

Ready and waiting.

A saviour.

When all hope was lost, they would be scooped up and taken on board. Every last one of them.

They would be cared for. They would be fed, they would be given cool, fresh water, clean, dry clothes and a warm bed to sleep in.

They were told that they were being taken to safety.

And they believed it was true.

105

THEY WERE HOUSED below decks with no view of the outside world, but they did not care. What was there to look at? Ocean and more ocean? No. It was good to be below decks. They finally felt secure, and that was all that mattered.

Not long into the voyage they were visited by the ship's doctor. A very pleasant, careful physician who spoke crisp, clear English that was easy to understand. The doctor wore a white coat and made them feel cared for. They were all weighed. They were all measured. They were all asked simple questions and given simple examinations. They were even given blood tests. Everything was written down. The doctor was meticulous. At the end of the visit, the doctor smiled and shook their hands.

> *This is a very good doctor. A very good doctor and a very good person.*

For the first time in many months, they began to feel excited. The torture and persecution they had fled was over. The money they had spent was now proving to have been worthwhile. They knew that when they next ascended to the upper deck they would see a new land ahead of them, filled with new opportunities. They would be safe.

They would be free.

Below decks, they lost track of time. There were no windows and no clocks. They ate when they were hungry and slept when they were tired. The ship was so large that it was impossible to gain a sense of how fast they were moving, let alone in which direction. No one would answer their questions about where they were headed. Not even the good doctor.

Eventually, a man descended the steep staircase that led down to the hold. He was very tall and very fit. He was dressed in black and had a blank expression on his face. He said nothing but gestured to everyone to follow him.

Naturally, and gratefully, they followed.

When they reached the upper deck they were surprised. They did not see land. They certainly did not see Sydney or Rome or Los Angeles. They did not even see sky. The ship had docked inside an enormous boatshed. Artificial lights illuminated the huge space, and black, cold water sloshed around the bottom of the cruiser.

They were efficiently herded off the ship and onto three large buses that were waiting below. They were chaperoned by more tall, athletic men, who were also dressed in black.

No one spoke. Most of the refugees still smiled and complied with the unspoken gestures. Once seated, a whispered chatter broke out amongst the passengers.

> *'Where are we?'*
>
> *'What is this place?'*
>
> *'Where will they take us?'*
>
> *'Are we safe?'*

But they were questions to which none of the passengers held the answers.

Two huge, automatic sliding doors at one end of the shed slid open and the bus headed out of the vast hangar. The passengers were surprised to see that it was pitch black outside. It was a cloudy night and there were no stars or moon to speak of. Just the soft amber glow of the occasional streetlight.

They all stared, bright eyed, out of the dark windows as they hurtled along a motorway. As the miles and hours ticked by some of the older passengers fell asleep.

Eventually, the bus rolled to a gentle halt. They had arrived at some type of secure facility. High barbed wire fences surrounded more featureless buildings. The bus glided into another large hangar, and the passengers were unloaded.

As they entered the building, they were each handed a backpack containing a change of clothes, some basic toiletries, snacks, and two bottles of water.

Many of the passengers were reassured by this, but still no one spoke.

They were taken up several flights of stairs and shown into single-gender bedrooms, complete with generic bunk beds. Six to a room. They were all exhausted and sleep came easily.

The next morning, they were woken early and were pleased to see daylight out of their windows. Although the views were impeded by a layer of thick fog and they still had no idea where they were, it was still a very pleasant sensation to see dry land.

The men in black ushered them through to a large dining hall. After filing through and filling their plates with fresh fruit, cereal, bread, juice, tea and coffee, they sat down at long benches and ate quietly and quickly.

It was going to be all right.

Most of them believed that they were in some sort of secure immigration facility, and that they were about to be processed and then released into the community.

They were half right.

They were about to be processed.

106

THERE WAS ONE man who stood out from the other staff. He did not dress in black. Instead, he wore a suit and tie and spoke with a lovely, cultured accent. They called him 'the Englishman'. It was clear that he had power.

When he welcomed the refugees to Britain, excited sounds filled the room as spontaneous chatter broke out among the group.

> *'Britain? Britain! Did you hear him?'*

> *'We have made it to Britain!'*

Wide smiles spread across tired faces. There was some brief laughter.

> *'My second cousin made it to Britain.'*

> *'My uncle is in Manchester.'*

> *'I can now send for my mother.'*

The Englishman then explained that they needed more medical checks before they could enter the general community. However, he assured them that there was nothing to worry about, and that the examinations would not take long at all.

The felt reassured, as surely the lovely doctor they saw earlier would take care of everything.

Throughout the day, one by one, they were taken to see the Englishman. They were all distracted about dreams of a new life, and they did not worry that none of those who went before returned to the rest of the group.

The optimistic ones assumed that they had simply left through another door, having completed their examination and been granted the freedom to make a fresh start into their new homeland.

Duc, from Haiphong in northern Vietnam, had lived a miserable life. As a boy, his impoverished and desperate parents had sold him to an affluent family, where he was put to work. His new 'parents' soon realised he was a bright and curious child, and so they allowed him access to books, which Duc devoured with great delight.

But the 'privileges' ended there.

For twelve hours a day he was at the beck and call of his new family. Hour after hour, day after day, he was subjected to carrying out an endless parade of mind-numbing, menial tasks.

A callous older 'brother' would torment Duc, and would regularly beat him. But books gave him a refuge into other worlds. He would read whenever he got the chance, usually until his brutal 'brother' would smack the book out of his hand and then punch him in the stomach.

Soon, Duc's imagination started to make stories of its own. He had read about magical far-off lands in Europe and the Americas. He would lie in bed at night and picture himself there. Places where he could be free. Places where he could read. Over the years, he hatched his escape plan. He never dreamt that he would make it to England.

Duc was ushered through to a small, sterile room. The Englishman smiled at him and politely shook his hand. The man then stared down at some papers and looked up briefly at Duc.

The Englishman was then joined by a woman. A nurse, Duc assumed. They urged him to sit on a chair in the centre of the room. He faced away from them and the woman gently bent his neck forward so that his chin rested on his chest. He saw the nurse unsheathe a syringe and the Englishman then drew up some type of fluid inside it. Duc wondered if he was to be given a vaccination.

'Sharp sting,' the nurse said.

Duc winced briefly, but within a minute he felt nothing in his neck.

'Hold still. This won't take a minute,' the Englishman reassured.

Duc held still. Who was he to question these people? They had saved his life. He could feel a vague sense of pulling and tugging at his neck, but no pain.

'There. All done,' the Englishman said.

Duc then had a strange experience. Some recent memories flashed into his mind, and then started to collapse on top of each other, like a house of cards. And then they were gone. He could not work out how much time had passed. But then time itself also collapsed. It too was gone.

The nurse helped him to his feet. He rubbed his neck. It was still numb. She ushered him out through a different door. He quickly turned around before the door closed behind him, only to see another refugee, a young woman, being guided to sit down on the chair.

Duc was then forcefully led by the arm by another man, dressed in black, down a long corridor. He started to feel lightheaded. No, not lightheaded… confused. No… scared. No… *what was the word*?

What is happening to me?

It soon became harder to walk.

Where am I?

He stopped walking and looked around.

On a boat. No… a bus. No… in the water. No… Vietnam.

Assisted by the man in black, Duc was taken through another door and into a vast room. The last image he could put words to was row after row of his fellow refugees, lying on barouches, unconscious.

They were all face down.

***

Duc, his own name now long forgotten, moved silently among the Thornhill mob. He was driven by hunger and by survival. One of the group, catching an aroma of something edible, would move in a new direction and the others would follow. They would avoid the lights whenever they could. Their instincts, for that was all they had left, told them to do this, rather than any conscious thought.

Duc no longer existed.

Patient X had been born.

107

THE ENGLISHMAN STARED with enormous satisfaction at the neatly arranged line of syringes in front of him. Each one was filled with a pale, straw-coloured fluid.

The most beautiful hue in the world.

All he could do was look, because a thick layer of reinforced glass formed a protective barrier between the syringes and the outside world. Look, but don't touch.

I would love to hold one of you. Just one more time.

The temperature gauge of the isolated booth the syringes were held in indicated a constant thirty-seven degrees centigrade.

Precise body temperature. Just perfect. No risk of sample degradation.

He closed his eyes and imagined what each filled vial contained.

Logic.

Memory.

Dreams.

Hope.

Fear.

Love.

Hate.

When he opened his eyes again his thoughts turned to more tangible issues: *their market value.*

That was what brought the biggest smile to his face. Having a gift for numbers, he quickly calculated the monetary value per millilitre of fluid, the value per syringe, the total value of all samples combined, and finally—and most importantly—his cut of the total shipment.

There were two wonderful Lucian Freud paintings at Sotheby's that he'd had his eye on for some weeks. They were due to be auctioned in a fortnight. The reserve price for each painting was over four million pounds.

I might take both.

As he stared at the samples, he pulled out his mobile phone and dialled.

'The technique has been perfected,' the Englishman confirmed to the man on the end of the line.

'How do you know?'

'I was there to see it for myself.'

'At the lab?'

'Yes, of course. I was there for the entire process. The harvesting, the shipping, and the storage. It is one of the most beautiful sights in nature. In the universe. To see a human mind laid bare. Stripped back to its most basic, most wonderful form. It is really art, you know. It transcends science.' His voice was quivering with joy.

'And there are no problems in utilising it?'

'Not now. We had a few teething problems, but they've been resolved. We had believed it would be like other organs. That we would need to transport and store it cold, at around four degrees. To preserve it.'

'What happened?'

'The specimens are just too fragile. Larger, solid organs like hearts and kidneys need to be kept cold to prevent deterioration, but not these. This is where the early trials went wrong, and why we had no initial success. Then we worked out that they must be kept at the temperature of the normal, living brain. At body temperature.'

'So where are they now?'

'Half are securely stored in Geneva, purely for research, and half have returned with me to London, ready for transplantation. The facility has been cleaned and is ready to go again.'

'Very good. I have two more buyers lined up. I'm playing them off against each other, and prices are soaring! At this stage I think the Parisian consortium will win out.'

'Excellent. Your deliverymen need to be extremely careful when shipping these samples. They must, absolutely *must*, be kept at a precise temperature.' The Englishman's voice was loud and clear.

'Understood.'

'I don't need to tell you how valuable they are,' the Englishman reminded him.

'Yes, I know, I know,' the voice barked down the line with exasperation.

'When you have a final price, I will provide you with the specific location, and details of how I want the money to be transferred.'

He felt a tingle of excitement at the thought of all that cash.

'Okay.'

'And one last thing… you had better not screw me over, Lalic.'

But Ivan Lalic was already gone.

108

JACK MADE GOOD on his promise to take her out for a drink. It was an easy call, as he had one more favour to ask. Over more than a few gin and tonics, Zoe had started to open up about herself. She was very keen to show him various random posts she had made on Instagram and Facebook over the years.

'You could follow me, if you like,' she offered. 'On here,' she pointed at her open Insta account.

'Ahh, sorry, I'd love to, but forensic psychiatrists really can't have a presence on social media. Too easy to be hacked or stalked!'

She looked disappointed but also intrigued. 'Oh, you make it sound so exciting, Jack. Stalking, hey?' she said with a wink.

They ordered some food and he asked Zoe about her uncle, Sir Roger.

'Uggggh,' was her instant reply. 'He's such a knob! He barely even speaks to me at work. He probably just saw me as a charity case when he got me that job. But I had worked hard and I earned it.' She gestured with her finger for Jack to lean in close to her.

When he did, she whispered, 'Three times married, three times divorced. Stinks of cigars. His own son doesn't even talk to him. And... major gambling problems.'

Jack showed her he was surprised.

'*Major*,' she emphasised. 'But enough about him. Oh, I know! I know what I had to tell you! I dug a bit deeper into that chap you asked me about... Barnard?'

'Ah yes,' said Jack, suddenly interested, even though he was unsure where this was headed.

'Well there is *no* psychiatrist called Andrew Barnard in the NHS but...' she laughed out loud and took a moment to compose herself. 'There was a guy who came to see my uncle the other day for a meeting. It sounded pretty intense. Uncle Roger said he was some sort of posh science guy. He looked about the age you said, but his name wasn't Andrew Barnard. It was *Horatio!*' She laughed raucously again.

Jack couldn't quite follow.

'Horatio! Horatio Barnard! Oh my god, *what a name!* And I thought, *I must tell Jack.*'

Jack slowly shook his head.

'Horatio? Horatio Barnard?'

'Yeeeaaah.'

'Slicked back hair? Expensive suit? Air of superiority about him?'

'Yes, yes, and *definitely* yes.'

'Did your uncle say anything else about him?'

'No. He doesn't tell me anything. But I remembered that you'd asked me about Barnard. So I looked him up on the Health Department database. He is a big-time researcher. He gets oodles of funding from my uncle. Massive amounts! Millions of pounds for his lab. All paid for you by you and me with our bloody taxes!'

> *Horatio Andrew Barnard, Delegate, UK Department of Health and Private Research Facility.*

She pulled out her phone again and showed him snaps of a bikini-clad weekend away to Ibiza with the girls.

> *It's time to move.*

He ordered more drinks and asked her if she'd managed to do the other favour he'd asked. She nodded as she sucked on a straw and then happily told him where the department had archived all of the old paper files that had been kept for patients admitted to the previous forensic psychiatric facility. He had been impressed that the records at the new NTC were fully electronic and paper-free, and had understood that the paper notes were eventually going to be uploaded and digitised, but due to the massive financial hit the health budget had taken due to Covid-19, that project had been put on hold. Indefinitely. As such, the files were just sitting dormant in cardboard boxes in a storage facility. And Zoe had found the location of the building where they were being stored.

'Oh Jack, we could go together,' she slurred. 'Maybe get lost in there… have an adventure in amongst all those aisles and aisles of boxes.' She giggled.

Maybe not.

The evening was getting late, and Jack wanted to be careful not to give Zoe the wrong impression, but he feared that horse had already bolted.

109

JACK HAD TOLD the unwitting receptionist that he needed to dig out some patient files for a clinical audit process he had been asked to undertake by none other than Professor Mortimer. He hoped she would not question him.

She didn't.

He flashed his hospital ID badge in front of her face and signed the visitor register with an indecipherable squiggle. She barely even gave him a glance.

'*Here*,' she handed him a stack of unpopulated patient file cards. 'Make sure you fill these out… *in full*… if you plan on leaving this building with *any* of the records.'

'Certainly.'

'In *full*.'

'Got it.'

Thankfully, her phone then rang allowing Jack to make his way into the storage area.

He gently closed the door behind him, and a cold shiver ran down his spine as he realised he was surrounded by hundreds of boxes containing the tormented lives of thousands of criminally insane people. Some files dated back almost a century.

He felt he was being watched, but convinced himself it was just anxiety kicking in.

Jack was very grateful that the notes were archived in alphabetical order, rather than by patient ID number. The only problem now was where to look, as it would be a physical impossibility to go through every box.

Think, Jack, think.

He chose a random set of files in the desperate hope that it may trigger some idea, some plan, some memory that may set him off in the right direction.

As he flicked through the records of a now deceased serial sex offender from the sixties, he remembered something curious: he had overheard Sarah speaking to Barnard a few months ago in the staff tearoom at work.

They were unaware that Jack was nearby and they were speaking in hushed tones, but he was sure that Sarah had said 'but Andy, be careful. They might put two and two together. He's like Elle. Remember her?'

'Elle?' Barnard replied with his usual disdain.

'Yes, Elle. Just like her. And the other girl... Em.'

Barnard nodded in agreement.

Jack stared at the thousands of files in front of him.

Elle... Em... Elle... patient... Em... patient...

Patient L and Patient M.

He then thought of his own enigmatic, non-verbal patient on the ward and realised that for admin purposes he was known as 'Patient X'. A formal designation for the NHS records.

It was worth a shot, so he moved along the boxes until he found the 'P' section. He scanned the rows until he found 'P-A-T'

Jack flicked through the files.

Patanowsky.

Patar.

Patel.

Patenson.

Paterson.

Patient A.

His eyes lit up as he pulled out the musty manila folder. There were remarkably few pages of notes. The patient, a tall male of African appearance and uncertain age, had been admitted around two years ago, and had only stayed on the ward for three days. He was charged with assaulting a teenage boy who was walking home from rugby practice in Southampton. The documented clinical profile was almost a carbon copy of Patient X's.

Strangely, there was nothing recorded as to his discharge address or his eventual legal status at the time.

The discharge diagnosis, completed by Dr Barnard, was 'malingering.'

'*What?*' Jack exclaimed to himself. 'So he was just faking it, was he, Barnard?'

Jack had assumed that Patient X was given that name because 'X' was an unknown quantity. He'd also assumed that Patient X was unique.

But he was shocked to realise that 'Patient X' was one in a line of many others.

One of 24, to be precise.

Starting with 'Patient A'.

Patient B was on the ward for less than twenty-four hours. An unidentified Asian female, also unable to provide a history, who had struck a fast-food worker with an iron bar by the M4 motorway. And, once again, there was no discharge address and no legal status.

The diagnosis from Barnard this time was 'personality disorder.'

And so it went on. Patients C, D, and E. They all had remarkably similar clinical presentations, and all had the same overseeing psychiatrist: Dr Drew Barnard.

And all of their medical management was taken care of by one registrar: Dr Sarah Wellington.

Not one of them had ever been reviewed by Nathan Mortimer.

Jack did not want to be caught with the original paper files, so he pulled out his iPhone and snapped as many photos as he could of the patient details and notes.

When he was done, he stuffed all the notes in the half-empty 'Z' section of the file compactus.

Jack realised that Barnard and Sarah had worked together to make sure that any previously trafficked patients who had escaped from the network would be taken care of.

It seems they had not counted on Patient X.

And they had certainly not counted on Jack Giorgio.

He then remembered Sarah pressuring him into discharging Patient X very soon after his admission. He was surprised at the time, but could also understand her point. Now it made even more sense.

Patient X was the first one of these individuals to be admitted to the NTC. The updated security protocols employed at the new forensic unit made the job of keeping any such patients under the radar extremely difficult for Barnard and Sarah.

But how the hell did they get these twenty-three previous patients discharged? How did they move them on, given that they were part of a broader legal and medical system?

A hunch told him that this was the last piece of the puzzle.

110

THE MAN, DRESSED entirely in black, had been following Jack for some time, waiting to make his move. When Jack turned a corner and entered a dimly lit laneway, the man did not hesitate any longer.

He approached quickly, from behind.

Jack did not hear him until it was too late.

A thick arm wrapped around the doctor's neck like a python.

'Don't scream. Don't say anything. Walk with me. I won't hurt you. I promise.'

Jack shuddered, but he instantly recognised the voice.

'What are you doing, Joel? What do you want?' It was hard to breathe, such was Joel's incredible and surprising strength.

The two men walked along the dark street, looking like a couple of drunken revellers staggering home to sleep it off.

When he realised that Jack was complying with his request to walk with him, Joel eased up, ever so slightly, on his grip. Jack breathed deeply, grateful for the small reprieve.

'Where are we going?'

But Joel remained silent and just kept walking, pulling Jack along with him. When Jack looked around at his face, he saw that Joel had a steely purpose in his eyes.

Real intent. I hope you are not psychotic, for both our sakes.

'Is it the planes?' Jack asked.

After about a minute, Joel stopped and let him go.

'No,' he replied, in a monotone voice. 'No planes.'

By now they had reached the edge of a small park. Given the hour, it was deserted. Joel gestured to Jack to join him there. He reluctantly followed.

'Sorry for all of this, but I have to be careful and I needed to see you. You have been kind to me, Doctor Jack. Cared for me. Treated me with dignity and respect. You actually *listened* to me. Thanks to you I am feeling much better. Much clearer.' Joel's voice certainly sounded more vibrant.

'That should be the norm, Joel. But sadly, it is the exception.'

'My father and Professor Mortimer both just wanted me out of the way. Quiet. Sedated. Not causing any trouble. For either of them.'

'I'm sorry. It is not fair at all. You did not choose to have this illness.'

Joel nodded in agreement.

'Well, I'm sick of being locked away by them. Sick of being in that horrible place of Mortimer's. I never, ever want to go back there again.' He looked at Jack with wide, pleading eyes.

'I can understand that,' Jack said. 'But how did you get out? I thought Mortimer said you weren't ready to be discharged?'

Joel glanced away, before turning back to Jack with a strange look.

'I thought the same, but then the professor came to my room and said, *"It's D-day. Discharge day! You've got yourself a free pass out of here. Now fuck off!* I was so shocked. He had never spoken like that before, but I didn't question it. I just grabbed my things and got the hell out of there.'

Jack agreed. It was very unusual for Mortimer to speak and behave like that. In light of Mortimer's illness, though, it all made sense.

Impulsive.

Erratic.

Sick.

Dying.

Joel showed Jack his arms. The wristband tracker that alerted staff if he left the ward had been removed. It seemed as though his discharge was legitimate.

'I'm sorry about putting my arm around your throat, but I was worried you would not meet me or come with me, and that you would send me back to hospital. But I do trust you, Jack. I trust that you see me as a person, not just as my symptoms. Christina would have really liked you.' Joel looked sad.

'Christina? The girl who died?'

'Yes.'

'You knew her, Joel?'

'Oh yes! We were on the ward together. She was my friend. She was beautiful. Very smart, too. Especially when she talked about art. I could listen to her for hours. She was also funny. She had a wicked sense of humour. She could memorise so many numbers at once! Her memory was amazing. I think that's how she got out of the ward. She knew all the codes. She escaped. And then I heard she was killed.' Joel looked very sad.

'She was on the ward before she died?'

'Yes, right before. Her father knew the professor, and Mortimer insisted she be admitted to his ward. She was also being given this new treatment by Mortimer. Like he did with me. An implant in the back of the neck. I don't know if it helped *her* but it didn't help me!'

Jack nodded: 'So that was what you ripped out of your neck?'

'Yes.'

'But you don't know what happened with Christina? With her implant?'

'No. In the weeks before she died I had less and less contact with her. My father didn't approve of our friendship.' Joel looked like he might cry.

'Why didn't he approve, Joel?'

'*She is trouble, boy, stay away.*' Again, Joel did a perfect imitation of his father's voice. Jack suppressed his laughter. 'After that, everywhere I went, I had one of my father's bodyguards with me.'

'That sounds oppressive.'

'Yes, it was. I gave them the slip, or so I thought, that day I went to the airport. But I am well now. My sister has said she will help me. I am sick of living under my father's rules. I don't care about his money. I have more than enough to get by. I've hidden enough away for myself over the years. I won't live like a king, but at least I will be living *my* way.' He smiled. 'I've even sold my Porsche, Jack.'

'But what about your treatment? You will need to stay on medication, Joel. I worry that if you don't take your medication you could end up really unwell again, and at risk.'

'I know. I wish you could treat me, Jack, but I know that after tonight it will not be possible. You have helped me to feel so much better, like I am really alive. Before I left the private ward I stole three boxes of those new pills you started me on. They really help. I am calmer, clearer, and there are no side effects. Don't worry, I will find a way to stay on my meds.'

Jack hoped more than anything that this was true, but he had his doubts. He had heard the same valediction made hundreds of times before by patients who would then be off their medication at the first opportunity.

'But Jack, there is something you need to know. Something very important that could change everything.'

'What's that?'

'I know that my father is involved in illegal activities. But not just weapons. I think they would call it crimes against humanity. I would go to the police, but with my history they are not going to believe me. They will just call me paranoid. And I don't know who to trust anyway, with all of my father's connections. But you… I trust *you*, Jack. You are very clever, you have credibility and can explain things so well, you can tell them these things.'

'What things, Joel?'

He then said something that made Jack's eyes widen.

'But be careful Jack, my father is a *very* dangerous man.'

Joel leant in close to Jack and whispered an eight-digit code into his ear.

111

As HE WAITED, Jack reread the magazine article he had taken from Cerise's flat. His eyes found the accompanying photograph of Cerise Lyon and Jose Navarro in Geneva.

In small print under the photo he read:

Photograph: Sam Wellington.

The photo credits that accompanied the other newspaper articles he found amongst Cerise's documents were the same.

Sam Wellington.

Jack thought back and realised that the only people at the NTC who had met 'Cerise' in person when she was with him were Sarah and Mortimer. He then recalled that when he introduced Sarah and Cerise to each other there was a very subtle hesitation, but then they seemed to make small talk as if it was the first time they had met.

You knew one another.

He needed to get some urgent answers, so he arranged to meet Sarah at their usual espresso bar. He told her that he wanted to discuss her providing a character reference for him for his medical defence lawyer in relation to his suspension.

'I just want to get back to work at the NTC,' he had lied on the phone to her.

She joined him in a corner booth. 'How are you holding up, Jack?' she asked with superficial concern.

'Ah, you know, okay I guess,' he said as he nervously sipped his coffee. 'How is Patient X?' he asked.

She looked surprised.

'Oh, well, much the same I expect.'

'Or maybe I should ask: *where* is Patient X?'

'*Where?* What do you mean?'

She looked stunned.

He kept his reply vague, to see how she responded, 'Oh, come on, Sarah. I know all about what's been happening.'

He let the broad statement hang in the air between them and sat back with his coffee. He waited. He could sense she was unsure how to respond.

After a minute she spoke tentatively. 'I am not sure what you mean, Jack. I'm not following.'

He decided it was now or never. 'So what was the final diagnosis? Malingering? Personality disorder? What did Barnard conjure up *this* time?'

'Conjure up?' she blandly repeated.

'Yes. After 24 patients it must get quite tricky to find a new, plausible diagnosis. One wouldn't want to discharge all these patients with the same diagnosis. It might start looking suspicious, wouldn't you say, Sarah?'

A look of horror washed over her face.

> *Bullseye.*

***

He ordered them both a second coffee.

'So take me back, Sarah. When did you first meet Sandrine? It's important I know that detail.'

A look of resignation appeared on her face.

'Not long after I got to Africa. I could tell pretty quickly that she was not quite *right*. You know what it's like… a shrink can detect these things.'

Jack nodded and encouraged her to continue.

'I met her at a regional clinic I was posted to with MSF. She said she was high up in a big pharmaceutical company, she really knew what she was talking about. She was so switched-on and engaging, and, most importantly, was promising to get free medication for the locals. Not just antibiotics and birth control. She said she could also get antipsychotic and antidepressant medication into the clinic for my patients. *I couldn't believe it.* Tens of thousands of pounds worth of medication for the desperately poor and severely ill. Naturally, I jumped at the chance. We became friendly and she was so interested in the clinic and the work I was doing. But the meds never arrived. And when I finally pushed her about it, she seemed to... *shatter.*'

'Shatter,' Jack softly repeated to no one in particular.

'Yeah, she seemed frightened and, frankly, extremely paranoid. She went on and on about MTR and conspiracies and Interpol. Then she vanished. So when I saw you with her here in London, I was shocked. I had to look twice to be sure. I was confused when you introduced her as Cerise Navarro, as I'd known her as Sandrine. But I also knew there was a scientist at MTR called Navarro, so I thought maybe they were related and it kind of made sense. In truth, I didn't really know what to think or how to react. What were the odds, Jack? You seemed so happy together and she looked so much better. She clearly adored you and it seemed like your love was somehow making her better. I didn't want to get in the way of that.'

Jack's sadness was starting to feel a bit overwhelming, so he moved the conversation on by producing the newspaper and magazine articles with Sam's name on the photo credits.

'And this? How do you explain your husband being the photographer for this piece?'

She didn't flinch. 'Sam was never in Africa purely as a journalist. That was his officially role, as it was easier for him to move around that way. But really, he was part of the private security surveillance detail for high-paying corporations, including MTR. He thinks I never knew about his side-gigs, but I always did.' She laughed. 'Can't hide anything from a psych, hey?'

Jack did not laugh.

Sarah continued, 'He had also seen Sandrine hanging around the edges of MTR, so they started to chat. She convinced him that she worked there and he told her about my work with MSF. She was fascinated. You have to understand, Jack, that Africa changed me. Really changed me.'

   Yes, into a psychopath.

'In what way?' he asked.

'I realised I had come from absolute privilege: growing up white, Western, middle class, intelligent, educated. I'd pretty much been handed a wonderful life on a silver platter. But what I saw there, working with MSF, I could never have imagined. The abject poverty, the total corruption, the complete lack of basic healthcare. Money diverted from medications into mansions. Even in the Twenty-First Century. So what was I to do? Just forget about all that I had witnessed and experienced? Erase it from my memory and return to the same Western merry-go-round of study, work, BMWs, beach houses, dinner parties and private schools? For what?'

She looked very sad.

'So what *did* you do?'

'I had always loved science, Jack. Adored it. The building blocks of the mind. It was why I became a psychiatrist. To merge the basic biology with the individual person. But in Africa, I lived with humanity's despair to such a shocking degree. It made me even more determined to make a difference.'

He nodded.

'I had done all this research. It was all on the clinical and cognitive side of the mind, but I lacked the technical, refined molecular neuroscience techniques. I thought if I could just perfect some type of cheap, reproducible, fundamental techniques for these people who had nothing then I could help so many at minimal cost. But I didn't have the background in that basic neural receptor work.'

'Enter Barnard?'

'Precisely. Barnard is brilliant. He plays the fool but in reality, he's a genius. A twisted genius, but a genius all the same. Where you and I see humans, all he could see was *subjects*. Tissues. Cells. Chemicals. That was all the human mind was to him. But he came in with all the ground-breaking techniques and, importantly, the money. He had the backing. He promised me that we would achieve so much, save so many lives together. Blah, blah, blah. I believed him but it was all bullshit.'

Jack could not decide if Sarah was an innocent party or not. He urged her to continue.

'I was seeing dozens of patients a day in my clinic, which meant that I always felt as though I wasn't spending enough time with them. But Barnard would step in and speak with them. I thought he was helping, but he was recruiting for his experiments. I remember Sandrine noticed this too, and she was wanting to spend more time with Barnard.'

'More time?' Jack asked.

'Yes, I remember once walking into the back of the clinic after hours and seeing the two of them chatting in hushed tones. There was a teenage boy with emerging schizophrenia, face down on the bed, sedated. Barnard was explaining to Sandrine his views about how it was possible to gain direct neural access through the back of the neck. He was too guarded and wary to tell her anything about what he was really doing, though. They both hovered over this boy's neck like a couple of vultures. Sandrine was utterly engrossed. I will never forget that.'

Necks.

She was engrossed.

'We had some early disasters with patients. It was so bloody primitive at the start. I realised where it was all headed with these poor souls and so I protested. I spoke up. I said I would leave. I would go to the authorities. Barnard threatened me. He blackmailed me. Told me he had connections and that they would get to Sam. I was scared. I was forced to collaborate with him, but then we started making breakthroughs. Genuine pioneering discoveries.'

Jack was stunned. The coffees were slowly going cold in front of them.

'And then the research stopped?' he asked.

'Well, the *published* research did. But the *work* continued at a furious pace. More money came in. The more refinements we made, the more successful it was. And the more private and underground it became.'

'More *successful?*'

'Yes.' She stared at him soberly with wide, piercing eyes. 'Live and complete Homo sapiens neurocognitive extraction via gamma-magnet extraction and implantation. Authored by Sarah K Wellington and Horatio A Barnard. Unpublished original research and field trials.'

'Bloody hell,' Jack whispered. He felt a tremor rip through his entire body. 'Mind extraction? But *how?*'

'It was brilliant in its simplicity. You know how an MRI scanner works to capture highly detailed anatomical images of the body? Your body is placed in what is essentially a huge spinning magnet that forces all the negative and positive ions in your body to line up and say "cheese". Well, Barnard developed a tiny neuromagnet that lined up and extracted the positive and negative ions specific to certain nerve cells in the brain. That's not entirely accurate. It's not the brain *cells* exactly—they are left intact—but the neurotransmitter receptors *inside* the cells are targeted and extracted by the gamma magnet. The final missing step, the step that I had suggested, was to add a biomarker, acetylcholine—the "thought chemical"—to make sure that what was being harvested was tailored *specifically* to the parts of the brain responsible for higher human thought. It was *thinking* we were after, not the basics of life… and *voila.*'

'Jesus.'

'Barnard initially told me it was only going be to used so that better mental health treatments could be developed at a much faster rate. When I saw that it worked, I believed him. Stupid me. It was a complete success. In the end. But so many innocent humans suffered because of this. It became a horror show. At first, most of them died immediately. But then the donors started to live. Which was worse. When I say "live", this isn't really an accurate description. *"Exist"* is probably a better word. There was simply no point doing animal research, as the mind was human-specific. So we went straight to people. I was so convinced that the greater good was eventually going to be served and that millions could be helped. I truly believed that. And now, Jack, you must believe *me*.'

He didn't know what—or who—to believe. He reached into his pocket and retrieved the small, white device he had found in Cerise's flat. He gently placed it on the table in front of Sarah. She look perplexed.

'And this, Sarah? Is this what you are talking about? Barnard's little horror show?'

'What? Where did you get that?'

She deftly snapped it in half and it examined it.

'What is it, Sarah?'

She gave a short laugh which irritated Jack.

'It's a piece of plastic, Jack. It looks a little like the cartridges that Barnard loads with the gamma magnet, but it's nothing more than a useless imitation.'

This was what Cerise and Mortimer were passing off as Positrex? Nothing more than a piece of plastic? Jack was mortified at the severity of their shared delusion. He returned to Sarah.

'And in London, why did you continue working with Barnard? On the ward?'

'Like I said, he was blackmailing me. I'd hoped that leaving Africa would put a stop to it, but he followed me here and started threatening my children's safety, as well as my husband's. *My children, Jack!* So I was stuck at the Tindal Centre. When Patient X was admitted I thought it was my chance to get out of it. I thought I could gather the evidence and link the patient to Barnard and… and… and then you arrived. I hoped you could see through it all and be the one to finally expose Barnard.' She was close to tears. Jack recalled all the snide comments Barnard had made to her about her children.

'But, Sarah, who was backing him? Where was the money coming from?'

She suddenly looked very nervous. Scared. Her eyes darted around the café.

'What's going on here, Jack? Who are you, really? What are you doing?'

'I'm just after the truth, Sarah. The truth. Remember *that?*'

She threw him a cold look.

'I *can't* say. This is bigger than all of us, Jack. So much bigger. You have to see that!'

She suddenly stood up.

'Bigger?'

'Yes, Jack. You need to think big. As high as it can go. But be careful Jack, these people don't muck around.'

She suddenly got up to leave.

'And Jack…'

'Yes?'

'Keep your Italian personality in check. Don't be so… *cavalier.*'

112

JACK HIT THE ground running.

He needed time and space to think things through.

> *The final elusive piece.*

It was right there in front of him. He could feel it.

Within fifteen minutes of setting off along the Embankment he felt like he was nothing more than a pair of legs moving a body. His mind started to clear. It felt like all the static and white noise had flowed out of his ears, nose, and mouth.

Pure thoughts remained.

The sweat started to accumulate on his toned body.

His mind kept taking him back to Sarah. To their final conversation.

Again.

And again.

She seemed frightened.

> *Who backed Barnard?*
>
> *This is much bigger, Jack.*
>
> *High as it can go.*
>
> *Bigger.*
>
> *Big.*
>
> *The biggest.*

He passed by the MI5 building at incredible pace.

> *Keep your Italian personality in check, Jack.*

Italian.

Don't be so cavalier.

Such a specific word.

Cavalier.

Italian.

In check.

Cheque.

Cavalier.

And then it dawned on him.

She was telling him something.

Cavalier.

Italian.

Cavaliere. In English it means 'knight'.

Knighthood.

Sir.

But not Sir Nathan Mortimer.

Who else?

Much bigger.

As high as it can go.

He stopped running and stood by the Thames staring into the cold, dark water.

Big Ben chimed and he could see the Houses of Parliament.

Under UK law, the one and only person who had complete discretionary power over the ultimate housing and disposal of forensic psychiatric patients was the Secretary of State for Health and Social Care.

Typically, it was the judiciary or the medical staff who decided where such patients were to be held. So, of course, such a power was only invoked in exceedingly rare circumstances, as the government always wanted to allow for completely independence between the courts and the Department of Health.

He pulled out his phone and looked at the photos he had taken.

He magnified the images on file after file, and saw the same signature on the discharge papers of all 23 patients.

> *Sir Roger Maxwell, Secretary of State for Health and Social Care.*

He had the final link in the chain.

> *Maxwell!*

Jack quickly looked around, as though someone might be able to hear his thoughts, given they were now screaming inside his head.

Sarah Wellington was providing the medical care.

Horatio Andrew Barnard had the technical expertise to harvest the minds.

And it was all lubricated and funded by Sir Roger Maxwell.

Which left Nathan Mortimer… *absolutely nowhere.*

'He's not involved,' Jack whispered to himself. 'He doesn't even know. I think Portman has been after the wrong guy.'

But then a question popped into his mind:

> *Who was providing the transport and the muscle?*

113

JACK PUNCHED IN the code that Joel had given him and held his breath.

A moment later the elevator doors slid silently open, and he stepped inside. The small, black camera glared down at him.

He travelled up to Lalic's penthouse. The front door was unlocked, as had been the case on his previous visits. Lalic clearly assumed that no one would be able to break the code to access the lift: and if they did, they would be confronted by his personal security detail, which would quickly have them wishing they'd not made it that far.

If he wasn't so tense, he would have shuddered and then laughed at the gaudy nouveau riche furnishings. He quickly moved through the lounge room and past the kitchen.

It was then that he saw him.

Lalic's enormous bodyguard, Bruno. He strolled past the other entrance to the kitchen and moved out onto the balcony. Jack watched from the corner of the kitchen as Bruno lit up a large cigar and took a sip from a crystal tumbler of what looked like Lalic's single-malt whiskey.

Careful, Bruno. Don't let the boss catch you.

Jack quickly dropped down onto his hands and knees, and quietly crawled through the kitchen. From the other side, he could see the heavy black boots of Bruno through the thick, double-glazed glass door. The bodyguard was facing out over the balcony, clearly enjoying the views of the city, along with his boss's whiskey and cigar. It seemed that Bruno was unlikely to be in a rush to get back inside.

Jack pushed on towards Lalic's private study.

He moved through the huge master bedroom. The bed was a mess and clothes were strewn all over the floor.

In contrast, the private study that was located immediately behind the master bedroom was immaculate. A white iMac sat neatly in the centre of a spotlessly clean desk.

Jack hoped that he would accurately recall the conversation he'd had with Joel in the park.

> *'There is one other password you need. For my father's computer.'*

> *'What is it?'*

> *'What else could it be? PianoMan.'*

He sat down at the desk and switched on the iMac.

As he waited, he heard a booming male voice speaking in an angry tone. It was Bruno. Jack froze and listened.

He waited for the heavy thud of Bruno's footsteps, but none came.

> *He must still be out on the balcony.*

He could only hear Bruno's voice.

> *He must be on the phone.*

The gravelly voice spoke in Italian. Not the formal, official language of the north. Jack recognised the dialect: Calabrese.

'... baby, no, I was not with Francesca on Saturday night. I was *working*. The boss needed me for a job. Don't get so angry. You are crazy!'

> *Woman trouble, Bruno?*

Jack turned back to computer screen and entered the password. It was correct. He breathed a sigh of relief.

> *But who needs passwords when you've got Bruno?*

He swiftly scrolled through the files and documents that Lalic had on the hard drive. Most of them related to the financial details of his 'legitimate' businesses, like the Rolls Royce dealership.

Bruno's voice suddenly became clearer.

He's opened the door!

'Baby, no! You can't come here... because the boss doesn't like it...'

Jack heard the gentle clink of the crystal glass being deposited on the kitchen bench. He then heard the balcony door close again, followed by the slightly muted sound of Bruno pleading with his lover.

Jack kept searching. He was amazed at how many companies, both real and dummy, Lalic controlled.

Eventually, he found a folder titled 'Imports/Exports' buried deep inside a string of other folders. When he opened it, he found an enormous spreadsheet containing names, dates of birth, countries of origin, and what appeared to be final destinations.

There were many hundreds of entries.

He jammed a USB stick into the computer and coped the files as quickly as he could. As they transferred, he kept reading the screen.

When he dragged the spreadsheet to its extreme right border, he found further columns that were more cryptic.

He read across the headings, which appeared to be in code.

PC.

RX.

TR.

He then looked down the first column, the one titled PC.

PC? PC?

He stared down at the letters appearing underneath. Each individual person appeared to be allocated to one of three subsections.

Several were allocated to 'GO'.

Others to 'ARA'.

But, by a considerable margin, most were allocated the letters 'MTR'.

MTR.

> *MTR.*

He looked back at the top of the column.

PC.

> *Pharmaceutical Company.*

It quickly fell into place. RX was the old-fashioned medical abbreviation, meaning 'treatment prescribed'. These must be the companies who were buying the harvested minds. They could then run their own lab tests on them.

The other column, TR, related to minds that were sold, to be transplanted into the highest bidders.

> *Transplant Recipients.*

The fees paid were astronomical.

He also noticed under the heading 'LOCN' the letters 'STN' repeated several times over.

> *LOCN?*

> *STN?*

> *STN?*

It then hit him.

LOCN: This could be an abbreviation for 'location', in which case, 'STN' would be an abbreviation for a particular location. But where?

He typed the search terms 'location abbreviation UK STN' into his iPhone. The first thing that came up was 'Stanstead airport code', but it seemed unlikely that they would be flying the donors in. He scrolled down and found a list of freight location codes on the UK government website. STN. Southampton. Of course! It would be so easy for them to make use of the busy shipping routes.

He looked back at the spread sheet. Another 'shipment' was due in the early hours of the following morning.

It was annotated.

> *Tx Lx.*

Jack had seen that a million times before: Treatment Location.

Next, in parentheses: *(Nty).*

He quickly opened up '*maps*' on the screen and switched to satellite mode, zooming right over Southampton. His fingers trembled as he scrolled with the mouse over a large, isolated building.

He looked up the ceiling as he whispered, '*Netley.*'

A message flashed up on the screen informing him that the file transfer was complete. He had the entire contents of the 'Imports/ Exports' folder.

> *Evidence.*

He yanked the USB stick out of the back of the iMac, but before he could stand up a huge hand wrapped firmly around his wrist.

'What the *fuck* are you doing?' demanded Bruno.

114

Bruno forced Jack out into the lounge room and sat him down on one of the leather sofas before positioning himself between the capture doctor and the front door of the penthouse. He then pulled out his phone and dialled.

'We have an unexpected visitor.... Yes... Doctor Giorgio.... Yes... No... I don't know...'

He kept his eyes on Jack the entire time. He then switched into one of the Slavonic languages, so that Jack had no idea what was being said.

He finished the call. 'Boss will be here in thirty minutes'.

It was clear to Jack that he would be unable to out-muscle this guy. He would have to outthink him.

If I sit here and wait for Lalic, I'm dead.

'Thirty minutes?' Jack asked in the fluent Calabrese he learnt as a boy.

Bruno looked bemused and was clearly unsure of how to respond.

Excellent

'Hmm,' Bruno grunted. A text message alert pinged brightly on his phone. He quickly read it and visibly winced.

'Trouble with the girlfriend?' asked Jack, again in Calabrese.

Bruno ignored him and sent a response to the message.

Jack made a mental list of everything he could glean about Bruno, to see if there might be any weaknesses in his formidable armour.

Mid-twenties. Physically imposing. Likely to be ex-military—there was some sort of regiment tattoo on his inner wrist.

So why did he leave?

No. He didn't leave. The tattoo suggested he was loyal to them. So he was forced to go. Kicked out.

Why?

Drugs? No. Too obvious. And he doesn't have the body of a drug user.

Too impulsive for an elite special unit?

His height and physical prowess would have taken him far when he was young, but if he had been given too much responsibility too soon, he could have cracked. That seemed plausible. The man had lost it in some way.

After he was kicked out of the military, he'd then found well-paid security work with Lalic. Easy job. Easy money. Easy access to cigars, expensive cars, penthouses, women. Poor Calabrese boy makes good in London. But under the surface, he was still lost. That's why he'd been playing around behind his girlfriend's back. He was still trying to run away from his demons. And women were an easy place to run to.

He's Impulsive. Give him a sudden dilemma. A sudden conflict. Knock him off balance. He might just lose it.

Bruno was still standing with his back to the front door.

Jack waited until Bruno was checking his phone again. Distracted. Suddenly, Jack's eyes widened and he stood up. He straightened his arm and pointed a finger past Bruno.

'Lalic!' he cried. 'You got here faster than expected!'

As Bruno dropped the phone and spun around, Jack ran for the balcony door and bolted to the far edge of the railing.

In an instant, Bruno was standing at the balcony door, his jacket off, his pistol drawn and aimed at Jack's chest. He was tense and breathing hard. A few droplets of sweat had formed on his forehead.

Fight or flight. Let's get that adrenaline flowing, Bruno.

Jack climbed onto the balcony railing. He could see back into the penthouse. In his haste, Bruno had left his phone behind on the floor.

No time to text the girlfriend back now, Bruno.

'Get down now or I will shoot you,' Bruno said in Calabrese.

'If you shoot me, I will fall backwards. The moment I hit the ground, a crowd will start to form. Someone will call the police, and they'll be here within minutes, at the most. After all, this is Knightsbridge. The crowd will be pointing up to this penthouse and will dutifully tell the police that the poor dead man fell from *up here.*'

Bruno took a tentative step forward and then a step back. The gun was starting to waver. He looked behind him into the lounge room.

'If we are still standing here when Lalic arrives, I will jump,' Jack said, again in Calabrese. 'I imagine that you will have quite a few questions to answer if that were to happen, Bruno.' Jack produced the USB stick and waved it in the air.

Bruno's mobile phone started ringing, causing him to flinch.

'Is it Francesca or is it Lalic?' Jack asked with a smirk. Bruno was distracted. He took his eyes off Jack as he turned to look inside. 'It doesn't really matter either way. They both have control of you!' Jack laughed loudly.

'Shut up!' Bruno yelled. 'Just stop this fucking talking!' He waved the gun above his head.

His phone rang again.

'What are you going to do Bruno? You'd better decide quick smart. Are you going to shoot me? Are you going to answer your phone? What if it's Lalic? Quick! Hurry up! Lalic will be here soon... or maybe there's been a change of plan and he needs to speak to you...'

Jack edged closer back to oblivion as Bruno stared back at his phone. The armpits of Bruno's tight t-shirt were beginning to reveal dark patches of sweat.

The phone rang for a third time.

'Maybe it *is* Francesca. Or one of the other whores you've been screwing?'

Bruno took a step towards him. '*Shut the fuck up!*' he said in an angry tone. He looked around again.

The phone kept ringing.

More sweat had formed.

'How much does Francesca charge you per hour?'

'What?!' He inched closer to Jack.

> *Keep coming. Keep coming. Get angry, Calabrese boy.*

'Because your mama charges me one Euro!' Jack said with a smile.

'*YOU FUCK!*'

Bruno ran at Jack, who was now perched up on the corner ledge of the balcony. The bull was charging. He dropped the gun and ran with both arms straight out in front him, ready to throttle Jack.

Jack crouched down as low as he could go, until his muscles were burning. Bruno was inches from him, baring his teeth, blind with fury.

Jack held his nerve and waited until the very last moment.

Bruno lunged for him. Jack sprung high into the air and over Bruno's head. He landed hard on the balcony, but recovered himself enough to reach out and grab Bruno's pistol. He aimed it at the back of Bruno's head, as the bodyguard was still facing away from him.

'I've got your gun, Bruno. Don't move, and don't turn around.'

Jack swiftly stepped back inside and locked the heavy glass door behind him.

The moment he locked the door, Bruno turned and charged at it.

Thank God Lalic spared no expense on the security glass.

For a moment, Jack entertained the idea of taunting Bruno, but quickly decided against it.

Stay focused. You're only ten minutes into a marathon.

Instead, he found the remote control for the metal security shutters. He watched with relief as Bruno's livid face slowly disappeared, as the metal curtain came down at the end of a particularly disturbing Punch and Judy show.

115

JACK QUICKLY GRABBED Bruno's phone and sent a text message to Lalic:

Giorgio locked in your ensuite.

He then slipped the phone into his pocket. He then rifled through Bruno's jacket pocket and found a set of car keys. The heavy platinum ring was embossed with the distinctive 'RR' logo.

Jack hurried to the kitchen and slid into the huge walk-in pantry, closing the door behind him.

Then he waited.

He held the gun at the ready, and focused on his breathing. His many years of running had given him great control over his respiration; a skill that he was now incredibly grateful for.

Within a minute he heard voices and footsteps out in the apartment.

Lalic and… a woman. It must be Misha, his other bodyguard.

> *'…won't take long…'*

> *'…Bruno's message…'*

> *'…great pleasure…'*

He held his breath as he saw the shadows move right past the pantry door.

When they had passed, Jack quickly moved out of the kitchen, through the living room, and headed straight for the front door.

> *Do I have five seconds? Ten?*

'Bruno?' Misha called.

'Bruno?' Lalic repeated in a louder voice.

The last sound that Jack heard as he gently closed the front door was the deep thud of a large fist banging on the balcony window.

***

Jack hit the 'unlock' button and the orange indicator lights of the Rolls Royce Phantom flashed twice. He slid onto the plush leather seat and started the twelve-cylinder engine. The car was so well insulated from outside noise, and the motor was so refined and quiet that he had to hit the accelerator pedal a few times to convince himself that the car had actually started.

I am stealing a Rolls Royce owned by a psychopathic arms dealer. I never thought my life would end like this.

In the rear view mirror he could see that the elevator doors remained open, and were now perpetually frustrated by Bruno's thick leather jacket which lay across the door sensor. The lift's doors would begin to close, hesitate, re-open, stutter, and attempt to close again.

That should buy some time to get a head start.

Jack hadn't really considered how he would get out of the underground carpark, other than accelerating as hard as he could and smashing through the door, but he was relieved to discover that the Lalic had fitted the Rolls with a remote control that was connected to the automatic garage door, and he was soon cruising out onto the streets of Knightsbridge.

The dramatically darkened windows gave him some visual protection from the outside world, but he knew it wouldn't be long before the car was located.

He quickly set the GPS and headed west for the M4.

The sun soon set, and Jack felt slightly more reassured. There was something about the cover of darkness that made him feel more invisible. Well, as invisible as one can feel in over two tonnes of gleaming Rolls Royce.

It then occurred to Jack that a man such as Lalic would always travel with a degree of protection. He flicked open the numerous storage compartments in the front cabin of the Rolls.

Nothing.

But Lalic would surely be driven.

He looked into the rear view mirror to the spacious back seats. The distance was vast between himself and the rear of the car. He would need to pull over if he was going to search for a weapon, and he was not sure it was worth the risk. He was sure the car would be fitted with some type of satellite tracking device.

They will be coming for you. They will be coming.

He put his foot down and headed past Belgravia and down Cromwell Road. He spotted a short, dark driveway in Earl's Court and steered the Phantom towards it. He slowly glided to a stop and turned the lights off. He sat in the car for a few moments, with all the doors locked, and looked out through the rear view mirror again, this time to the world beyond the confines of the car. He could not detect any movement and so, with the engine still running, he quickly crawled over to the back seats.

After locating a small bottle of expensive cognac, two crystal glasses, and a dozen thick cigars, all housed in a bespoke walnut container bearing the initials '*IL*', Jack finally found what he was searching for.

The small black pistol felt heavier than he would have expected. It also felt extremely cold as his fingers folded around the grip. He assumed that it was loaded, but he was not sure how to check.

He read the small, ribboned name embossed on the flat barrel.

Walther PPK.

007! Jesus, this guy really is in love with the West.

Pistol in hand, Jack climbed over to the front seat and drove on, towards the M4 and Southampton.

116

JACK REASONED THAT Lalic must have figured out where he was headed, but as far as he could tell he was not being followed. He assumed he was being tracked but had no clear idea how to tell. He tried to remain vigilant, but he missed the black Range Rover several cars behind him.

I just need to get there first.

He needed back-up, so he called Portman as he drove, explaining what he had discovered and where he was headed.

'You should have waited for me,' Portman sounded concerned more than angry.

'There was no time! I have to stop anyone else from being harmed. I have to get there before any more minds are lost forever.'

The drive took four hours, but he finally hit the outskirts of Southampton. It was well after midnight, but as he closed in on his destination, he found that he had never felt more awake. More *alive*.

Jack had told Portman where to meet. He hoped he was right, and that Portman would keep up his end of the deal. He did not want to face two psychopaths on his own.

But he also knew that he had just one shot, if they were going to get Lalic and Barnard. And tonight was that one shot.

One shot.

Jack knew he'd have to abandon the Rolls before he reached the hospital. It was too much of a risk to continue driving—especially given how conspicuous Lalic's car was.

Seeing Jack pull into a narrow, dead-end side street confused the two men following him.

Why had he done that?

Was it a trap?

They held back for a moment and then proceeded with caution. They climbed out of the Range Rover, but left the headlights on. Once they'd established that the Rolls Royce was empty, they hurried to the narrow pathway at the end of the alley.

Nothing.

A mobile phone rang inside one of their pockets and was hastily answered.

'Yes. He is.'

Moments later, a second SUV with pitch-black windows pulled up.

Bruno was at the wheel.

The near-side rear window silently slid open.

'Get in,' Ivan Lalic commanded.

117

WITHIN MINUTES, JACK had settled into a smooth stride. He pushed images of Cerise out of his mind. Running often reminded him of her. His feet began to feel sore after around fifteen minutes or so, but instead of ignoring the pain, he decided to focus on it.

After a further fifteen minutes the pain had become a steady, dull ache. Jack kept on running and did not dare to look behind him. He could feel tension in his upper body, and worried that at any minute he would feel a large hand grab his shoulder and pull him to the ground.

Is this what Christina went through?

The narrow streets were as good as deserted at that time of night. At times he would dash past late-night revellers who were making their way home from parties or pubs, but they were too wrapped up in themselves to pay any attention to Jack.

He allowed himself to slow to a walk when he crossed the bridge at Pilgrim Way. When he got to the other side, he allowed himself the luxury of looking over his shoulder.

Nothing.

He looked out towards the English Channel, and he thought he could make out the silhouette of a massive, dark cruiser.

He continued to walk once he had crossed the bridge. He headed towards the harbour, making several more twists and turns as he snaked his way towards his ultimate location.

He knew it was not enough to simply locate the hangar where Lalic's ship would be stored and the refugees unloaded. The transplantation work needed to be done in a more discreet setting. A medical facility.

After a few more turns, he finally arrived at his destination.

***

The Netley Hospital had been built in the 1850s and operated for over a century, until it eventually closed in the late 1970s. Florence Nightingale had been a critic of the hospital's design, but it had been quite a monument to maritime medical care.

But now, it had been left to decay.

Or so people believed.

The great physicians who practiced there in the nineteenth and twentieth centuries would be turning in their graves if they knew what was taking place there.

Jack checked his watch. It was quarter past one in the morning.

He checked behind him. Still nothing.

He crept through the hospital grounds. There was no one around. He thought he could see a dim light coming from inside the abandoned building, but the grounds were incredibly dark.

> *How far away are you, Portman?*

Jack heard voices in the distance. It was a foreign language that he could not quite decipher. He followed the sounds, and the conversations gradually became louder and clearer as the voices echoed off the old stone walls.

> *Eastern European.*

He entered one of the central courtyards, and darkness swallowed him whole.

118

INCH BY TINY inch, Jack quietly moved towards the dim light that was just visible through a distant window. When he reached the building, he tried to gently prise the window open. After a bit of encouragement it slid up, the catch long since rusted away in the maritime air.

He dared not use his mobile phone torch, so he crawled through the opening and walked with his hands stretched out in front of him, feeling his way through the shadowy corridors, moving in the direction of the light.

The light became brighter and the voices became louder.

Then they suddenly stopped.

Footsteps.

A door slammed.

Then silence.

In the quiet, Jack took his chance and swiftly moved closer to the source of the light. He could see his surroundings now. The corridor was littered with the decaying remnants of obsolete medical care. Old drip stands, dusty glass beakers, broken chairs, a tattered grey straitjacket, the odd medical textbook.

His mind suddenly turned to Mortimer. The professor's words ringing in his ears, '*Have we really come that far, Jack?*'

Portraits of some of the great medical pioneers lined the walls.

Jack scanned their faces. Charcot, Jenner, Lister, Cushing, Florey. All staring down. A galaxy of medical stars.

Hanging proudly over the door at the end of the corridor was none other than Sigmund Freud.

How fitting.

Jack wondered if the doorway marked the entrance to the part of the hospital that had been used as a psychiatric asylum. He even stepped past another old discarded straightjacket.

He gripped the door handle and slowly turned it. The door swung open, revealing a stark, brightly lit treatment room. He walked in and closed the door behind him.

The room was incredibly well stocked. Not only was there a hospital bed, there were also collection tubes, syringes, needles, torniquets, bandages, and medications. Anyone would think it was a fully functioning medical clinic.

Not a torture chamber of misery and death.

He pulled out his phone, snapped as many photos as he could, and quickly sent them to Portman.

A door led through to a second room that contained what appeared to be a glass-fronted incubator the size of small fridge. It was about a quarter full of vials, which contained straw-coloured specimens. It was like nothing he had ever seen. The temperature was set to 37 degrees centigrade.

Human body temperature.

Human brain temperature.

Storage of the human mind.

More photos.

Still no sign of Portman.

One final door led through to a small, dark room.

A light suddenly flicked on. He felt an arm around his chest and the cold, hard blade of a knife at his throat.

'Do not fucking move, Giorgio,' a familiar voice hissed into his ear.

119

Lalic released his grip on Jack, and moved round to face him, although he the knife dangerously close to Jack's throat.

'You know, Jack, it's true what they say. Human mind is greatest machine on Earth. Amazing. I realise this in Yugoslavia, before war. Not from the scum who buy weapons from me. They were simple. They live on greed.'

You might count yourself among that number, Lalic.

'But it was common man,' Lalic continued. 'That really make me think. They fight to live. They fight for survival. I see decent men do terrible things just to stay alive. To protect their family.'

'And, let me guess, you soon realised that they would do anything to escape?' Jack said.

'Precisely,' Lalic confirmed. '*Anything.*'

'So, you stepped in to organise their transport.'

'The more desperate a man becomes, the more willing he is to believe,' Lalic said simply.

'You preyed on innocent people. You exploited their love. Their love for their families, their love of life, their love of freedom.'

'They agreed. They make choice. I just offer them a way. Like I tell you: I can make problem. I can solve problem.'

'They didn't know what they were agreeing to, Lalic.'

'Is business, Jack. You wouldn't understand.'

You are a true psychopath.

'Now, you give me back USB stick and then Bruno have quiet word with you.'

Time to change the subject.

'Okay, Lalic, I will. But first I need to tell you about Joel. It is *very* important.'

'What is so important?'

'I know where he is, Lalic. I can tell you.'

Lalic laughed.

'Is that all? You know *nothing*, doctor. He is in private ward. Locked away. No more fucking planes and airports,' Lalic nodded with certainty.

'Oh, *is* he now? I don't think so. Why don't you check the tracker on his Porsche? If he is securely locked away, then his car should be safe and sound, parked in his garage.'

As Jack expected, Lalic couldn't resist. He pulled out his smartphone, opened the tracker app and stared at the screen.

'*What the fuck!* Manchester! What he do there?'

'Just because his car's in Manchester, that doesn't mean he is,' Jack said quietly. 'His bracelet tracker from the ward should tell you where he is.'

Lalic dialled a number. Jack knew he was calling the private ward.

'Hello? Is Lalic here. How is my son?'

Jack couldn't hear the reply, but he knew what they would have said.

'What the fuck you mean you don't know?'

Another stuttered response.

'*GONE WHERE?!* What the fuck! What does tracker say?'

A further reply.

'Why tracker is off?'

Jack's fingers inched toward the Walther PPK inside his coat pocket.

'When this happen?'

Closer.

Closer.

'I can't fucking believe you let him go?! He still *SICK!*' Lalic was shaking his head violently.

Closer.

His fingers wrapped around the handle.

Keep talking.

Tighter.

'Mortimer did *WHAT?*' Lalic was lost in the moment. His arm fell to his side, the knife still clenched in his hand, but no longer an immediate threat. It was Jack's chance.

He slid the pistol out from his pocket and aimed it squarely at Lalic's forehead.

The man looked utterly shocked.

He ended the call.

Jack cocked the gun.

Lalic handed over the phone and dropped the knife.

Jack quickly directed Lalic back through into the treatment room. He instructed Lalic to remove his pants and lie down on his generous stomach.

Jack rifled through the well-stocked medication supplies. He knew exactly what he was looking for.

In a huge syringe, he drew up a wonderful combination of a highly tranquilising, high-dose antipsychotic, coupling it with plenty of liquid midazolam, a sedating benzodiazepine.

'You will have some delightful dreams, Ivan'.

'Fuck you.'

'Now hold still… just a little *prick*.'

In under a minute, Lalic was out like a light, and would be for many hours. For added insurance, Jack removed his belt and used it to tie Lalic's hands to the side of the bed as securely as he could. He wheeled the snoring psychopath into a dark, empty room off the corridor and closed the door behind him.

120

JACK HEADED BACK towards the main treatment room in the abandoned hospital. Again, he heard muffled voices nearby, and then a door slammed shut.

A soft vibration from inside his coat told him that he'd received a text.

A text.

He pulled his phone out, but before he'd had a chance to read the message, the device was grabbed from his hand by a man dressed in black.

The familiar voice of Bruno then demanded he hold still as he dragged Jack into the treatment room, using just one hand. The other hand was still clasped tightly round Jack's phone, tauntingly waving it like a carrot in front of the helpless doctor as he was hauled along the corridor.

Jack winced as the huge Italian threw him onto a chair in the centre of the room.

'*Stay!*'

A moment later Barnard walked in.

'As usual, you are right on time, Doctor Giorgio. Punctual bastard, aren't you? I thought Aussies were relaxed about such airs and graces. Anyway, welcome to my private ward.'

Come on, Portman, find us.

'Go to hell,' Jack spat.

Bruno stood over him, arms folded, like a grinning colossus.

'Now, you always loved the teaching sessions at the NTC, Jack.

But I think it's your turn to learn something new. Tonight, we're going to be focusing on *technique.* You see, old boy, the days of theoretical research models are over,' proclaimed Barnard.

'For too many years, for too many *decades*, psychiatric research has been held back by nineteenth century thinking. We have been starting at the wrong end of the problem.'

Jack shook his head. 'You can never justify what you have been doing, Barnard. You have murdered innocent people and destroyed the lives of dozens more. You have taken the one thing that made them human: their minds.'

As he tended to do, Barnard ignored the criticism and carried on.

'For too long, it was the drug companies that called all the shots in psychiatry. They made the drug and *then* found the mental illness to match it to. Does that seem right to you, Dr Giorgio?'

Jack remained silent. He knew it was useless to intervene.

Where are you, Portman?

Barnard continued, unperturbed. 'Take social phobia. It didn't even exist as a diagnosis before the advent of the SSRI antidepressants, for Christ's sake! You've got to hand it to them. It's so fucking smart, Jack. Make the drug. Find a disease, market the disease, then provide the treatment. Brilliant!' Barnard smiled, shook his head, and looked up to the ceiling. 'Brilliant,' he repeated.

Jack wondered if Barnard was about to cry with elation.

Where the hell was Portman?

'*BUT*,' Barnard said loudly, his gaze fixed on Jack. 'This approach was doing the mentally ill, the *genuinely* sick, no good at all. Their needs were being ignored. No one was getting back to basics. No one was looking at the *science*. No one was serious about finding causes for these illnesses. No one wanted to find the ultimate cures. I mean, why would they? If the drug companies *actually cured* people, they'd be out of business.'

Jack interrupted. 'That's bullshit, Barnard. Thousands of researchers have been working on those very things for decades.'

'Oh, *have* they? I don't think so. Way back in the sixties we could take the heart from a dead man and put it in a live one. In the *fucking sixties*, Jack! And yet, today, we are no closer to stopping hallucinations. To stopping delusions. To halting the negative symptoms of schizophrenia. Well... I am going to change all of that.'

He was sounding like Mortimer now.

'Don't pretend you were motivated by some pure philosophy that would deliver the greater good for humanity. It was greed, Barnard. Pure and simple,' Jack said angrily.

Come on, Portman!

He imagined Portman, wearing his stupid *Roma* cap, wandering around the labyrinthine corridors of the hospital.

'But then it occurred to me... if I can get rich off the minds of these lowly scum, these refugees, then just imagine what I could get for *your* brilliant mind, Doctor Giorgio!'

He deftly donned a pair of black surgical gloves as he spoke.

'I mean, *your* mind must be worth, what... *ten million? Twenty?* You have already learnt so much, and yet you are so fucking *young*. Some of my clients who are entering their "mature years" would love to get their hands on the mind of the brilliant Doctor Jack Giorgio!'

Jack stared at Barnard with horror.

'I'm looking at a little side business, now that we have perfected the harvesting technique. A venture that doesn't need to involve idiots like Lalic. I have established a more bespoke service for some of my wealthier clientele whose minds may be in need of a little *tune up*.'

Jack suddenly thought of Mortimer.

I have a special, private ward Jack, for special clientele…

He decided to play to Barnard's malignant narcissism and delay as much as possible by keeping him talking about his favourite topic: *himself.*

'I must say, Barnard, I *am* genuinely impressed. Mind transplants. Brilliant. Genius. Sarah explained the extraction technique, but how did you manage part two? The actual implantation?'

Barnard grinned widely and stood still.

'Oh, I am *so* glad you asked, Doctor. And you are correct: it is genius. After I realised that the harvested material needed to be stored at body temperature in order to survive, I required a mechanism by which I could reverse the harvesting process. But of course it is not as simple as just injecting the receptors into a new host.'

Jack stared at him, his eyes pleading with him to keep talking.

'Glutamate!' he loudly proclaimed.

'Glutamate? The excitation transmitter?' asked Jack.

'Absolutely, old bean. Nature's turbo charger. By infusing each sample with just a single microgram of glutamate, the harvested receptors were woken up and able to spread like wildfire right through the cerebral cortex, taking over the functioning of the host's old mind. Brilliant.' He laughed darkly and continued, 'Great minds, such as yours, could find a new brain *and* a new body… I could spread you around a bit. Oh, yes! A little Jack Giorgio *here*, some *there*. After all, why should only one person have all of you?'

Jack shook his head in astonishment. 'This is lunacy, Barnard. You will never…'

Jack's phone, which was still grasped in Bruno's huge, sweaty hand, began to ring cheerfully.

Barnard gestured to the huge Italian to pass it over.

Jack could see the name on the screen.

Portman.

'Answer,' Barnard commanded. 'Send him away.'

Jack took the phone and accepted the call.

'Yes?'

'Jack, thank God. Where the hell are you? This hospital is like a fucking rabbit warren!'

I need to think fast.

How can he find me?

'Portman, listen to me. You need to stop. Right now!' Jack implored.

'Jack... *what are you talking about?*'

He hoped Portman would catch on.

'Trying to stop a genius like Barnard is *insanity*.'

Barnard looked satisfied. So far.

Come on, stay with me, Portman.

'I mean it, Portman. Going up against someone like Barnard is a one-way ticket to the psych ward.'

'Psych ward,' Portman whispered.

Jack thought he caught a hint of recognition from Portman.

'Yes. Exactly...'

Barnard signalled for Jack to wind up the call.

He hung up, praying that he had given Portman enough.

121

JACK WENT SILENT as Misha entered the room and joined the party.

She and Bruno now stood either side of Barnard, but their eyes never left Jack.

Barnard moved to a stainless-steel chest of drawers and slid one of them open. From what Jack could see, it contained a range of surgical instruments. Barnard appeared to be checking them as Bruno and Misha moved closer to Jack.

Where are you Portman?

'What make are those surgical gloves, Barnard? I have never seen black surgical gloves before. They look amazing.'

He hoped an appeal to Barnard's narcissism would lead to more talking and less incising.

'Well you wouldn't have, old boy. They are one of a kind. The material is infused with an anti-biomagnet barrier. Damn potent this little bugger.'

Barnard held up a tiny implantable metal device between his gloved fingers.

'Don't want my precious DNA mixed in with yours now, do I?' he laughed.

'I think it will be easier if I show you how it works. If you'll be so good as to hold still, old boy,' Barnard said with his back to Jack. 'It will be easier for all of us that way.'

A nurse entered the room, wheeling a hospital bed.

'Helen?' Jack exclaimed with shock. 'What the hell are you doing here?' Bruno and Misha now had hold of Jack's arms.

'Oh, yes,' Barnard said. 'Helen realised that I could offer her much better career advancement than she would ever get working in the NHS.'

He again laughed loudly, but the nurse remained silent. She could not bring herself to look Jack in the eyes.

'I've refined the technique even further, Helen,' Barnard said, still sorting out his instruments. 'The bed is much better than the chair. More accurate and less chance of resistance.'

Bruno and Misha forced Jack out of the chair and onto the hospital bed. He briefly thought of struggling but realised it would be useless.

There was still no sign of Portman.

'I want him face down. I need access to the top of his neck. Right at the base of the skull.'

Jack felt a warmth gently cascading up the veins in his arm and throughout his body.

The sedative. It won't be long now.

His eyes flickered as he tried to fight the drug that was coursing through his body. But he knew it was futile. He used all that he had left in his being to conjure up an image of Cerise before his memories and his mind were gone forever.

Running with Cerise.

Kissing Cerise.

Waking up with Cerise.

Holding Cerise.

Cerise.

122

THE PORTRAIT OF Freud fell to the floor and smashed as Portman rushed in, his firearm at the ready.

He didn't hesitate to put a bullet in each of the two guards as they instinctively moved towards him. They instantly slumped to the ground.

Barnard was standing over a comatose Jack Giorgio, holding a sharp steel surgical instrument in one hand, and, Portman guessed, what must be the implantable device in the other.

The nurse had her back to him. She gasped in surprise when she spun around.

'Don't move a muscle. Either of you,' Portman commanded. The pistol was aimed squarely at Barnard's chest.

'I wouldn't do that if I were you,' was the reply. 'The procedure is at a very precarious stage for your boy here. One slip from my hand and I will hit his brainstem. Which means that he will die instantly'.

'There is nowhere to go, Barnard. Even if you take out Giorgio, it's over. There is nothing left for you. Interpol and the UK Coast Guard have just intercepted the ship. They have freed the refugees, all unharmed. Maxwell has been arrested. Lalic is now in custody and will also be arrested, as soon as he comes round. There will be no more victims. No more harvesting.'

Barnard hesitated, and then moved his hand towards Jack.

A gunshot rang out and Barnard collapsed.

123

As HAD BEEN arranged, the front door to the opulent Chelsea mansion was unlocked.

An unnerving quiet had descended on the building, but Jack headed straight up the ornate staircase to the top floor, in line with the instructions he had been given. From the landing he could only see three rooms. He assumed that one would be the master suite.

He tried the first door, but it was locked.

The second opened into an enormous dressing room, complete with 'His and Hers' walk-in wardrobes, a dressing table, a lounge suite, and floor-to-ceiling mirrors. A further door led into a two-way bathroom.

On the other side of the bathroom was the bedroom.

And lying in the bed, gasping for breath, was Mortimer.

Jack could see his body had wasted away to nothing more than a frail skeleton wrapped in a layer of paper-thin skin. He seemed to be alone.

An air humidifier whirled away in the corner.

'Who's that?' the frail voice called out, all authority drained from it.

But before Jack could answer he asked another question. 'Is it Tuesday? Tuesday is air encephalogram day. I will prepare the patient.'

>   *He's delirious. Air encephalograms have not been used to image brains for over fifty years.*

'Who's that I say?' Mortimer tried to sit up in bed but was forced, through overwhelming fatigue and dizziness, to slump back down on his pillow.

'It's Jack. Jack Giorgio.'

'Aaaahhhh. Jack.' He seemed relieved, but who really knew which emotions were cascading through that diseased brain.

'Take me to Geneva , Jack,' he mumbled.

'Why Geneva?'

'More treatment. My chemo. More time.'

> *Ah of course, it was state-of-the-art cancer treatment he had been getting in Geneva. He hadn't been researching Scion.*

Jack walked closer to the bedside. Mortimer's eyes were closed. His breathing was shallow and rapid.

> *It won't be long now.*

A magazine fell to the floor behind him causing Jack to jump. He swung around and saw an obese, elderly nurse, fast asleep in a chair in the far corner of the bedroom. She started to snore.

He leaned in closer to Mortimer.

'Can you hear me, Nathan?'

Mortimer nodded.

'Tell me the truth about Christina Beauchamp-Alard,' he demanded.

'Christina,' Mortimer softly repeated.

'Yes. You need to tell me now.'

'Next week. After the conference.' His breathing became more laboured.

'No. *Now.* There is no time left.' Jack grabbed the dying man by the shoulders. The lateral points of his clavicles felt hard and sharp. He was worried that they might actually pierce the emaciated skin that covered them.

'Christina. So much promise.'

His breathing was more irregular.

Cheyne-Stokes breathing. The final throes.

'What. Happened. To. Christina?' Jack asked loudly and clearly, causing the nurse to shift in her chair. She remained asleep.

'She died,' Mortimer whispered.

'Yes. *Before* she died. What happened?'

Mortimer coughed violently. A huge plug of rust-coloured phlegm sprung out of his mouth, narrowly missing Jack.

'Scion. Cure. She would make me a God'.

Jack was sure he could see Mortimer's lips curl up into a slight smile.

'Scion. Did it work, Nathan?'

'NO!'

The smile was gone.

His eyes widened and he looked straight at Jack. His bony, cold hand slid up and found Jack's. It was like ice. Again, the dying man tried to hoist himself up. Jack supported his head as he rose.

'It was all a dream. My dream. It was all a lie.'

He exhaled deeply with a soft groan, and Jack took his weight as he slumped back.

His eyes remained open.

Open. But lifeless.

124

JACK RE-WATCHED THE video of Christina. Portman, who sat next to him, also stared, wide-eyed.

'She was scripted,' Jack confirmed, to himself as much as to Portman. 'She is pretty convincing. Beneath her psychosis, she was a very bright woman. A part of her probably also wanted to believe that the miracle cure was out there—and who could blame her? But she soon realised that it was all lies and that she had to escape. She didn't want to be part of Mortimer's sick delusion. We won't ever really know if she deliberately threw herself under that truck or not. Either way, I hope she is at peace.'

'Unbelievable,' Portman whispered, fixated on the screen.

'Mortimer's narcissism made him so determined to become a medical immortal that he was willing to believe anything. He knew that his time was running out, and because the cancer had spread to the frontal lobes of his brain, he was incredibly vulnerable to suggestion, and his grandiosity was amplified. The tumours made him a sitting duck.'

'And Sandrine?' asked Portman.

'For sure. She fed into his madness and his ambition with her belief in Positrex Scion. She had him completely convinced. She even had the very believable false data to back up what she was telling him.'

'You shrinks have a term for that, don't you? For when two people feed into one another's madness?' Portman asked.

'Yes, it's a French term. We call it a "folie à deux"—literally a "madness for two",' Jack confirmed. 'It's pretty rare, but it certainly does happen. And as we've seen here, it is very dramatic when it does. Two brains, even sick brains, are more powerful than one.'

'So, if I have it right, Jack: Mortimer was always driven by narcissism and ambition, but he became psychotic as a result of the brain tumours and Sandrine's own false beliefs?'

'Absolutely right. By the time he met Sandrine, he was already unwell, and was clearly suggestable enough to believe anything she told him'. Jack looked away. 'But I guess he wasn't alone there'.

Portman stopped the video and looked sympathetically at Jack. 'Have you heard anything more about her? Has she contacted you at all?'

'No. And no'.

'Between you and me, I was given some recent intel on her. It seems she may be getting some treatment for the thing you said she had. The Leuko thing.'

'Leukodystrophy. Do you know what sort of treatment?'

'A transplant of some kind. A *legitimate* transplant.' Portman smiled uncomfortably.

Jack felt relieved, even though he knew that such a treatment was likely still in its infancy. 'Well, I hope it's successful,' he said earnestly. 'I really do hope that she will be okay.'

'We all do, Jack. We all do'.

?

HALF. FULL. SHORT. BLACK.

JACK SHOT DOWN his hot espresso and called the waitress over so that he could order another.

Portman.

Jack noticed that he was back to wearing his tacky 'Roma' cap. Before he could say anything sarcastic, Portman seemed to read his mind.

'I know, I know,' he said almost apologetically. 'But I've become somewhat attached to it'.

Jack imagined that back in his house or apartment or train station locker or wherever the hell he lived, Portman had an eclectic collection of assorted memorabilia that he had acquired on various cases around the world.

'That cap! Makes me think of being set up by that actress in the hotel. I can't believe they went to those lengths to frame me. I should have just hung out with you, Portman.' They both laughed.

The waitress came over with Jack's second espresso, and he took a grateful swig before placing it back on the table.

Portman pointed at the coffee cup.

'Half full or half empty, Dr Freud?'

Both men laughed loudly again.

'I thought you might like to know that Ivan Lalic's extradition back to his homeland has occurred, and the whole trafficking chain is dismantled. Lalic will never see the light of day again. His life of luxury is going to be nothing more than a memory. The prisons over there are no walk in the park, Giorgio.' Portman shook his head.

'Somehow I have a feeling he will survive.'

Portman sighed and looked away. 'But it looks like you were right about Mortimer. We've found absolutely nothing to connect him to the trafficking. It seems he was just a deluded old man. It was all Barnard and Maxwell. Even Sarah Wellington was totally cleared in the end. She gave us more evidence to nail Barnard. It seemed that she genuinely had entered into the original research with good intentions. She tried to get out when she knew what was *really* happening.'

Jack shook his head.

'Oh, and your young friend Zoe, who sends a giggling *"hi"* by the way, got us access to her uncle's bank accounts and the shipping documents he'd falsified for Lalic, so that evidence was also very, very helpful. It clearly showed that the international trafficking ring were taking huge payments from clients for the transplants and then funnelling that money through Maxwell and the Department for Health and Social Services. It then came out clean, as 'research grants', which allowed Barnard to continue his work. And around and around it went.'

'What will happen to Maxwell and Barnard?'

'Barnard has fully recovered from his gunshot wound, and they're both facing over a dozen very serious charges. The evidence is conclusive, so there's little doubt that they'll get off. They're both in line for a lengthy stretch'.

'How the mighty have fallen!' said Jack. 'Sharp suits, fancy apartments, adoring women, and now…'

'Prison clothes, cell checks, and let's hope Barnard has a sharp memory and a vivid imagination, because it will be a *long* time before he is with a woman again,' Portman laughed.

Jack couldn't help but smile along with him.

I wonder who will take over Barnard's TV spot?

'You never know, Barnard or Maxwell may show up for treatment in your prison clinic one day.'

Jack shook his head and swallowed his coffee. He frowned.

'No, I don't think so. I don't see myself going back to London. There's just been too much...' He broke off as he thought of Cerise.

'Sure,' said Portman. 'I heard she's getting that stem cell treatment now because of you.'

It was the first time Jack felt any real sense of compassion from him. He slipped his Ray Bans on and held out a hand across the table.

Portman shook it firmly. 'You've done a great thing for the world, Jack. A great thing. It won't be forgotten'.

It doesn't feel great.

'I don't know whether to say thanks or you're welcome or go to hell. The world will never know, but the real hero in all this is Joel Lalic. With all of his challenges he still found the integrity and courage to do the hardest thing of all; stand up to his monster of an old man so that he could help us to expose the truth'.

'That he did,' agreed Portman.

'Portman, you do all this work for Interpol, tracking people down. Do you ever do any private work?'

'What do you mean, Jack?'

'Like looking for people's lost relatives?' Jack asked shyly.

'Interpol tends to frown on such activities. Why?'

'It's okay. It was just a passing thought. Forget about it'.

Jack let go of Portman's hand and strode outside. Once the road was clear, he picked up his pace and quickly crossed to the other side.

By the time he hit the beach, with the brilliant blue Mediterranean stretched out in front of him, he was running.

www.ingramcontent.com/pod-product-compliance
Lightning Source LLC
Chambersburg PA
CBHW071342020726
47502CB00001B/210